The Shots Against Us

Cassandra Moll

Cover design: Caravelle Creates

First edition: November 2025

ISBN: 9798991826037(paperback)

Other Titles By Cassandra Moll

The Maple Grove Series
Beautifully Broken
Daring Destiny

The Golden City Series
The Boards Between Us
The Holiday Delay (Novella)

For the girls who use humor to mask their emotions—
You don't have to do that.

But you're funny as hell.

The Shots Against Us

Cassandra Moll

Prologue - Brooke
10 Months Earlier

There are two places I feel trapped in this world—my parents' dinner table and inside of a pair of sheer fucking stockings. I knew I should have ditched them and gone bare underneath my red strapless dress, but it's cold as balls outside and I've always been a girl who's more mini skirt than full-length gown.

If my mother were here, she'd say it was a nod to my poor choices, and Dad would simply agree. As for my older brother, Blake... well, he would try—and fail—to hide his smirk, knowing damn well that his white picket fence, beautiful daughter, and high school sweetheart don't help my case.

But despite the bitter winter winds tonight, this satin number just screamed Spark the Flame gala with its color that twinkles like embers from a fire. So, common sense—and my mother's nagging voice—be damned, it had to be *this* dress.

Now, I have to deal with the constant tug-of-war going on underneath its hem. It's as if the nude material doesn't know if it wants to fall down or ride up, and I'm stuck dealing with the aftermath of its indecision. The crotch is too low, but the waistband is squeezing in all the wrong places. I've barely made it to the ballroom's double doors before I decide my first stop—after a much-needed drink—will be to ditch the nylon covering my legs. Thank God I followed my Aunt Ivy's advice and *shaved every inch,* just in case.

As if this wasn't bad enough, the start of my night was no better than my current fashion crisis—my tights and my job apparently both on my bad side. I've been at The Gilded Pub for nearly a decade, waiting tables and occasionally slinging drinks behind the bar. What started out as a way to make good money while I *figured things out,* as my mother put it, has quietly turned into my long-term job. And truth be told, I don't *always* hate it.

Tonight was a particularly shitty shift though. Our expo called out, which left me checking for dipping sauces and adding pickles to plates in addition to taking orders. And as always, I helped behind the bar. On top of all that, the Diet Coke button on the soda machine was jammed... again. So, not only did I have to hear customers whine, but I myself had to go my entire shift without the comfort of my work-beverage of choice. Add in that I was slighted in tips more than once by patrons with greasy fingers and shallow wallets, and you have yourself the customer service trifecta.

I've never been one to believe that a paycheck should come bundled with misery. I'd spend double the time making half the cash sitting behind a desk somewhere else, and for what? To slowly watch my life dissolve into pencil skirts and microwaveable lunches? *No thanks.* The idea of spending the next twenty years observing the seasons change through the flowers in a cubicle vase sends shivers down my spine.

I don't know exactly what I *want* to do long-term, but I sure as hell know what I don't, and settling just to appease my parents isn't on the list. According to them, thirty is the age where all the clocks start ticking—career, marriage, babies—deadlines disguised as milestones. I never understood that pressure. Never felt the need to satisfy some sort of checklist. They just can't wrap their heads around that. Most people can't.

Except Ivy—wild, unapologetic Aunt Ivy. She's the only one who never flinches when I say I'm still figuring it out. She doesn't believe in ticking clocks. She believes in timing—and that's not the same thing.

So I'm here.

At a notorious gala.

Tell me that's not an accomplishment, *Mom.*

Who would have thought that my best friend Alex Bennett, lifestyle blogger and single mom to my twelve-year-old bonus nephew, would find herself at an event for the Golden City Flames—one of the NHL's hottest teams right now. Not only that, but her son Cooper is being recognized as a spotlight player for their outreach program that works with youth hockey teams in our community. As if it could possibly get better, the guy in charge of all this—hot, rich, super sweet, professional coach, Levi Montgomery—is the dream guy she's banging. Talk about going against the grain. *God, I'm so jealous.*

But I love this for her.

Walking into the dimly lit room, accented in red back light that streams up from the floor, dozens of people wander around, spirits high like the cocktails in their hands are not their first of the night. I missed the main event. I knew I would. But at least I'll still get to show my support for my two favorite people.

Scanning the room, I don't see Alex anywhere. Knowing her and Coach McHottie, they're probably finger-banging in a bathroom some-where. Those two can't keep their hands off each other, and something about a toilet and a sink seems to really do it for them lately. I do, however, spot Cooper seated with a few men in suits in front of a plate full of food.

Deciding I should say hi to the guest of honor before caving to my growing need for alcohol and naked legs, I deviate from my beeline toward the bar and walk up behind Coop.

"Hey, there he is," I say, placing both hands on his shoulders and leaning over him so he can see it's me.

He turns in his seat and attempts a smile, his mouth full of what I assume from the mound of meat and glistening buns on his plate, are the remains of a slider. "Ha Aun Book," he makes out through full cheeks.

Rolling my eyes playfully at his lack of words—and manners—I grin politely at the rest of the table. "Hi, I'm Cooper's Aunt Brooke."

The gentleman to Coop's right, with glowing dark skin, a trimmed beard, and a plate that matches my nephew's, offers me his hand. "You're Alex's friend, right? Erik."

My palm connects with his in a hearty handshake. "That's me. And you're Levi's assistant coach?"

He nods. "Yup, me and Gavin over there." He points to a man across the table, so engrossed in showing his phone to the person next to him he doesn't even notice Erik's gesture. To be fair, his screen displays the most adorable puppies, and if it weren't for the way I suddenly feel eyes on me, I would pull up a chair and ditch everything else to see those little fur balls.

"Very cool," I answer, suddenly distracted. Someone's gaze is burrowing through me. Pulling back from Cooper and the guys, I scan the room.

Almost instantly, I lock eyes with the source of my branding sitting two tables over. The culprit is looking at me, drinking me in—studying every inch. He seems familiar, but I can't quite place him in his cobalt blue suit and crisp white button-up that pulls across his chest. His overgrown hair is swept back away from his face, and his light eyes are steady on me. *He's fucking gorgeous.*

Tearing away from his admiring gaze, I lean down to Coop. "Hey, congratulations, buddy. I'm going to grab something to drink and walk around a little. You okay?" He nods, still chewing.

I wrap my arms around him, and he does the same to me. "I'll be back."

Releasing him, I turn to Erik. "It was nice to meet you."

He shoots me a warm smile and nods. "Likewise."

It takes everything in me not to glance back, but I need alcohol, like, yesterday.

Spotting the bar nestled in the far corner, I head in that direction. It's your typical reception setup with the drink selection sitting out on display and no stools in front to keep the line moving. There are only a few other people waiting, which I take as my sign from the gala gods that it's time for a hefty glass of wine. On the short walk to the wooden bar that's painted a stain so dark it almost matches the black outline of the Flames logo behind it, the mystery man's face pops into my mind.

He's smoking hot, undoubtedly younger than me, but there was history painted in his clear blue eyes. Most guys who spend that much time admiring me have dilated pupils and hooded lids. But he wasn't undressing me, at least not that way. He was stripping my layers as if he was reading my soul instead of getting me naked, and that alone made me want to lose these stockings for reasons other than their annoyance.

I run through the names of the people Alex has talked about as I approach the counter. Coaches, Levi's friends, his brother, but none of them stick out as the one I'm now admittedly wet for underneath these god-awful tights. Something about how he so casually made my stomach flip—how he was sitting so relaxed but made me feel anything but—intrigues me more than I'd like to admit.

A man capable of that must be accustomed to a life like this. I bet his pants aren't driving *him* crazy. He's probably used to a suit that hugs him in all the right places. I, on the other hand, am more of a ripped jeans and cropped-tee kinda girl.

It hits me that he has to be an athlete. He's too young to be a coach or in some sort of team leadership role. He must be a Flame. Growing up only a year younger than Blake, I can hang with the guys better than most girls, but I don't make it a habit of watching sports in my free time. The only games I've seen lately are those of the hockey team my best friend and her son have been associated with for the last few weeks. There are athletes from all over Golden City here to support the Flames, but he has to play hockey if he seems familiar.

I think back to the few games I've watched, and none of the players' actual faces come to mind from behind their helmets. There's not many I observe too carefully except maybe the panty-dropping showman I'm admittedly intrigued by. The one who failed his drug test earlier this week and... *oh my God.* I pause in my tracks at the same time I reach the counter. *That's it.*

The mystery man.

He's Drew fucking—

"Anderson! My guy, what's goin' on?" The bearded bartender calls to someone behind me. I don't turn around, but a presence lingers nearby in the same way that the eyes from earlier did.

"What's up, man?" The words are spoken all but into my ear and send goosebumps up my body, making me suddenly glad that the skin on my lower half is covered.

"Tough week, huh? What can I get ya?"

There's a shift beside me as the man I can now confirm is Drew Anderson, the Flames' starting forward, leans his forearms on the bar. "I think she was here first," he says, and once again I know he's looking at me without even turning my head.

I finally face him, making eye contact for the first time since I connected the dots. This close, his irises look like two crystal clear oceans you'd see on an island, the blue of his suit only further enhancing them. I rush to take him in, immediately realizing the reasons why I didn't put two and two together sooner.

This is not the Drew Anderson that I've seen on TV. That guy is in full hockey gear, his helmet rarely off, and when it is, he's dripping with sweat or squirting water seductively into his unruly hair. He's flashy and bold, and even when he's not trying to showboat, just the way he handles his stick or plays with the puck makes it look like he's performing.

But not now.

Now, he's swapped his gear for a suit that was clearly made for his impeccable body. His locks are gelled back rather than falling on either side of his forehead, and he's calm—almost despondent—as if he's trying to blend in rather than be the star of the show.

"Right, no, of course," the bartender says quickly, bringing me back to the moment. "What are you drinking?"

I reluctantly turn away from the guy I'm used to drooling over through the screen in my living room. "I, um—red wine please," I stutter, simply caught off guard by my realization. I use the time it takes Drew to ask for his beer to fully make my way back to the present, and when I do, I add on to my order. "But, like big, please." I hold my hands up, one about six inches on top of the other, palms facing in. "Heavy pour." The bartender smiles politely before turning to grab our drinks.

"Rough night?" Drew asks, tilting his head toward me. Thankfully, I'm not easily thrown, at least not on the outside, because... wow. *This guy.*

"Work sucks." We take our drinks from the counter in front of us.

"I know," Drew says, immediately taking a long pull of his beer.

I smirk, trying to decipher if his answer was coincidental or if he understood the musical reference, as he takes a second sip. "Rough night?" I mimic, stepping aside, surprised at how watching his throat move up and down ignites a heat between my legs.

He shifts so he's standing next to me again. "Rough fucking week."

For a moment we stare at each other, and it's as if the rest of the ballroom falls away. Drew goes back to looking at me like he was at the table—like he's memorizing me from the outside in. His gaze slinks down my chest, past my hips, and over the tights I now wish I had removed *first*.

I'm not shy about copying his movement, trailing my eyes down his well-built body. This man is like a Greek god, and this is *with* clothes on. He's taller than me, but not by much in my heels. He's maybe 6'2" or 6'3", but his presence is that of an actual giant. His frame is broad, the threads of his clothing pulled tight around his obvious muscle, and the hand around his beer tells me what he's packing underneath has to be proportionate.

When our gazes meet again, his eyes aren't the clear water they were before. They're dark and murky, more like an ocean at night than a Caribbean sea. His jaw ticks as he adjusts his feet so he's closer than he was before, both of us aware that whatever is happening here isn't your typical friendly conversation.

"You want to talk about it?" I ask, twisting my shoulders to search the room for Alex and Cooper—to give myself any excuse to turn away from his unrelenting eye contact. Alex is still nowhere to be seen, and Cooper is now at the dessert bar, a plate in each hand, as Erik adds pastry after pastry on top of each growing pile.

"Not even a little," he says, pulling me away from the sugary scene.

"That good, huh?"

He takes another sip. "Better now."

My chest warms, but I maintain composure and ignore the way my body reacts to those two words. Unsure of what to say, I simply nod, and a silence falls between us.

I can't explain why I'm drawn to him. I've felt it since I first saw him on the big screen. There's no denying the specimen that is the man in front of me, especially when he's flying across ice and sinking pucks into the net. But he was always untouchable—figuratively and literally. At minimum, an ice rink sat between him and me in Levi's box in the stands. Not to mention, I'm at least five years his senior. But that's what fantasies are for.

Now, though, he's not a fantasy.

Well, he is, but... he's also here.

Taking a big gulp of wine, I buy myself a few seconds. I'm not one to lose my words, but it's been a night already, and I'm draining fast. Honestly, what I could really use is a good release—and if the man I've salivated over for the last few weeks wants to give it to me, who am I to stop him? I'm not going to throw myself at him like he's probably used to, though—I didn't spend the last thirty years letting my parents down to start kissing ass now.

But if he wants to shoot his shot... he will.

Tipping my chin back down, I almost hit his nose with the stem of my glass. *Did he move closer while I was savoring the rush of wine to my head?* His scent surrounds me, the perfect combination of spice and earth notes—Dior? Tom Ford?—something expensive. Maybe it's the time that's passed, or the fleeting buzz my first sip gives me, but I start to doubt that this is anything. Could he be acting cordial and just so happen to have ridiculously intense—and insanely sexy—eye contact? *Or maybe these stockings are finally starting to cut off circulation to my brain.*

"Well, I'm going to g—"

"Do you want to get out of here?" Drew cuts off my attempt to end... whatever the hell is happening here, and my mouth goes dry.

I have half a glass of wine left to buy time before I answer, and I use every last drop to do so. Throwing back what's left, I contemplate if this is really what I want. Is it possible that Drew's using me as one of his many hookups to right what's gone so wrong for him? Probably. Would I be using him for the same exact thing? One hundred percent, yes.

It's clear we have some sort of weird connection, but I'm not delusional. This is a one-time deal—a random hookup to cure some sort of mutual misery. No part of me thinks this is some kismet meet-cute where the famous athlete and the thirty-year-old black sheep bond over temporary intimacy, then fall madly in love. But sex has never meant much to me—yet another way I let down mommy dearest. So, whatever this is, doesn't matter anyway.

"That's a little presumptuous, don't you think?" I tease, making sure I don't look *too* easy.

He narrows his eyes in my direction. "Is that a no?"

Walking to set my glass on the edge of the bar, I take a deep breath as my back's turned to him. On the exhale, I spin around and step toe to toe with him. "Definitely not a no."

Let's lose these fucking stockings.

Prologue - Drew
That Same Night

The bathroom door clicks shut, and I lock it behind me, turning to see this mystery girl already pulling off those things women wear under dresses. That fast, she has them past her hips, making me regret not just reaching behind me to turn the brass knob.

"Right to it, huh?" I ask, the stretchy material now in a heap at her ankles, her strappy heels already off.

"What? Oh, no." Her voice is breathless, and though it might be from the effort it seems to have taken to roll the elastic down her thighs, I'd like to think it's because of me. "These things were driving me crazy. Honestly, they would have come off either way." She pulls her foot from each of the holes and tosses the tan ball of fabric right into the trashcan.

Huffing out a laugh, my gaze falls down her tight and curvy body pretty fucking obviously. *Holy shit.* I don't know who this girl is or where the hell she came from, but she's fucking stunning. More of her skin is showing than not, her dress held up by only her chest, and she fills it out flawlessly—a perfect mix of classy and sexy. But as much as I love it *on*, I'd much prefer it on the goddamn floor.

After the week I've had, this gala was literally the last thing I wanted to do. I've spent the past forty-eight hours dealing with the aftermath of the random drug test I failed, and it took everything in me to even get out of bed, let alone face the entire athletic community of Golden City.

I had been having a rough... month, and when I started dropping the ball on the ice, I outsourced—self-medicated. My sounding board has been gone for a while, so I looked for support where I knew I shouldn't. Then I got caught. And now? Well, now, I don't know where it all leads. Except for tonight. Tonight, I'm taking back control. I'm leaving this fishbowl I'm swimming in, and I'm seeking relief in the stranger that I can't keep my eyes off of.

All of a sudden, the girl reaches behind her. She unzips her dress with the slip of her hand, and peels it off, letting it fall to the gray-tiled floor. All the while, her eyes are fixed on mine until I can't stop them from dropping to her matching black set.

"Your move, Anderson," she says, leaning back to place her palms on the sink. The white porcelain is stark in contrast to her tan hands around it and the dark lace now on display. She has random tattoos stickered all over her skin. Some phrases here, a word or two there, some pictures I can't quite make out because I'm trying to take her all in. *So fucking sexy.*

Blowing through my lips, I stride toward her slowly. "You might regret that."

She tilts her head and narrows her eyes. "Eh, I don't think so. But it's already been a long night, so if you don't mind..." She tilts her chin as if to gesture me over, and I comply without question, darting to her.

I first spotted her when she walked in alone, my gaze fixed on the exit from the moment the speeches ended as I waited for my chance to leave. Instead, I caught sight of the rest of my night, all legs and confidence in her little red number. It's ballsy to show up at these things by yourself. There are a lot of people with power, and some plain old rich assholes, to just float in casually unconnected to one.

When she went straight for the kid, the fact that I had never seen her before made a little more sense. She must be related to Coach's old lady. That would explain the way her toned body made my dick twitch like Monte's girl's does—respectfully, of course. But as I really read her, analyzed her movements like I would an opponent's, something else reeled me in.

It was how her eyes never once lingered on anyone. A few dozen pros all gathered together and a puck bunny would foam at the mouth. But this fucking goddess beelined it for Cooper, then went straight to the bar, her independence evident, bravado clear.

Sort of like it is right now.

"You okay with this?" I ask, tracing her collarbone with the tip of my finger. Goosebumps spread up her neck, her lips parting as I follow them north.

"You're asking now that I'm half-naked in front of you?"

A lazy smile spreads across my lips. "Well, when I asked if you wanted to get out of here, I didn't exactly mean the lobby bathroom." Though *that didn't stop me from following her into the single stall like a goddamn puppy.*

She turns her lips in and winks at me. "It's fine," she says, reaching for my coat. "I have to get back in there after, and there's apparently something I'm missing about doing it against the sink." My brow creases as she undoes my button. "Not like that, it's—just forget it. Come here."

She pulls me by my jacket, slipping her hands underneath the flaps at my shoulders. I let it fall to my elbows before I take it off and hang it on the hook that sits on the back of the door.

"So, you know me," I say, turning back to her. It's more of a statement than a question considering she called me by name, but there's no missing the despair in my voice.

Looking back and forth between my eyes, she studies me for a moment, unflinching.

No judgement.

No assumptions.

"*Know* you?" She shakes her head. "I understand who you are, but I wouldn't say I *know* you."

My lungs fill with air for the first time in two days. Everyone has had even more to say about who I am in the last forty-eight hours. I'm sulking, going through a crisis, a disappointment, or my personal favorite—a total buzzkill. They're mad that for the next few months I'll be riding the bench instead of performing for them. They don't care about *me*. They don't even *know* me. And this total stranger might be the first to see that.

"What's your name?" I ask hesitantly, sliding my palms past her cheeks.

"Kiss me," is all she says in response.

Inching closer, our lips barely touch. "Tell me, baby."

With that last word, her mouth presses to mine.

I consider objecting, pulling away and insisting that I learn the name of the one person who hasn't mentioned my biggest regret. But when her tongue grazes my lips, asking for permission, my whole body melts into her. I open and allow her in, and *holy fuck*, this might be the best kiss of my life.

It's not even the way she tastes—although her mouth could easily be a delicacy—or the way she runs her teeth gently across my bottom lip, somehow knowing exactly what I like. It's how our mouths fall instantly into a rhythm like they're already familiar with one another. Like they were meant for each other. Like every other kiss either of us has ever had was just practice for this one.

The girl with no name drags her fingertips down the length of my back, and I arch into her, realizing I'm still wearing my clothes. Normally, I'd be naked in less time than it takes for a woman to ask how many points I scored in my last game. But this girl has me humming without an inch of my skin exposed.

Slipping my hands between us, I keep our embrace as I find my top button. In response, Mystery Girl places her palms over my knuckles and pulls back breathlessly. "No time."

She drags our hands, still wrapped together, to the waist of my pants, letting out a soft whimper as her fingers brush against my hard cock below it. "Just these," she whispers, her face still so close to mine that our heavy breathing mixes together.

I can't help the smirk that forms between us despite the fact that my dick thinks this is anything but funny. Most women either want the full treatment or are pissed if I do decide we're making this quick. They want the full show—the guy they've imagined. But here, I don't think I could be anyone else even if I tried. Luckily, she doesn't seem to care. And for once in this situation, I'm not calling the shots.

"You're bad, aren't you, Mystery Girl?"

She purses her lips, and I swear I catch a roll of her eyes despite how close our faces are. "Not bad," she says. "Well... maybe." She snickers, then wraps her hand around mine and brings it between her legs. "But right now I'm just more ready than anything."

She guides my first two fingers under the black lace, right between her legs, and *holy shit.*

She. Is. Drenched.

"Fuck," I groan, sliding them up and down her center. "You *are* ready, baby."

"So, what are you going to do about it?"

With no hesitation, I shove both fingers inside her, her pussy already slick enough to dive right in. She moans as she lets her head fall backward, tightening her grip on the sink. Pressing my body to hers with my cock throbbing against the pants I still haven't taken off, I bring our cheeks together and speak softly in her ear. "You like that, Mystery Girl?"

I inhale, my breaths coming in quick bursts like it's the end of a game and I've played every minute. When I do, the perfect smell of citrus intertwines with the air, and suddenly fruit is fucking erotic.

"Yes," she exhales, and my thumb moves in response, finding her clit and beginning slow circles.

"Tell me what you want."

"Keep going," she answers definitively. "Faster. More."

This girl knows what she likes, and she's on a hunt to get it. Normally, girls think it's a novelty just to be with me—something they don't really care about experiencing because it's the accomplishment they're more concerned with. But not her. And I'm willing to give her whatever she wants.

"Play with me," she says breathlessly as I kiss and nip at her neck.

I pull back to ask how I could possibly do that *more,* only to see she's pulled the cup of her bra down and out of place. "You're fucking perfect," I say without thinking.

She bites her lip to hide her smile and, at the same time, reaches out and runs her palm along my hard, constrained cock. "Not too bad yourself."

"Oh, babygirl, you haven't seen anything yet." With that, I lean down and take her peaked nipple into my mouth, rolling my tongue over it like it's a goddamn lollipop.

She cries out when I suck it hard, and I press my waist to her leg to give myself some much needed friction.

As if the contact was permission, my mystery girl's legs start to quiver. "Oh my God, Drew."

The sound of my name falling from her lips is better than any high I've ever felt. It's completely unexpected and downright unexplainable, but this girl is like a drug I've never tried, intriguing and bold, but completely foreign to me. Yet one little hit of her leaves me desperate for more.

Needing to ride out this feeling, I drop to my knees, swapping my thumb for my mouth until she falls past the edge. I savor every second of her release, maintaining my movement as she pulses against my lips.

"Holy shit," she pants as I loosen my suction. I stand and kiss her with my coated mouth.

"Mmm," she hums, running her tongue past my lips. "You are... that was..." Her gaze drops to my cock that's finally free thanks to my use of the time she's taken to gather her thoughts. "That thing is..."

"Impressive?" I tease, a playful raise in my brow.

Her eyes darken as she glances back and forth between my face and what she sees between my legs. "We'll see about that."

A growl escapes from deep inside me as I once again drop to my knees for this girl and pull her thong off of her hips. "Fucking hell," I say, seeing her on full display. *She is everything.*

I rise slowly, dropping my forehead to hers. "Tell me your name."

"Don't worry about that," she says, reaching for me. I groan as she strokes me from base to tip.

"Why can't I know?"

The corners of her lips tug upward. "Where's the fun in that?"

Sliding my hand into her hair toward the base of her neck, I tug gently so she's forced to look at me. "Who are you?" I whisper more to myself.

"Does it matter?" she answers despite it being rhetorical. "In five minutes, our worlds will fall back into two completely separate orbits."

My head snaps back, my brows furrowed. "Woah, woah, woah... five minutes? I don't know who you think you're dealing with but—"

Her laugh cuts me off, not because of the noise but because of my reaction to it.

A goddamn angel.

"You know what I mean."

Palming her face, my expression turns serious as I speak to both of us. "It doesn't have to be that way."

She half-rolls her eyes, then tilts her head. "It does," she says simply. "So, take it or leave it."

I don't know who this girl is, but I know that I've never met anyone like her. Most women I sleep with offer so much, there's not an ounce of mystery left between us. But not this one. She offers me nothing, leaving me completely in the dark—baffled.

And so fucking captivated.

Answering without words, I reach under her arms, picking her up and sitting her full ass on the sink. She leans back and braces her palms on the sides as I reach down for my pants to take out my wallet. Reaching into the pocket, I feel only fabric. My heart starts to race as I reach into the other.

Nothing.

No, no, no. This isn't happening. I'm sure panic riddles my face as I shove my hand into every slit of my blue suit pants but still come up empty.

"What's wrong?" she asks, shifting one hand to stroke the inside of her thigh.

I swallow hard at her movement before dropping my pants and my head at the same time. "Fuck." *As if this week could get any worse.*

"What?" she repeats.

Heaving a deep sigh, I look up at her, almost wincing from how much I want this girl. "I left my wallet at the table with my phone."

She narrows her eyes before I continue.

"No condoms?" I say as if it's a question. *Is she not putting two and two together? Because I'm freaking the hell out right now.*

She bobs her head back and forth like she's considering her next thought. "Well, I take the pill religiously... and I can tell you right now that *I'm* clean."

I stare at her blankly. "I, I mean—we get tested all the time for this shit. I know I am too."

"Well..." Her teeth run across her bottom lip, and I can't help myself.

I snap to her and do the same with mine. Kissing her again, I sink my tongue into her mouth, and she rocks her bare pussy against the base of my aching cock. "What are you saying here, baby?" I ask helplessly.

"I'm saying I'm good with this if you are."

I instantly panic.

We don't fuck raw. It's a locker room rule. A team rule for Christ's sake. Even Gavin and Erik make weird old man jokes about *no glove, no love* on a weekly basis.

But look at her.

Something in me knows this isn't some weird sort of setup. That shit happens to people all the time, and in my line of work you learn quickly that there can always be ulterior motives. But *this* doesn't feel like *that*.

This feels like a chance to have the girl I've been drawn to since the moment I saw her. The chance to be inside the girl I feel weirdly connected to. And I have no fight left in me. I want her. Now.

Knowing I'll regret not doing this more than taking the risk, I kiss her one more time with all I've got, then line my tip up with her entrance.

Without any more waiting, I shove deep inside her, and we both cry out as I take her... bare.

1
Brooke

"Oh, for Christ's sake!" I yell, striding back into the kitchen, dirty dishes in one hand and three dollars in the other. "If one more group of college kids leaves me half the tip they should, I'll lose my mind."

My coworker, Tessa, lets out a laugh as she refills a tray of empty cups. "Gotta love cheesesteak night. Now that school's back in session, there are even more people here for five dollar sandwiches, forgetting that we do the same amount of work to serve them their half-price meat."

I groan. "I know. God, I'm getting too old for this shit." Pointing to the broom leaning against the wall in the back of dry storage, I continue. "I can practically hear that thing calling me to go out there and shoo them all away."

Tess, who's just a few years younger than me, rolls her big blue eyes as she places four sodas on a tray. "Cranky old lady style, huh?" she asks. I nod, and she mirrors my gesture. "Nothing like a couple dozen college kids to remind you you're not as young as you once were."

Scooting past her, I dump the stack of saucy plates I bussed from my last table into the bin by the dishwasher. Then, I shove the three measly bills into the pocket of my apron. "And here I am trying to convince my mother thirty's the new twenty."

Tessa scoffs. "It is. Just not when your income depends on the cheap wallets of kids barely legal to drink."

I point a finger at her as if to say she nailed it, then reach for my diet soda stashed on the back of the metal counter. Taking a long sip, I slurp up what's left, popping the lid off to fill it once more. "I seriously need to find a new job."

"You've been looking, haven't you?" She glances around the corner of the doorframe into the dining room to scan her tables. I focus on the hiss of the soda machine in an attempt to calm my sudden unease.

"Yeah," I sigh. "But everything somehow seems even worse than this or boring as hell. And thanks to the lack of letters beside my name, I'm apparently not worth enough per hour to even pay my rent."

Picking up her tray, she balances the drinks on her hip with one hand and places the other around my forearm. Giving it a squeeze, she smiles sympathetically. "Sorry, babe. Something will come up. I know it."

That's easy for her to say. Tess is a college grad who studied education. She had her own classroom for a while until she started nannying and homeschooling full time instead. She waits tables every once in a while for her "slush fund," as she calls it—money she can use from her occasional shift to indulge in new shoes or go away on a girls's trip. But it's not her full-time income.

I love Tess, but it's not the same.

I paint a smile as I take another sip of caffeine. "Girl, I hope so."

With that, Tessa heads back into the madness, and I remember back to when I used to make up stories about *why* young customers shorted me in the first place. I told myself that they were saving for their first car or spent the rest of their cash on condoms and lube. Those measly dollars were what was left after taking their girl on a date or betting their friends they could shotgun a forty. Now it's not fun or cute, it's annoying. And it's only recently that this mental shift started.

I've had a transformative last couple of months—possibly the next *Great Awakening*. It was a quiet change, a slow progression, a gradual unraveling of the world around me that finally made it click. But I, Brooke Larkin, have decided... it might be time to put down roots.

It began when Alex and Levi started getting more serious. Alex was always my kindred spirit—my twin flame. Neither of us ever did anything conventionally. Al dropped out of college, had her son young, and began her life as a single mom avoiding men that resembled her ex.

I skipped college, more interested in going with the flow than waking up at eight a.m. to torture myself by sitting through lectures. Then, bounced from bar to restaurant to bar-restaurant, going out and dating around. Neither of us had it all together, but we were fine that way.

And then she met Coach McHottie.

The two of them pretended to keep things physical for awhile after they met, but soon enough, they were madly in love. Before I knew it, Al had a boyfriend and was taking steps toward her dream job, quitting The Gilded Pub here with me to start writing for Spark the Flame.

Within a few months, the two were engaged, and around that time is when things really started weighing on my mind. I was never anything but happy for her, but it was the first Jenga piece to be shoved out of the tower I called my life. Alex was now doing something that she loved with *someone* she loved. And I no longer had my single ride or die with me at home or here at work to laugh about unsolicited dick pics or complain about our aching feet.

Suddenly, my nights were lonelier and my tip pocket lighter. My bed felt emptier even when someone was in it, and my shifts just a little longer. Even the stories people told at the bar started feeling more pointed. Like the hot guy with tattoos who talked about how in love he was with his girlfriend was rubbing it in that he was building a life rather than drinking through his problems.

Shortly after Al and Levi's courthouse wedding, my brother found out his wife was pregnant... again. Here I was, going about my same routine, and Blake and Amy were having another baby—making two full humans before I did, well, really anything significant. The selfish bastards already have my niece, who takes after her aunt and is basically perfect. Still, they just *had* to grow another one. Add in my mother's constant nagging about growing up and settling down, and it's no wonder my thinking started to shift.

My entire life, my mother has pressured me into this mold she assumed I should fit. The one that she so willingly fell into, then handcrafted for me to do the same. The one that says I should be more settled by now—career, relationship, house, kids. But I was never quite on board.

The whole situation was only made worse when I turned thirty last year. God forbid a woman in their third decade of life isn't at least one husband and a few kids deep. I swear Mom wore black to my birthday dinner not because it made her look slimmer, but because she was mourning any chance I had at not winding up a cat lady.

Her sister and I laughed about it all through dessert.

My Aunt Ivy is Mom's opposite. Where my mother is structured, living in quiet judgement, Ivy is chaos wrapped in charm. She's fun and free and lives life in the fast lane. She's never been married, and is far from settled down—always hopping on the tour bus of some cover band or spelunking in a crystal cave.

Ivy says there are two types of people in this world—those who follow the map and those who burn it just to see where the smoke goes. Some people are like Mom—they think there's one correct order to the way life unfolds—a blueprint—and anyone who veers off course is likely to be left behind. But others, she insists, are like her. They don't need directions because there's no finish line. The journey is the destination.

I wish I fell into *either* category. It would have made things easier. I never considered living in a vintage camper to follow the moon like Ivy has—or taking an impromptu trip to Morocco because my tarot cards told me to—she's just built differently. But I obviously haven't lived life step-by-step like Mom has either.

Lately though, I've felt pulled in my mom's direction. I've realized that pissing her off may have been my favorite part of resisting. That, and avoiding all that comes with it. But watching everyone else deepen their roots has me contemplating putting down some of my own. I'm not saying I'm ready to freeze my eggs or allow Mom to trade me for a brood of chickens, but I'm starting to consider taking some small steps towards building a life as an evolved adult.

The problem is, I'm not exactly sure where to start. It's hard to switch up routine after thirty years of doing things *my* particular way. I've kept my eye out for a new job, and I've been looking for a real relationship, but both of those things are difficult to commit to when you've had the same job and sex life for the last ten years.

Difficult in general.

My mind flickers back to Drew Anderson hovering over me—still fully dressed from the waist up—his slicked back hair falling loosely onto his forehead with each pounding thrust. His cerulean eyes were locked onto mine, unwavering, as he asked me over and over to tell him who I was—begged me like his livelihood depended on it. *He* was different, that's for sure. Someone who, in other circumstances, might make rerouting my path a little easier.

But that would never happen.

He doesn't even know my name.

I don't know exactly when I decided to keep my identity a secret. I just knew I wanted to be the one making the rules. The one with the power as I let the guy I had been drooling over for the last few months rail me against a sink. At the time, I hadn't yet had my epiphany, so I leaned in and did what I always do. I kept it casual, light, fun.

Unforgettable.

Maybe a little too much considering I'm still thinking about it after all this time. For someone who says she doesn't get attached, Drew's been hard to shake. But something about him struck me—stuck with me even after all this time.

I was caught off guard by the fact that he seemed different than I expected—more raw. Real. His intensity, the way he growled into my ear—it felt like we were connecting on a deeper level than maybe either of us are used to. Add to that his solid thighs, rock-hard ass, and *holy shit*, his massive—

"Brooke!"

The sound of my name rips me from the memory of Drew's perfect... everything, and I look up from where my gaze burns a hole in the red laminate floor of the kitchen. Trisha, our very goth—very unfriend-ly—hostess, stands in front of me, her expression blank behind her thick black eyeliner. She's naturally blunt, aggressive, and borderline hostile, but when she's standing by the restaurant door, she can turn it on better than anyone I know. It's scary how she can be two completely different people, but you get used to the slight fear she instills in you every time she comes to tell you that she's seated someone in your section.

Sort of.

"Sorry, did you say something?" I ask, taking another sip of my soda before returning my drink to its slot next to Tess's.

She stares at me briefly, and my gaze wanders awkwardly around the kitchen. I've learned that avoiding eye contact makes you feel less like she has a voodoo doll of you at home.

"I said, I sat you. Table twelve." With that, Trish turns on her heels, mumbling under her breath.

Normally, I would laugh off her attitude—that girl is one puzzle I don't care to piece together. But I have no capacity to feel anything right now except for the paralysis of my mind thanks to her last damn word.

Twelve.

For the past ten months, anything that reminds me of Drew "Best Sex of My Life" Anderson, makes my stomach drop, my palms sweat, and my chest flutter with a weird anxiety. I've had one-night-stands, sure, but none of the others still sit in the back of my mind. I don't think about any of them when I'm alone at night or sleeping with the guy I've gone on a few dates with, who is dull as dishwater but hung like a horse—*Sorry Shane, it's nothing personal.* But seeing Drew in the news, hearing him speak in an interview, having customers seated at *his* number's table... all of it brings memories of that night flooding back to me.

Cracking my neck to either side, I roll my shoulders in an attempt to release some of the tension. *Get it together, Brooke.* Drew Anderson was a one-off. He's the Flames' star forward for God's sake, and he's not without baggage, that's for sure. I know I'm just starting my *real* journey into adulthood, but something tells me pursuing a young celebrity isn't the most promising start.

Besides, it was my idea to make sure our bathroom sexcapades stayed within those four white walls. Who's to say he'd even remember holding my naked body against them while he slammed into me, my weight held effortlessly in his chiseled—

Holy shit, I've officially lost it.

Glancing into the dining room, I find table twelve, a booth with dark stained wood and red pleather seats tucked into the back corner. I snicker when I see who is seated there, hands intertwined on top of the table, their plastic menus casually pushed to the edge. I would swear they did this on purpose if they knew about that night. But they don't. No one does. And ideally, I'd like to keep it that way.

Strutting over to them, I mouth the words to the song echoing around the room, resetting myself to the beat of the music. "Your love would be so damn nauseating if you guys weren't so disgustingly hot," I say when I finally reach their table.

Alex rolls her eyes before glaring up at me. Levi chuckles, leaning back into the cushion behind him, his hands slipping from Alex's grasp. "Hey, Brooke," he says, draping one arm on the back of the booth and turning his body to face me.

"McHottie," I say curtly, nodding to him. Levi shakes his head and smiles as I slide into the booth next to Al. "What are you guys doing here?"

Laying her head on my shoulder, Alex wraps her arm around mine now resting on the table. "Can't we just come see my best friend while she's working on cheesesteak night?"

I look down at her suspiciously, then over at Levi, who immediately raises his palms in the air. "Don't look at me," he says. "I'm actually here for the sandwich." He reaches for the specials menu tucked into the metal holder at the back of the table and pretends to be captivated by the faded image of chipped steak and melted cheese wedged between a long sub roll.

Al's head slips off of my shoulder as I turn toward her and raise my brow. "So, are you going to tell me why you're really here or do I need to sic Trisha on you."

"Front of the house Trish or the *real* Trish?" she asks with wide eyes.

"I haven't decided yet."

With a shiver, she shakes her head. "Forget it. Both give me the creeps." She scrunches her face up before continuing to answer. "I need a favor."

I nod in faux understanding. "You guys want to borrow my handcuffs, don't you? I told you, you're always welcome to any of my—"

"Oh my God, no." She slaps my arm as a laugh rips out of me. "That is not what I mean."

I glance at Levi, who has his eyebrows cocked and his lips turned down, looking over the cheesesteak card. "Speak for yourself," he whispers not-so-under his breath as he returns it to its place in the holder. Alex looks at him as her mouth falls open, and he, once again, holds his hands up in surrender.

"What do you need?" I ask through a giggle, turning back to my blushing friend.

"The Flames' first game is next week in Grand Oaks—"

"Wait a minute. Isn't that the place where you guys started all this?"

"Uh huh," Levi answers.

"And where you banged for the first time," I add on.

"Mhmm," Alex says, her cheeks growing more pink by the second.

"And where Levi first went all *good gir*—"

"Yes!" she yells. Levi rubs his forehead trying to hide his smile, and I snicker.

"Yeah, it probably sounded just like that." I wink in his direction, and Alex groans before dropping her chin into her hand, her elbow resting on the table. "Okay, okay, I'm done. So, the game is in Grand Oaks..."

She huffs out a breath, then sits back up. "The game is in Grand Oaks, and we were thinking maybe we'd go back and try to sneak in some time together to celebrate our—"

"Your one year bangiversary?" I deadpan.

Alex closes her eyes and inhales deeply like she does with Cooper when she's about to lose her patience. She takes a few calming seconds before opening them back up. "Something like that," she answers simply. "But I would need someone to take Coop."

"Oh, I'm surprised he wouldn't go with you. Not for the banging part. But the hockey part."

Levi crosses his arms over his chest and leans his forearms on the table. "That's what I said."

"He'll be bummed to miss the game," Alex explains. "But last time he came because the trip was part of the spotlight. I don't want the guys or coaches to feel like they have to babysit on their first away trip. They do enough of that at the rink."

I glance around to make sure Trish hasn't sat anyone else in my section, but find nothing but empty tables. Thank God. I'll be cut soon, and I'm ready to hightail it out of here as fast as I can.

"Well, you know I'll take my nephew whenever you need me to, but I gotta say, I'm with Cooper on this one. I'm so jealous. Not because of the game..." Tilting my head toward Levi, I grin. "No offense. I just wish I got to get away with a sexy hockey play—coach. A sexy hockey coach." The words fall out of my mouth before I can catch myself. *Dammit.* I blame Trish for the idea of Drew now sitting at the front of my mind. And I blame Alex for my sudden desire for a steady man.

If my best friend notices the flush that creeps up my neck, she doesn't say anything. She's too busy looking at Levi with suspicion.

"Wait, what?" I say, feeling like I missed something.

Levi clears his throat. "I said, why don't you join us."

"To which I said... excuse me?" Now Alex is the one who crosses her arms in her usual *what did you just say* pose.

"I didn't mean it like that. You know you're it for me, Bennett." He winks playfully at his wife before continuing. "I was just thinking that instead of Cooper staying home with Brooke and missing the game, what if Brooke came with the three of us to Grand Oaks? I could get the two of them their own room, and they can hang out like they would at home, but Coop wouldn't have to miss the game live."

Alex shrugs her shoulders. "Works for me. I didn't think of that. I was just hoping we'd have our *own* room, that's all. What do you think, Brooke?"

I'm staring at her, but once again, I'm not quite listening. This time it's not the image of Drew in the venue bathroom that's debilitating me. It's the one of him on the ice, his hair dripping with sweat, his body looking even more powerful in full gear. I know from experience what it's like to be in the same space as *that* Drew Anderson. Especially after the night that we had.

When I watched him win the Cup last season, just months after our moment together, it took everything in me not to glide over to him on the ice after we all flooded it to celebrate the win. Just being that close to him with no boards between us made the air feel charged by more than the victory. It's the reason I decided to duck out early—to "let Alex, Coop, and Levi have some time alone to celebrate." I couldn't risk him seeing me and coming over. Or worse—risk him seeing me and ignoring me completely.

For a second, I contemplate saying no to the trip. Apologizing to Alex and Levi and making up some sort of excuse as to why all of a sudden I've changed my tune about taking Cooper. But I can't do that to them, or my nephew, and I damn sure can't tell them the real reason why I'm suddenly sweating through my shirt. I'm not sure either of them would appreciate finding out I slept with Drew, or even worse—that I'm attempting to make some big life changes and being that close to temptation might detour my plans.

So, instead, I paint a smile and channel my inner Ivy—fearless and spontaneous. I slide out of the booth hoping the distance between us will keep them from smelling my hesitation, and I agree to putting myself in the same rink—the same fucking hotel—as *him*.

"Sounds great," I say, my voice cracking halfway into the second word. "I'm sure it'll be a kickass time."

2
Drew

"**D**rew, the first game of the season is just a few days away. How are you feeling?"

Running my hand through my soaked hair, I hike up the grip on my stick and bare my weight against it. "Yeah, we're feeling good. The guys put in a lot of work this off season, and we're eager to get started."

Emma Dean, a reporter for Golden City's local sports channel, nods in understanding. She's a regular after practices, especially when there's buzz around a big game. "I'm sure you are. And you're coming off a Cup win. How do you think that will affect your mindset heading to Grand Oaks this week?"

"It won't affect us at all," I say without hesitation. "We know we'll have a target on our backs. Every team, not just the Gladiators, is gonna deliver their A game, but we'll be ready."

Emma leans in closer, her overly sweet floral perfume mixing with my post-practice sweat in the worst possible way.

She's objectively good looking, with her nice clothes, slicked-back ponytail, and perky tits she always makes sure to show off. But she's not my type. I like my women a little edgier—ripped jeans, inked skin.

Chocolate hair, matching eyes. Women who smell less like flowers and more like... citrus.

"And how about you personally?"

Emma jolts me back to the interview with the start of her next question, and I'm grateful I'm still wearing my padded hockey pants to cover the part of me that's stuck on *her.*

"Are you feeling like you might get some residual kickback from last year's failed drug test?"

Without hesitation, a scoff falls from my lips. Emma raises a brow as I roll my eyes and shake my head. Countless goals, dozens of wins, and a goddamn Cup—yet this is what it always comes to. It used to piss me off, but now it's entertaining. That one mistake is the bone they can't stop chewing on. Well, they can't shake me if that's what they're going for. If there's one lesson that's been nailed home these last few months, it's that it's easier to stop caring when you stop feeling altogether.

Inhaling deeply through my nose, I smack my lips, grinding the blade of my stick into the floor. "Guys chirp us about everything. I've been doing this long enough to tune them out. At the end of the day, they're still worried about me when I couldn't care less about them."

She laughs, tilting her microphone back. "You don't feel the need to defend yourself?" she asks, an eyebrow raised. Several of the guys around me chuckle under their breaths.

"The scoreboard will do plenty of talking," I say, looking right at the camera.

Her expression falters, a cross between impressed and uneasy, but she continues. "After everything last season, you seemed pretty quiet. We didn't see many of your usual moves—trick shots, celebrations, crowd work. Even your social media presence has gone dark..." She tilts the microphone toward me, waiting.

She raises an eyebrow, and I give her a blank stare. "Is there a question there, Emma?"

My voice is smooth and deliberate as I drag my tongue slowly across my lower lip. Her mouth parts slightly, and to the average viewer, she is preparing to respond, but I catch the slight hitch in her breath as her eyes track my movement. *Two can play this game.*

"I think Golden City wants to know if we'll be getting our icon back."

A quiet chuckle rumbles in my chest as I consider my answer. I kept my head down after the failed test, trying to move past this. To let it all blow over. To let myself process it all. I spent most of last season either suspended or under scrutiny. My P.R. manager and I thought maybe toning down my infamous antics might help them forget. Let me breathe. Give me time to sort myself out.

It backfired.

All it did was give them a silence to fill with their own bullshit—and time for me to realize I don't want any of it.

Slipping into the role I know best, I smirk, letting my arrogance take the wheel. "Who says he ever really left?" I wink at Emma, then turn away, leaning my stick against the side of my stall—a clear signal. This conversation's over.

"That's right," I hear over my shoulder. I don't have to turn to know Brett Burns, our best defenseman and my best friend, is standing next to me. His voice is almost as annoying as his laugh, but we love him for it anyway... usually. I throw him a side-eye as I stand back at attention, residual tension still hiding in my jaw from Emma's last question.

"Cap's *been* back. Can't keep Superman down, can ya?"

I smile softly, but swallow hard. Emma shakes her head and gives a tight-lipped nod. She faces the camera and starts signing off as I go back to removing my equipment.

"Thanks, Drew. Nice to see you again," she says, turning back to me once the red light blinks off.

I tip my chin up to her before peeling off my shirt, pretending I don't notice the way her eyes linger on me. She's not subtle. None of them are. Sitting on the bench to remove my skates, I consider the last few minutes while the guys dick around in the background.

I didn't ask to be put on a pedestal. The media, my dad, the whole goddamn world—they're the ones who decided I was untouchable. But the second I slip, they're the first to throw stones. I crossed a line, yeah. But the truth is, all of it—my ego, my game, even the drugs—serves the same purpose. To hold up the version of me *they* created.

"Yo, that little news hunny wants her some Anderson pie, doesn't she?" Burnsey throws his shoulder into mine before sitting on the bench that runs along our stalls. "You gonna hit that or what?"

I blow a heavy breath through my lips before responding. "What?" I ask, trying to drain my voice of irritation.

"Ms. Microphone with the knockers. She's always givin' you the eyes." He wiggles his brows up and down, and mine crease in annoyance.

All the puck bunnies are the same. They're just looking for attention and would love to get it from someone with a reputation like mine. Who wouldn't want a taste of the Flames' wildfire?

Well, now it's worse.

"Not this time, Bursney," I say casually, despite my crawling skin. "She's all yours."

Burns arches a brow and nods. "Sweet!" He pauses a moment in thought before he turns back to me. "You think she takes that camera in the bedroom?"

The guys around us, including our goalie, Carter Ward, pause in their tracks before they erupt into laughter. Brett glances around with his eyes narrowed and his arms wide.

"What? She might! Anderson, come on, don't act like you wouldn't like a little role play. I'd let that girl give me a post-game interview." He smacks my arm with the back of his hand, a devious grin across his lips. "She could talk into *my* microphone, if you know what I mean."

I shake my head as I pull off my sock. "Dude, nobody has any fucking clue what you mean."

Burns scrunches his face and falls back from my stall. "You know, like a blowj..." His voice trails off as it's met with awkward silence. He scans the room, waiting for someone to join in his enthusiasm. Instead, Ward huffs out a laugh and shakes his head as he slips his other leg into his shorts.

"You're a strange bird, Burnsey."

Brett rolls his eyes, then flips him off. "Says the fucking goalie."

When I'm stripped down to nothing but my signature gold chain, I wrap a towel around my waist and move toward the hallway in the back of the room, ignoring the ongoing conversation about Brett's sex life that continues burning ears around me.

Heading to the showers, I finally let the weight of the interview settle. Sometimes I don't know what's worse—hearing this shit or pretending it doesn't get to me. I hang my towel on the hooks outside of the wet area, then walk to the first shower head—*my* shower head—and turn the water on.

I don't bother to let it warm up before I brace my hands on the black-tiled wall and let it cascade down the back of my head as it hangs between my arms. Letting the sweat from practice and the disgust from this whole situation rinse off of me, I allow my mind to drift back to last season.

I'm not sure I can pin-point exactly where it started. The team shrink that Monte wanted me to see might have had an opinion if I actually went. I'd say I had just fucking had it—the pressure building and building over the last several years. Add in that we got fucking robbed of the Cup two seasons ago, and the dam was bound to break. I hate being the underdog. I was never allowed to be. So when my game started to slip from all the bullshit, I made an executive decision.

I knew I was playing with fire the moment it happened. It wasn't my first time trying coke. But this time it wasn't a hit at a party. This time was different, calculated.

This time I needed it.

It was the morning after another shitty game. My dad called me, his words like salt in an open wound. He told me he didn't understand why I was struggling, that my team was counting on me. My *city* was counting on me. *You're better than this, Drew, so be better.* That's Dad—never satisfied. The guy who couldn't make it past the collegiate level playing for the Grizzlies, but expected me to go all the way.

According to him, I can always do more, play more, score more... *be* more. He's holding me to my potential, he says. *"You're capable of reaching the stars, Drew. I'm not going to let you settle for walking the earth."* But I don't think he realizes how easy it is to shoot for the moon and lose all sense of grounding. There's no gravity in space. Nothing anchoring you down.

My natural talent has always been able to carry me, but that means I'm not allowed to have off days. I knew how the drug made me feel off of the ice—like I was incapable of stopping even if I wanted to—so when I fell into a slump, I figured maybe it could do the same thing *on* the ice.

And, fuck... it did.

As soon as the dust hit my bloodstream that first time before practice, a switch flipped back on inside of me. I didn't just have energy—I was weightless. It was like I was flying—gliding across the ice like I was hovering over it, my body moving without me asking it to, my knowledge of the game—where to be, when to bob, and how to weave—happening on autopilot.

It was exactly what I needed. Enough to lock me into the game and drown out everything else—be the man again. Half the time, I didn't even need a second bump. That first hit—those first thirty minutes—were enough to snap me into gear. To remind me who I am. Who I had to be.

That I was untouchable.

Until I wasn't.

And the fall was brutal.

"Yo, man. What's the plan for tonight?"

Brett breaks me from my trance, twisting on the shower head next to mine. Grabbing the shampoo from my shelf, I answer. "I don't know. Haven't really thought about it."

He stands back from the spray and rubs his palms in front of his face. "Come on, man. It's a new season, and this is the last weekend before the opener. We gotta do something."

Running my hands through my overgrown hair, I pause at my nape, gripping my neck and letting my elbows fall forward. My head lolls back, putting pressure on my grasp, my fingertips naturally pressing into the tension at the top of my shoulders. A flash of my mystery girl's hands massaging me in the same spot snaps me back to life.

She's always there.

Almost a year later, and I still can't shake the way she made me feel. The way she saw *me*. Or just didn't care about the rest. And ever since, every one-night-stand, every meaningless hookup, has been a failed attempt at chasing that high. At feeling anything again.

"Hello?" Burnsey sings.

I open my eyes and see he's too goddamn close to me considering we're both buck-ass naked. "Dude, personal fucking space." I dip my head backwards, allowing the stream of now piping hot water to wash away the suds. "Save it for Emma."

His eyes dart to mine as I smother a smirk. He splashes water on his face and uses both hands to wipe it away. "My bad, bro," he laughs. "Just trying to start the season off right."

My eyes slink slowly shut as I duck back under the water. I let it wash over me in an attempt to rid myself of everything I'd like to say—everything I'd like to do except *that*—just everything in general.

But it doesn't work.

It never does.

Inhaling deeply, I give myself one more beat of honesty before I slowly start to nod, falling back into the persona I can fake better than the real thing. "Yeah, " I say as I let out my breath. "Party at your place."

Shifting back toward the wall, I reach for my body wash before I pause and look back at Burns. "No fucking reporters."

3

Brooke

Packing for my chaperoning trip to Grand Oaks, I give every article of clothing a little too much thought. Every top I pull from my closet, all the jeans I hold up, any piece of underwear I consider throwing in my bag—each decision more important than it should be.

Realistically, the odds of running into Drew are pretty slim. Sure, we'll be staying at the same hotel. And yes, I'll be watching him play the Gladiators. But the chances are small that we actually interact. I can't exactly picture the star of the Flames casually roaming the hotel lobby when he could be doing literally anything else. Besides, Cooper's old enough to handle himself around the team if they were to invite him out like they have before.

So, in reality, it's not so much seeing Drew that rattles me. It's how he would act toward me if we did run into each other. In my mind, he's the guy who read my soul with just a glance, begged to know me when I tried to keep him at a distance, ruined me like no one else has.

On the ice, he's a showman. Hell, that's what caught my attention in the first place. In uniform, he's all smooth moves, hard shots, and quality entertainment. Confident. Calculated. Charismatic. But he seemed so different when he was with me. He knew what he was doing, and he damn sure wasn't shy, but it was as if the version I got of him was stripped down in more ways than one. He seemed deeper. Thoughtful. More complex.

The internet is riddled with pictures of Drew all over Golden City—all over the damn world for that matter. But I don't see *him* in any of them. Not the guy I caught a glimpse of that was full of undiscovered layers. There are none with those steel-blue eyes that saw right through me. No strong yet graceful stance that held me in his arms. The pictures seem like just that—an image. Unless that's who he really is.

I guess it's hard to know which version of him is a show from our one interaction. But it doesn't matter anyway. Even flirting with that idea is counterproductive to what I'm trying to do, which is get my parents *off* my back.

A dull hum sounds from my mattress, which means either my vibrator's gone rogue or my cell phone is ringing under my pile of clothes. Tossing a handful of sweaters, a leather jacket, and my favorite pair of jeans to the floor, I locate the source of the sound.

"Hello?" I answer, bringing it to my ear and turning down the country song playing through my laptop speakers.

"Hey, Brooke. It's Levi."

It takes me entirely too long to put a face to the name and process that my best friend's husband is the voice on the other end. "McHottie? Why are you—wait, is Al okay?" My brain gets whiplash, flipping in three directions from my mental ramble about Drew, Levi's call, and now my sudden concern for Alex.

Levi chuckles. "No, no, she's fine. She gave me your number. I actually need another favor."

Plopping onto my bed, I let out a deep breath. "You know, Al didn't really sound too thrilled about the—"

"It's not about the handcuffs," he says, beating me to it.

I scoff playfully, running my finger along the frayed knee of another pair of denim. "Mhmm, not yet. So, what's up?"

"Listen, I know you're into the whole social media thing."

"You mean that I *have* social media, Levi?"

He laughs before saying, "Okay, fair. But Bennett also says that you're actually really good at it."

"She told you about my detective work, didn't she? Well, put me in Coach! Who do you need me to stalk?"

Levi sighs, and it's as if I can hear him roll his eyes through the silence that follows. That or maybe he's considering how much investigating I did into him before he and my best friend started hooking up.

"Thanks for the offer, but I'm good," he says, his voice laced with amusement. "I was actually wondering if you'd take a few pictures and put some stuff together for the game this week while you're there. Our social media manager left at the end of last season, and we sort of shit the bed on replacing her fast enough." He exhales sharply in defeat. "She apparently had content scheduled to be posted through the off-season and a few images for the start of the season. But our new girl can't start until she finishes up a project at her current job, and the Cup champions can't really go into our first game without any advertising."

I raise an eyebrow, shifting my phone to my other ear. "I mean, I know how to take decent pictures and throw a caption underneath. And I guess you could say I keep up with trends and stuff, but I'm no professional."

"That's okay, anything's better than nothing. Alex said you do it for The Pub?"

"Yeah..." I say skeptically. "My cocktail pics are top-notch, if I do say so myself. You throw that baby in portrait mode and—"

"Yeah, I have no idea what that means. But you know what you're doing?"

I shrug even though he can't see me. "Sure, I know my way around."

"Okay, well, I need someone in the interim until our replacement can start." He pauses, like he's gauging my reaction. "What would you think about filling in until she gets here?"

"For just the first game?"

"Um, yeah. Or maybe, oh I don't know... the first dozen games? Say, a month or so?"

"A month?" I echo loudly.

"Yeah," he drags out. "I know. It's a little last minute, but you know this isn't my thing. It's not Jack's either—our owner—so we sort of both thought the other guy would handle it. I'll pay you, obviously. I know you'd need to take off from the restaurant."

I exhale heavily, contemplating his offer.

"You'd really be helping me and the organization out," he adds, then sighs. "It's either you or Burnsey's gonna try to do it, and God help us all if that's the case."

"Who?"

"Never mind," he says playfully.

"Wait, what about Al? She's basically doing that for Spark the Flame, isn't she? She wouldn't want to do it?" I ask, assuming he's already thought of his wife, who is working for the team's community outreach program doing almost the same job.

"Yeah, but the gala's next month. So, between the blog and Spark the Flame, she has basically zero extra time. She's actually the one who thought you might be interested." He lets a silence fall between us as I gather my thoughts. "You can think about it if you need to."

I hesitate, considering there's a good chance that my taking pictures of the team would involve my being *near* the team... and a certain first line forward. But I *have* been looking for something new, and I'm sure I could get my shifts covered at The Pub. I guess temporary is better than nothing. Plus, I can hear Levi's desperation, and damn it if I don't have a soft spot for Coach McHottie thanks to how happy he makes one of my favorite people.

I inhale deeply, giving myself one more second to reconsider. "Yeah, alright," I say instead. "I can do it."

He blows out a heavy breath as if a weight's been lifted from his shoulders. "Thanks, Brooke. I owe you. I'll make sure to get you the specifics."

"No worries. I get the gist." I grin as I raise a brow, scheming. "Oh, and hey, Levi?"

"Yeah?"

"You keep me posted on those handcuffs."

Half a second passes where I think he may be thinking it over before he clears his throat. "Goodbye, Brooke," he says dryly.

I laugh as the line goes dead.

Okay, so maybe I won't be avoiding Drew as much as I had hoped. But this is a good opportunity to explore other career paths. And besides, there are other players on the team. He can't be the only one the media wants to see.

Deciding it's necessary—for research purposes—I click open the Instagram app.

Pulling up the page for @GoldenCityFlames, my vision is flooded with a sea of red and black. The last few images are marketing their first game against the Guardians, and before that, there are posts of new players they signed over the summer. Their contract years and values are listed next to their pictures with an overlay of the Flames logo and text that says "Welcome to G.C." There are also some trade alerts, this season's game schedule, and a couple of filler reels with player quotes and interviews—all things I think I can handle. If anything, they're actually a little duller than I expected them to be.

After sliding past another couple of posts, my thumb instinctively presses to the screen, pausing on a picture of a familiar face looking every bit as untouchable as he always does with any sort of glass between us. The post is of Drew on July second in his red jersey with a gold chain that lays on top. His hair looks freshly tossed, and his smile is more like a smirk, his left eyebrow raised slightly. The caption says, "HBD Drew Anderson! This Flames' forward turns twenty-five today. Happy birthday, number twelve!"

"Twenty-five," I whisper to myself. *Holy shit.* He's *barely* twenty-five. That means when we hooked up, he wasn't even—yep, not even old enough to have a quarter-life crisis.

I swipe right, and it takes me to a short video clip the old social media manager must have asked him to send her. It's him holding the camera out in front of him with probably a hundred people in the background, party music bursting through the speakers. He's wearing a black button-up shirt that sits halfway open, his gold chain shimmering every time the moving lights glimmer past it. He looks good—sexy. My heart-rate kicks up like it only does when you're doing—or *feeling*—something that you shouldn't.

"What's up, G.C.," he yells over the song. "Just wanted to say thanks for all the b-day shout outs." He swallows quickly, his eyes darting to either side of the camera. "I appreciate all your support over, uh, this past year. Twenty-four was... well... I learned a lot."

He pauses for just a second, looking past the camera instead of directly at it, before another guy comes up behind him and throws his arm across his shoulders. Drew glances back at him before switching his demeanor, but if you're paying attention, you'd notice his smile is dimmer than it was before.

"Anyway, I gotta go tear it up with these assholes, but... I love you guys."

A girl with long, wavy red hair slinks up to him and places her hand on his chest, just as the video comes to an end. I roll my eyes, brushing my thumb as fast as I can back to the first picture.

Scrolling down, I glance through the comments. There's everything from basic birthday wishes to insults, bro responses to thirsty messages.

BBurns_06: HBD, my dude! Here's to an epic year.

Sp0rtsBr01980: Over. Rated.

JustCallMeLola: Holy hell, for the sake of my vagina, please do not get hotter with age.

Shay_Bae: I have a present he can unwrap...

Hockey.Fan.4Lyfe: This guy's twenty-five? Way too old to be acting like he does.

RedHotRedHead21: What a wild night, babe.

Rolling my eyes, I try to ignore the way hate heats my chest and how that last one churns my stomach. Instead, I focus on the fact at hand.

I knew Drew was young. In fact, I vaguely remember Alex telling me about it this past season, but at the time it was all a pipe dream. In reality, the difference between thirty-one and twenty-five is only six years. That's not even one dog year—barely a first grader. Maybe I shouldn't admit this, but I've had underwear longer than that. It somehow just feels different when it's the years between our ages.

At the time, the numbers didn't seem as wildly different as they do now. Maybe because the way he acted—the way we connected—felt like we were one and the same. But now, ten months, countless headlines, and one new life goal later, his age is just an added reminder that we're not just living in different stages of life—we're on completely different planets.

So, the man's a good lay. But this seals the deal—that's all that it was. This time last year, *I* wasn't even ready to start building a life for myself. There's no way a twenty-five-year-old professional athlete who lives a life of lust and luxury would be even remotely on the same page.

Glancing around, my clothes suddenly all seem like completely acceptable choices. Jean jacket? Perfect. Black denim? Great. Combat boots? Works for me. Of course, I want Drew to remember that night—it still stands out to me for so many reasons. But I'm no longer afraid of how he'll act toward me. It doesn't make a difference. He could be my intriguing mystery or the world's charming Romeo—it's irrelevant when we don't make sense either way.

My phone vibrates again, this time in two quick buzzes. Grabbing it, I find an incoming message from my brother. I swipe it open and groan aloud.

Blake

> You better not be bailing on dinner again. I'll see you in a half-hour.

Damn it. The last few weeks, I've been lucky enough to be scheduled at The Pub during my family's weekly dinners. Apparently tonight, my luck runs out. I consider bailing anyway. I have things to pack and *now...* Instagrams to stalk. But I do miss my niece—and the rest of my family, I guess. And it *has* been awhile since I've had to play a game of Dodge-Mom's-Passive-Aggressive-Critiques-Of-My-Life-Choices.

I do like to stay sharp.

I grab my nearest jacket from the pile—my sage green bomber—and shrug it on over my black t-shirt and jeans. I slip into my combat boots, which are already piled next to my bag, and make a mental note to put them back there later so I don't forget them for our trip. *Ugh, our trip.*

Just like that, the image of seeing Drew up close and personal crashes into my mind, and there's an instant pulse between my thighs. Luckily, the next wave of thoughts brings with it the reminder that no matter how I remember him, he's not the guy from that night last year. He's Drew Anderson—hockey all-star, Golden City hero, ladies' man.

A twenty-five-year-old phenomenon.

And now, even Mom and I have more in common.

4
Drew

Stretching over to my bedside table, I groan as I attempt to end the constant fucking whirring coming from my phone. When I finally reach it, I crack one eye, leaving the rest of my body plastered chest-down onto my California king. Peeking at the time, I let out a heavy sigh. *God dammit.* I have to get up. Not that it matters really—sleep doesn't help much when it's your soul that's tired.

It's game week, and we have to travel to Grand Oaks in a couple of hours. I'm ready physically, but I'm not sure I'm prepared mentally to step back into the season. Never being out of the public eye is exhausting. Even during the off-season, there are always cameras and signings, interviews for something—the draft, training camp, Flames events. But these next nine months will bring even more unwanted attention.

I've grown used to being a topic of conversation in the hockey world. People love me, they hate me, they can't decide which way they lean more. There's no winning when it comes to the media. If I don't score enough, my contract's questioned. If I score too much, I'm not a team player. I'm used to being ridiculed and held to a ridiculous standard.

But now, there's an unforgettable drug test added to the list.

Pushing myself out of bed, tomorrow's game creeps to the forefront of my mind, but I'm not worried about the Gladiators. They were in the middle of the pack last season—not much of a threat. It's the perfect game to kick us off—to set the tone. Get in, show out, and remind G.C. who the hell I am, then ride that wave into the rest of our schedule.

I'm halfway between my bed and my master bathroom when my phone vibrates in my hand. Looking down, I see the incoming number and immediately throw the device back onto the mattress. *Nope. Not today.*

My dad calls every so often, his way of making sure he's still a voice inside my head. Usually it comes before a big game and goes something like this:

"Hey, champ. Big game coming up. You ready?"

Like always, I'll respond, *"Yeah, Dad, I'm ready."*

Then comes the unsolicited advice or insight—*"Remember, their goalie favors his left side." "Don't forget to keep your feet moving." "Try not to get caught on a long shift like you did last game."*

I'll nod along, either agreeing or complying—whatever it takes to end the conversation—and he'll sign off in his typical manner. *"This is your game, champ. You're a star. Don't let them forget it."*

Only what *he* forgets is that stars don't shine. They fucking burn.

I thought when I finally made it to the NHL, he might ease up. This is what he trained me for since I was three and first stepped onto the ice. But now, instead of reminding me of what I'm working toward, he just likes to make sure I don't overlook everything I have to lose. And lately his motives are even more loaded.

I'm not sure when playing professional hockey became *my* dream. Or if it ever really was. Mom always reminded me of the *real* reasons I was playing the game—have fun, meet friends, make myself proud. But Dad was quick to follow up with reminders of his own—stay focused, train hard, don't waste the gift I was given. Unfortunately, those first few weren't beaten into my head for as long as the others.

I glance in the mirror, and a light pink patch of bruised skin right above my collarbone stands out. "Fucking hell," I say, leaning into the glass for a closer look.

I didn't realize Maddie—Mandy?—went so hard last night before I left. Twisting around, I glance back at my reflection. Faint claw marks trail down my spine, and I blow out a breath. She was hot, but not brand-me-before-my-first-trip hot. Fine enough to let off some pregame steam with an added bonus of helping to get Jane off my case.

My P.R. manager, who to no one's surprise was pushed on me by my dad, makes it a point to keep me in the headlines. To keep me on the fans' radar and hold up my image. In fact, that's exactly what she was hired to do—take my rookie self, who spent his life in a hockey rink instead of with friends or girls, and make him "worthy" of my contract.

It was simple, really. What guy just starting out in the league doesn't want to become the face of a franchise? To fuck beautiful women, drink in penthouses, and say exactly what's on their mind? Soon, though, that transferred onto the ice as well. You can't only wear the mask half the time. But as time went on, the novelty of all of it faded until I stopped wanting to do any of it.

Spinning back toward the mirror, a memory springs to mind. My mystery girl. The only one that's left an impression. It's been so long, but it feels like yesterday. I wonder if she remembers me—if that night left any sort of mark on her the way it permanently inked itself on me.

Besides the fact that she was fucking breathtaking, she was also the only girl that's stuck with me in a blur of other hookups. The only one who was more than an hour of relief. The only one who treated me like an actual human being.

Everyone wants Drew Anderson—hockey star and bad boy. They want a thrill or to check me off their bucket list, only caring that they have a story for their damn group chat. They want the hair, the tattoos, the chain—the image. They don't want *me*.

But she seemed different.

Gripping the sink on either side of the porcelain, I picture her legs sitting between my arms. Her chest heaving into mine as I wrap my hand around the base of her neck and pull her close.

Suddenly my bathroom smells like citrus, and her voice echoes inside my head.

"I wouldn't say I know you."

Yeah. She seemed *really* fucking different.

Wiping my face of the mental image I have of her straddling my torso, I push off of the sink. I crack my neck to both sides, then run a hand through my hair. Time to get moving. I've got a plane to catch.

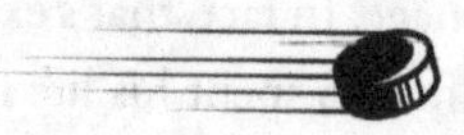

There's nothing like the roar of the engine bouncing off the Golden City streets before an upcoming game. Cruising through the city, I always make sure to take my bike the long way to the arena. Something about the ride helps clear my head—no calls, no coaches, no cameras. The only pressure is from the weight of my bag on my back or my grip on the throttle as I weave through the morning's traffic.

My Ducati was the first thing I bought when I signed with the Flames. At this point she's a few years old, but I like her broken in. It's a machine—high performing, built for speed, perfect for pushing limits—a goddamn superbike. It's painted a sleek matte black, which attempts to conceal the power underneath, but there's no hiding all it has to offer. With its gold suspension bar as the perfect contrast, the whole design creates a tough image to cover the intricacy of the beast that lies beneath it.

The growl from the engine morphs into a high-pitched wail as I speed down the street—the roar mixing with tight crackles and snappy shifts that announce its arrival before you even see it coming. The Ducati's bold. Loud. Aggressive. It's not a sports bike—it's a fucking statement.

And that's exactly what I was going for.

Zipping through downtown Golden City toward the arena, the sun beats through my black warm up jacket, the perfect touch in the cool October air. I soak in the commute as I bend down the roads, which aren't as busy as they might have been during rush hour. There are still plenty of people milling about—shopping, running, grabbing their mid-morning coffees. But the ease of the drive now is exactly what I need before a day like today.

I love this city. Always have. It's the perfect combination of small enough to feel like home but big enough for me to feel almost insignificant. With my helmet on, I'm just another city dweller rolling through the streets. No one knows if I'm off to throw on a ten-million-dollar jersey or push papers at my nine-to-five.

Here, on this bike, I can be whoever the hell I want to be, and no one would know the difference. Shit, no one would fucking care. On these two wheels, I can be exactly who I want to be—me. It's just a shame that it ends here, as I turn onto the arena's street.

Pulling into the covered lot, I ride directly to where my teammates' sports cars and SUVs are parked in our secure designated area. Easing into my spot, I settle my weight backwards, cut the engine, and stomp down the kickstand with the heel of my black boot. Savoring my last beat of silence and fresh air, I remove my helmet and run my hand through my hair.

I spot the black and red shuttle parked by the back entrance, the Flames logo sparkling from the morning sun. It's the first sign of a new season. We're back to traveling, hotels, and pregame rituals. I'll do my thing, some of the boys will tape their sticks in exactly the same way at the exact same time. Others will eat the same meal they've had before every other game and drink Gatorades with only a certain color cap. Burnsey will take his hour-long nap, Ward will tap his stick against the goal posts to the beat of *Eye of the Tiger*, and Petrov will do... well, I don't actually know what he does. Either way, I'm not sure if I'm ready for any of it. It's all just a precursor to what's coming. But I have to be.

Sliding off the bike, I work my shoulders to relieve some of the tension my backpack caused while I was crouched over the handles, then set my helmet on its spot behind the seat. Strolling over to the bus, I run my thumb side to side along the bottom of my chain—the closest thing I have to reassurance. At the same time, Burnsey runs to catch up with me from his blacked-out Hummer.

"What up, broski? Big day! You ready?" He claps me on the shoulder as we head toward the bus.

I nod slowly, sliding my backpack down one arm and tucking my keys into the front pocket.

Burns falls into step beside me as I throw it back over my shoulder. "I stay ready. You know this," I say just a couple feet from the door.

He taps his elbow into mine, a cheesy grin resting on his face. "Atta boy."

We walk the few steps it takes to get to the stairs leading onto the bus. Brett matches his pace to mine, and I take slow, steadying breaths until Brett stops abruptly, turning around to face me.

I blink with genuine confusion. "Can I help you?"

He shoves his hands into his pockets and narrows his eyes. "You good, man?"

I shift my weight, already feeling the walls go up. "Burns, you just asked me that."

He shakes his head as he adjusts the strap of his duffle bag hanging off of his shoulder. "I asked if you're *ready*. Now, I'm asking if you're *good*."

My stomach drops the way it always does when someone threatens to cut a hole in the facade. Brett's my best friend—obnoxious as hell—but the guy is solid. He's got my back no matter what, both on and off the ice. He's the only one who really gets how heavy this past year has been, but even he doesn't know the full story.

Brett has his own reputation to uphold as the team clown, always diving onto the ice or back flipping on skates. But it's not the same. People don't ride him the way they do me. And with his picture-perfect family and golden retriever vibes, pressure doesn't seem to stick anyway.

"I'm good, man," I say, dropping my hand onto his shoulder. I decided a long time ago that I wasn't going to burden anyone else with my secret. I damn sure don't plan to start now. "Just locking in. You know how I get."

He studies me for a beat too long before nodding slowly. "You sure?"

"Dude..."

"Alright, alright." He laughs, his hands up in surrender. "New season, same Cap."

I roll my eyes, tucking both thumbs under the straps of my backpack, then toss the kid a bone. "I was thinking about switching up my pregame routine though."

Burnsey's face twists up like I told him that he and Ward were swapping positions. "You mean you aren't gonna disappear to a secluded spot to listen to your angsty shit beforehand?"

I shake my head, biting the inside of my cheek. "I mean, I didn't say *that*. But I don't know, just mix it up. Maybe start slow and change up the night before first." I let out a heavy breath. "Try to make this season as different as I can from last year's, ya know?"

Burns nods in understanding, or at least the half he can, and offers his usual easygoing grin. I don't want to distance myself from the boys more than I usually do, but I also need *something* to change this year. If it can't be my game or my persona, maybe a few extra hours of peace is a good place to start.

Brett looks down at his gold Rolex, then back up at the bus. "Alright, I get that. But give me the next twenty-threeish minutes at least. Sound good?"

I huff out a laugh. "Yeah, bro. You got it."

His smirk grows into a full-on smile as he turns and walks onto the shuttle. Pausing to let him climb the stairs, I bring my first two fingers to my nose and pinch the bridge. *Here we go.*

I take one deep breath before walking onto a bus full of guys who need me to be at the top of my game, and trying to pretend I don't feel like I'm drowning.

"What's up, assholes!"

"Drewww," they all drag out in unison, their voices low and lazy.

I smile and tip my chin up, heading right for the back.

Twenty-three minutes until we board the plane.

Twenty-three minutes until the season begins.

Twenty-three minutes until I'm back to being Drew motherfucking Anderson.

Or at least who he pretends to be.

5

Brooke

I have successfully gone almost the entire first day in Grand Oaks without running into Drew, and I haven't decided yet if that's a good thing or a bad thing. Part of me is dying to see him. I want to know if he'd even recognize me after all this time—and if my body would remember him in person the same way it does when I see him on TV.

The other part of me, though, is happy to avoid the situation altogether. I'm not sure what would be worse—the two of us gravitating toward each other like we did ten months ago or the illusion of the connection I thought we had burning to the ground.

It helps that Al, Cooper, and I have gotten to do our own thing. McHottie flew with the boys and they had a team meeting this afternoon. So, once we got to Grand Oaks, we decided to explore a little before checking into our hotel.

This town is adorable. It's almost the same size as Golden City, but it gives off a much cozier vibe. There's a small park in the center with walking paths and a water fountain where people throw their coins, and benches on nearly every street. There's a dog park and a flourishing community garden, and the light poles are adorned with banners. Each one contains the names and faces of one citizen who went off and changed their little corner of the world—business owners, authors, a cellist in the Boston Philharmonic Orchestra.

The main strip is lined with more indie shops and small boutiques than name brand stores, and all the food places seem more Mom and Pop than franchise business. There's a bakery we stopped in for lattes and cinnamon buns when we first arrived that was decorated with twinkle lights and hanging plants.

And then there was the pizza place.

Al and Coop both raved about it on the car ride here, but damn, that shit was good. The restaurant itself was awesome—the perfect combination of modern and traditional. There were black and white tiled floors, red leather chairs, and pictures of Italian mobsters framed on the walls. Not to mention Mr. Tall-Dark-and-Handsome throwing pizzas behind the counter. My first reaction was that I'd let his beard do unspeakable things to my inner thighs, but then future-Brooke showed up, waving her red flag and cockblocking me like the responsible grown-up she's trying to become.

All in all, our exploration of the town was great. But as late afternoon approached, Cooper and Alex were both itching to get to the hotel to see their boys.

"So, what time is everyone leaving me on my own?" I ask, now laying back on Alex and Levi's king-size bed, flipping through the room service menu.

My best friend pauses her hand mid-swipe of her lashes before sticking her mascara wand back into the tube and finding me in the reflection of the mirror on the wall. "I'm sorry you'll be on your own tonight. You're welcome to join me and Levi. I didn't realize the assistant coaches would invite Coop to dinner with them."

"Wow, Mom, thanks a lot," Cooper chimes in, glancing up from his phone at the foot of the bed where he's been watching highlights from some other games this week.

Alex spins around and parts her lips to explain, but he peers up and smirks at her. She physically settles, her shoulders dropping back down from her ears as she turns to me and sits back on the desk. "Levi and I are just going to the hotel restaurant. You should come."

Dropping my chin, I raise one eyebrow and cross my arms over my chest, remembering exactly what went down in *that* restaurant's bathroom last time Alex and Levi were here. Not to mention what happened back in his hotel room afterwards. I peek over at Cooper, who looks completely invested in his screen, but at the ripe age of thirteen, he's always listening.

Glancing back at Al, it's clear from the color of her cheeks that she can read my mind. "I think I'll let you and your husband enjoy your dinner, but thanks." She tries to hide her smile as I continue. "I'm actually kind of excited. This is the first night I've had off in a while. I'll probably just hang out and wait for Cooper to come back so we can order one of every dessert on the menu and charge it to the Flames' account."

Alex and I look at Cooper, who shrugs without glancing up from his phone. "Works for me," he says.

We both laugh as Al turns back toward the mirror. "What about dinner?"

Sitting up against the headboard, I cross one foot over the other. "Al, don't worry about me. I can order that too, or run out and grab something. I'm here to babysit, remember?" I wink at Alex right before Coop's head snaps back in my direction.

The look he gives me is borderline feral as I move the tip of my foot toward him. "I'm kidding," I say as I smack my shoe against his thigh. "I can't wait to watch Zombie Tsunami."

Now, it's Alex's head that spins around. "Isn't that rated R?"

Swinging my legs to the side of the bed, I hop off the mattress. "Maybe," I say, striding toward her. With my back to Cooper, I lean in to whisper. "But I'm pretty sure whatever you and Coach McHottie will be doing in *your* room would be rated worse than that."

Her whole chest lights up pink as she tries to fake devastation, but the second our eyes meet, we both completely lose it.

"You're probably right," she says softly.

Grabbing my purse from the desk, I toss it over my shoulder. "Oh, I know I am. Come on, Coop. Let's head to our room and let your mom finish getting ready."

I wrap my arms around her and squeeze tight. "Have fun tonight. We'll see you at breakfast in the morning."

She tightens our embrace. "Thanks again for doing this."

Cooper steps up behind me, and I move toward the door to let him hug his mom goodbye. "You listen to Aunt Brooke," Alex says sternly.

Cooper rolls his eyes teasingly. "Have fun, Mom. Tell Coach we have a big game tomorrow. I want you both home at a decent hour."

Alex and I shoot each other a cocked brow. Cooper strolls past me and walks right out the door.

Flicking off the TV after only half an episode of Food Truck Wars, I decide I'm starving. This is why I can't watch shows like this. Especially when I'm not at my apartment with showtime snacks readily available.

Cooper left about a half hour ago to meet up with Erik and Gavin, the Flames' assistant coaches. Tonight the team is doing their own thing for dinner, so they decided to try out a restaurant downtown. With Levi out with Alex, there was room at their table, and when they found out Cooper was coming, they insisted that he join them. It's sweet how they've bonded with Coop since his spotlight for the Spark the Flame program. He spent about a month interacting with them a few times a week—joining them on the bench and at practices, even attending meetings and a coaches breakfast. And now, with Alex and Levi married, they see each other more than ever.

All I asked was that they have Coop back to our hotel room in time to watch the new zombie movie and fall asleep sick to our stomachs on dessert. My nephew may be getting older, but he's still one of my favorite people to hangout with. They made no promises, but if they know what's good for them, they won't come between me and movie night with Coop or some molten lava cake.

Now, though, I'm on my own for dinner. I contemplate ordering room service and eating a toasted veggie panini, fries, and a carton of ranch in bed—this is as close to a vacation as I've gotten in a while, and I might as well indulge. But it's also my first time in a five-star hotel and my one—or at least safest—opportunity to explore it.

Crawling off the mattress, I walk the four feet it takes to get to the bathroom. I tousle my brunette, collarbone-length hair and use my fingertips to fluff it at my roots. Leaning onto the white and gray quartz countertop, I bring my face just inches from the glass and spin my thin gold nose ring so the spot where the metal clamps together is hidden underneath.

This was my most recent addition to my look. Every once in a while I get the itch to go under the needle, either piercing or ink. I have a dozen tattoos stickered on my body. Nothing overly big or extravagant, but enough that you can see at least a few unless I'm dressed for a blizzard—another thing about me that drives my mother crazy.

Sometimes I wonder if it's really the permanent markings on my skin that she can't stand or the idea that it's the only thing I've really committed to in life. Part of me would like to stay single forever if not just to watch her squirm. But then I think about why I'm here alone and my best friend is off doing God knows what with the man that she loves, and I'm reminded that driving her nuts isn't worth it.

Barely.

Reaching over, I flip on the light to check my makeup more closely. The room is immediately illuminated in an offensive brightness that most hotel restrooms offer, but because this one is *fancy,* there aren't just fluorescent bulbs in the ceiling. The mirror is backlit by an LED strip that erases every shadow and ensures there is no running from fine lines or wrinkles. And it leaves me feeling way too exposed.

I tilt my chin from side to side, then lean in closer, before once again pulling away from my reflection. I'm no witch, but *man.* Drew's now not the only thing I'll be hiding from in this hotel. Smacking down the switch, I use just the light from the main room to check my reflection. *Much better.*

Maybe it's the idea that I'm currently hiding away from a twenty-five-year-old. Or maybe it's my mom's voice that seems to live inside my head, reminding me my clock is ticking. But right now, I feel every bit of thirty-one.

It's then that I decide a seat at a bar that's not The Pub's and a cocktail *I* didn't mix is calling my name. Maybe there will be an older single guy there sipping a scotch. A little flirting never hurt, and there's no temptation when I'm coming back to Cooper. But nothing says young and vibrant like someone buying you a drink. And who knows, maybe there's a boyfriend waiting there for me.

Digging through my suitcase, I grab my favorite leather jacket and slip it on over the cropped gray t-shirt I've been lounging in. I never changed out of jeans, but these faded Levi's are more comfortable than any pair of leggings. So, I tug on the high waist, slip my feet into my combat boots, and head for the door.

Single and starving. Party of one.

6
Drew

Ignoring my dad's call yet again, I step off of the elevator. Walking down to the hotel bar, I slip one hand into the pocket of my athletic joggers and tug at the collar of my Flames hoodie with the other. I decided to switch it up for dinner. It's not much of a change, but maybe it's enough to shift the energy this season. Normally, I'd grab food with some of the boys if we aren't eating as a team, but I thought some alone time would do me good. Give me a minute to myself before having to perform for millions of people.

The lobby hums with familiar sounds as I make my way through it—the low murmuring of guests, the dings from the elevator, the shuffling of suitcases being dragged along the floor. But as I pass, those noises are slowly replaced with calming jazz music as I step closer into the far corner of the room. The lights grow dimmer, and the chaos fades, the combination of it all creating the perfect easy ambiance. *Exactly what I need.*

The hotel bar is one long, sleek counter lined with about a dozen leather stools and a warm glow that travels the length of the marble. Shelves of all the highest priced liquors sit behind it on a wall made of a deep cherry wood. There is a young couple on one end, both sipping white wine, an older guy on the other nursing a whiskey, and a dude with his back to me sitting right in the center.

The guy in the middle is built like a tank—tall, broad shoulders, biceps bulging from his too-tight shirt. He has a head that's twice the size of mine and is wearing a velour tracksuit. *Wait a minute.*

The only person I know who still owns one of those things is...

"Petrov?"

I pull out the stool next to a familiar face, confirming it's my teammate. He lifts his eyes from his phone before glancing over at me slowly. Sitting in front of him is what's left of a sandwich, an empty soup bowl, and... *is that a fucking Shirley Temple?*

I stare at the glass topped with maraschino cherries a minute too long, and when I look up at him, he's staring at me blankly, his expression unreadable. He's either planning my death or waiting for me to initiate conversation.

"Why aren't you out with the guys?" I ask, sitting down on the seat and shifting it closer to the counter.

He brings his gaze back to the device. "Because I never eat with the team," he says in his thick Russian accent, his deep voice cutting through the otherwise smooth, rhythmic music that surrounds us.

My brow creases as I consider his answer. "Really?"

He slides his thumb upward, scrolling on the screen. From this angle, his Notes app is partially exposed, short lines of writing stacked in a paragraph on the open page. "Really," he says curtly.

"Why?"

He sets his phone on the bar and turns his body toward me. "I like *me* time. I sit. I eat. I write." His hand slides to his phone mindlessly, and when he bumps the screen with his thumb, it lights up. "Then tomorrow, I am ready."

His words are blunt and rough around the edges, but they land. They seem out of place but are exactly what I'm hoping to get from tonight.

Making no effort to hide that I'm peeking over at his app, I scan the contents. "Is that... poetry?" I ask genuinely confused.

Alexei Petrov is known for a lot of things. He's massive, menacing, and manhandles opponents on the ice like they're flies he's shooing away.

He's infamous for sinking pucks into the net from the top of the circle, and leading the league in assists. He speaks very little and grunts quite a lot, and I'm not sure I've ever heard him string more than a few broken sentences together, let alone a poem.

"I like it," he says without blinking. "Poems don't have to make sense to mean what you want them to."

Completely dumbfounded, I continue to stare at him, waiting for him to break out in a smile—for the punchline of his joke. But I'm met with nothing.

"Wait... you're serious?"

He wraps his huge hand around his phone and flips it over on the bar. "I am serious."

I nod to myself, genuinely impressed. "That's cool, man... really fucking weird, but cool, I guess."

Standing, he towers over me, bracing his heavy hand on the counter. "Please keep my secret," he says in a clipped, hushed tone. His voice is innocent, but his face tells me he'd crush my skull if I disobeyed.

Reaching up, I clap him on the side of his arm and can't help it when a laugh escapes my lips. "You got it, buddy."

Petrov grunts in his typical manner, throws a crisp hundred on the bar, then turns and walks away without another word.

I follow his exit, still somewhat confused, and suddenly needing to read every single poem written by Flames' starting forward, Alexei "The Storm" Petrov.

Still laughing to myself, I turn back in my seat and—

Holy shit.

It's her.

Sitting just a seat apart from Whiskey Guy, who is probably in his forties, is Mystery Girl. *My* mystery girl. I freeze, stunned that she's here and shocked that my body didn't somehow already know that hers was this close.

Her head is turned towards the guy who is smiling back at her, eye-fucking her over the glass of his drink. My blood starts to boil as I watch the two of them interact, too far for me to hear their conversation, but close enough that her easy laugh hits a little too hard.

She's holding a glass of red wine in her hand, and I lick my lips, tasting it there as my mouth remembers her flavor even after all this time. With a quiet inhale, I turn back to the counter as the bartender approaches, and use the time to figure out my next move.

"What can I get for you, sir?" the woman asks. Her hair is pulled back into a tight bun that looks like the ones figure skaters wear, her black pants and matching black button-up, both sleek and spotless.

"Water, please," I grind out, all the while avoiding the scene to my right.

The bartender nods politely. "And anything to eat?"

My jaw clenches as *she* shifts in her seat next to me.

What a loaded fucking question.

Anxiety builds in my chest as I consider that she may not remember me. Here I am, her presence shooting straight to my dick, losing my shit that she's here after thinking about her every time I was *in* someone else these last ten months, and she might not even remember our night.

Or worse.

She may regret it.

The bartender continues to wait patiently as I let my thoughts spiral. When I have enough of myself together, my usual order pours from my mouth—my night-before-a-game meal—no menu necessary. "Grilled sirloin, quinoa, steamed broccoli."

She smiles, then turns away, and I steal another glance in Mystery Girl's direction. Her back is now completely to me, her body shifted, so she's fully facing the guy at the end. He's invested in whatever she's saying, staring at her intently, and I use the opportunity to really take him in.

He's in a white button-up with the top two buttons undone and a grey vest that hangs open down the middle. His brown hair is pushed back in a shorter version of how I style mine for formal events, and his salt and pepper beard is trimmed tightly across his jaw.

He no doubt has money, maybe coming from a meeting or some sort of work conference. He's looking at my mystery girl like she's the rest of his night, and suddenly I'm hell bent on making sure he's wrong.

Her laugh once again slices through the room—*and my chest*—and it's all I can take. I push my stool back from the bar and move to the empty seat next to hers, doing everything in my power not to plop myself between the two of them.

If she notices someone now behind her, she doesn't move. The citrus that pours off of her perfect body lights me up, and at the same time, the bartender goes to place my water down where I once was before. Finding that stool now empty, she searches for me, then spots me in my new seat and swings in my direction.

"Your meal will be out shortly, sir," she says, placing the glass in front of me.

I thank her, speaking louder than I need to, but keeping my voice steady despite my racing heart. I make a mental note to tip her with all the cash I have when I realize my plan is working.

Our words grabbed my girl's attention.

My favorite mystery slowly spins toward me. I get a glimpse of her as she flashes me a casual grin before turning away once more. For that half of a second, my confidence wavers as my heart sinks into my ass. But then, she snaps back in my direction.

We lock eyes, mine never having left the back of her head, and hers grow wide as her lips part slightly. *God, she's fucking beautiful.* Even with the look of shock on her face, it's exactly as I remember it except now she has a small gold hoop hugging the side of her nose. *Even better.*

We each seem to freeze for a beat, staring at each other, but after another moment, her lips close as she swallows hard. It's the first time I let my eyes leave hers, but watching the way her throat moves up and down is worth it. It reminds me of how it felt when my hand was around it and she did the same thing before she called out my name. *A perfect fucking memory.*

My eyes drop down to her chest as it starts moving in quicker, deeper waves, and the effect her reaction has on me—watching as the puzzle pieces click into place—is undeniable. My jaw tightens, my heart hammers against my ribs at this point, and my palms are only cool because of the glass of ice water I'm strangling in my hands.

Thankfully, this is what I'm used to.

"Hey you," I say as her eyes finally begin to trail down my body. They dart right back to mine as the words fall casually from my lips despite the ache in my forearms. I'm now digging them into the bar top to keep myself from pulling her onto my lap, but she doesn't need to know that.

Her mouth opens briefly before she closes it again, looking back over her shoulder at Whiskey Guy. I forgot he was here. He should be pissed that I'm about to steal the attention of the girl he's been flirting with all night, but when our eyes meet, he throws me a genuine smile and rises from his seat.

To his credit, as much as I want to hate the guy, he walks over to where I'm sitting and offers me his hand. "Drew Anderson, in the flesh."

I stand, not missing the way Mystery Girl's head tilts upward as she follows my movement. I take his palm in mine. "How's it goin', man?"

"Going to the game tomorrow, actually. Can't wait to watch you kick off the season." *Fuck. Mr. Toolbag's a nice guy after all.*

"I appreciate that. We'll put on a show, don't you worry."

He drops our grasp and taps my shoulder with the back of his hand. "With you, I don't doubt it."

I force out a laugh. "It's what I do best."

He nods, and I drop my chin to find Mystery Girl still watching me intensely. I pause for one deep breath to take her in again before turning back to him. "Hey, listen. I'm sorry, but I'm gonna have to steal your girl here."

He tilts his head toward hers, and I do the same. She paints a smile for him, and he mimics the gesture. "Oh, all good. We're not together. Do you two know each other?"

Our eyes meet, and hers reflect back the same way they did the first time we saw each other—pure, sincere, free of judgement.

"Old friend," I say, without pulling away, and I swear those same irises darken. I get lost in them, a silence falling between the three of us until Whiskey Guy clears his throat quietly.

Reluctantly, I rip my gaze from hers and offer him a tight-lipped nod, shoving both hands into my pockets. He looks at me knowingly and holds out his palm once more.

"No worries at all. You guys catch up." I shake his hand firmly before he extends it to her. She takes it all too quickly, and the whole interaction sparks a heat in my chest. I'm so consumed with my physical response to her that I almost miss his next few words.

Thankfully, I don't because they're everything I need.

"It was nice to meet you, Brooke."

My entire body tenses.

Brooke. Holy shit.

She has a fucking name.

7

Brooke

My arm freezes as Steve releases my hand. It slowly falls to my side as I shift my body back toward... *him*.

Drew is here.

Of all the times I thought I'd be able to escape him, we somehow ended up in the exact same place.

And now... he knows my name.

Steve was a nice guy. He's traveling for work—the head honcho for some law firm—and is headed back home after tomorrow night's Flames game... to his wife of twenty years. He told me he was married just a couple minutes into our conversation. Apparently, I really don't know what a husband looks like. He didn't offer to buy me a drink—maybe that should have been my first sign—but he was good company for a while, talking about how real estate around here has really sky-rocketed. Future-Brooke thought that was good to know.

But then *he* showed up.

I don't know how long he's been here. The last I saw to my left before turning toward Steve was a massive man on his phone with a thick Russian accent. He was quiet, other than the occasional slurp of his soup, typing away on the device that looked hysterically too small for his enormous hand.

But when the bartender came over and spoke to the person behind me, the sound of his voice sent shivers down my spine. It was two words—*thank you*—but the way they crawled from the guy's throat felt familiar. I *knew* that voice even if I couldn't place it. It only took one fleeting moment before curiosity got the better of me. I turned slowly in an attempt to match the sound to a face, but my brain glitched. I smiled politely—reflexively—in a moment deserving of so much more.

It was only when I had spun halfway back toward Steve that it finally registered whose eyes I just locked with. Drew drank me in like a top-shelf liquor—slow, deliberate, savoring every drop—and I gawked at him like a deer in fucking headlights. He looks so different tonight than he did at the gala—relaxed, casual—but captivating all the same. Just like that night, his eyes pulled me in, my mind scrambling to read the depth hidden behind them.

Now, those eyes avoid me, his body pulled in tightly against the bar as he wipes at the condensation that's built up on his glass. When Steve called me by name, there was no missing Drew's reaction. His body language stiffened as if he was holding his breath. I took it as a sign that I must affect him the same way his presence here affects me. But now, I'm not so sure.

As he sits back in his seat, the vibration of potential in the air briefly settles into something different. Jealousy? Bitterness? Hurt? His shoulders slouch forward slightly, his eyes narrow on the rim of his glass as the muscles in his neck tighten and loosen as if his agitation falters so quickly you might miss it if you look away.

But I don't.

Rotating toward the counter, the rest of my wine calls me from the corner of my eye. As if she can read my thoughts, the bartender walks over and tops it off.

"Oh, uh—thank you," I say, giving her a closed-lip smile.

"Sure thing, hun." She nods and walks away, and when I peek back over at Drew, he's back to looking at me with a raised brow and a confident aura.

"So... *Brooke*."

My cheeks warm as I grab hold of my drink like the life-line that it is. I take a large gulp before he huffs out a laugh. The sound, thankfully, slices through the intensity between us, and my shoulders relax slightly as I take another sip. *Just for good measure.*

He watches as I set my glass back on the bar. I take a deep breath, mentally shaking off how much he's thrown me and regaining my composure before holding out my palm. "So... I'm Brooke," I say, my voice almost lyrical.

Drew looks from my extended hand back to my face and makes me wait just a beat before he turns, staggering his legs with mine so his knee sits dangerously close to my inner thigh. He meets my hand with a firm grip, and shakes it slowly, the contact alone causing a heat so low I'm afraid he'll feel it through his joggers.

"Drew," he says simply, but the fervor in his eye contact makes it much more intense. The tension is palpable, my heart and breathing rates both picking up speed from just his first name, and I find myself shifting in my seat to cause some friction. *God, Brooke. Keep it in your damn pants.*

Realizing I've been holding his palm in mine for far too long, I drop it, inhaling deeply. Attempting to allow the smooth jazz in the background to regulate my nervous system, I occupy myself by spinning my wine glass on the marble bar.

The bartender, who is a saint for keeping judgement off her face as she saunters past me, places a plate in front of Drew. "Your steak, sir."

She spins the porcelain so the meat is closest to him, then drops a fork and knife on either side. "Can I get you anything else?"

Drew catches me staring at his meal. "Did you order yet?"

I shake my head quickly. "No, actually. I, uh... I hadn't gotten to it because I—."

"Because you were flirting with the old guy?" A flash of irritation crosses his face before it settles into a cocky grin.

My mouth falls open as I prepare to defend myself and a *married* Steve, when his expression falls casual again. "I'm kidding. Order something. I'll wait for you."

Still stuck on his comment, I stutter. "I, uh... I will in a second. You don't have to do that."

He sits back in his seat definitively as if to prove he's waiting. "I'm not going to eat in front of you."

I crease my brow, leaning forward slightly. "It's fine, it'll get cold. Just eat."

Still facing me, he places the tips of his fingers on the side of his plate and slides it closer my way. "Okay, then you eat mine, and *I'll* order another."

My face floods with confusion. "What? No, then I'll be the one eating in front of *you*." He stares at me blankly. "That's stupid."

I reach out and slide the plate back to where it started. He exhales heavily, sits up straighter on his stool, and moves his legs back under the counter. I shouldn't miss their close proximity to mine, but it's as if they suddenly cranked the air conditioning in here.

"Could you please box this up for me?" he asks the bartender, who until now, was watching our interaction like a tennis match.

Her face remains free of judgement—or annoyance or confusion—as she responds immediately. "Of course, sir. Can I get you something else?"

Drew turns just his head toward me and sucks his teeth. The gesture triggers a memory of his tongue on my neck, in my mouth, sliding down my—

"I'll take another order of the same thing, please. And whatever she's having."

My mouth falls open as the bartender smiles with her eyes in my direction. "Drew I—"

"Order, Brooke."

My lips snap shut as I tuck a hair behind my ear. *Damn it.* Another reason past-me was smart not to give him my name. Subconsciously, my body must have known that hearing it slide from his lips would make me picture him naked.

If only to put the poor server out of her misery, and to provide some relief for the professional collectedness she's surely been faking, I obey. "A veggie panini, please. With fries."

My eyes fall closed slowly as she walks away, and when I open them, they find Drew looking at me curiously. "What?" I ask.

He shakes his head. "Nothing."

Sitting my elbow on the bar, I rest my temple on my fist. "No, go ahead. Let's hear it."

"That was just a lot of fuss for you to order a salad between two slices of bread."

I sit up straighter, rolling my eyes. "Very funny."

"I'm serious. I would have thought all that back and forth would have led to at least a burger. Maybe a filet? A nice chicken sandwich."

I squint in his direction with fake irritation. "I don't eat meat." He freezes where he is, his brow cocked slightly. "Save it," I say, not interested in—or capable of—any sort of innuendo.

It takes him a second to realize what I'm saying before he lets out a chuckle. The laugh travels through me—such a genuine sound coming from someone who seems larger than life—as he holds his palms up. "I was just going to say, there really is a lot that I don't know about you."

His words sit between us, the mood in the air shifting from light-hearted to heated. We're both thinking back to that night, and we know it. I just wonder if he's thinking the same thing I am. *Even if I may want it to, it can't ever happen again.*

"I didn't expect to see you here," he says, his voice now softer, pulling me from my thoughts.

I nod slowly, then drag out my words in pieces. "I sort of expected to see you. At some point. Obviously." *Just not until there was a sheet of glass between us.* "But I didn't think it'd be here." I point to the marble and glance around the bar.

"You know Coach's girl, don't you?"

I smile thinking about *my* Alex and how now she's seen as *Coach's girl.* "Yeah, she's my best friend. I'm here keeping an eye on Cooper so she and Levi can spend some time together on the trip."

The corner of his lip tugs up, and the movement reveals a deep dimple in the middle of his freshly shaved cheek. I find myself turned on again until I realize his youthful smile is just a gentle reminder of the age gap between us.

"I always forget Monte's real name is *Levi*."

Something about the statement—or maybe my current situation—strikes me so funny that a laugh rips from my throat. Drew's eyes fill with awe before suddenly growing darker. Out of nowhere, his gaze drops to my mouth, and the mood instantly switches back to one more fitting for our circumstances.

"Why wouldn't you tell me your name ten months ago?" His jaw is now tight, his face serious.

"Oh, come on, who doesn't like a little mystery?"

He shakes his head. "I'm serious. What's the difference between me and Whiskey Guy from earlier?"

"Who?" I scan the bar until I realize who he's talking about. "You mean Steve?"

"See, *you two* are on a first-name basis." He speaks with swagger, but his eyes couldn't tell me a lie if they tried.

"I had no intention of sleeping with *Steve.*"

His pupils dilate—which I'm blaming on the ambiance of the bar—but his shoulders physically relax. "So, you only keep your name a secret from any guy you plan to take to bed?"

"Or bathroom," I add quickly.

We both laugh, but I'm instantly transported back to when the same face next to me was buried between my thighs below said restroom's sink. Flooded with warmth, I slide out of my leather jacket and let it fall between my ass and the back of the stool.

Drew makes no attempt to hide the trail his eyes leave on my now-exposed skin before he brings them back to mine. "I don't buy it."

Inhaling deeply, I turn my body once again toward his, resting my hands in my lap. "I was different then. And he wasn't *you.*"

Drew runs his hand through his hair and takes my eyes with him. He faces me and folds his arms across his chest. "And what's that supposed to mean?"

"I wasn't looking for anything serious."

He nods, his eyes narrow. "And the second part?"

I scoff. "You're the star player of the team my best friend's husband coaches. My name didn't really seem relevant." I take a sip of the wine

I almost forgot was here and take a vested interest in the way the liquid swirls when I brush the stem of the glass between my fingers.

Drew copies me, his mouth finding the rim of his water as he lets a sip fall between his lips. I'm sure it's not meant to be seductive, but I hang on to the movement like it's the climax of a movie. When he pulls away, his lips glisten from the drink, and my vagina clenches in jealousy.

As if to torture me, he licks them nonchalantly before setting his cup back on the bar.

"Who says nothing would have come from it?" he asks, sitting forward in his seat. His hands fall between his legs, and his knuckles graze my thigh. Thankfully, they land where there's no exposed skin from the rips in the denim, or I would be a dripping mess.

"You're Drew Anderson, remember?"

He rolls his eyes aggressively. "I was Drew Anderson that night too."

"It's different."

"How?"

"Because we were hooking up in a hotel bathroom, not out in the real world."

He reaches up and brushes a stray hair behind my ear, catching me completely off guard. "Felt pretty *real* to me."

Everything from my chest up radiates with heat. I clear my throat, trying my damnedest to act unaffected by his touch. "Drew, come on."

He leans back and shakes his head, his voice now just above a whisper. "Don't act like I'm crazy. You felt it too, I know you did."

My mind falls into a fit of chaos. He's *not* crazy, and neither am I. I knew from the second our eyes found each other that night that there was a weird chemistry between us. It's still here now—a magnetic pull that goes beyond our obvious physical attraction. But that doesn't change reality and the circumstances we're dealing with.

I swallow the lump in my throat and remain persistent. "You're literally famous, Drew."

"And?" He shifts slightly forward on his seat, his body moving closer to mine.

"A superstar."

"Okay."

"An icon."

"Uh huh." Every time he speaks, he closes a little more of what's left of the tiny gap between us, and my lungs lose an inch of air.

"My friend's husband's player."

"So?"

When I can barely breathe, let alone speak, I let my final—yet most important point—fly from my lips.

"Drew... you're fucking twenty-five."

His face drops slightly as he looks back and forth between my eyes. "What's that got to do with it?"

A laugh comes out with my shallow breath.

"Everything."

8

Drew

*F**uck me.*

As if the girl from the gala wasn't already making herself a permanent spot in my mind, she had to show up *here*. At our first game. And even more perfect than I thought.

The only thing about her that I didn't find adorable, intriguing, or fucking sexy as hell, was the fact that she already wrote me off ten months ago. Part of me loves that she's not like anyone else I've slept with, trying to take as much of me as I'm willing to give. But most of me can't stand the fact that I finally found someone I wouldn't mind seeing more of, and she's already convinced herself that *we* would never happen.

After Brooke—fucking *Brooke*—laid out all of her excuses, refusing to admit that there's something between us, she asked the bartender to pack up her food and split. Short of chasing her through the hotel lobby, there wasn't much I could do besides watch her walk away. But *damn*—even that I didn't mind.

She thinks I'm too young, too famous, too well-known, and too close to her social circle. I don't know her despite our two interactions, but I'm almost positive this girl isn't afraid of what other people think. No, she's worried I'm not the guy to settle down with. That I'm not old enough to want anything serious, especially with my job and reputation.

She might be right. Shit, I've never really thought about it before right now. I'm twenty-five, in the prime of my career, or at least trying to get back there, and I'm a fucking mess inside. But a "normal" life sounds pretty great right now—maybe exactly what I need.

My saving grace is that I know she's here for Cooper, which means she's at least sticking around Grand Oaks until the game. That gives me time—and real inspiration for my season kick-off performance tonight. Dare I say, it's a little true motivation to put on the show I know I have to anyway.

Skating around the ice for our morning practice, my mind seesaws back and forth between her and the game. Thinking about the two, I scoop a puck onto the end of my stick and toss it in the air. When it falls, I kick it back up with the side of my skate then catch it smoothly on the blade again, mindlessly occupying my time before I'm interrupted.

"Yo, where were you last night?" Burnsey asks, skating over to me. He smacks the bottom of my stick with his, knocking the puck loose so it falls to the ice. "Starving yourself part of your new pregame ritual?" He slides the disc back and forth as I follow its movement.

"Nah, I grabbed food at the hotel bar. Thought I'd try the solo thing for once." *Turns out I didn't exactly end up alone.*

"Ah, goin' all Stormy on me, eh?" The Canadian in him slips through his words as my eyes fly to his.

"You knew about that? That Petrov never eats with the team?"

Burns freezes, his lower half still hunched over his stick. "Bro. He's *never* eaten with us." He laughs as he continues. "He's too cool, apparently. I don't know what the hell he does on his lonesome, but God forbid you ask him about it at warm ups the next day."

He shivers dramatically, and I crack a smile. I can picture it now. Burns bein' Burns and in everyone's business, meanwhile Petrov puts the fear of God in him to protect his little poems.

"And you call yourself our captain," he mutters, shaking his head.

I know he's messing around, but my face immediately turns. I push off my back foot and glide just inches from him, our blades nearly kissing. "Don't."

He holds his gloves up to his chin. "Dude, I'm *joking*. Chill out."

I pause, regaining my composure. I even threw myself with that one. I fall back, my breath still spewing out in quick spurts, and clear my throat. "Yeah, sorry, man. My bad."

Burns throws a punch at my chest. "It's all good, Cap. Hey, everything's gonna be fine. You're back. Fuck that testing bullshit. You're *Drew Anderson*—our guy. Hell, you're *Golden City's* guy. Just give the people what they want. Be you."

I let out a dry laugh at the infamous saying. *But that's the problem.* I can't do both things at once.

A whistle saves me from having to respond and draws both of our attention toward Monte. He's at center ice, tapping his stick rhythmically like he's growing impatient and has somewhere else to be—which, knowing his girl is sitting back in his hotel room waiting for him, he probably does.

Burnsey nudges me with his elbow. "Come on, Captain." He pushes forward just a few feet before he turns backward on his skates and winks. "Showtime."

That one word snaps me back. I shake it off and skate toward the circle, trying to leave the weight of everything else behind me.

"Alright, big game tonight, boys. I want a lot of touches this morning. Lots of passes, lots of shooting. We're just gettin' warm."

I nod, swirling the handle of my stick in my hand. "Line it up," I call after Monte's finished.

He looks at me and tips his chin up, our silent communication to get a drill started. I mirror his movement, but catch a glimpse of red and black in the stands that sticks out like a sore thumb against the bright yellow and dark green of the Gladiators' arena.

I let my eyes wander to the source as I spin toward the corner of the ice where the boys are waiting.

And I see her.

I freeze, watching her as she looks down at her phone, her lower half covered by the seats in front of her. She's wearing a black leather jacket that's on full display, though, with a white and red stripe down the front—one meant to wear while on a goddamn bike.

And my dick responds before anything else.

"Drew, lets fucking move," Monte says, nodding toward the guys.

Despite his impatience, I coast closer to him. "Hey, uh, Coach. Why is—who's that?"

Monte peers over his shoulder in the direction I nod and pulls out the mini notebook he keeps tucked into the pocket of his warm ups. "The new social media manager," he says, flipping through the pages.

"Wait, what?" I ask without thinking.

Coach glances up at me and wrinkles his brow. "Come on, Drew. I know you know all about Instagram." He smirks as he skims his notes on the page his book is opened to.

I shake my head, reacting to both his comment and my attempt at trying to wrap my head around my thoughts. "No, yeah, I get that. I just mean—"

"She's my wife's friend. She's just filling in until the new girl starts permanently." He goes to turn another page but pauses with his fingers clenched around the paper. "Don't get any ideas. No messing with her or any dumb shit. I don't want you guys being assholes." Monte flips the page and continues, this time mumbling under his breath. "Alex will have my fucking head."

With my mind stuck on her, I barely hear him as he shoves his notebook back into his pocket and takes off for the guys.

Why didn't she say anything last night when we talked about her being here? She had to know I'd find out. I start to feel some type of way about her lying by omission, thinking maybe she isn't as different as I thought she was, when it hits me. *No.* She wasn't trying to keep it from me. She's *scared*. Scared to tell me, scared to be near me... *holy shit.*

Scared to admit that this is exactly where she wants to be.

The realization lights the same fire in my belly that starts when I first walk out through the tunnel—when the crowd hums my name like they do when my number's called in the starting line up. It's a fire that's sparked at the start of a game that reminds me that it's time to be on. Time to secure what's mine. Time to hold on to everything I have to lose.

With that growing flame low in my gut, I turn to find Monte talking at the bench with Max, our equipment manager. Taking advantage of the time, I push forward just enough to close a bit of the gap between me on the ice and Brooke in the stands. When I'm a few yards away, I stop harder than I need to, spraying snow and whistling one quick, sharp sound.

Brooke finally glances up from her phone, and when her eyes meet mine, I know I was right. This girl, who doesn't seem scared of anything, is terrified of what she feels for me.

"Good to see you again, Mystery Girl." Her lips fall open as I push off my blade and glide backward. "Make sure you get my good side."

An hour later, practice is over. I don't know how much warming up I actually did for the game, but my body is fucking ready for Brooke. I spent the last sixty minutes half dicking around on the ice, half performing for her. As if I didn't already have enough roles to play, apparently now I'm showing off for a girl who's made it abundantly clear I can't have her again.

I think that's my biggest problem. Brooke's not just some prospect that I stumbled upon out at the bar one night. I've had her. I know what it feels like to be buried inside her—raw for that matter—and I know how it feels to be near her even *with* clothes separating us.

She can refuse to accept it all she wants, but there's something between us. It's physical and palpable, and the fact that she's denying it only makes me crave it more. But I'm not going to let her forget. Not that easily at least.

The boys are piling off the bench toward the locker room as Brooke saunters down the stairs in the stands closest to the tunnel. For the first time since practice started, she's within a reasonable distance from me, even if she's avoiding eye contact and has her hands tucked into that fucking jacket.

"Hey," I call up to her, catching her eyes and those of the last few players still heading out. "Aren't you gonna come with us?"

Burnsey, who I could kiss for finally picking the perfect time to put his nose where it doesn't belong, hangs back and drapes his arm over my shoulder, pulling his helmet up to rest on his forehead.

"Yeah, Jenny used to go all behind the scenes for interviews and shit for the 'Gram.' Maybe catch some skin while we strip down. You in?"

Brooke goes wide-eyed for a second before regaining her composure. "No, that's okay." She pulls her hand out of her pocket, and with it comes her phone. She holds it up and says, "I think I got enough for today."

Brett leans into me. "Aw, the new girl's bashful," he whispers.

My mind flashes back to the image of Brooke sitting relaxed and completely naked on the bathroom sink with her perfect pussy on display. I blow out a slow breath as her bold words ring inside my head. *"Keep going." "Faster." "More."*

"Yeah, I don't think that's it," I say, my voice coming out weak.

"Well, shy or not, she's totally hot."

I resist punching him as he nods again toward Brooke. "We don't bite," he says louder. "Unless you're into that sort of thing." Brett raises his brows in her direction and laughs before nudging my shoulder and heading out through the tunnel.

Brooke and I are the last two in the rink, and her dark eyes are still on me. "You get some good content?" I call over the rail that sits between us, desperate to continue talking.

"Good enough," she says, sticking her hands into the back pockets of her jeans. Her jacket pulls open with the movement, revealing an inch of skin just above her waist. My eyes immediately drop to the tanned sliver, and she notices.

Without even thinking about it, I step closer to the stands, looking up at her. She doesn't exactly seem thrilled, but she doesn't walk away either, which is good enough for me.

"You didn't tell me about the job," I say.

"You didn't ask."

My head drops forward as I try to hide my smirk. When I look back up, she's wearing a weak smile too. "Fair enough."

A silence falls between us that's not necessarily uncomfortable, but definitely charged.

"Listen, Drew, I—"

"Brooke, I think—"

We both speak at the same time, then snap our lips shut simultaneously. "You go first," I say, leaning my weight on my stick.

"I was going to say, considering I'll be working with you at least for a little while, I think we should—"

"We should probably go on a date," I say, cutting her off. Her face falls flat. "Sorry, I know I said you could go first, but something tells me I'm not gonna like the end of your sentence."

She tilts her head sideways and crosses her arms. "Drew, we talked about this."

"No," I say, shifting my feet. "You rattled off a list of excuses and are calling it a conversation."

"They aren't excuses. They're facts, and they make total sen—"

"Bullshit."

Her head snaps back. "Excuse me?"

"You heard me," I say. I hook my hand on the lowest rung of the rail and lean in. "You don't strike me as the type of girl who gives one fuck about any of that shit you leaned on last night." Her throat moves up and down as her arms fall loose, just enough for me to notice.

"Admit it, Brooke. You still want me." Her cheeks flush the perfect shade of pink, and I feel it fucking everywhere. "The same way I want you," I add, my voice low but confident.

Her lips part slightly as Burns goes and resorts back to his impeccable timing, popping into the space at the end of the tunnel. "Yo, Cap, you comin'?"

"I'll be right there," I call to him. I turn back to Brooke, her arm now pulled across her chest.

"It's okay," I say, stepping back from the railing. "You don't have to admit it. We both know the truth."

I tap the metal with the blade of my stick, and she blinks hard. I start to walk away but pause after a few feet and turn back to see her still watching me. "I'll see you around, Mystery Girl."

Then, I wink and walk away.

9

Brooke

*H*oly *shit.*

What the hell did I get myself into?

This is going to be harder than I thought—especially if Drew isn't going to let this go. Maybe working for Levi, even temporarily, was a bad idea. It may even be a sign that I should retreat from this whole putting down roots thing. If I was a weaker person, I might have caved. Instead, I stood there dumbfounded with my mouth ajar, chest burning, as Drew winked and disappeared under the tunnel.

It doesn't help that I was reminded all morning of the way he stretches or how his smile shines even behind his mouth guard. Not to mention the charm that the world—and *I*—get sucked right into. Drew spent that practice dominating the ice. He's powerful and captivating and draws your attention. He might not literally be the biggest on the team, but his presence is unmatched.

Of course, the other guys aren't shabby either. A few times I forgot *I* was the one doing *Levi* a favor taking pictures from the outside of this boy aquarium. It sounds bad considering I should be professional—and future-Brooke definitely wouldn't approve of comments like this—but every player on this team could totally get it. Burns is hilarious, I'd damn sure let Petrov throw me around, and their goalie can bend his body like a goddamn pretzel.

But Drew is just... Drew.

He really is a star. My God, he takes his helmet off for water and it's an image of perfection. Of course, he has his usual antics, but it's also so much more than that. He's a natural out there. I mean, the guy gets paid millions of dollars to play—but hockey isn't just what he does, it's part of him. His skates and his stick are like an extension of his body—his movements on the ice like rehearsed choreography.

Honestly, I'm jealous.

Most of my life I've felt like I have no real purpose. I know my worth and that there are things I'm good at, but sometimes it feels like I'm the one person who hasn't found their true calling. No, I don't feel *behind* like Mom might think I am—and I don't often let it show—but it does get to me. Unlike Aunt Ivy, who thrives on flying by the seat of her pants, I do have *some* desire to at least find my place in the world. It just hasn't come that easily.

Today was enlightening. I never considered myself a creative type—there haven't been many opportunities to use things like photography or content creation in my day-to-day life. But I had a lot of fun, and it turns out I might not be half bad at this.

It was easier than I thought to come up with a list of ideas before seeing the boys in action. I actually managed to get a few decent shots too, which is key. The logistics, though, still throw me a little. How close can I get? Where should I stand? Do I follow the boys into the locker room or is Brett Burns just fucking with me? It's all things I'd figure out, eventually. But none of it matters for the short time I'll be here.

I did make a mental note to check in with Levi after this weekend to see if the team has a nice camera lying around. I'm thinking a Sony or Nikon might create images better than what I threw in portrait mode on my iPhone. I did Yearbook Club back in high school so that I could get out of class to walk around and "take pictures." I think I'd remember my way around a lens. Maybe not as vividly as I'd remember my way around a Swisher under the bleachers after fifth period... but it would come back to me, eventually.

Sitting in the stands now, waiting for the game to start, I swipe through the couple of photos that I favorited from earlier today. Most of them include Drew in some way or another, but after about five minutes of practice, I knew that's how it would be. I don't think it matters that I know what he looks like when he's coming undone. I think anyone watching the team would find their eyes drifting toward him.

My scroll wanders to a series of images I took back to back. The first is of Drew balancing the puck on his stick held parallel to the ground. The second is of the puck in the air, half a second after he tossed it, and the third is of him with his skate turned sideways, the disc just centimeters from touching the blade.

They're silly really and have nothing to do with the first game tonight. But the simplicity makes him look so... accessible. If you took off his practice jersey and deleted the view of the million dollar arena behind him, you wouldn't know if it was a guy out back having fun on his pond or a professional athlete preparing for battle.

This is the Drew that I connected with. He's softer than the guy I know from the media. Genuine. Human. The pictures are a reminder that I wasn't crazy—another version of him must exist. But they're also a visual representation of what I know I can't have.

A puck smacks the glass in front of me and I jump, startled. A kid two rows down yells something at the ice and claps his hands. I laugh awkwardly, then glance back at my phone, suddenly self-conscious about my internal monologue and deciding whether or not people could hear it aloud.

"Hey, that's a good one," Alex says from over my shoulder. I quickly swipe out of the photos as if she'd somehow be able to know what I'm thinking, and throw her a smile as she finds her seat.

"Yeah, I figured I could put some casual photos up on the page's stories, then pick a few to put in a carousel."

She looks at me blankly. "Huh?"

"My God," I say, shaking my head. "You and Levi are perfect for each other."

A blush creeps up her cheeks as she shrugs her shoulders. "I know."

"Someone had a good night last night." I raise my brows in her direction as she squirms in her seat.

"And a good morning." She winks as her grin grows into a smile.

"Jesus, you two fuck like rabbits." I roll my eyes, scanning the ice. "I'm so jealous."

Alex nudges her shoulder into mine. "You still going through a dry spell?"

I spin my body toward hers, leaning back in my seat. "Excuse me, it is not a dry spell when it's *by choice*. I told you—I'm trying to be good—giving myself the chance to really meet someone."

"And I'm so proud of you," Al says as she locks eyes with Levi stepping onto the bench.

He tips his chin up at her, then runs his tongue over his top teeth, his one eyebrow cocked flirtatiously.

I sigh audibly, watching their interaction, my gaze wandering naturally to... *him*.

Drew drops to his knees and begins thrusting into the ice, taunting me with each motion.

"B, you're the bravest person I know and fiercely independent," Alex says, her hand landing on my arm. "It's the pot calling the kettle black, but you just have to put yourself out there. With jobs *and* with guys."

"Uh huh," I say, attempting not to get lost in the rhythmic movement of Drew's hips.

"I'm serious. You got this."

I nod mindlessly. "I know." Drew slides onto his stomach, grabs his stick, then pops up into a textbook push-up position.

"Brooke!" Alex hisses as he starts banging out reps. "Too bad he's not ten years older," she laughs, and now she's got my attention. "Or even five, for that matter. You'd clearly have no problem opening up for—I mean *to*—him."

My jaw clenches as my whole body tenses. Alex's face crinkles as she scans mine that's probably dropped a few shades in color.

"Brooke..."

I flash a tight-lipped smile, taking a vested interest in the Dunkin Donuts' advertisement posted on the boards. "Would you say the Dunkin Donuts' pink is more magenta or—"

"Hold on." She pulls on my arm, literally forcing my hand. I slowly turn so I'm finally facing her. "Am I missing something right now?"

Breathing in deeply, I buy myself time, scanning her dark denim jeans and tight long-sleeve Flames shirt. When our eyes lock again, her lips drop open. "No."

"Mhmm."

"No."

I nod slowly.

"When?"

"At the gala. Took a play from your book."

She gasps, her eyes growing wide. "You did it in the *bathroom*?" she whisper-shouts.

I purse my lips. "Definitely worth the hype."

Alex opens her mouth ready to agree, then snaps it shut and shakes her head. "But how? Why?"

I huff out a laugh. "I'll let your imagination handle the how." I wink, tapping her knee with mine. "And why?" I throw my arm toward the ice. "Look at him!"

I instantly find Drew amongst the sea of red. In perfect timing, he takes off his helmet, runs his hands through his hair, then lifts his jersey to wipe sweat off his forehead, leaving a glistening six-pack completely exposed. I catch a glimpse of a tattoo on his ribs I didn't know existed and curse past-Brooke for insisting he leave his shirt on.

"You know what," Alex starts, and I cringe, anxious about what may come next. "That's fair." I smile as we both gape at Drew as he pushes off the bench, glides backward effortlessly, and licks his lips before bringing his helmet back to the top of his head.

"But why didn't you tell me?"

I swing back in her direction. "I guess I thought you'd make a big thing of it."

She scrunches her nose, creases her brow, and folds her arms across her chest. "With good reason," she says, leaning into me. She lowers her voice. "Brooke, he's *twenty-five*."

"What are you trying to say?" I deadpan.

Alex rolls her eyes. "You know what I mean."

"Yes, Al, I know what you mean. But that was ten months ago." *Not that I'm counting.* "I didn't have any plans of settling down yet. I was still out having fun and going with the flow." *Before I realized everyone in my life was moving on without me.* "Blame the old Brooke."

She nods in understanding as she looks down at the ice. "Just promise me that won't happen again. You're on a good path—finally figuring out what you want. And I'm guessing whatever that is doesn't look like Drew Anderson."

I lean back in my seat, exhaling as I watch Drew skate a quick circle, then tap gloves with a teammate. "Yeah," I mutter, more to myself than to Alex. "I know."

That's the hardest part. The one thing that might have felt right in the moment isn't anything that could be sustained long-term. Like it or not, I'm drawn to him, but the Drew I got behind a locked bathroom door isn't the Drew I'd get out here. Hell, he's not even the twenty-five-year-old I'd get in the real world. A professional athlete's world is a whole other ball game even if you aren't the golden boy. And the combination of the two is deadly. The things I could ignore while we were entangled on the porcelain sink would flash like warning signs any other time.

The problem is that's sort of how I feel about everything right now. The change in dating, my makeshift job, this half-hearted attempt at adulthood, *feel* good but seem just out of reach.

I sigh at the thought, and just then, Drew's eyes lock with mine. He freezes in his tracks, and I think maybe I'm seeing things until Alex leans over and says, "Does *he* know it was one and done?"

As if to answer, Drew slides his shield up, revealing those baby blues. He smirks, then pulls his bottom lip between his teeth. Now *I* freeze, unable to react, but also not wanting to. Suddenly, Cooper's voice floats over to me on the other side of his mom as he takes his seat. Alex's body shifts to face her son, but I'm still paralyzed by Drew's attention.

The horn bursts through the arena, signaling the end of warm ups. Both teams make their way to their respective benches, but still, Drew and I stare at each other. The lights dim as the crowd around me hoots and hollers for the players as they skate off the ice and dart into the tunnel toward the locker room. Finally, Drew slowly slinks toward the boards, all the while, his eyes still on me. When he gets to the gate, other players step past him to leave as he comes to a stop.

When he's one of the few people still on the ice, he lifts both thumbs and forefingers in two C shapes facing each other, just inches apart in front of his face. I look to Alex to see if she's watching—and if she can possibly explain what the hell is happening—but she isn't.

When I turn back around, Drew turns his head, framing one eye between his hands, and closes his lid, lifting and lowering his one pointer as if he's holding a camera and taking a picture... of me.

My mouth falls open, my only movement. How do I react to that? What do I do with rows of fans sitting between us?

Fortunately for me, I don't have to respond because before I can, Drew flashes me a charming smile and steps into the tunnel.

Then, just like earlier, he's gone.

10
Drew

"Well, we won. The Gladiators came at us harder than we thought, but we were able to stay ahead of 'em. Burnsey made a ridiculous one-timer goal from the blue line, and Petrov managed to escape without too many minutes in the box. Ward had a wild glove save on a breakaway too. But I guess you saw all that, huh?"

Pulling one leg up, I rest my elbow on my knee, rolling a blade of grass between my fingers. I let my eyes wander, following the shadows the lush trees cast across the ground on an otherwise bright fall morning.

"Tried out my new celly—another TikTok dance the fans ate up. That'll cost me. I know, I know... it's stupid. I don't know, Mom. I've been so done with this shit since last season. Nothing's felt the same since that fucking test. And it's crazy how much has changed in me since I've had to go back to being *that* guy. But it's like I have no other choice. When I did get to take off the mask, even briefly, the silence... Mom, it was so much louder than the noise."

Suddenly, my alarm rings out, mocking me for appreciating the quiet. Sighing, I click it off, then push to stand. "I'll figure it out. Don't worry." I brush a stray leaf off of the speckled tombstone before bringing my hand to my lips, then pressing it to the marble. "I'll be back soon. I still have to tell you about the girl." I laugh, slipping my headphone back into my ear. "I love you, Mom."

I turn away from the site, and as if on cue, my screen lights up with my dad's name. I hit decline like I have the last few times he's called and, instead, click the next song on my playlist so that it rattles loudly through my ears. Taking off toward the path leading out from the cemetery, I continue my run—my feet landing on the stone road in time with the beat—and my thoughts on the game.

Like I knew I would, I fell right back into step. For sixty minutes of playing time I was exactly who I was supposed to be. I'm not sure I'd know anymore how to be anyone else. It's muscle-memory—a conditioned response. The second my skates hit the ice, *he* takes over. A man on autopilot wearing a mask because out there, under the lights, surrounded by the roar of the crowd, he knows exactly who he is.

The rest of the time it's not so clear.

Sometimes I stress thinking Mom would be disappointed in me. For losing myself or investing so much time in being someone I'm not. But then I remember that wasn't her way. It's crazy to imagine, but I think my dad would be more pissed off if I stopped being the person he trained me to be—the person he built—than Mom would have been for not being myself.

It's part of the reason I've been avoiding him and didn't hang around for his post-game lecture last night. I figured switching up my pregame ritual seemed to come with benefits, maybe changing other things would help a little too. Plus, I don't want to hear what he has to say. He's on a new kick, and it's the last thing on my mind.

Following the path, I weave through headstones, some worn and aged, leaning with the weight of time, some with fresh dirt packed in front of untouched marble, the names and dates written across the front still stark and prominent as if they were written in bold. I can't hear the crunch of the gravel underneath my feet thanks to the music, but I feel it.

I didn't always visit. When Mom died my sophomore year in high school, I couldn't bring myself to terms with talking to a rock—with admitting that it's now my only way to speak to her. I was shocked and pissed off and instead of dealing with her death, I just sunk further into hockey. Letting Dad schedule as many extra hours on the ice and releasing any grip I still had left on my future—the hold only Mom encouraged—was my way of coping. You don't have to face the truth if you create a new reality. It was the only way it felt manageable.

I guess not much has changed.

But in the last few years, I've found it peaceful. I first visited after I signed with the Flames. I wanted to be the one to tell Mom that I finally made it. Not that anyone else would have done it because I don't think Dad's been here since the funeral. But, since then, I've come back a few times a week just to fill her in. Part of me thinks I'm just hoping one day she'll talk back—give me permission to release some pressure and have fun like she used to. Until then, I enjoy the peace this place brings—the solace I get from knowing there's no pretending in here. I don't know any of the backstories that belong to these people, but their graves are a good reminder that we're all human after all.

Stepping out of the cemetery, through the iron gate that swings ever so slightly when the wind hits it just right, I continue my run down the back streets of Golden City. Right on cue, the familiar scent of Drippy's coffee shop wafts past me at the corner, as I pass the row of luxury brownstones that I'd kill to live in. They hold so much history compared to my highrise. But back when I was first looking for places in G.C., they didn't quite fit the brand I was attempting to build.

These are seasoned. Riddled with history and charm from their rounded bay windows to grand stoops begging for quiet mornings and lingering conversations. There's history in the stone—stories of those who have lived inside them over the last two-hundred-years woven into the walls. They're occupied by long-term residents or settled families—couples starting over or roommates looking for calm in the chaos of the city.

My apartment is nothing like that. It's new, chic—low-maintenance, high-luxury—and just a few floors above the action. There's a spa and gym, a pool, and a concierge service, and floor-to-ceiling windows that overlook the steady flow of passing people and moving headlights. The view is a constant reminder of the city's pulse—and it does nothing to help slow me down.

But running past these brownstones always stirs something in me. I'd love to feel like I belong somewhere quiet and lived in. My place is perfect on paper—sexy and young. But despite the statement it makes visually, with its glossy exterior and intimidating presence, there's still a part of me that would prefer the more understated beauty of something real.

Picking up speed, I turn down a narrower street as the rest of the city wakes up around me. The song in my ear changes to a classic that Burnsey has named one of my angsty songs as I squeeze past a mailman and dodge a few papers tossed carelessly on the sidewalk. Increasing my pace again, the complete opposite of the slower beat of the drums in my ear, I all but sprint further into the busy part of the city.

Closing out the end of my run in the direction of my apartment, I always give it all I have left. It's funny how I run to escape the noise, yet I find myself moving faster as I head back toward it. The last few days scroll through my mind, driving me to dig even deeper, my sneakers pounding the pavement with each heavy step. The test, the trip, my dad, the game... *her*. All of it so simple, yet so fucking complicated.

Before I know it, I've passed my building, my pulse thumping, chest heaving, as I finally decrease my speed. Jogging the length of another street, I eventually stop, pulling my phone from my pocket and silencing the music, letting the buzz of the city replace its tempo. Plucking my headphones from my ears, I slip them into the pocket of my mesh gym shorts, rip my t-shirt off and slap it over my shoulder, then place my hands on my head. I spin around to find my bearings, my heart and breathing-rates slowly recovering. There are a few dozen people already out and about, so I step closer to the darkened windows of a storefront beside me.

With one heavy exhale, I drop my hands to my knees, sucking in air through my nose as I take my swinging gold chain into my mouth. My head hangs between my arms as the door to the building begins to open, and when I slowly lift it, I freeze, my body still bent, the metal still clenched between my teeth.

"Oh, hi."

I stand up slowly, my eyes dragging up the view in front of me, the jewelry only falling from my lips because of the new curve of my mouth. "Mystery Girl."

Brooke, who looks hot as hell in an off-the-shoulder cropped sweatshirt and leggings, her hair slicked with sweat and tucked behind her ears, rolls her eyes. "What was all the fuss about learning my name if you aren't even going to use it?"

A chuckle escapes me as I bring my hands to my hips. "Hello, Brooke."

"Twelve."

I still, cocking one brow, then shake my head. "What are you doing here?" Realizing I don't even know where *here* is, I step back, glancing up at the building.

Before I can finish reading the sign, she says, "I just did a workout class."

I finish scanning the name—*Beats & Barbells*—then look her up and down. "Please tell me it was old lady Zumba."

She smothers a smile. "Something like that."

I wipe my brow with the side of my hand, struggling to hide the stupid grin on my face as her eyes home in on the ink on my exposed skin. "I saw the posts from the game. And the stories." My cheeks grow warm thinking about Brooke taking a series of photos of me, and I thank God my face was probably already pink from my run. "They were good."

Brooke adjusts the strap of her puffy black bag that hangs off her shoulder. "I have to ask Levi for a real camera, but they turned out better than I thought."

"You had a handsome target."

Now *her* cheeks glow. "Yeah... Brett *is* easy to look at."

Tilting my chin down, I roll my tongue over my teeth. "Don't play with me, Brooke."

At the same time, a man in short spandex shorts and a tight black tank top reaches for the door. Brooke smiles at him, and he smiles back devilishly before throwing me a wink. I nod, flattered, and Brooke steps aside, forced to move a foot closer to me.

"Drew, it's not happening. I told you I—"

Before my brain catches up with my body, my hand is in her hair, and my mouth is on hers. Maybe it's the runner's high lowering my inhibitions or the word *believe* written underneath her collarbone egging me on. Or maybe it's just the idea that I finally fucking feel something—but suddenly I can't hold back.

Brooke inhales quickly, her body tensing as her lips remain still, but just when I think I should retreat, she melts into me for the briefest of moments, resting one hand on my ribs. Her lips part slightly, but although I'm dying to sweep my tongue across hers, I don't. Instead, I pull back before she can.

Her expression drips with surprise, but I felt it. It was there—her acceptance. Her contentment.

Our eyes lock, both sets searching the other for a reaction.

Realizing my hand is still threaded in her hair, I pull it back, holding our stare. "You're..." I start. Brooke looks at me with wide eyes, waiting anxiously for what might come next. "Really sweaty."

My arm falls the rest of the way to my side as Brooke shoves her hand into my chest. "Ass," she snaps.

"For the kiss or the comment?"

She crosses her arms as her bag falls to the crease in her elbow. "Both."

"You sure you're mad about the kiss? Or are you just mad that you liked it?"

Brooke parts her lips, ready to speak—or argue maybe—but nothing comes out. I step just an inch closer and add, "That you like *me*."

She swallows, and my whole body reacts to the movement of her throat. "It's not happening," she says.

"That's not a denial."

Brooke blows a breath through her lips, then tucks her hair behind her ear. "I'm not the same girl I was ten months ago, Drew. I'm not looking for a fling anymore. I want strings. And roots." She grinds the toe of her shoe into the pavement and avoids my gaze. "I'm trying to finally plan for a future."

"Okay," I say skeptically, realizing that should scare me more than it does. But instead, I'm just happy that she finally gave me something back. "And what's that have to do with me?"

Brooke looks at me blankly. When she chews on her cheek, reality hits me. "Is this seriously because of my age? What year are we living in again?"

"It has nothing to do with me being embarrassed that you're younger than me—by a lot FYI." This time it's *my* expression that's unwavering. "But I know how *I* was living less than a year ago, let alone six..."

I can't help the way a smirk tugs at the corners of my lips. *Fuck, I love that she's older.*

"I'm serious," she says. "And *I* wasn't a goddamn hockey sensation."

"And how do you know that's not exactly what I want too?"

"Oh, come on, Drew. I'm not an idiot. I watch the games. I see the pictures."

On cue, her words from our first night together rattle in my mind. Suddenly, my hand reaches for her chin, placing it between my fingers, the reality that none of that shit is real sitting at the forefront of my mind. "And what happened to admitting you don't know me at all?"

Brooke gasps, her eyes darting to my mouth. I know she won't just believe me if I tell her, especially after my impromptu kiss. And who could blame her? I pay a shit-ton of money to make my life exactly that—believable.

This time I don't try to hide my grin. When I finally speak, I'm not sure who I'm talking to more—her or myself. "Actions speak louder than words, Mystery Girl."

11

Brooke

I've been walking for—honestly I'm not even sure how long now. I always walk home after a workout class to cool off and soak in another twenty minutes of endorphin-filled bliss. Sometimes I grab a coffee from the corner shop or a smoothie from the wellness place right down the street from the gym, but today? Today I've used every block—and more, apparently—to stew over mine and Drew's little run-in.

I passed my apartment at least five minutes ago. But the slight October breeze and constant whirring of cars taking their passengers to work or the store—or the moon for all I care—crafted the perfect backdrop and white noise for dissociating over something that shouldn't have even happened in the first place.

Drew kissed me.

He fucking kissed me.

Right in the middle of the goddamn street.

So, there was no tongue involved. And it lasted maybe a total of three seconds. But this was no kiss from my grandma, God rest her soul. No, this was a *you know you want me* kiss that held up the entire sidewalk.

Who does that besides Golden City's star forward? I should have known the Flames' number twelve doesn't mind causing a scene. People slowed down, gawked, some stopped altogether. But he didn't notice. I guess he's immune to that by now.

I'm pissed at him. Not just about the kiss, but for not dropping all this. I'm trying to do Levi a favor, and honestly, I'm having fun. I spent hours last night splicing footage and adding in images to create a post to highlight the team's first win. And it came out great. Turns out creating reels and pairing them with the perfect song might be one of my strengths. If I could just apply that same energy to finding myself a solid man that's not a half-dozen years younger or at least one that *listens* to me. Or, better yet, a job that might exist two months from now.

The truth is, if I *was* giving Drew even the slightest green light, I'd probably love this whole thing. I want a man who takes charge. Who goes after what he craves and can put me in my place—almost. But I'm not giving him that signal. I've told him no, and he's acting like this anyway. I say it's not happening, and he asks me out. I blow it off, and he smacks his lips to mine. Add in everything else and it's exactly how I would expect someone his age to behave. He's certainly not doing himself any favors.

I know there are people all over the world in their mid-twenties who are perfectly settled. Hell, Blake seems to have come out of the womb with his life sorted out. But not those throwing parties in their penthouses, with a different woman on their arm every night or a reputation as Golden City's bad boy. I didn't wait this long to settle down only to be *let* down instead.

Drew takes the ice every game to be the center of attention—to make big moves, leave a lasting impression. It's not a bad thing, just not exactly what I'm looking for. I don't want someone who constantly seeks validation from the world. I'm where I am this late in life because I *haven't* cared what people think.

Even if Drew magically had the epiphany that I had six months ago, it would take him at least that long to get to the point that I'm at—and even I barely have a handle on what the hell I'm doing. Not to mention that I have six years on the guy. I'd have to imagine that growth would be proportional. If it took me half a year to make the switch at my age, it'd take him way longer than that.

As if my mother can hear my ticking clock from across the city, my phone starts buzzing in my bag. When I pull it out, *Grace* is written across the screen, mocking me with its irony.

"Hello, Mother."

A scoff crackles through the speaker. "Hi, Brooke."

I glance around, finally noticing where I am—leave it to my mother to ground me without even trying. I'm entirely too close to Drippy's coffee not to make a pit stop.

"What's up, Mom," I ask, crossing the street—and my fingers—hoping she doesn't ask me about, well, any part of my life at the moment. My lips tingle with the reminder of Drew's, and I shove the thought of telling my mother a professional hockey player kissed me on the street into my back pocket in case I ever feel like giving her a coronary.

"Are you coming to dinner tonight?"

I reduce my pace leading up to Drippy's as if I'll be able to remember the nonexistent dinner plans we had if I'm moving at a slower speed. "Mom, it's Monday," I say, pulling my phone from my ear to triple check that it is in fact not Family Dinner Night.

"It's also Amy's birthday," she answers back.

Bringing my fist to my forehead, I mouth the word *fuck* as I approach the door.

"You forgot, didn't you?"

I roll my eyes. "When did we make these plans again?"

"Via group text on Saturday, Brooke. The one you didn't respond to until you sent a thumbs up emoji at the end of the conversation."

A quick memory rolls through my mind of my phone dinging continuously while I was taking pictures of the team, the drop-down notifications blocking my view. It didn't take long for me to silence the messages. When I finally opened the thread, a few dozen unread texts riddled my screen, and rather than catch up, I sent the emoji blindly instead.

"Oh, that's right," I lie.

"You didn't read them, did you?"

"No, I did, I just—"

"Brooke..."

"I didn't."

I step to the side to let a middle-aged man in ahead of me, smiling at him as if that somehow redeems me. "I'm sorry, Mom, I just had a lot going on this weekend, but I'll be there."

She sighs, and I can visualize her disappointed face on the other side of the line as clearly as the scent of Drippy's tempts me through the cracks in the door.

I didn't forget my sister-in-law's birthday in general. Kelli Cooke's new book is already wrapped in confetti paper and tied up in a satin bow, sitting on my dining room table next to Amy's favorite non-alcoholic wine. But I also didn't know we had dinner. It seems I've had a few other things—and people—on my mind recently.

"What time?" I ask just to further rile Mom up.

"Six, Brooke. Dinner is always at six."

"Like it has been every night for thirty-one years," I say overtop of her same words. "Yes, Mom, I know. I was kidding."

"If only you could build a life on that humor," Mom says passive aggressively, her voice two octaves higher than it normally is. "I'll see you tonight!"

"See you then!" I mock in the cheeriest voice I can muster.

Hitting the end button as fast as I can, I inhale one long, deep breath and shove my phone back into my bag before pulling open the door to Drippy's. I've never needed an extra large cup of caffeine as much as I do right now.

Stepping onto the stoop of my parents' brownstone, I brace myself for what's to come.

It's not all bad—Blake and I are really close, and I love his wife Amy. My niece, Selah, is almost two, and we already have a bond that could rival some of the best out there—Bonnie and Clyde, The Wet Bandits, Adam Sandler and Kevin James. But the rest of the attendants are way less cute and a lot more of a pain in my ass.

I love my parents. They kept me safe and fed and put up with more than they probably bargained for. But I always felt like I was on the outside. Like I was playing a game and losing because I didn't know the rules.

Blake belonged. He was all solid grades and good behavior. Always falling into step with Mom's predetermined plan without so much as a hiccup. He coasted through his teenage years—no late-night partying or questionable piercings like another Larkin I know—and then kept right on track through adulthood.

He and Amy went to the same college. He studied physical therapy, she studied nursing, and they both proceeded to land great jobs. Soon after, they got engaged, then married, and finally, bought the exact house I always pictured them in—red brick, welcoming front porch, and white picket fence to seal in the perfection.

That was never me.

I was always more bull than porcelain. More winding roads than Adult Highway, always detouring off of the more predictable path. My parents never said the words outright that they were disappointed in the way I acted. But it was there in Mom's backhanded comments and Dad's heaving sighs that cut through the silences.

I used to make light of it. Mom would complain I never had a boyfriend, and I'd hit her with, *"Well, at least a nonexistent man can't knock me up!"* Dad would ask me over and over if I was sure there was nothing he could do to convince me to go to college, and I'd answer with, *"At least this is one thing I'm sticking to!"*

But the humor only dulled the sting.

I can see the good in growing up on my own—the independence it gave me. The way I don't need anyone to make me feel whole. How I accept myself and my life for who and what it is, only deciding *now* that I'm ready to make any alterations. But that doesn't change that when I step through these doors I'll be the one dodging passive-aggressive remarks and being compared to a brother in a whole different league.

With one more deep breath—and one last regret that I didn't buy full-alcohol wine along with Amy's—I grab the knob. But before I can even crank my wrist to turn it, the door flies open, and Mom's pink cheeks and raised brows meet me at the door.

"I win," she says in a cheerful voice only *I* could spot as proceeding an insult. "We took bets on when you'd show. I said 6:05, and it's..." She lifts her arm to read her slim-banded watch. "6:04."

And there it is.

She smiles at me with only one corner of her mouth lifted. "So, I win."

"Not without going over," I quip, smiling as I step through the door, masking my discontent as usual. "Maybe next time, Mom." I lean over and kiss her cheek, then proceed through the hallway. "I assume everyone else is here already?"

"They're in the dining room," Mom calls out just as I round the corner and see for myself that the table is full.

My dad, my brother, and Amy with her swollen belly, all swing their gaze to me as I walk through the kitchen. Plates are already set on the table, steam still floating off of Mom's signature roast. No one except Selah has started eating yet, chunks of meat and two baby carrots set up next to a mound of mashed potatoes and some tan, lifeless cereal. When Blake calls out to me, her little eyes find mine, her hand mid-trek toward her mouth with a Cheerio.

"Book!" she screeches, and I'm instantly happier.

"Say Say!" I yell back, rushing toward her.

When I get to her high chair, I lean down, plop a kiss on her head, and steal a piece of cereal off of her tray, popping it into my mouth.

"Hey!" she whines, her face dropping on a dime to one much grumpier.

I laugh, tickle under her chubby little arm, and her smile returns, reaching each ear. "I missed you," I whisper, stepping behind her chair to the head of the table.

I lean down, squeezing my father's shoulders. "Hey, Dad."

"Hi, hunny," he says, tapping his fork, eager as always to get dinner started.

I move to Amy next who attempts to stand despite her unbalanced center of gravity. "Oh, sit," I say. "Happy birthday." I hand her the bag with the book and set the bottle of useless wine on the table.

"It's good, I've read it. Two words—pumpkin muffin."

"Umm, yes," she says, fanning herself. She reaches up and squeezes my arm. "Thanks, Brooke."

I smile, then continue moving to Blake, who is already standing, waiting for my embrace. "Hey, big brother."

Blake pulls me into a hug and squeezes hard. "For the record, I purposely took the L and said you'd be here at six on the dot."

Pulling back, I look him up and down and keep him at arm's length. "Your loyalty is unmatched there, Blakey," I laugh.

Blake nudges my shoulder and chuckles. "I know. Someday you'll thank me by letting me be right for once."

Rolling my eyes, I find the empty chair across from Selah and drop down onto it, sticking my tongue out to her as Mom walks in the room.

"Nice, Brooke. The perfect thing to teach your two-year-old niece," she mutters sarcastically, grabbing the rest of the roast off of the counter in the kitchen.

Rather than argue, I simply wink at Blake and shake my head. "So, Amy, how are you feeling?"

She sighs heavily. "About being older or fatter?"

The rest of the group pauses, Mom still standing with her hands on the serving platter placed at the center of the table. I shrug my shoulders. "Both, I guess."

I reach for the open bottle of red sitting in front of Blake and grab it at the bottom. He clamps his hand around the neck, teasing me by resisting my pull, before finally letting go.

"The older part is fine. What's another year?"

I cock a brow in agreement, pouring myself a hefty glass, and Mom definitely notices, her eyes drilling a hole of judgement into the side of my head. It's not Amy that she's silently criticizing—her life is as full as Selah's cheeks with potatoes. But it's a totally different ball game for me, who is competing with a nonexistent clock and still has nothing to show my opinionated mother.

"Work's getting harder though. Being on my feet for my whole shift has been way worse this second time around."

"Yeah, *that* sounds horrible," I say, bringing my glass to my lips. "I know what it's like waiting tables for a double, and I'm not carrying a mini-person strapped to my front... no offense."

Amy shakes her head and rubs the side of her belly. "None taken. This thing gets bigger everyday."

"Uh, yeah, babe," Blake leans over. "That's kind of the point. You're growing the next Golden City athlete in there."

My ears perk up at just the word *athlete* as Mom tells everyone, "Eat up!"

Without thinking, words fall from my lips that I regret the second I hear them aloud. "Speaking of... I've kind of been working for Levi, doing some social media content for the Flames."

You'd think I'd said I sent Levi *up* in flames with the way Blake freezes and Mom's fork falls from her hand with a clang.

"Wait, like hanging with the players?"

"Brooke, did you get a new job?"

Blake and my mom speak simultaneously, both of their faces lit up like Christmas trees. I scan the table to find Amy and Dad still casually eating and Selah tossing a mushy carrot off of the side of her tray.

The vegetable hits the floor and the plopping sound seems to echo off of the walls, the room otherwise silent with full mouths and hopeful ears.

"Yeah, sort of," I say, answering the easier of the two questions first. "I'm not really *hanging* with them." *Just getting accosted on the street.* "But I was around them all weekend and will be again these next few weeks."

"That's so cool." Blake smiles, shoving a forkful of meat in his mouth. "Get me Anderson's autograph, will ya?"

My cheeks heat, either from his comment or the steam from my food—which is what I'm choosing to believe. I push the pile of cooked vegetables up against the mound of mashed potatoes on my plate as if they're forming a gravy dam.

"I, uh, can sure try," I stammer out, noticing Mom still sitting on the edge of her seat.

"And no, Mom," I answer reluctantly. "I'm just filling in."

My mom's whole body slouches, her lips pursed as she picks her fork back up and nods slowly. "I should have assumed, I guess," she says softly, then quickly turns back to Amy and Blake's side of the table.

"So, did you guys pick a na—"

"For now," I swallow hard, sitting up straighter, as if my posture can hide the bullshit in my tone.

For the second time tonight, the words spew out without me thinking, and I want to blame the wine, but I'm only three sips in. Instead, I blame the way too young for me, tattooed—*did I know he had two sleeves before I saw them this morning?*—sexy hockey-god that has thrown me off yet again.

"I'm filling in for the Flames until their new girl starts, but I realized I'm pretty good at it. I like it too." I grab my wine glass and take a big gulp. "I decided I'm going to use this as a way to build experience for my resume. Hopefully I'll find something permanent and get myself a big girl job. Finally be able to quit The Gilded Pub."

"Ah, that's awesome!" Amy says cheerfully, clapping quietly. Selah copies her mom, smacking her hands together and screaming, "Yay!" at the top of her lungs.

"Hell yeah, little sis," Blake says next. "You'll definitely find something. Content creation is huge right now."

Dad nods in approval, chewing his latest scoop of roast and Mom—well, she looks speechless after something I've said for maybe the first time ever.

"Well..." she begins, running her tongue along her teeth. "If it all works out, that'll be an answer to prayers."

I nod, gulping down the rest of my wine. "Yeah," I say.

If it all works out.

12

Drew

Pushing open the door to the locker room, I naturally fall into my usual path over the stark Flames logo on the center of the carpet. I head for my stall without looking up from my phone, the last chorus of my current hyper-fixation song coming to a close. The noise blasting through my headphones at full blast fades out as my shins hit the bench in front of my space.

Swiping out of my music, a laugh quickly replaces the beat, and my head swings toward the direction it comes from. At the same time, Ward walks over to me, nudging my shoulder.

"Yo," he says.

"What's that about?" I ask too quickly, tipping my head toward the back of the room where Brooke is laughing unnecessarily loud at whatever Burnsey just said.

"Uh, I don't know?" he says, taking them in. "I just got here like thirty seconds before you."

I nod, my eyes still lingering on Brooke who hasn't spotted me yet. Taking advantage of the time I have to drink her in, I let myself really admire her for the first time since that night at the gala.

Her black denim jeans hug the curve carved perfectly above her hips, her graphic t-shirt tied up in a knot, sitting just above the button. Her hair hangs in loose waves, framing her face that's locked in on Brett's, which is driving me crazy.

What's worse is that she looks so relaxed right now—her weight settled on one boot, her hands dipped casually into her two front pockets. The smile she's wearing is easy—like she's shooting the shit with a friend. Nothing like she is with me.

For a second, it rubs me wrong. I can't quite place it at first, but something about the way she's acting bothers me, and it goes beyond the fact that my charming friend is clearly leaving an impression. When she lifts her hand to tuck her hair behind her ear, a small butterfly tattoo reveals itself on the bottom of her forearm.

Dropping my backpack onto the bench, I inhale deeply then turn on the ball of my foot. I get only a few strides closer before Brooke and Brett both turn my way. I didn't realize it was there before—I guess when her hands were pushed back, pressed against the sides of the sink, I didn't notice. When she was in that motorcycle jacket or her slouchy sweatshirt, I didn't notice either. But now I do. And it hits me why her behavior's nagging at me.

That first night Brooke and I were together, she was like a butterfly with me—bold, beautiful. Her wings wore a pattern that was intricate and unreadable, but they were fully spread. Free.

Now, she's different. Still gorgeous—still elusive as hell—but her wings are tucked, her colors turned inward like she's hiding them away. Like she's keeping them from me.

I know she said she's changed since then—that her priorities have shifted, and I don't fit into the rest of her life like I did that night. But I fucking hate that she's not being herself around me. Not acting with me like she is right now. I want the Brooke from that night back. Even if her plans have changed.

Shit, I just want Brooke, period.

"Yo, Cap, what's goin' on?" Brett holds out his hand, and I clap mine to his. Stepping into him, I bring my other palm to his shoulder, all the while, locking eyes with Brooke.

"What's up, man?" We separate, and he crosses his arms. "Coach asked me to give the new girl a little facilities tour before everyone started droppin' trow."

Brooke smothers a laugh, and I grin more at the way her lips meet in a dimple than at Burn's stupid comment. "How far did ya get?" I ask.

"Uh..." Brett looks over my shoulder toward the entrance, then back at his feet. "To about here," he says, rocking back on his heels.

I nod, give Brooke a quick once-over, then look back at him. "How about you let me take over?"

"Nah, it's all good, Cap. I don't—" I lower my chin and cock a brow. "Oh," he drags out. "Oh, okay. I see you." He nudges my arm, then turns to Brooke and fucking bows. "My lady."

"Brett, you don't have to—" she attempts.

"Get the hell out of here," I say lightheartedly, shoving him back toward the stalls.

He stumbles away, leaving just Brooke and me nearly pressed up against the giant flat screen that hangs on the wall.

"Brett was doing a good job, you know." Brooke crosses her arms and nibbles at her bottom lip.

I dare to take half a step closer to her and shove both hands into my back pockets. "I'll try to do better."

Brooke swallows, dropping her arms and standing up straighter as if I'm talking about more than the tour.

Because I am.

"Alright, well, where were we?"

"No, he was right. We literally only made it this far. I think you got here like two minutes after us."

"Oh." I nod toward the short hallway behind her. "Let's hit the showers then."

Brooke's lips part slightly as I brush past her, only half-grinning to myself.

I walk the few feet it takes to cross from the locker room into the showers, feeling Brooke at my heels as I do. "Alright, well, I'm guessing you'll never need to see this again, but here's where we all get naked."

She glances over slyly, rolling her eyes. "Yeah, I know Levi gave me free reign, but I have a feeling the organization might have an issue with their players being exposed on social media."

"True," I agree. "Which is kind of a shame. Some of the guys have killer shower voices."

Brooke drops her head in an attempt to resist responding, but she fails. "Now *that* I'd love to see."

"I'll try to record it sometime," I say, causing Brooke to look at me curiously. "The audio, I mean. Just the audio."

She nods through a smile. "Do you ever harmonize? Maybe drop some bars?"

Now it's my turn to gape at *her*. Not just because of what she says, but that she's continuing conversation at all. "Drop some bars?"

She huffs, shoving my chest like she did before, my skin filling with goosebumps like it also remembers. "You know what I mean."

I shake my head. "No, I don't harmonize." I lean into her. "Or drop bars. That's not really my style of music."

"What do you listen to?"

I purse my lips, inhaling deeply. "Angsty shit," I say, going with Burnsey's favorite description.

Brooke tilts her head, looking me up and down. "Huh... I can see it."

I don't ask her why although the question threatens to burst from my throat. Brooke lit up the second I mentioned music. I'm not risking all of that coming to a grinding halt by going too deep on my end—even if she strangely makes me want to. Instead I say, "How about you?"

"Oh, I definitely sing in the shower. Bars too." She looks at me sideways, giving me maybe the first authentic smirk I've seen on her.

I flash her one back. "I mean, what do you listen to?"

"I like everything."

I nod, though I'm a little disappointed—and pretty surprised—that her response is so cookie-cutter.

"But not in the way that most people say," she continues. "Like they could listen to whatever and be fine with it."

My attitude weakens as she steps forward, beginning a slow circle as she continues taking in the room. "I genuinely think there's good in all music. Country calms you down. House pumps you up. Rap songs have that beat that makes you feel alive. And the angsty shit?" She turns around, smothering a smile. "That's the kind of stuff that makes you feel like you're dying inside. But in a good way, ya know?"

She turns back around, continuing to circle, but I don't move or speak because I don't want her to stop—talking or reading my soul. "Like you're being ripped apart. Stripped raw." She completes her journey, landing back in front of me. "Seen."

Looking into her eyes, I find her again. The girl from the gala that somehow sees *me* whether or not she even realizes it. "Exactly," is all I manage to say, though my voice comes out soft.

Brooke shrugs her shoulders as if she didn't just perfectly explain why I fill my head with the lyrics I do, despite the shit I constantly get from my teammates. "So, anything else to see besides the drains you all piss in?"

My brain is caught so off guard by her words—and my sudden rewiring—that I stand there motionless, my mouth open and eyes wide like a goddamn idiot. Brooke waits, searching my face for an answer—or maybe any sign of life—before I finally shake my head of her sadly accurate statement. And my heart of her perfectly sculpted words.

"Uh, yeah, you weirdo," I finally manage to push out, acting unfazed despite feeling the opposite. "No sinks though... if that's what you're looking for." Her guard instantly flies back up, her lips pressed into a flat line. I sigh, dropping it before she completely disappears again. "Out this way."

I spin around toward where we entered the showers—a few minutes and one life-changing conversation earlier—and walk ahead of her. When I step back into the hallway, I turn toward the only other door in this direction.

"Next stop," I say, pressing my thumb into the sensor by the frame.

When it unlatches, I push it open, and Brooke walks up from behind me, stepping into the space. "Holy shit," she says, the view in front of her bringing her back to me. "This is like a five-star resort."

She glances around, taking in the grey and white marbled steam room, top of the line sauna, and glistening cold and hot tubs that fill the space. There are TVs in front of every amenity and every luxury you could possibly imagine—heated flooring, a stocked mini fridge, towel warmers. It's all newly renovated and pristinely polished, showing off every cent put into it.

"Yeah, we're pretty lucky. I probably don't use it all as much as I should, but a lot of the guys hang out here at night and watch games while they chill in the hot tub and stuff."

"That's adorable," she says, her eyes still full of wonder. "I can't believe you don't take advantage of this."

"Eh, I usually kill time in the bay." Brooke stops to dip her hand into the pool. "The shooting bay," I clarify, unsure of why I'm even telling her this.

"Where's that?"

"On the other side of the facilities."

"Can I see it?"

I lean against the doorframe as Brooke stands and brushes her wet hand on the back of her jeans. I'm definitely the jealous type, but I'm not sure I've ever been envious of a woman's own limb until right now.

"Oh, it's not much to see. Nothing like this."

She shrugs. "That's okay. I want to see everything."

I nod, pushing off of the wall, surprised at how at ease I feel. "Alright then," I say. "Back this way."

I lead Brooke back down the hall to the locker room where more guys are slowly piling in. Petrov catches my attention as he observes me with an unreadable expression. I tip my chin up to him, and he tilts his forehead down in response as Brooke catches up behind me.

I let her pass, ignoring Storm's weird reaction, and instinctively setting my hand on her lower back to guide her in front of me. She continues walking despite my touch, but my fingertips don't miss the initial jolt she had when they landed on her. Electric, like any other time we've touched, which might throw her off, but doesn't surprise me at all.

I nudge her toward the locker room door and let her lead this time, ignoring Ward's wink and Brett's fucking pelvis thrusts after they're out of Brooke's sight. Flipping them off over my head as we enter the hall, I grab her wrist, then tug her in the right direction.

"The gym's over there with basically any equipment you could possibly imagine." I point towards a glass wall where you can see a line of dumbbells and a few treadmills, which doesn't even scratch the surface of what's inside.

"You use that a lot." She doesn't ask it as a question, and I can't pass up the opportunity to mess with her.

"What makes you say that?"

She glares at me. "You know."

A chuckle escapes my lips. "I lift often, yes, Brooke."

"No cardio?"

I glance at her side-eyed. "Oh, I do plenty of cardio."

I purposely increase my speed so that I'm a half a step ahead of her. "Through there is the trainer's room," I say, pointing to another door and changing the subject. "There's a taping station and an ice bath. Some stretching machines and massage tables." I look over at her quickly, a lazy grin creeping onto my face.

"I'm not saying a word this time," she says, holding her hands up in surrender.

"You know, you don't have to be afraid to flirt with me, Mystery Girl," I say, stopping at our destination. Now that I'm here, with her, I'm oddly anxious about entering the one spot I frequent so often.

She blows through her lips. "Actually, I do because apparently you can't take a hint even when I spell it out for you."

I laugh, instantly put back at ease by her stubbornness, and run my tongue over my bottom lip, unlocking the door with my finger. "That's because you can't spell for shit."

I push it open, then step inside, and Brooke follows as the door closes behind her. We walk through the equipment room that leads to the shooting area, the walls lined with sticks of every size and color, gloves hanging from hooks from floor to ceiling, and skates sitting on the mat running the length of the wall. Brooke pauses at the sharpening machine, looking at it closely before continuing past the racks of spare visors and cages and crates of tools stacked on top of each other.

When we make it through to the shooting bay, she stops at the synthetic ice. "This is it?" she asks, her eyes sweeping over the space.

There's not much in here—two non-regulation nets with goalie cutouts, a cracked set of plastic targets, a video monitor for speed and playback, and a dozen loose pucks scattered across the surface. Her response doesn't throw me.

"That's why I love it." I walk over and grab a spare stick leaning against the wall, scooping a puck onto the blade and tossing it in the air. "It's simple." I catch it and let it drop. "Quiet."

Brooke shoves her hands into her back pockets again and closes some of the gap between us. "I would have thought a guy like you would prefer the high-end spa or the decked-out gym."

Of course she did. "Hmm, yeah." I wind up, smacking my stick into the puck with a crack. It flies through the air and into the target in the top corner of the net. "You'd think."

Brooke's eyes sink into the side of my head as I reach for another disc. She doesn't press me, which makes me *want* to explain.

"I started coming here as a rookie. Late-nights, early mornings—whenever I needed a break from it all. An escape from the chaos. I guess it stuck. Now it's just... my spot."

I shrug, then shoot again, burying the puck into the opposite pocket. "In here it's just hockey. Kind of like when I used to play in my driveway in middle school." I smile at the memory, pausing to lean my weight on the blade grinding into the tile. "God, I'd be out there so long my mom used to have to drag my ass inside."

Brooke smiles, soft and knowing. "Well, I'd say the obsession paid off. She must be proud."

Inhaling deeply, I swallow hard and let the comment roll off of me as best I can. Standing up straighter, I slide another puck my way and wind up again. "I hope so," I say, flicking my wrist.

Brooke's forehead creases, and before I can stop myself, I continue... again. "She died when I was fifteen."

I never say that out loud. Of course my teammates know, but even so, it's not a topic that we ever talk about. But she always seems to have this effect on me. From the moment we spoke at the gala, I was different around her. Now, there's something about her being in this space with me—or just something about *her*—that makes me open up again.

Her eyes grow wide as she strides over to me. "Oh, Drew. I'm so sorry. I didn't know."

Her energy shift catches me off guard, and my mouth reacts before I can stop myself from pushing her away again by doing too much.

I step to her. "There's a lot that you don't know about me, Brooke."

She searches my eyes, hers wandering back and forth between the two. When she doesn't instantly deny me, my hand pushes the moment, moving from the stick to tuck her hair behind her ear. That quickly though, my mind catches up, and I pull it back down.

No, not this time.

Brooke licks her lips, her gaze dropping to mine. For a second I think *she* might lean in—this spot, my confession, stripping down her walls. Still, I don't waver.

Your move, Mystery Girl.

She hesitates another moment, and just when I think she may actually do it—might finally let go for just a second—the keypad hums from the other side of the door.

"Oh, shit. My bad, guys," our equipment manager says, halting in his tracks.

Brooke steps back quickly, clearing her throat, but my feet—and eyes—stay planted.

"All good, man," I say, without looking away. She's flustered, clearly affected by our conversation—by me. *So, why is she resisting so much?*

"We were just, uh—he was—" she stammers.

"I was just showing her around," I offer through a sigh, finally turning to Max. "She's helping with social media for a while."

Max chuckles knowingly, walking to a crate of pucks in the corner of the room. "Well, don't let me stop you." He picks it up and heads back toward the door without so much as another word.

When it latches shut, I look at Brooke who is chewing at her bottom lip, arms folded tight like she can't trust herself otherwise.

She's gone again.

"Should we keep moving?" I ask, my voice rougher than earlier.

She glances around the room, but this time, it's not the simple space it was before. Now, it's filled with a depth that she doesn't seem ready to dive into. "I don't know. Maybe I've seen enough for today."

I consider arguing—contemplate questioning what the hell is going on. But I don't.

I'm used to this.

"Yeah," I say instead, nodding slowly. "Maybe you have."

13

Brooke

"Brooke!" Levi calls to me from the bench as I scroll through my list of polling questions for the boys. My plan is to stick around for practice and grab some pictures, then video them coming off of the ice and answering one for the camera.

Standing from my seat in the row right behind him, I step up to the boards. Levi tosses something small over the glass, and I fumble my phone trying not to let either fall through the seats.

"That's the key to Jenny's old office. It's down the hall from mine. Drew reminded me I never gave you any of her equipment. That's my fault. Use whatever you need."

I'm caught off guard by just about everything he says—office, Drew, equipment. Mostly because I've never had an office before. Not that it's really *mine,* of course. And Drew—he just keeps surprising me.

"Thanks, I'll take a look while you guys are out there."

Levi nods, then holds his phone screen up to the glass. "These are the job requirements I forgot to show you last week."

I scan the list. There's nothing on there that I didn't expect—or already Google. Capture photos and videos, create content, schedule posts, track trends, collaborate with the marketing team, and interact with fans online. Most of it is either obvious or something I won't be around for long enough to worry about.

"This is all very professional of you, Coach McHottie," I say, tapping the glass where his now blacked-out screen is still displayed.

He rolls his eyes, pulling the phone back down and swiping up on the device. Pressing it back to the glass, he says, "And this is what I can offer you for the time you're here. That is, if Burns and Anderson didn't already scare you away with their *tour*."

I grin, glancing down at the screen, then back up at Levi, who's looking over his shoulder as the guys start funneling onto the ice. Leaning in closer, I double check the number.

"I don't think that's right," I say, calculating. "You only asked for a month."

Levi turns the phone back toward himself, nods, then flips it to me again. "That's the number, Larkin."

I do the math once more, and I know I didn't go to college—*sorry, Mother*—but I'm not stupid. And I know money. That easily matches what my pay would be for the next month at The Gilded Pub, plus more, and that's without dealing with college kids on cheesesteak nights. I already got Tessa to cover my shifts for me for the time being. Luckily, she's in-between her regular gigs and was eager to take them.

Mentally thanking Tess—and Alex for banging the fucking coach like I so graciously suggested—I smile. "Sounds good to me."

Levi pockets his phone. "Cool," is all he says before he turns around, steps off of the bench, and starts skating toward the boys.

I take one look at the team, spotting the goalie, who, thanks to my studying over the last couple of nights, I now know is Carter Ward. *Take that, college.* His legs are bent in a way a girl could only dream, but with my new temporary salary in mind, I shake the immediate thought and head back toward the tunnel.

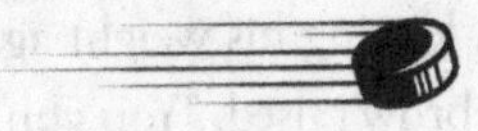

"If your hockey stick had a name, what would it be?" I ask the next player off, sticking the tiny wireless microphone out over the tripod.

The player, who I believe is Ellis but could easily be Hughes—I'm getting better, but I'm not *that* good—stutters. "Uh, I, um... Hercules."

I smile politely.

"No, Thor."

I nod, pulling the microphone back.

"No, wait..."

I shove it back in front of him, inhaling deeply, my mouth still formed in a forceful grin.

Ellis-Hughes stands straighter, the corner of his lips turning upward. "Excalibur."

I nod, and thankfully, Ward steps up behind him, saving us both from any more indecisiveness.

"Claus."

I snort out a laugh. "What?" He simply shrugs and continues walking by as Petrov's presence shadows above me.

Still half giggling, I swallow down his massive size, tip my chin up to him, and hold out the mic. "Hey, Alexei, if your hockey stick had a name, what would it be?"

He pauses, contemplating, then glances down at his stick. After a moment of consideration, he looks back at me. "Volshebnaya Palochka."

"Oh," I say quickly. "That's, um—wow. Okay." He stares at me, his expression as unreadable as it normally is. After another beat of silence I assumed he would fill, I ask, "And what does that mean?"

"It is the same as you say *wand*." We both look at each other blankly. "Because with it I make the magic."

My eyes go wide as I tilt my head. "Huh. That's so... poetic."

He nods assertively then walks away. I track his movement, dumb-founded by the intricate depth of such a large man. When I turn around, Drew is standing there, leaning his weight against his stick, his helmet unstrapped and one eyebrow raised. "You gonna ask me?"

"Yeah, sure," I say before swallowing. I take an interest in my phone to ensure it's still recording and notice through the view of the camera that Drew is watching me.

The way he looks at me is different than I would have expected. *He's* different than I would have expected. I think back to our conversation earlier in the shooting bay. The way he spoke up for me with Levi. Everything about that night at the gala.

But that's only *him* some of the time.

And that's only one of our problems.

I reach my arm out to him, clearing my throat. "What would your stick be called if you had to give it a name, Twelve?"

Drew narrows his eyes and runs his tongue along his top lip. "Maybe—"

"The Hammer," Brett says, stepping up to Drew and throwing his arms over his shoulder. He knocks his glove into Drew's stick, and it falls to the rubber ground with a thump. "Look, Cap. You *dropped* it."

Drew scrunches up his face as he looks at him sideways, then puts his arm behind him and shoves him forward. "Get lost, Burnsey," he says through a chuckle.

Burns lets out his infamous cackle as he falls into step backward, away from us and the video. "My stick's name is Dixie, by the way! Dixie Normus!" he calls to us as he continues down the hall.

"You wish, bud!" Drew yells, then rolls his eyes to me.

"I'll just edit all that out."

"Good idea."

I tap the record button on my phone to stop the video. "I think I have enough anyway."

A silence falls between us. It's not uncomfortable, but definitely charged. Every interaction I have with Drew feels weighted. Not nec-essarily heavy, but dense. Maybe it's because I know how I feel—hell, I know how *he* feels—but I won't act on it. Maybe it's because we really do connect. But it always seems like there's a depth to our interactions—electric chemistry, intense banter, loaded questions. Like if I just let myself give in, we might fall from the cliff we're teetering on.

It gets me thinking that if I want to do my best here, I'm going to need some of the novelty to wear off between us. I can't work with him every day for a month, thinking there's some sort of unsolved mystery inside of him—some unlocked potential. I need things to be easy and casual. I need to see him as the man that he is and not the man I wrote him to be in my head that night. I need to see the Drew that the world sees—but for myself.

"What's your typical day look like?" I ask, capitalizing on the motivation I have.

He pulls his neck back, justifiably caught off guard. "Um, it's different all the time, honestly."

"Do you think you could show me?" His eyebrows shoot up before he blinks them back down, attempting to hide his surprise. "Maybe let me sort of shadow you for a day?"

His brow wrinkles slightly. "Like for content?"

Like for peace of mind.

I shrug. "Sure."

He mulls it over, silent while maintaining eye contact. When his lips crawl into his signature grin, my body reacts as it usually does, and I start regretting my decision. "You sayin' you want to hang out with me, Mystery Girl?"

"No, I—that's not what—"

He adjusts his stance, shaking his head. "I'm fucking with you, Brooke. Jenny did this before with Ward. Why she'd want to spend the day with a goalie is beyond me." He blows out a breath as if his opinion's exhausting. "Those dudes are weird as hell."

I catch myself snickering, and he definitely notices. "But yeah," he says, striding half a step closer. "Sure. You can be my shadow."

I nod and remove my phone from the tripod clamp. I shove it into my back pocket as he continues.

"Under two conditions."

I peer up at him. "No dates."

He cocks his head back and looks me over quickly. "Well, someone's awfully confident." My gaze turns to a glare. "But no. That's not one."

"I'm listening."

Drew switches his stick to his other hand and tugs one glove off, tucking it under his arm. He removes his helmet next, balancing it on the top of his stick and runs his free hand through his hair. "The first is you have to lean in. You want to spend a day in my shoes, you're walking in them right alongside me." When my eyes finish their quick detour to his hair raking, they return to his. And of course, he's smirking at me knowingly. "You have to commit, Mystery Girl."

"Perfect," I say, dripping in false confidence. "That's exactly what I've been working on."

"It'll be good practice then."

I tip my chin down, popping a hip out and scooping up the tripod. "And the second condition?"

His voice flattens, his tone serious. "I say what makes it into the highlight reel. If there's something I don't want on social media, you have to respect that."

His final term throws me. Mr. Spotlight doesn't want his life on full display? Instinctively, my thoughts go to something messy—something dangerous, risky, maybe a bad habit he can't seem to shake. But in that case, I wouldn't want to post it anyway. I'm not trying to stir up trouble for the one guy who could possibly write me my first ever *real* letter of recommendation. And honestly, seeing he's still got shit he's dealing with would only help me with the real reason I want to tag along.

"Yeah, okay. Deal," I say. "You get final say."

"Alright then. Tomorrow?"

"Sure, what time?" I lean down, shoving the tripod into my black, quilted bag, the end of it jutting out of the top.

"6:30?"

I snap up, the bag in my hand swinging with force and landing on my shoulder, the metal rod sticking out practically taking out an eyeball. "In the *morning*?"

Drew chuckles. "I can pick you up if that's easier."

Why did I think that this man would need his beauty sleep? Maybe time to flush out the hangover? "Oh my God, you're serious," I deadpan.

"Uh, yeah, Brooke. I'm serious."

My ass starts vibrating as my phone goes off in my jeans. First taken aback by the time and now distracted by the message, I don't manage much more than an, "Um..."

I slip my cell from my pocket and glance at the screen. *Unknown Number* is sitting on top of a new text. I slide it open curiously.

UNKNOWN NUMBER

In town for a few hours, Brookie. Meet me for coffee?

My current attitude does a complete one-eighty. There's only one person in the world who calls me Brookie, and the last time I saw her, she had just swooped back into town after spending Christmas in Iceland under the Northern Lights in nothing but her birthday suit. *Typical Ivy.*

The excitement I gain from my aunt's text replaces the dread from Drew's early wake-up call. Suddenly, I'm oddly okay with starting the day at such an ungodly hour for anything but Ravi's sunrise hot yoga class. That, mixed with my anxiousness to fly to Drippy's as fast as I can so I don't miss even one minute with Ivy, finally gets me to answer.

"6:30 is fine," I say with borderline excitement. Drew creases his brow, and I tilt my phone at him. "My aunt is in town. I have to go. But I'll see you tomorrow."

I'm already turned halfway to the exit when I twist back around. Drew is still in the same spot he was in before, his lips still curved upward, his eyes still on me.

"My apartment's on Eleventh!" I call back. "Feel free to be late!"

The door to Drippy's jingles with the announcement that someone new is walking in. My eyes beeline for the entrance, and sure enough, only twenty minutes after she said, *Be there in five!*, my Aunt Ivy waltzes in.

I smile, watching as her silver waves bounce off of her shoulders, her bright red glasses halfway down her nose. The top she's wearing looks every bit hand-sewn that it probably is, striped in royal blue and bright yellow, draped over her floor-length cheetah print skirt. Her platform sandals, which are the same cerulean as the stripes on her shirt, peek below the ruffled hem as she turns in my direction.

"Over here!" I call to her from the two-top table shoved into the corner of the cafe.

I love Ivy dearly—her stories maybe more—but she doesn't spare any details, and more than once, nearby patrons have gotten a little nosy. I've learned that rather than have them shoot us a look, or worse, have them join, it's easier to separate us and other customers.

Ivy spots me over her glasses, her face lighting up as she strides in my direction. When she reaches the table, I stand, and she greets me in typical Aunt Ivy fashion.

"Brookie," she sings, kissing one cheek. She grabs hold of my shoulders, stretching out her arms to put space between us. "Have you lost weight?" I shake my head, a lazy smile on my lips. "Done a full-body peel?" I repeat my answer. Ivy hums, looking me up and down. "I got it!" she cries, her voice already too loud. She leans into me, bringing her hands to my cheeks. "You've been rammed by a stud who's hung like a moose, haven't ya?"

A snort bursts through my nose as I shake my head once again.

"Not even that hockey-playing one you gave the honor to before?"

I feel my face turn the same color as her fire engine frames. "Definitely not," I say.

Ivy drops her hands. She stares at me an extra beat as if she's contemplating my honesty. "Well, you're absolutely glowing, whatever the cause," she eventually says, then she kisses my other cheek and whispers. "But we'll circle back to that last one in a minute."

"It's so good to see you too, Ivy," I say, taking my seat and praying her sporadic thoughts direct her anywhere else. "Where have you been?"

"Oh, darling," Ivy sighs, lifting her glasses so they sit perched on her head, her hair now pushed away from her face. "I've been a little here, a little there. You know how I am. I don't belong to one place."

She lifts the steaming cup of oolong tea I preordered for her, sniffing it and smiling at me through the misty haze.

"Why *didn't* you ever settle down?" I ask abruptly, holding my Americano in my hands like I need it for survival. I take a sip as Ivy sets down her round Drippy's mug and unnecessarily stirs her tea with the small spoon rested on top of the matching saucer.

She doesn't answer right away. Instead, she watches the way the tea swirls with the motion of the spoon like the center of the spiral may reveal the future—or maybe the past. The silver clinks once against the rim before she places it back onto the dish and looks up at me.

"Settle down," Ivy repeats, her voice full of subtle amusement. "Such a funny phrase, isn't it? Like life is something to just comfortably skate through."

She pauses, then lifts the mug to her lips. Her lipstick leaves a faint trace on the porcelain. "I tried once," she adds, her voice unusually hushed. "But he liked quiet nights and board games, and I..." She laughs more to herself than to me. "Liked parties with strangers and one-way tickets."

I sip my coffee, the rich espresso bitter against my tongue. Her words sink in, most of my heart swelling at the idea of a beautifully mundane life with someone who knows what brand of ranch dressing you like and remembers to fill the water on your nightstand. But the part of me that is still holding on to the life I lived ten months ago, still aches for even a fraction of the freedom I know my aunt embodies.

"Do you ever regret it?" I ask, almost hoping she does.

Ivy smiles, deep creases rushing from the corners of her eyes. "Only on rainy Sundays or empty park benches. Or when I see someone like you."

My gaze darts from the rim of my cup. "What do you mean, someone like me?"

My aunt hunches over her as if she's preparing to tell me a secret. "Someone brave enough to have both."

My eyes narrow as I adjust in my seat. "I don't understand."

"I know you, Brookie. I see you. You want to take root in this fruitful garden of life, but on your own terms. You didn't fold under the pressure of your mother to become something you're not, but you didn't run away to join me either."

I brush my thumb across the porcelain of the mug and scoff. "That sounds indecisive, not brave."

"Why can't it be both? What's so wrong with not having everything figured out all at once? With keeping some cards close to your chest?" Ivy inhales slowly, reaching across the small wooden table, placing her hand on top of mine. "If I've learned anything from all the places I've been and people I've met, it's that there's no answer to this life. It's not one size fits all. Not knowing exactly where you'll end up isn't *wrong*, Brookie. It's the journey."

I stare down at the hand covering mine—warm, steady, wrinkled with time. My throat tightens unexpectedly, a lump of emotion rising in my chest that I force to stay put. "I used to be so sure, ya know? So confident about how my life was playing out. Lately though, I don't know, there's something about everything happening around me that makes me feel like..." I exhale, blowing through my lips and looking up at her eyes that somehow seem to twinkle. "Like I'm being left behind."

Aunt Ivy wraps her hand around mine fully and smiles softly. "Oh, darling, you can't be left behind when you're the one in the driver's seat. Some people may be going faster or slower, some may pass you altogether, but you're all headed to different places. All operating different vehicles."

I grin and shake my head. "Well, it sure feels like I'm on a rickety shaggin' wagon, and they're humming past me in their Cybertrucks."

Ivy lifts her hands and waves me away. "Those things are ugly as all hell."

We both let out a laugh. "I know," I say, still chuckling to myself.

"See," Ivy beams. "That's not your style anyway."

I nod, thinking of Alex. It seems like, until recently, she and I were chugging along together, laughing about our rusted bumpers and bum wheels. Now, though, she's the one in the electric car, her head out the window, waving to me as her man pulls away.

"Maybe it's *becoming* my style," I say, my voice unsteady.

It's still hard to admit this out loud. That my future might look different than I thought it would. That I'm starting to open myself up to judgement—about my decisions and feelings.

Ivy paints a slow smile. "Seasons, leaves, the tide, the moon." She pauses, then takes a long sip of her tea.

I crease my brow, waiting expectantly, watching her eyes fall closed as she swallows it down.

"Some of the most beautiful things in life change, Brookie," she says, her tone full of wonder. "And one of them is you."

14
Drew

olling up to Brooke's apartment, I'm borderline nervous. Not to be around her—*that* I'm excited for. But for her to see my life from this side. I've never done this—allowed someone to follow me around. Partly because I like to soak in every ounce of peace I'm capable of finding in my day, but mostly because that would break through the facade.

People don't want to see Drew Anderson, the guy who wakes up early to lift *before* the workout. There's no excitement in watching me bust out reps in the bay or hype myself up to be the face of a brand. They damn sure don't care to see me visit my mom or avoid my dad's phone calls.

The parts of my life that they want are in front of the camera or behind the glass—no one wants to see Clark Kent out of costume. So, it's better to allow the illusion that I just show up and show out. No lows or complaints, definitely no staged dates or forced outings—we all do better with rose-colored glasses.

I couldn't say no to Brooke, though. Turning down an entire day with her would have been a missed opportunity. Besides, there's no hiding from her. From what I can tell, she sees through the bullshit—or better yet, is ignorant of it. And I don't think I could fake how I am with her even if I wanted to.

Stomping my foot down on my kickstand, I lean my bike to the side and swing my leg over. I pull my helmet and backpack off and sit both on my seat, sliding my phone from my pocket. There's one message written across the screen. I swipe it open, knowing I'll regret it instantly.

Dad

> **Drew, call me back. I have thoughts.**

I scoff as I usually do after reading Dad's text, then drop my phone back into my pocket, taking a deep breath before I walk up to Brooke's building. For the first time since I rode up, I fully take in the neighborhood.

It's not a shit-hole by any means, but I'm definitely not on the west side anymore. Trash is built up along the side of the can that sits under a dying tree on the sidewalk. There's no one around, but rap music drifts faintly from one of the nearby houses. The paint on the front of her building is weathered, the pots by the door empty except for dried mulch that looks like it's sat untouched for years.

I'm not surprised by the view I guess—we live in a big city, most parts of town look like this or even worse. And Brooke isn't the type of woman that I'd necessarily worry about. But it's an obvious contrast to my living situation. Sometimes I forget how different we are. It's easy for that to be the case when I'm nothing but comfortable when we're together.

When I get to the stairs, I pause, only now realizing I don't know which apartment is hers. I hesitate briefly before I realize the names are listed on the wall by the entrance. A wave of anxiety flushes past me at the idea that literally anyone can stop, simply read a sign, and know who lives here. There's not much privacy in my life, but you can't even get into my building without ID or permission.

Maybe being Drew Anderson has its perks after all.

Running the pad of my thumb under my chain, I climb the last of the steps leading up to the door. I scan the list, my finger trailing down the names until it lands on the one that lights up my senses. I reach for the buzzer, clearing my throat and mentally rehearsing my greeting, when the door to the building comes flying open.

"Shit!" Brooke squeals, halting in her place only inches from running into me.

"Good morning, Mystery Girl," I say, tucking my hands into the front pockets of my joggers.

Brooke scans me head to toe, her stoic demeanor cracking ever so slightly when her eyes make their way back to mine. "Morning," she says, attempting to look unfazed. "You didn't have to come to my door. This isn't a date, remember." She looks at me, her expression full of half-assed warning.

I glance around, admiring the quiet streets, the sun just barely peeking up from the horizon. When I swing back to her, I ask, "Do you often go on dates at 6:30 in the morning?"

She narrows her eyes at me, then swallows and relaxes. "Well, no."

"And let's not forget that this was *your* idea."

"Uh huh."

"Not to mention, the city still being dark at the ass-crack of dawn gives more danger than ambience, don't you think?" She rolls her eyes and swings her arms over her chest. "I'm just trying to be a nice guy here, Brooke."

In perfect timing, a drunk with long matted hair stumbles down the street across from us, waving and singing some sort of show tune. I finish my sentence with my body turned toward him. "But if you'd like to walk out alone, by all means, be my guest."

When I spin back around, Brooke's hand is falling from where it was lifted, waving. "For your information, that is Frank, and he is a very nice guy." I clench my teeth, more bothered than I should be. "And I can handle myself, thank you very much."

A scoff slips through my lips, and I hold my hands up in surrender.

"Can we just get going?" Brooke asks, her eyes wandering behind me. "Where's your driver?"

I stare at her blankly. "My *driver?*"

She widens her eyes as if to say, *duh,* and I smirk. "I'm a big boy, Brooke. I can get myself where I need to be."

Her head pulls back in surprise, but this interaction is nothing I'm not used to. "Okay, where's your car then?"

My smile grows bigger. I turn around, walk down the steps, and cross the sidewalk to my bike. Picking up my helmet, I perch myself on the seat and tap the spot next to me. "You ready, Larkin?"

Brooke stares at me, her arms slipping back down to her sides, her face no longer in shock or annoyed. No, I've seen that look before. *Fuck me, this girl is turned on.*

She descends the stairs slowly, only speaking when her feet hit the sidewalk. "We're riding around on this thing all day?"

I nod definitively. "You wanted a day in my life."

Pulling on my helmet, I turn, reaching into my backpack and producing hers. I hand it to her, sliding the straps of my now empty bag over my shoulder, then swing my leg around so I'm sitting on the front end of the bike. Brooke doesn't move. I start the engine, and it roars to life, as I look back at her. "Don't want to be late."

She licks her lips, rolling them in on each other, then tucks her hair behind her ears and slips the helmet on. "These things aren't considered safe, ya know," she warns, placing her hands on my shoulder and hoisting herself on as if she's done it a million times before. It hits me that she's trying to convince herself more than me considering her movement tells me this also isn't *her* first time.

I don't answer right away, my brain misfiring from having my mystery girl tight against me, her legs straddling mine for the first time in too long. I wait expectantly for her arms to slide around me, but when they don't come, I realize she's waiting for my answer.

I blink hard, bringing myself back to the question, then turn over my shoulder.

"I can handle myself, thank you very much."

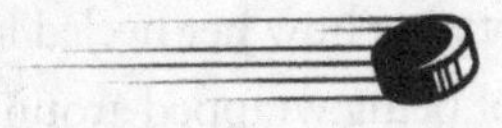

"So, what's first?" Brooke asks, handing me her helmet. Her cheeks are a nice rosy pink, and her chest is rising with each short breath. Either she's cold even in her black leather jacket with a thick sweater underneath, or she's just as fucking flustered from that ride as I am.

No one's ever been on the back of my bike. There was never a situation where that would even make sense. My teammates and I are tight, but I don't want their husky thighs wrapped around mine, and if I'm ever with a girl, it's because we're on a date I didn't plan or she's coming home with me—neither of which warrant the opportunity to sit their ass on my seat. But I didn't think twice about taking it today. With her.

This is my usual morning. My typical routine. My daily ride. I didn't think to switch it up just because Brooke would be with me, which says something. But holy shit, I should have prepared myself.

Brooke's clearly comfortable on the back of a bike. She didn't startle when we hit a bump or awkwardly clasp her hands in front of me, and she knew just the right angle to lean to when I made a sharp turn. Just those thoughts alone turned me on. Add in that she applied just the right amount of pressure to the outside of my thighs and that her hands dropped into my lap every time we hit a red light, and I'm surprised she couldn't feel my excitement through my sweats. *Unless she could.*

It took everything in me not to graze her calf when we came to a crosswalk or drop my hand to her knee when I was cruising down an open street. But I'm trying my best to stop putting moves on her. At least for now. At least until she stops fighting it.

"Back and bis," I say, shaking my head of what I'd rather be doing and setting both helmets on my seat. "Then a little breakfast, and there's film before on-ice this morning."

Brooke purses her lips as we head toward the entrance. "Not as exciting as I thought it would be."

I look over at her, noticing how her heeled boots only accentuate the legs I'm still dreaming of being wrapped around me in a whole different way since the ride over here.

"Who knew Drew Anderson was so... normal?" She smirks, but her words hit me harder than she means them to.

"Not many people," is all I say before scanning my finger and pulling open the door.

Brooke stays quiet for a while, the two of us walking side-by-side down the hall toward the gym. When we get there, it's empty like I knew it would be. The team has lifts later today, but I always get one in on my own.

I do some of my best thinking in this space. There are no lights, no performance, no sound other than the thunking of dumbbells or the clink of a barbell landing in its spot on the rack. You can't fake your way through a workout or pretend you're someone you're not under the weight of a bar. In here, it's just me—the *real* me—and headphones on blast to drown out the silent noise.

"I'm usually the only one here, so make yourself comfortable." Brooke looks around and walks toward a square of mats in the corner of the room. "I usually lift with headphones in, but we can talk if you want," I offer, torn on what I hope she picks.

"Are there speakers? Can you play your music out loud? I won't bother you with conversation, but maybe your angsty shit will tell me something."

We both smile, Brooke at her comment, and me at the idea that she somehow read my mind.

"Yeah," I say. "I can do that." I walk to the system in the corner of the room and connect my Bluetooth to it. "Any requests?"

I turn back to Brooke shaking her head, allowing the strap of her purse to slide down her shoulder. She sets her bag down and crosses her legs, her knee peeking out from the intentional hole in her jeans. "Nope," she says. "This is a day in *your* life."

"Alright then." I hit play on my workout playlist, and Thirty Seconds to Mars comes blasting through the speakers.

My head bobs to the beat as I look at Brooke for her reaction. She's mimicking my motion, scrolling on her phone. I take in the scene—this girl, this song—and am more ready than ever to throw some weight around.

The song plays as I stretch myself out, doing some warm up reps as Brooke continues messing around on her screen. As it fades, I pick up dumbbells to do my first real set of curls, waiting for the next one to begin. My new favorite NF song comes drumming out, the one with lyrics about breaking down, having loud thoughts, and how the spotlight leads to a mask and self-hatred. The one I relate to all too well.

I bang out my next set, getting lost in the rhythm, only realizing Brooke's watching me when the music fades out.

"Well, that was... definitely angsty," she says.

I force a laugh, knowing I relate more to that song than she probably realizes. When the next one comes on, she goes back to her phone, and I move on to my next exercise. Halfway through bent-over rows, I pull my sweatshirt over my head, and toss it by my backpack. Brooke looks up when the fabric slaps against the rubber floor, her gaze bouncing from the bundle of cloth to me.

Before I can overthink it, her head slinks back down, her attention once again on her device. Over the next couple of minutes she takes some pictures of the gym, a few of me in between sets—grabbing water or setting plates on a bar—and types away.

"What are you doing?" I ask, lowering the barbell to the mat.

"Just drafting out some captions for my next couple of posts. I want to get some pictures of the facilities up before your first home game. A little look inside the arena." She turns her phone to me, an image she must have just taken of the dumbbell rack up on the screen. "Plus, I still have to put up the stick-name video from yesterday and figure out what I want to make with everything we do today."

"So, is this what you usually do?" I ask. "For work?"

She shakes her head, putting her phone in her lap. "No, I'm really a waitress and bartender. But I'm trying to find a new job." She plays with a string hanging from the rip in her jeans. "I do think I'm okay at this, though. And I like it. I'm considering trying to find something permanent, actually."

I pick the bar back up and begin curling it toward me. *She really is making big changes then.* "Is that all part of your new plan?" I grunt out between reps.

She tilts her chin down at me. "Yes," she says bluntly.

I nod, finishing out my set and dropping the weights to the floor. "So, what is it? New job, husband, couple of kids?"

She grins to herself, her eyes growing wide. "If my mother had her way."

"She's not happy with your life right now?"

Brooke lets out a cackle, tucking her hair behind her ear. "Not even a little bit."

Walking over to my stuff, I grab my water bottle and take a long sip. "And how about you?" I ask, resting my hand on my hip to catch my breath. "Are you happy with it?"

Brooke looks at me and tilts her head, either caught off guard by my question or unsure of her response. "I used to be," she answers simply.

A silence falls between us for just a second as the current song fades out. "I know the feeling," I say just as the next one begins.

Brooke looks at me in disbelief. "Oh, yeah. I'm sure you *hate* all of this." She gestures around the gym, both of us knowing what she really means. I lick my lips, considering my response, when the beat from the song begins to pound against the speakers, saving me from spilling my secrets and creating the perfect ending to the conversation.

Before moving on to my next exercise, I tear off my shirt and lay it down with my hoodie. As I make my way back and get down on all fours, I notice Brooke tracking my movement.

"You know, you should really be down here with me."

She closes her lips, and her throat moves up and down before she sits up straighter. "Drew I—"

"Doing pushups, Brooke," I laugh. "You're supposed to be leaning in, remember?"

Her cheeks turn that pink again, and now I know I was right before. She felt it just like I did. Just like we always do.

"I can't work out in these clothes," she says, gesturing to her outfit.

"Well, you could always take them off."

Her mouth falls open, and I try to hide my smile as I get into a pushup position.

"You would like that, wouldn't you?" she quips, which shocks me in itself.

I push off my hands and sit back on my knees. "Yeah, actually. I would." Her cheeks blush although she doesn't say anything. "But you know that already."

She shifts in her spot and tilts her head sideways. "Why though?" she asks, narrowing her eyes at me.

I answer with a quick smirk, then shrug my shoulders. "You're hot."

She throws the piece of thread she's been balling between her fingers my way. "Shut up."

We both let out half a laugh. "What? It's true." She rolls her eyes, and I resist every urge I have to stride toward her and lift her so we're standing toe to toe, chest to chest, before I add on. "And maybe that night stuck with me."

Brooke moves her head up and down, dropping eye contact. "Yeah," is all she says.

"I'm sorry, what was that?" I ask, cupping my hand by my ear and leaning closer.

She peers up at me, her volume raised with concision. "I said, yeah." She runs her nail along the thread of her jeans, mumbling under her breath something entirely too close to *me too*.

I want to push. To make her say it again. To make her scream it. But I don't. Because that's where I'll lose her.

"It'll be nice to spend some real time together today," I try to say casually, just a hockey player making polite small talk with a team employee. But I mean every word.

She answers by rolling her tongue over her teeth. "This is work, Drew."

I sigh, then mock her. "I know that, Brooke." Leaning all the way forward, I drop my weight back onto all fours. I walk my hands out so

I'm in the push-up position, then catch her staring at my arms as they strain against my weight.

"Always with the excuses, Mystery Girl."

15

Brooke

"**A**lright, so the guys are good with that?"

Levi looks at Drew, who must agree because he stands to leave, but I don't hear his response. Instead, for what must be the tenth time since this meeting began, I have to stop myself from nodding out and all but falling asleep.

Drew's mornings are boring as hell. And holy shit, I'm tired. Not only did I wake up way before an already ridiculously early wake-up call, but I've spent most of the morning masking my true thoughts and feelings about this man. I swear everything he does is sorcery—casual gestures and routine behaviors, somehow received by my brain as meticulous foreplay.

It was hard enough having to sit on the back of his bike—his fucking *Ducati*, with its sex appeal and steady vibration—without trailing my fingers toward his crotch. But then to see him throw heavy weight around, sweaty and shirtless with his tattoos on display, talking to me about how that night—*our* night—meant something, had me ready to fucking lose it.

Luckily, breakfast was a nice reprieve. I ate fruit, he packed in like three thousand calories, and we both chatted with some of the other guys in the lounge. Film afterward wasn't bad either. It was actually interesting hearing them analyze what looks like regular hockey to me in almost a foreign language.

But then came practice.

It's bad enough that I already feel like I'm walking into some sort of erotic club every time I see the team on the ice. These men make flying across frozen water look easy with stick handling that gets me wondering what else they can do with their hands. And the hitting? Who knew that was such a turn-on? Not to mention the goddamn stretching. But add Drew to it all after the foreplay—I mean *morning*—that we had, and this dry spell is feeling more like a drought.

Needless to say, this meeting? The perfect reset.

"You ready there, Sleeping Beauty?" Drew whispers to me as Monte clicks away on his computer.

"I was not sleeping," I hiss, glaring at him, though it's more directed at myself. I didn't realize anyone would notice, but this is definitely not the kind of impression I'm trying to make on my interim boss.

I stand, attempting to look more awake than ever, and Drew gestures to the door.

"Hey, Brooke," Levi says before either of us takes a step. "Can I talk to you for a second?"

"Oh..." I look at Drew who shrugs his shoulders. "Yeah, sure."

He throws his thumb behind him. "I'll just wait outside."

I nod and turn back to Levi. "What's up, McHottie?" I say out of habit. Levi turns his head slowly, and I force a smile. "Sorry, I'm trying not to do that at *work*." I put air quotes around the last word, and Levi laughs.

"It's all good," he says. "I just wanted to see how you were doing. Make sure the guys aren't giving you a hard time."

I catch myself before I look back toward where I know Drew is waiting on the other side of the door. "It's actually going great," I say, thinking of all the content I've made in the last few days. "I'm realizing I really like doing this stuff."

"Well, you're good at it too." Levi sits forward in his chair and clasps his hands under his chin, his elbows resting on his desk. "Jack just called and said his daughter was busting out laughing at the stick-name video you posted this morning."

"Wait," I interrupt. "Did you actually figure out how to watch it?"

Levi blinks at me blankly. "Yes, Brooke. I figured it out." He inhales deeply, and on the exhale he adds, "Eventually."

I smother a smile, raising my brows. "So what did *you* think?"

"I think Burns is an idiot," he says quickly. I may have decided to leave some of that in. "But I also think it was funny as hell and just the kind of thing we need to keep the fans engaged and in good spirits this season."

Pride rises in my chest, a feeling I'm not too familiar with. "Well, good. I'm glad you all liked it."

He sits back in his seat, moving his elbows to the arms of his chair. "We did, so keep it up."

"I will," I say, turning toward the door.

"Oh, and Brooke," Levi calls after just a few steps. "You're smart to play Anderson up. He's the money-maker around here. The fans and front office will eat that up."

I tip my chin down, not really sure how else to respond other than with that or the truth, and Levi doesn't want to hear that I'm spending time with my old hook up so the anomaly wears off.

"I'll see you at the game tomorrow."

"See ya then," I say, his comment marinating in my mind.

As I push the door open, I can't shake a nagging feeling attached to it. When I step into the hall, I spot Drew standing at the end, looking at framed pictures. His face is serious, his hands are in his pockets, and one piece of hair is flopped down on his forehead. That's when it hits me—why Levi's comment feels so off.

From here, Drew doesn't look like a *money-maker* or the guy you see all over the internet. He's the player who likes to shoot around by himself. The athlete who works out at sunrise and listens to music that hits you like a punch in the gut. He looks like the guy whose morning practically put me to sleep. And whose mom died when he was too young to drive a car.

Drew glances over at me and smiles, his face brightening in a soft way, where his eyes relax and the corners of his lips get lost in deep dimples. As always, who he is with *me* isn't who everyone else seems to know. The change makes me think of what Aunt Ivy said. *Why can't he be both?*

As he saunters over to me, I replay her question in my mind. I come off strong, independent, and confident. But sometimes just a hint of emotion can suffocate me. And I feel like I'm standing still when the rest of my world is forging on without me. I want to settle down and find something serious, but at the same time, that means opening up... and I can't stop drooling over the twenty-five-year-old who banged me in the bathroom. Maybe Drew can be both of those people too—the playmaker from the internet and *my* guy from the gala.

"You ready for a little downtime?" Drew asks, stepping up to me and tearing me from my mental detour.

"As long as there's sustenance involved."

His head falls forward as he lets out a chuckle. "Sure." I breathe a sigh of relief, and he grins.

"I know, it's a lot. But I only have one more thing a little later today."

"Okay, so what now?"

"Well," he says, sticking his hands into his sweatshirt pocket. "We could hang here or head back to my place. For a tour," he adds quickly. "Maybe chill a little."

Biting the inside of my cheek, I consider my response. "Well, what would you normally do?"

"Probably head home."

"Alright," I nod. "Home it is."

I wouldn't say I'm surprised by how lavish Drew's penthouse apartment is—my best friend's married to his coach, and I know where they live. But I am shocked at how different it is from what I pictured.

Call it stereotypical, but I assumed Drew's place would be riddled with beer cans. Maybe have some controllers sitting out on the couch, a woman or two still in his bed. But the apartment I stepped into is nothing like that.

Not only is his place spotless, but it's also practically bare. There's no elaborate art on display that costs more than my car, no wall-to-wall bar stocked with any liquor you could possibly want. There is a small cart staged in the corner, with crystal glasses and a few top-shelf bottles, but that's about it. There's a gaming system tucked under the TV, the same one Cooper has, but the furniture barely looks lived in. There are no pictures on the shelves or walls, and the fridge has not one magnet stuck to it.

"Did you just move in here?" I ask, peeking through the first door I see. It must be a spare room because there's a bed in the center with an end table next to it, but there's just a fitted sheet, one single pillow, and a blanket folded and laid at the bottom.

"No, since I got drafted." He walks into the spotless kitchen, drops his keys on the vacant counter, and leans his forearms on the empty island. "So, like six years?"

I join him and lean my hip against the marble surface. "Where's all your stuff?"

He shrugs, glancing around. "What do you mean?"

"Like art?"

"Don't have any."

"Decorations?"

"Don't need any."

"Pictures?"

"Of what?"

I laugh almost awkwardly. "I don't know. Friends? Family?"

Drew leans down and pulls a blender from the cabinet underneath him. "There's a picture of my mom in my dresser drawer."

I tilt my head side to side, considering his answer. "Don't you want it to feel homey?"

He squints his eyes, slowly setting the machine's lid on the island. "It's where I live. Can't get much more *homey* than that."

Drew clears his throat, and I realize I've been staring at him longer than could be considered normal. "I'm sorry if my place isn't as Cribs as you thought it'd be."

My body freezes. "Wait, you know what that is?"

He rolls his eyes, turning toward the fridge. "I'm twenty-five, Brooke. Not fifteen."

Just the reminder of his age makes my stomach drop. So, he knows the MTV show I practically grew up on. That doesn't change that he's living in a whole different decade.

"Your place is great," I say, changing the subject back as he dispenses a handful of ice into his hand. "Just different than I thought it'd be."

His brows lift, then fall back down as he drops the cubes into the blender. "The best things usually are."

I hold his gaze, trying to read him, and he holds mine, challenging me.

When I'm determined that I'll fall into him if I don't look away, I switch topics once again.

"So, what are you making?"

He stares at me another second, not even attempting to hide his shit-eating grin. "You'll like this," he finally says, ripping open the fridge.

"Why's that?"

"Because it's pretty much a salad blended to a pulp."

I purse my lips at his attempt to tease me. "Is it good?"

"Honestly?" he asks, pulling out a bag of kale and a carton of almond milk. "It tastes like ass, but it's all I'm supposed to drink before a shoot."

"A shoot?"

"Yeah, that's our last stop. I have a photoshoot for Tom Ford in... fifty-three minutes."

I'm instantly taken back to that night at the gala when his cologne invaded my senses in the best possible way. Suddenly the space between us feels more like inches than feet, his bare kitchen backlit by the glow of red accent lighting. The mood shifts, but only to me. *Why couldn't I have waited until after all this to decide to keep it in my pants*. Regardless of the timing, my body can't seem to forget that night, and I have to check myself before I beg him to relive it.

I swallow down the words that threaten to escape the same way they did ten months ago.

Kiss me.

"What's in it?" I ask instead.

Drew points to the two ingredients on the island. "Just this, protein powder, and a banana. Sometimes I add other stuff depending on what I'm feeling."

I wince. "That sounds kind of terrible."

"Yep." Drew pushes up the sleeves of his sweatshirt, and I beg myself to look anywhere but his black and gray tattoos. "It helps if you pretend it's a mint chocolate chip milkshake."

"Does it?" I ask, actively fighting my wandering eyes.

"Well, you can tell me yourself." He takes a few steps toward the cabinets and grabs two glasses from the bottom shelf.

"Oh, no. I'm okay. I'm not really hungry."

He sets them both on the counter next to the appliance. "You're leaning in, remember. Plus, you haven't eaten since you picked at a bowl of fruit and called it breakfast. *This* is your sustenance."

Heat grows between my legs as my smutty brain interprets his words as an "eat kink," and I shut it down the only way I know how. "Sorry we can't all pack away an entire day's calories in one sitting."

Drew places his palms on the counter and leans his weight into his arms. The veins that shoot up his forearm are impossible to miss, and the temperature in his apartment rises too many degrees.

"Well, now you know why," he says, completely unaware of his effect on me. "We're about to make the only other thing I can eat until tonight, and even then, it's the night before a game. I can't get too crazy."

The mention of hockey is the reminder I need to silence the sex-deprived parts of me just enough. *This is work.* "Well, we better make this the best damn milkshake you've ever had then."

Moving next to him, I pick up the kale and grab a handful from the bag. "One scoop of ice cream," I say, dropping the leafy greens into the pitcher.

Drew smiles, shaking his head, before grabbing a banana from the hook on the counter. Peeling it, he breaks it off in chunks, dropping them in one at a time until the whole thing is sitting on top of the kale. "Two scoops," he says, a cheesy smile on his face.

I tip my chin down confidently before grabbing the milk. I unscrew the lid and hover it over the blender. "I guess milk can still be milk?" I ask.

Drew nods through a laugh, moving his palm to the bottom of the container. His hand grazes mine on its journey, and I thank God his massive grip is holding the weight of the carton I would have otherwise let slip through my fingers from his touch.

He lifts it slowly, the creamy liquid falling from the spout in an oddly erotic way, or maybe it just seems like that because of how he looks at me as he does it. His eyes are locked on mine, and for a second, I almost forget that we're making a green smoothie and not undressing each other.

When he tips the milk back, I snap to the moment, looking around the kitchen.

"Vanilla?" I ask.

Drew looks at me, confusion written on his face.

"Protein powder," I whisper.

His mouth forms an O shape, and I'm drawn to his lips. "I was gonna say..." he starts, moving to another cabinet and producing a tub. "Nothing vanilla about me, baby." He says it jokingly, throwing me a wink as he unscrews the top, but there's my smutty mind again, dropping to her knees.

"Just put it in," I order with a roll to my eyes. He gapes at me, and I exhale heavily. "You know what I mean."

He obliges, filling the scooper from the container with the sweet white powder and dropping the protein into the blender.

"That it?" I ask, picking up the lid. I almost have it on when he holds up a finger, telling me to wait. He walks to the pantry, bringing with him a small bag of tiny black beads. "Chia seeds?"

He winks again and shakes some in. "Chocolate chips."

We both smile, and it hits me just how *normal* this is. The showman, the playboy, the Flames' franchise forward, simply making a smoothie and pretending it's a treat instead of a makeshift meal. At 6:30 this morning, I never would have guessed I'd be joking around with Drew in his kitchen. I pictured some hockey, sure, and okay, there's a photoshoot later, but I would have imagined more limelight than banter—more cool guy than boy next door.

Drew reaches past me, the movement putting him so close to me I can smell the body wash he used after practice. The smell, the proximity, my body's natural reaction—all of it causes a panic in me.

Without thinking, I push the start button, desperate to do anything but run my hands through his hair—hear anything but his name fall from my lips. The second I do, dust flies from the blender, green chunks of soggy kale flying in every direction.

"Oh my God!" I squeal over the whir of the motor, my hands flying to my face.

"Oh, shit!" Drew yells.

"Turn it off!"

He nudges me out of the way, his fingers fumbling the buttons, the sound only changing from the settings he's hitting rather than the off switch. "I'm trying!"

Droplets of sludge continue raining down on us both, the grinding blade now mocking us at full speed.

"Drew!"

"Brooke!"

Finally, the buzzing stops, the chaos of the noise and the kale confetti ending with it. I drop my hands slowly, the aftermath of the unfortunate event painted all over the kitchen, our clothes, and my mortified self.

Drew and I both stand frozen, his gaze glued on the appliance from hell. When his eyes make their way to mine, we stare at each other for just an instant before both of us lose it. We bust out laughing, me wiping tears away from my milk-splattered face as he's doubled over, bracing himself on the now-messy island.

When our laughter slows, and we catch our breaths, Drew stands back up, looking down at himself.

"I'm so sorry," I say, embarrassment creeping back in.

Drew shakes his head, lifting the collar of his shirt over his nose to wipe it clean. "Don't be," he says. "I haven't laughed that hard in years."

"No way," I reply, peeling leaves off my arms. "You have yourself plenty of fun."

Drew pauses, his expression growing serious—almost heated.

"What?" I ask, taken aback by the shift.

"You don't get it yet, do you?" He turns his whole body to me, using the pad of his thumb to brush a seed from my cheek. His knuckles linger near my jaw as his eyes travel down my face.

My lips part, but I don't know what to say. "Drew, I—"

"Nevermind," he interrupts. "Don't answer that." He steps back and offers me a polite smile. "Let's get you cleaned up. I have a shirt you can wear."

16
Drew

I have a lot of clothes. Style's part of my image and brands send me shit for free all the time. Most of them are basics—plain t-shirts, jeans, joggers, boots—all way too expensive for what they are, but it comes with the territory.

I was never really attached to any specific piece, though. I don't have lucky socks or a hoodie that reminds me of a particular moment. But the second my black v-neck landed on Brooke's shoulders, I had a new favorite.

Her leather jacket was wiped clean, her jeans somehow blocked by the wall of the island. But her sweater? There was no saving that thing after the smoothie explosion. I gave Brooke her pick and let her look through my closet for whatever she needed. But she came out with exactly what I assumed she would choose—because it's what I would have chosen for her.

When she entered my living room with it knotted at her waist, one sleeve pulled lower than the other so the V of the neck fell just slightly off-center, you would have thought she was in lingerie—or that same black bra from our one night together. That on top of the fact that our mess making might sadly be the first time in months that I've had genuine fun, and I was once again reminded of why I'm drawn to her.

Now, sitting in my chair on set, in the steel button-up shirt and black jeans from wardrobe, with a woman named Melissa dabbing my face with a brush, I still can't take my eyes off of her. We keep having these moments. Ones where I act so out of character, yet more myself than I ever get to be. Brief blips of time where I think she may finally lean into this—to *us*—or where I might finally convince her. But she doesn't. And I won't force it either.

"Alright, Drew, we're ready for you." Jane, my P.R. manager, struts over with her earpiece in as always and both of her phones stacked in one hand. She glances at Brooke standing in the corner of the room, whose big eyes are wandering the set like she's in a magical forest. "I still can't believe you're letting the social media girl follow you around."

I watch as Brooke walks over to the product table, leans in to smell the cologne, then looks around like she hopes no one saw her sniffing the bottles. I smile as her eyes find mine, and she tries to act like it never happened.

"Why's that?" I ask, my eyes still on Brooke.

Jane snaps her gum and folds her arms over her chest. "Uh... because I've strongly advised against it since you made the best decision of your life and hired me six years ago. Not to mention, you never want your *real* life discussed in anything we do."

I peer up at her and her teasing smile. "There's not much going on today that could cause any issues."

"What about the date with Cheyanne tonight?"

I exhale heavily, dropping my forehead between my thumb and fore-finger. "I forgot."

Jane adjusts her footing, jutting her hip out. "Drew," she says bluntly.

"Jane, honestly, I'd rather spray that cologne into my eyeballs."

Jane sucks in a deep breath. "Yeah, well..." she says, blowing through her lips. "We have a deal, remember? I keep you relevant, which in turn, makes it so you can continue playing for whichever team you'd like. And you... well, and you listen. Besides, just give the people what they want, ya know what I mean?"

"There is no way the *people* want to see me out with Cheyanne Sinclair, which is one hundred percent a fake name by the way."

Jane creases her brows and nods her head rapidly. "Oh, no doubt." She looks me up and down, then pops one more button open on my shirt. "But fake name or not, your fans want to see you out. With girls. Painting the town that sexy Flames' red."

She winks, and I slip my chain under my thumb and run my finger along the cool metal. "Yeah," I sigh. "I guess."

Jane claps me on the shoulder, her way of telling me that my side of the conversation's over. "Besides, she co-starred in that alien movie that just came out. That's kind of cool."

"It was zombies," I deadpan.

"See!" she squeals. "It's like you know her already."

"Drew, I'm ready when you are." Isaac, the photographer for today, waves me over. I hop out of my chair and take my spot on the X marked on the floor where I'm supposed to be standing.

"I'm ready," I say, shoving one hand into the front pocket of my jeans.

Isaac nods, his camera in hand, then turns around and calls over his shoulder. "Hey, iPhone girl." I follow his gaze to see he's talking to Brooke. "No photos besides mine. And hand him that black bottle, would ya?"

Brooke's perfect chocolate eyes grow before she attempts to regain her composure, quickly slipping her phone into her pocket and moving back toward the table. She grabs the only black bottle of cologne and walks toward me hesitantly. When she's just a foot away, she holds it out.

"Thanks," I say, taking it. I toss the bottle and catch it again in the palm of my hand. "My shirt looks good on you by the way." She rolls her eyes unconvincingly. "Sorry you can't take pictures."

She shakes her head. "No, that's okay. Just good to see you in your element."

I scoff. *My element.* "Right."

"Alright you two, we have work to do." Isaac stares at us impatiently, his camera now hanging around his neck.

Brooke purses her lips, then fades into the background. I spend the next twenty minutes twisting my body into different positions—neck turned, shoulders squared, some with the bottle and some without. I peek at Brooke every once in a while, but I don't let my gaze linger long enough to read her expression.

I know this is what she expected from the day—cameras and lights, open shirts and gelled hair, a crew of people working for me. And yeah, that's true some of the time. But I thought maybe she was starting to see that my life isn't what she sees online. That the one designed to make people believe I'm something that I'm not isn't real. Or at least I hoped so. But her reactions tell me she might not be there yet.

That's okay. I can wait.

"Good work, Drew," Isaac says, standing from where he was crouched for the last couple of shots. "We're going to grab some with the girls real quick, and then we'll get you out of here."

"Okay," I say, holding still so Melissa can gel a loose hair into place. I use the time to scan over to Brooke, who is jotting something down in a notebook. She glances up and smiles at me casually before going back to whatever she's writing.

She's bored, I'm sure. Hell, I fucking am. But I like her being here even though I know it's not exactly by choice. I'm tempted to let myself think about what it would be like if someone *was* here just for me. Not for a picture or a paycheck or to be a face to their brand. But someone who was here to support me, and tease me for wearing makeup, and listen to me bitch about just wanting to go home. I'd kill for that to be Brooke if she'd ever look past all her excuses. If she'd forget that I'm younger or admit that she feels something anyway.

"Hey, Drew."

Two voices harmonize as identical twins step out from behind the backdrop of the set. They're good-looking girls—blonde hair, nice racks, legs for days in the excuses for skirts that wardrobe put them in. They're definitely friendly judging from the way both girls drape their arms over my shoulders as they move beside me. And I'm sure they're very sweet. But all I can picture is Burnsey telling me about twins that he saw do very unsister-like things in a dream he once had. They smile at me flirtatiously, and I smile back, though it's more at the mental image I have of Burns reenacting the scene like it was a goddamn Broadway production than at them.

Isaac starts directing us, telling me to stand strong, and both girls to act as if the cologne is a pheromone making me irresistible. The twins, whose names I still don't know because Isaac just keeps referring to them as *the girls,* take advantage of his direction, clinging to me, their hands on my thighs, around my biceps, and slipped underneath my shirt. I'm told to ignore their wandering touch—to look anywhere but at them or the camera as if I don't even notice they're hanging on me.

It's easy enough, this is a job after all, and that's my natural response even when it's not. I start in one corner of the room, finding objects to home in on that are just beyond the lens, listening to Isaac tell me to pout or look stern or stick my hand into my pocket.

When I've done a few to the left side of the camera, I shift so that my gaze lands just outside of the right. And that's when I see her. Brooke—or at least a version of her. But it's not the same girl with her head in her notebook, borderline bored, or even the one who handed me the bottle with her usual faint attitude and a roll of her eyes.

No, this Brooke is alert—arms crossed, eyes narrow, lips pressed into a firm line. To everyone else, she's simply observing attentively. But I've watched *her* watch *me* all damn day. And this? This is not that.

I freeze on her as her eyes flint back and forth between one twin and the other. The photographer tells me to hold my position, and at the sound of my name, we lock in on each other. We hold our stares for only a second before Isaac speaks again.

"That!" he yells under the lens of his camera. "Yes, Drew. Stay just like that."

I hold my expression—the one I couldn't change even if he asked me to. Whatever face I'm making is my natural response to seeing Brooke so reactive, and my guess is that it's dark and primal—like my thoughts about her.

She doesn't waver either, her eyes mirroring that same intensity. *Is my mystery girl... jealous?* The idea alone does something to me, and it takes everything in me not to dart off this set and explain that to her the best way I know how.

We hold our gaze for another few shutters of the camera, her mouth the only thing about her relaxing—her lips falling apart ever so slightly. It's only when Isaac yells for what must be the second time that we're done that I rip my eyes away from her, realizing I'm the only one still standing on set.

A crew member from wardrobe walks over to me, handing me my worn-in jeans and faded USA Hockey t-shirt. With my eyes still glued to Brooke's, I slowly unbutton the shirt that I'm wearing, letting it fall open and onto the floor. I tear off the tight jeans next, adding them to the pile. Brooke watches intently, making no effort to look away, and I find myself pulling my pants on as quickly as possible to cover my dick's natural response to her attention.

After what feels like forever, yet still not long enough, Brooke tears her gaze from me and starts packing up her things. I finish dressing myself and say my goodbyes to Isaac and the crew.

"Don't forget about tonight," Jane says when I tell her I'm leaving. "You're meeting her at Josephine's on Third. I already have the paps set up."

I sigh, taking a vested interest in my boots. "What time?"

"Reservation's at six."

I glance down at my watch, then my head snaps back to her. "That's in like an hour." Jane stares at me straightfaced. "And I still have fucking makeup on."

"Well, you better get home and get showered." One of the phones in her hand buzzes on top of the other, and she accepts the call, tilting the speaker away from her mouth. "Or better yet, leave it on," she whispers. "It'll make your cheekbones pop." She slides her phone back into place and tips her chin up at me. "Jane Simpson."

I roll my eyes and groan, turning around and nearly running right into Brooke. I'm instantly calmed, the idea of spending the rest of my night on a publicity stunt suddenly not so bad with her in my presence.

"Oh, hey, sorry. Are you ready to go?"

Brooke tucks her hair behind her ear, avoiding eye contact with me. "Mhmm."

I grin to myself, noting her change in demeanor from earlier, but keep my thoughts to myself. Instead, I nod toward the door, dropping my hand on her lower back as she steps toward it. She sucks in a quick breath but continues moving.

We walk in silence until we get outside, both of us stopping when we get to my bike.

"Where to now?" she asks expectantly.

I grab both helmets off the seat and hand one to her. "Your place, I guess. There's not much else to see."

A glaze of disappointment coats her eyes. "That's a tame night for Drew Anderson."

"Yeah, well..." I contemplate telling her about Cheyanne, but decide against it. "Game tomorrow."

"Right."

Neither of us say anything else. Instead, we wait another beat of silence before sliding on our helmets and hopping onto my bike.

I purposely turn out of the lot toward the long way back to her apartment building. Despite my time constriction, I'm not ready for our day to end, and I'm damn sure not in any rush for my date with Cheyanne.

Something about this ride is different. Maybe it's that we're more comfortable now. Maybe it's because this is the last one of the night. Or maybe I was right—something switched in Brooke during that photoshoot. Either way, she seems even closer than before, her hands resting by my hips, her legs pushed all the way forward so her front is flush against me.

It's charged. Like at any point I could pull over to the side of the road and without hesitation, we'd fall into each other. After a few red lights, I give in to temptation, taking a risk and dropping my palm from the handlebar to the outside of her thigh. She doesn't pull away like I thought she might, or startle even. Instead, she somehow sinks into me further, her legs hugging mine a bit tighter.

When I pull onto her street, anticipation rushes through me, a similar feeling to how I am on a windup, when the next few moments will determine the projection of the play. The score of the game. The reaction of the crowd.

Putting the bike into park, I let her swing her leg off before stomping my kickstand down and stepping off. Brooke hands me her helmet, and I throw it into my backpack before setting mine and my bag onto the seat.

"I'll walk you up," I say when she looks at me sideways.

There are no questions or objections. She simply nods and moves forward. At the top of the stairs, we turn into each other.

"Thanks for doing this today," she says first. "It was good content." I grin. "Fun even."

Cathartic.

"Was it what you expected?" I ask, my brow lifted upward.

Brooke looks at her feet, pressing the toe of her shoe into the pavement. "Uh, no, actually."

My smile grows wider. "I feel like that's a good thing." She doesn't answer, and I'm afraid of what I'll do with too much idle time between us, so I continue talking instead. "Well, have a good—"

"Do you want to come in?" She cuts me off, her eyes like a cartoon's when her brain catches up with the words that poured out. "Oh my God, no." She brings her hand to her forehead. "What am I doing?" she whispers to herself. "Pretend I didn't say that."

I stand there, completely dumbfounded by every word that just spewed out. I open my mouth, then seal my lips again, still unsure of what to say. "Brooke, did you just..." I start.

"No, I didn't—well, technically yes, I—"

"*Un*invite me in?"

"Yes," she answers quickly. She sighs, her shoulders slumping forward. "Yeah, sort of."

I drag my hand slowly down my face, borderline afraid to make my next move. "Do you see it now?" I ask softly, holding my breath. "Me?" I take one step forward, so our chests are almost touching. "*Us?*"

Brooke's head falls into her hands, leaving her words muffled. "Shit, I don't know."

"Hey," I whisper, pulling her wrists away from her face as I lean into her. "Talk to me."

She slowly brings her eyes to mine, and I actively stop myself from sliding my hand into her hair and slamming my lips to hers. She goes to speak, but as soon as the first word forms on her tongue, my phone vibrates twice from my pocket.

I ignore it, but either she's using it as an excuse to stay silent or she's easily distracted. "Tell me," I demand, slipping my palms over her cheeks. Again, the buzzing sound goes off, three hums this time, before Brooke can say what's on her mind.

I slide my phone out of my jeans and read the messages that riddle the screen.

Jane

> Josephine's at six.

Jane

> Don't be late.

Jane

> I mean it, Drew.

Jane

> Remember the last time you went rogue on me.

Jane

> GIVE THE PEOPLE WHAT THEY WANT.

"Fuck," I groan, rubbing my forehead with my first two fingers. I contemplate bailing on Cheyanne to stay with Brooke, but Jane's right. The only thing worse than failing my test last year was the fans' reaction to my mortality. We're off to a good start this season, and I don't need any drama—or hate—ruining that.

Or this.

She looks at me confused, rubbing her arm with her opposite hand. "What?"

"This is the worst possible timing," I say reluctantly. "But I have to go."

"Oh." She nods quickly, taking half a step backward.

"Or I could stay," I add, instantly regretting my first answer.

Brooke shakes her head. "No, no, you should go. I'm not, I don't even know—"

"It's been a long day," I say, stepping to her again. "Why don't you think about whatever you were trying to say, and we'll talk tomorrow. Before morning practice?"

She looks at me with bold eyes, failing to hide her concern, but I remain steadfast. *I'm not going anywhere.*

"Yeah, okay. Let's talk tomorrow," she finally says. "I'm sorry."

This time I really do slip my hand behind her ear, but instead of pulling her mouth to meet mine, I drop my forehead to hers. "Don't be," I say softly. I pull back, pressing a kiss to her temple. "You've always been my mystery girl."

17

Brooke

Stepping into my apartment, I close the door behind me, and the first thing I do is bang my head against it. "Why?" I groan, my voice sounding every bit as obnoxious as Drew probably thinks I am.

I was doing so well—ignoring his flirting, staying level-headed, keeping my mind on the future prize. But almost ten hours together was just too much. I couldn't take it anymore.

I did okay in the morning, only glancing up occasionally to scan his chiseled body, which thanks to his tattoos, is quite literally a work of art. I even maintained my cool when he admitted that our night together might have meant something to him—despite that I stupidly agreed. But after the smoothie incident, I started wearing down... quickly.

Wrapping myself up in his t-shirt didn't help—the one that smells like him and hangs on me three sizes too big, yet still looks adorable tied up in a knot. Neither did the moment right before we sprayed green juice all over his apartment where he was nothing but cute and approachable. But then to see him at the photoshoot? I thought witnessing the surreal parts of his life would bring me back to reality, but it only drove me crazier. Justified or not, it bothered me to see other women hang on him—in real life rather than through photos on the internet. But when he barely looked at them—his eyes on me rather than the leggy blondes beside him—I didn't know how to react. The last thing I thought I'd see was *my* Drew living in *his* world.

It got me thinking more about my talk with Ivy. About how there's not a one-size-fits-all solution to life. How it's okay to change and having a destination is great, but the journey there might be the best part. Seeing this side of Drew today, the one where he was two people at once—the guy the world knows and the one I'm really starting to see—made him even more irresistible. But who says it has to be all or nothing?

There was a time not long ago that I used to mentally reprimand my mother because she sees the world in black and white—follow the steps or you're doomed to fail. But like Ivy said, maybe it's okay to have a destination and still figure things out along the way. Maybe I *can* want stability without shutting out every person who doesn't tick all the boxes. Maybe the goal is still the same, but the path there is a little... beautifully gray. Or at least that's where my brain—and honestly, my sex-deprived vagina—were steering my thoughts when we left the Tom Ford set.

So, now, I'm sitting here, my forehead pressed against the door, trying to decide if inviting Drew in was brave or unhinged. Was it a bold, healthy risk? Or was it just me caving under the weight of lonely nights and thoughts of him, trying to justify why letting him in *might* actually make sense?

Before I can decide—or give myself a concussion—my intercom rings. I jump backward, then freeze, as if whoever pushed the button can now see inside my place. An anticipation flies through me. *Did Drew change his mind?*

Without second thought, I hit the buzzer by my door, allowing the person to enter. I guess the reasoning doesn't matter anymore—my variety of excuses, irrelevant after just one day together—because the second I think he's here, my body springs to action, welcoming him in.

Actions speak louder than words, Mystery Girl.

Ugh, maybe Drew was right.

Bounding sideways toward the mirror by my door, I run my hands through my hair and readjust his t-shirt. I make a mental note that I should probably give it back to him, but part of me hopes it'll be his to clean up after his visit to my apartment.

A few moments later, there's a quick knock at the door. Moving toward it, I inhale deeply. It registers how most of what I'm feeling is excitement. That our day doesn't have to end after all. That he came back.

That he's here.

Exhaling slowly through pursed lips, I rip the door open, a smile on my face and heat in my eyes. "I thought y—oh."

"Are you sick? You look a little flushed?"

I freeze completely, my mouth still open as Alex pushes through the door. She bumps past me, heading straight for the kitchen. "I brought sweet potato tacos from that truck you like," she calls to me as I continue to linger in the doorway.

I remain motionless, actively trying to wrap my head around how completely wrong I was in thinking it was Drew. To say I'm disappointed would be an understatement, and that alone blows my mind. I knew I was having second thoughts about how I felt about us, but to be borderline annoyed to see my best friend?

"I'm losing it," I whisper to myself. Shaking my head clear of the chaos, I reset and present with my typical attitude. "Well hello, Alex. Good to see you too. Hey, why don't you come on in?" I say loud enough for her to hear while throwing the door closed and rolling my eyes.

Alex shoots me a glare jokingly before sliding a brown bag across the counter and reaching into my fridge. "How was your day with Drew?" she asks, completely oblivious to the emotional hurricane still ripping through me.

"Uh..." I take the bag in my hands, rubbing the rough paper between my fingers, my mind actively trying to process what the hell kind of rollercoaster ride my emotions just took. "It was good," I say eventually. "Ya know, to be expected."

Alex pauses, her hand halfway to my wine glass cabinet. "That's it?"

I shrug, my eyes wandering everywhere but to hers. "I don't know. I guess?"

She slides her arm back down, twisting both across her chest. "Spill."

"Spill what?" I ask, reaching past her and pulling out two glasses. I pop the cork on the chilled white she took from the fridge and look at her sideways.

"Please tell me you didn't sleep with him... again," she says warningly.

I click my tongue, filling one glass. "I did not sleep with him." I move to the other as Alex waits for me to continue. I watch the liquid fall into the cup as I pray she fills the silence. When it's clear she isn't going to, I huff out a breath. "But I think I want to," I add quickly, slamming the bottle on the counter.

"I knew it!" she cries, grabbing her drink. "Brooke, no. We talked about this!"

"I know," I groan, taking a massive gulp of much-needed alcohol. "But Al, you didn't see him today."

She sets her glass on the counter and leans her hip against it. "Listen, I know he's all abs and aesthetics. And he's got those tattoos and that chain. And don't get me started on the hair that you just wanna—"

"Okay, slow down there, wifey," I cut in, shoving her hand back down that was raised to act out her words.

Alex clears her throat and takes another sip of wine. "Sorry," she mutters.

"Levi's been busier lately now that the season's kicked up, hasn't he?"

"So much," she says, bringing her glass back to her lips.

"Imagine how I feel," I say only partially under my breath. "But that's not even what I'm talking about." I nod toward the couch and walk over, plopping down on one side while Alex takes the other. "He just seems so unlike what I expected," I set my glass on the coffee table and pull a pillow into my lap. "Yes, he's Drew freaking Anderson, which means he's smug and edgy, but I'm into that. Especially when he's also kind of sweet, and sort of funny, which I like, and..." I sigh, letting my head fall backward into the cushion. "I don't know, maybe I was too quick to judge."

I stare at the ceiling, waiting for Alex's opinion. When it doesn't come, my neck rolls to the side to see she's sitting there, chewing her lip. "Say it," I grind out.

She winces like she's trying to hold back whatever it is that's sitting on the tip of her tongue. When my eyes go wide, telling her to spit it out, she squeezes hers shut. "He's twenty-five, B."

Lifting the pillow, I smother my face in it and groan. "I know," I whine. I let the cushion slowly fall back into my lap. "But maybe that doesn't matter?"

I glance back at Alex, who is wearing a polite smile. "Maybe," she says, her voice an octave higher than it should be.

I stare at her blankly. "Go on."

"Listen," she huffs. "He seems really nice. He signed all those jerseys for Cooper's team last year, and he is pretty great with him one on one. But, age aside, you see him in the papers. Plus, there's the recreational drug use I still don't have details on. I'm not saying there's anything wrong with how he lives—not *technically*—but you're trying to move on from that kind of life."

I blow a breath through my lips as Al pulls her phone from her pocket. "Whatever," I say, brushing it off. "It doesn't matter, anyway. He apparently had something to do after our day together, so he's probably out with some famous singer."

"Actress," Alex corrects.

"What!" I snap forward, trying to regain my composure as Alex peers at me from over her screen. "What do you mean?" I ask, my voice dramatically tempered.

She tilts her phone toward me, and I lean into it. A picture fills the screen—Drew in a black button-up shirt, black jeans, and his boots, his arm draped over a woman in a silver beaded mini-dress. The photo is on Golden City's gossip page with the headline, *"Is Anderson Putting the Sin in Sinclair?"*

"That's the girl from Zombie Tsunami," I mumble.

And he was literally just here.

"Oh, I know," Alex says. "Thanks to you, *she's* my son's newest obsession."

I offer her a closed-lip smile despite now being pissed at both Drew *and* Cooper.

Alex twists the phone back toward her and continues swiping on the screen as my stomach churns. Is Drew serious? *This* was what he had to do? *Who* he had to do?

I know I'm nothing to him. Hell, we're nothing to each other besides a player and a temporary social media manager for the same team. But with how things have been—with how things ended—I didn't think he'd be running off my stoop just to meet another girl.

He's the one who told me actions will speak louder than words. Tonight, I think both of our efforts are screaming at the top of their lungs. So, I only half-invited him in. But I put myself out there! And it was pretty clear that he understood what was going on in my messed-up mind, which also really says something. For him to skip right over it and into some zombie slayer's bed tells me everything I need to know.

With that thought, and the rest of the wine that shoots straight to my head, I take a deep, clarifying breath. "Okay, then," I say sharply. "That settles that."

Alex looks up at me as if she doesn't believe it. "I'm serious," I add. "Name one time I went after a guy who didn't want me back."

She purses her lips and tilts her head side-to-side as if she's thinking. "I got nothing."

"Exactly. And I'm damn sure not starting now. I'm getting settled, not settl*ing*."

Even if it's Drew.

"Well, alright then," she says, grabbing my empty glass from my hand. "One more to celebrate."

I nod definitively as she stands from the couch. This *does* call for celebration. The last ten hours—no, the last *week*—all I've been doing is fighting with myself. I can't want Drew. I *do* want Drew. It would never work. But maybe it could. Putting down roots is my goal. Putting down roots is a mindset. Settling is necessary. Settling is also scary as hell. Who says I can't have both?

Now? All of that can go away.

The inner turmoil was because the door was cracked open. There was a possibility that under the right circumstances—if all the pieces fell so gracefully into place—that in some universe, I could have the guy from the bathroom ten months ago, despite what he is to the rest of the world. That I could plan for my future despite currently being set on *him*. That maybe his advances irritate the shit out of me because I'm denying my heart—and my body—of what it truly wants.

But not anymore.

In reality, Drew just did me a favor. He slammed the door shut and gave me permission—not that I needed it—to finally let go of the glorified idea that with me he was different. That he was worth letting in. Maybe there *are* two sides to him, but they're not yin and yang. They're oil and water.

I sink into the couch, and at the same time, Alex comes back with two glasses of *red* and the taco bag tucked under her arm. I slide the paper out from her grip, placing the grease-spotted bottom on the coffee table.

"I figured this might call for the hard stuff," she says, handing me my glass.

I grab it from her easily and take a sip, but shake my head. "Nah, I'm good."

"Are you sure?"

Reaching into the bag, I pull out a taco. "Totally," I say, hoping it sounds convincing enough for her to drop it.

She lets out a chuckle and slides the food her way. "Remind me to never piss you off?"

My hands pause on the white take-out paper that the food came wrapped in, and I peer over at her.

"You can cut people out easier than anyone I know."

I shrug my shoulders, her words not landing like she means them to. I've been told my whole life how admirable it is that I can just brush things off. But sometimes it's not as easy as it looks. This decision feels right, but it doesn't feel *good*. Working with him for the next couple of weeks will be hard as hell, and not wanting him—another form of torture. But this is how I've survived my whole life, without caving under the weight of my mother's disappointment.

"I'm an independent woman, Al," I say, taking a massive bite.

"With a giant pair of scissors."

I fake a smile, grateful that this time the credibility of my words will be muffled by my mouth full of food. "Snip snip."

18
Drew

Looking at the clock on the wall, the red block letters seem to mock me as I check the laces on my skates for the third time. I've officially hung around the locker room for as long as I can, waiting for Brooke. Every five minutes I've peered into the hallway, making up a different excuse each time a teammate asked me what I was looking for.

One time I needed Ward, another I had a question for Coach, and when Burnsey asked, I just told him to fuck off like I usually do. The bottom line is there's still no sign of her, and that's a problem. Partially because I have to get out onto the ice like... now. And partially because I haven't been able to stop thinking about her since our little mishap on her steps.

I went out with Cheyanne last night because I had to. Because that's the deal that Jane and I made. But that never means I have to enjoy it. I thought about Brooke the entire time.

When Cheyanne batted her lashes, Brooke's eyes came to mind. When she flashed her smile, I thought of Brooke's. And when she threw herself at me, way too tipsy after two glasses of wine, all I could think about was my mystery girl.

Usually, my date and I agree that we might as well at least get a night out of it. Sometimes we're even on the same page, and we blow through dinner just to get to the fun part. But last night, no one but Brooke would have satisfied that craving. And there was no way I was sleeping with Cheyanne. She wasn't happy, but I was thrilled to go home. Ready to fall asleep and wake up, only to rush to the rink this morning.

For nothing.

"Fuck," I groan, standing from my stall and snatching my helmet from the shelf. I cross through the locker room, running my thumb under my chain. Pushing the door open to the tunnel, I attempt to talk myself off the ledge.

I've made it this long, I can wait until—

I exhale heavily the second I lay eyes on Brooke's chocolate hair, the front hanging in her face as she looks down at her iPad. She's leaning against the wall at the front of the tunnel, the perfect barrier between me and the ice.

"Hey you," I say once I'm next to her. She doesn't answer, so I reach out and brush her elbow.

She startles and lifts her head, her eyes darting to where my fingers still linger on her skin. When she sees it's me, she pulls out a headphone, her eyebrows shooting up before her whole face settles into a blank stare.

"Hey," I say, smiling. "I've been looking for you."

One corner of her lips turns up as she looks down at the screen in her hand. "Well, here I am."

Her tone's a mix of frankness and irritation. It takes me aback, but I brush it off. "I see that." I lean on the wall next to her, my hand now hanging by her leg. I sweep my thumb up the hem of her jeans and watch her swallow. "What's goin' on?"

Brooke clears her throat, her eyes still trained on whatever she's working on. "Not much, just trying to get this set up for after practice."

"Another question video?"

"Mhmm."

I'm thrown by her energy. Even when she was fighting this with everything she had, she was more open than she is now. Then, after last night, I thought we were getting somewhere. "Cool," I say hesitantly. I don't want to push her, but I don't want us to waste more time either. "So, do you still want to talk?" I lean into her, my attempt at grabbing her attention from the screen. "About last night?"

She finally glances up at me, but when she does, I almost wish she hadn't. Her eyes are cold despite her warm cheeks. "No, I'm good. I don't really think there's much to talk about."

I pull back, searching her expression for an explanation. "But, I thought you—"

"Listen, Drew." She turns fully to me, but as she does, she takes a step back, widening the gap between us. "I'm kind of busy here, and you have like a minute to get on the ice before practice."

She swings her iPad back up toward her chest, and before I can stop myself, I grab it from her hands. "Brooke, what's wrong?"

She narrows her eyes at me, her intention to look pissed, but there's a layer hidden underneath of something else. "Nothing," she snaps. "We don't have anything to discuss, and we both have things to do, so it's probably best to just—"

"Wait, are you serious?" I cut off her excuses, shortening the space between us again. My voice is low, my tone dripping with the same frustration that's ripping through me.

"Yes, Drew," she says sharply before she stands up a little straighter. "It's fine." She shrugs, dismissing me like this wasn't supposed to be the moment that everything changed for us.

"Yo, Cap. Coach needs you." In his perfect timing, Burnsey is at the boards yelling over the bench, his thumb thrown behind him where Monte is standing huddled with the boys at center ice.

I pause before answering, finding her again, questioning her with no words at all. She avoids my eye contact, crossing her arms over her chest and biting at her bottom lip. When she doesn't speak—doesn't even look at me—I call back to Brett. "I'm coming," I say dully, my eyes locked on her.

I hold out her iPad, all the excitement I've had since she first blurted out those words last night on her steps, completely depleted. When she takes it from me, our gazes finally meet. For just an instant, she looks like she might speak—offer any sort of explanation. But instead, she puts her earbud back in, tuning me out like I tune out the world.

Like I tune out everyone but her.

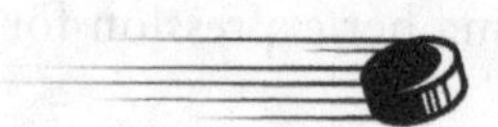

"No way, bro. Look at the pictures. It's definitely the one on the right."

"Yeah, but look at the left one. That's a statement right there."

Stepping off of the bench and into the tunnel, Burns and Ward's argument, about whatever the hell they must be looking at, ripples down the hall. They're standing next to each other in full pads, blocking what I assume is the situation I've been avoiding since Monte blew the final whistle. This time being last on the ice had nothing to do with wanting to hang back and talk, but still everything to do with Brooke.

I walk slowly, my swagger half because of the wobble from my skates on the rubber and half because I'm trying to get into the mindset that I typically don't have to fight off with her. The one that says I don't give a fuck about what happened *or* what you think. The one only worried about me—that can't get me hurt.

As I get closer, Petrov steps up behind them, placing his hands on their shoulders and pulling them apart. He slips in between them, his voice booming off of the walls of the tunnel as he offers his opinion. "I think the correct way is whichever way the giraffe prefers."

Brett and Carter look around him at each other, their faces riddled with both confusion and amusement. "Uh, yeah, I mean... for sure, Storm. That too."

Burnsey claps him on the back as Ward laughs off the comment, and the three move on, Petrov walking ahead of the other two who seem to hang back to whisper amongst themselves.

When their bodies are out of the way, everything I'm not ready to see comes into focus. Brooke is standing where she was before, this time with a tripod set up, holding a camera, and her iPad in her hands, facing outward. She has a smile on her face from her last interaction, and my jaw tightens knowing it'll fall flat when she sees me... just like it did before last night.

As I approach her, I wrestle with my options. I can stop and talk, either ignoring our current situation and pretending all is fine like I should, or continuing to push her like I'd like to. Or I could simply walk by. Ignore her and her question and let whatever is or isn't happening between us unfold as it may—keeping my distance.

With my face stern, I decide maybe blowing past her is best for everyone. I told myself I'd be patient. That her actions will speak louder than her words. But then I realize that's exactly what's happening. Whether or not she took it back, she invited me in. She finally gave me something. Then afterwards, she *told* me that we'd talk today about what happened. *Fuck that.*

I'm not going to let her go back to being scared. And I'm damn sure not letting her brush this off because of what? I glance down at her iPad. Two giraffes in goddamn neckties?

With that, I step to her, adrenaline pumping through me.

"Hi," she says awkwardly, once again looking anywhere but at my face. "So, the question is, would a giraffe wear his tie up here like this or down at the base of his—"

"*This?* This is what you were *so* busy with before practice that we couldn't talk about last night? A fucking giraffe in a necktie?" My words come out more harshly than I intend. But the blood pumping through me—a combination of post-practice flow and our current situation—seems to bubble over when our conversation from earlier boils down to a zoo animal in formal wear.

Brooke's eyes snap to mine, her hand flying to her hip. "Why, yes. No matter how ridiculous *Drew Anderson* thinks it is, this is my *job.*"

The way she says my name stirs something in me. It's bitterness and anger, hurt and frustration, and years of assumptions all rolled into one. Ripping my helmet off, I tuck it under my arm and rake my hand through my hair in resentment. "What the hell is that supposed to mean?"

Brooke blackens her screen, tucking her device into her bag on the floor, then stands back up, squaring her shoulders. "Exactly what I said."

I scoff, sucking my teeth and glancing behind me to make sure we're still alone. "So, we're back to this now? I'm *Drew Anderson,* when what? You're scared? When it's not just the two of us?"

I wait for her response, but it comes only in the form of her arms folding across her chest.

Something snaps in me that I would otherwise shove down. A disappointment I'd typically swallow—like a kid who's been so excited for his party, and when no one shows up, he acts unfazed. Only I don't act indifferent. Instead, like I usually do with her, I let my true self show through. For once, it's harder to hide the truth than to just say how I feel.

"So, who did you *uninvite* inside last night then, Brooke? Or was me being *Drew Anderson* suddenly okay because you saw me half-naked and covered in girls. Were you jealous, is that it?"

I mean what I'm saying, but not *how* I'm saying it. It's just that instinct kicks in, and like second nature, my I-don't-give-a-shit attitude takes over.

Her eyes narrow, full of rage, and her lips part in a way that shouldn't be sexy considering the bed I just made, but *fuck me.*

It definitely is.

"Actually," she counters, inching closer, her neck strained upward to get more in my face than she could otherwise with me in my skates.

Suddenly, my helmet flies out from my arm, and I whip around to see Max standing behind us with it in his hand. He nods at me once, either completely oblivious to the vibe or doing a damn good job at pretending he doesn't notice, then pulls my stick from my other hand.

"I got you, bro," he says, and I tip my chin up at him as he turns and walks away.

The encounter reminds me that we're right between the ice and the locker room and neither of us can afford the attention. But unlike my usual response, I'm not shrugging this off.

"Shooting bay. Five minutes," I grind out.

She rolls her eyes then reaches for the tripod. I grab her wrist as it hovers on top of the camera and lower my voice just above a whisper. "And so help me God, Brooke, you better be there."

Her eyes double in size, the movements of her chest that I definitely notice, picking up speed. She stills otherwise, her hand left resting on top of the camera as I let go of her wrist.

"Five minutes," I growl.

I take two steps away from her before turning back. "And by then you better have found your voice, Mystery Girl."

19
Brooke

Being that I can't cut through the locker room of naked hockey players after practice, I have to go the long way to the shooting bay. By the time I get there, I have maybe another minute until Drew arrives, and my heart is hammering inside my chest.

I'm not quite sure if it's due to adrenaline and how I'd like to rip into him for the way he put this all on me or the fact that I now have to wait here like a sitting duck because I don't have access until he arrives with his finger.

Our *discussion* in the tunnel was only somewhat expected considering I knew Drew would plan to talk about last night. I didn't, however, think he'd be so aggressive about getting answers from me, which proved to be hotter—and more annoying—than I thought.

Standing here, I'm not really sure what to say. He wants answers to why I've been so hot and cold, but honestly, none of them are justified. I guess if I admitted it, then yes. I was turned on all fucking day because of the parts of him that he exposed to me—physically and otherwise. And some of me did turn a shade or two of green when I saw beautiful models draped over him. But what really got me was how all day he was one way with me—and so openly interested—and then the second I gave him anything back, he hit the road to pick up the next girl. The problem is, none of that should matter.

But apparently it did.

After another minute and a half that feels like an eternity, footsteps finally thump against the floor. I slowly drag my head toward the sound, and *goddamn.* Drew knows how to come prepared for an argument. At least one against me.

He approaches me, his hair damp and slicked back, his gold chain sitting outside of a skin-tight, grey long-sleeve shirt that shows every curve and indent of his muscles. I can't even hide the way my eyes glaze over him, attempting to take in every inch from head to toe. When they get to the pants painted on over his impressive bulge and massive tree-trunk thighs, I literally freeze.

"Are you wearing leggings?" I ask, any edginess I was previously feeling completely absent from my tone.

"I didn't change out of my gitch yet," he says, reaching for the sensor by the door.

The smell that wafts toward me is a messy combination of his cologne and residual sweat, and I never knew that was erotic until right this second.

Drew pushes open the door, the boulders on his arm straining through the thin material as he holds it open for me. I crease my brows, swallowing my lust and forcing my attitude to take the wheel again. "What's a git—"

"Move, Brooke."

I don't even bother disobeying, not that I could considering my thirsty ass started walking into the bay the second those two words rolled off his tongue. I take the few seconds he needs to enter the space and shut the door behind him to drop my things and rechannel how I felt last night when I insisted I was fine with Al.

"So..." he starts, his frustration dulled slightly from time. "Start talking."

"What do you want me to say, Drew?"

"I want fucking answers, Brooke. An explanation," he says, his irritation building once again. "I didn't expect you to come hunt me down this morning and confess your damn love, but I at least thought we'd have a conversation."

"We're having a conversation right now," I quip.

He rolls his eyes and runs a hand through his hair. "A *real* conversation. About last night. I mean, am I fucking crazy or did you at least for a second think that you might want this?"

He gestures back and forth between the two of us, and my teeth clench despite the way my eyes dart to the floor. I watch as he rests his hands on his hips, my brain now torn between sharing his intensity and staring at his crotch through his second skin.

He pauses briefly, waiting for me to fill the silence, and when I don't, his arms fly in the air. "Okay, since you're not denying *that*, then what's the excuse this time?"

My head shoots up, my armor now in place. "There's a lot of *reasons*."

He raises his brows expectantly. "Like what? The fame? The image? Because I play professional hockey? Or is it because I'm on your friend's husband's roster? Because you do realize how you got this job, right?"

My lips drop open, wanting to argue, and my hand twitches at my side, desperate to wag a finger in his face. But he's not wrong. I know I only got this gig because Levi's married to Alex, and with how much it's changing my plans for the future, I'm actually so grateful that's the case.

He stops briefly before his eyes close slowly and scoffs. "You still don't think we could be on the same page because of my age."

I cross my arms over my chest, leaning into my last excuse. "You're twenty-five, Drew."

"And you're thirty-one, Brooke!" he yells. "And you don't seem to have it all figured out."

"Yeah, that's the point! Imagine how little I had *figured out* six years ago."

"Okay," he mocks in agreement. "So, is that it then? You're older than me, so I couldn't possibly want the same things as you?"

"You *don't* want the same things as me! It's clear as day. The parties..."

"Uh huh," he nods, sarcastically agreeing.

"The attitude."

"Yep."

"The..."

He narrows his eyes, waiting for me to continue. When I don't, he crosses his arms over his chest. "Go ahead. Say it."

"Listen, I'm not judging your test from last year, but..."

His arms fly to the top of his head, and he brushes his hands down his face. "I don't fucking do drugs, Brooke," he says matter-of-factly.

My head snaps back, and I hold my hands up in surrender. "Okay, well, you can't deny the women."

A bitter laugh sneaks from his throat. "The women, huh? It's funny you're pretending to care because it sure seems like I'm the one who wants you and you're—"

"*You* want *me?*" I repeat, unconvinced.

His expression melts into one of frustrated confusion. "What?"

I actually smile as I shove my hands into my pockets. "How was your date last night, Drew? Was that planned before or after you offered to stay at my place? What? I didn't invite you in, so you had to go find someone who would?" I stop mid-ramble, before starting a new one. "Ya know what? No, you are free to do whatever you want. And you should, really. But that's my point. *That's* what you want. And that's fine! That's what I wanted way past twenty-five. But if you're still there. If *that's* what you're looking for—then this..." I say, repeating his gesture from earlier. "Isn't going anywhere."

Drew turns around, rubbing the back of his neck before he whips back to me. "You have no idea what you're talking about."

"Oh, don't I? You do realize that pictures of you and the blonde actress you were with last night are all over the internet."

"Yeah, I do," he snaps back.

I let out a dismissive laugh. "Oh my God, and I'm the crazy one?"

"Yeah," he nods, his whole body on edge. "You are."

"And how's that?" I throw back.

Drew's lips purse as if he's fighting to keep his next thought in.

"That's what I—"

"It's fake!" he shouts, cutting me off and stepping closer.

"What?" I ask, otherwise stunned.

"Fake," he repeats just inches from my face. "Not real."

My mind attempts to interpret what he's saying, but that same erotic smell from before keeps distracting it. "I, I don't—what?" I stammer out.

Drew leans in, his arms wide. "It was a goddamn set-up, Brooke. A stunt. A chance for paparazzi to catch me out doing the shit my fans expect me to be doing. All. Fucking. Pretend. Just like the rest of it."

I search his face for any indication that he's lying, but his expression is strong, his eye contact steadfast. "But why? I don't understand."

He turns around, pacing a few strides before returning to his spot in front of me. "Because that's what people want from me," he spews out. "Because that's who they think I am. That's the guy I fucking snorted drugs to maintain."

I remain speechless, both waiting for him to continue and not knowing what to say. He blows out a breath, tempering his volume. "But none of that's real."

"Okay," I say unsurely. "So, what's real then?"

He blows out a breath as if he's considering what he does and doesn't want to share. "What's real?" he says under his breath. His voice grows louder, his energy rising once again. "What's real? Me bringing you *here,* that's what's real. Talking to you about my mom and music and all the shit that's *mine.* That I don't let anyone know. *That's* what's real."

My stomach flips as I take in his words. That the guy I thought he might be—the one who he seems to be with me—is really in there. And has been all along.

Drew steps to me so the tip of his sock grazes the toe of my boot. I physically react, my pulse racing and my chest rising to nearly touch his.

"And *this,*" he says, his voice almost a whisper. "*This* feels pretty fuck-ing real."

His breathing is heavy, and I hyper-focus on whether that's from his passionate rant or his body's response to his proximity to me. I get lost in his inhales and exhales, the sound both calming and intoxicating me all at once.

He somehow locks in on me even more than before, his mouth tight, his nostrils flexing under the strain of his breath. So many things fly through my mind—my mom's opinions, Ivy's words, Drew's actions throughout the day yesterday. The way my heart sank when I saw the picture of him with Zombie Girl.

And how I feel now.

A deafening silence settles in, one where not even a shuffling of feet in the hallway can be heard underneath the door. We stay like that, motionless—stuck in a game of chicken where no one speaks but no one pulls away either.

I replay the last thirty hours in my mind, every look, every laugh, every doubt and each defense. I have so many questions, but none that I can put into words with him standing so close to me like this. My brain runs through the list of excuses Drew justified for what feels like the hundredth time, when suddenly, his jaw grows tight, the only movement between the two of us.

My gaze lands on his gold chain shining like a light at the end of the dark tunnel of his shirt, and I flash back to it sitting across his sweat-beaded chest, damp and glistening. His ink on display, bold and vulnerable. My eyes resisting the urge to wander, my heart questioning his depth. His skin and true-self exposed just enough.

"Your move, Mystery Girl."

Or maybe not *enough* at all.

I barely finish my thought when I'm in his arms, mine arranged around his neck. I kiss him hard, and he reciprocates, our lips melting together like they're one, as always, our tongues greedy for each other. Before I have a chance to question it—even one moment to second-guess—Drew slides his hands to the outside of my thighs, lifting me so I'm forced to wrap my legs around his waist.

The perfect cock I know he's restricting underneath his thin compression pants fights against the spandex. It swells between my legs as he pushes on my ass, holding me firmly against him. The friction he causes at the apex of my thighs isn't even close to the amount of pressure that I need.

I whimper as Drew drags my bottom lip between his teeth, while simultaneously turning and walking us backward. We pause when my back hits the wall, both of us panting. He slides his hand into my hair and holds my gaze, speaking to me with no words at all before he kisses me once more.

Moments later, my legs unfold from around him as I slide down his chest, setting my feet back on the floor. Drew moves his other hand from my waist so both are tangled in my hair.

"This real enough for you yet?" He presses his lips to mine again as he drops his hands and brushes his thumbs past the fabric covering my nipples.

"I don't know, Twelve," I gasp, pulling away. "I think you can do better than that."

Drew dips down and nips at my neck, grabbing my hand and pinning my palm to his cock. "How about now? Pretty real?"

I inhale quickly as I feel every minute of how long it's been since he's been inside me. "Yeah," I say breathlessly. "Better."

With that, Drew grabs hold of my hips and twists them swiftly, spinning me so that I'm sandwiched between him and the wall in the best possible way. "This has always been real to me, baby," he says to my back before leaning in so I can feel locks of his damp hair fall onto my cheek. "And you won't leave this room without feeling every inch of that."

As if those words were a command, my fingers drop to the waistband of my jeans, readying them for him. Drew growls in my ear as I push my ass into him, and he watches my quick work over the button.

Before the zipper is even fully down, he steps backward, dipping his hands underneath the fabric on either side of my hips and pulls them down as they take my thong with them.

"Fuck," he mutters.

Without needing to be asked, I step on the back of each shoe, kicking them off, grateful that I decided on the zip-up combat boots this morning and not the ones that lace up the front. Once they're tossed to the side, I step out of my jeans and wait for Drew to make his move.

When he remains still behind me, I look back at him over my shoulder.

"What are you doing?" I ask, suddenly vulnerable with my bare ass on display.

He licks his lips. "Fucking memorizing this."

A heat creeps up my cheeks as I turn back around, hiding his words' effect on me. Seconds later, Drew shuffles behind me, and I move my hips, desperate for his touch.

Just to tease me, he lines the tip of his cock up with my middle and slides it up and down, my body already slick for him.

"Is this *image* too much for you?" he asks, his free hand brushing down the center of my back. "This attitude?"

I moan in response, pushing back into him as he continues his taunt.

"Answer me, baby."

"No," I blurt out. "God, no. Just... more."

With that, he shoves into me, filling me in the most satisfying way, my walls clenching around him like a lifeline. *It's been too damn long.*

I cry out, muffling my sounds by pressing my mouth into the back of my arm braced on the wall in front of me. "How about that?" he huffs out at the same time, buried inside me but agonizingly still. "Does that feel too fucking young for you, Brooke?"

"No," I pant, now even more needy. "Definitely not." When he stays motionless, I take matters into my own hands, shifting forward and driving back into him.

Drew groans, his hand flying to my hair. He wraps it in his fist and pulls me toward his chest. At this angle, his cock hits me in the most delicious spot, and once again, he's in control.

"Turn around," he whispers in my ear.

"What? But—"

He drops my hair and pulls out of me completely, leaving me empty and desperate.

For him.

"Turn around."

I do as I'm told, and before I can question him again, he picks me back up by my waist and shuffles forward. He pins my shoulders to the wall once more, only this time, I don't unwrap my legs. With one arm still holding me, he takes his other hand and lines his cock back up with my entrance. I settle onto it as he releases some of my weight, and the pressure from this position shatters me in the most welcomed way.

Pulling the hair at the nape of his neck, I stifle my sounds by baring down on his shoulder. I should probably care more that the last time we were in here someone walked right in, but I can barely remember my own name with Drew inside me.

"Look at me," he says, still pumping in and out.

I lift my head, my gaze landing on the same heated eyes that saw through me ten months ago. Drew drops his slick forehead to mine, and my hands drop to his biceps that are bulging from holding all of my weight not pinned to the wall. "I want this," he pants desperately. His eyelids fall shut as his breathing kicks up. "I want this," he repeats almost to himself.

His words bring me closer to the edge, and Drew's speed increases as my mind races.

This.

This is the Drew that I met ten months ago.

This is the Drew that I see when I'm with him.

This is the Drew that I knew existed.

This is the Drew that I *want*—my mother's opinions and future-Brooke be damned.

"Fuck," he grunts as he slams into me once more, emptying inside me as I ride my own high.

My legs squeeze his firm waist as my body quivers between his wall of a chest and the real one behind me. He presses his dewy lips to mine, solid but eager, as if he's ingraining it to memory. I meet his fervor, with all of my thoughts still at the forefront of mind.

"Tell me you want this," he says between breaths after breaking our seal.

I search his eyes and come up with nothing short of longing. I nod, agreeing to both myself and to him. "I think I might," I admit, swallowing any remaining hesitation.

He exhales through a boyish smile. "What are you saying here, baby?"

I chuckle softly, remembering those same words from that night. "I guess I'm saying I'm good with this if you are."

20
Drew

"Have I mentioned this is my favorite room?"

Brooke looks up from where she's buttoning her pants and shrugs. "Only ever with me in it, which is interesting."

She paints a sly grin as I stride over to her, pushing her hair back and away from her perfectly flushed face. "You must have that effect on me."

She smothers a full smile, leaning slightly into my palm. "I never told anyone that before, ya know?" She stands up straighter as she inhales slowly. "That I let my P.R. manager set those things up."

"That's really not you?"

I shake my head almost shamefully. "I mean, I guess it used to be. Sort of. Or who I became. But after everything went down last season... I just—I couldn't do it anymore. Couldn't fake it. At least not on my own."

She drops her head, pretending to still be playing with the waistband of her pants, and my hand falls with it. "Drew," she says, her voice cautious. "How would we even do this?"

I blow a breath through my lips and trail my fingers down the outside of her arms. "Talk to me," is all I say.

Brooke turns and moves to her stuff, crouching down and searching through her bag. I try my best not to stare at her as she does it but, *fuck, this girl is beautiful.* When I met her here, I had no intention of things ending up like they did. But that's what happens with me and her. Things escalate unintentionally, or at least for me they do. Every look burrows through me, every touch like a branding. Every conversation ends with me all but baring my soul.

After a few seconds of digging, she pulls out a claw clip, and like muscle memory, she twists her collarbone-length hair back into it. Her clip sits in her mouth as her hands work their magic, and all I can think of is how her lips tasted on mine.

"You just told me that part of this life of yours revolves around planned outings with models and celebrities." She pulls a few pieces of hair loose so that they frame her face. "Of which I am not, if you weren't aware."

"You could be."

"Oh, but I couldn't."

I chuckle softly. *If only she realized how much of a bonus that is.* My face grows serious again as I step closer to her, brushing my hands up and down her arms. "Yeah, but that's the point. I don't want that anymore."

"So, what? You're just gonna completely flip the script? Change your whole life around?"

"Isn't that what you're doing?" I ask quickly.

She nibbles her lip, considering my answer. "But I'll still be working for the Flames," she says rather than responding to my question. "I told you I think I might want to do this for real. I can't mess up the only chance I have at proving that I'm capable. I need this."

I drop my hands, and she slings her bag over her shoulder. I know what she's dancing around—she can't mess up the only chance she has because of me. Because she knows if we go all in—if we make this official—that pull we have toward each other is capable of dragging us away from everything else.

But maybe that's the point.

Grabbing hold of the strap of her bag, I yank her back to me and brush her chin with the pad of my thumb. "We'll figure it out, I promise."

She cocks a brow in her usual way. "How?"

I bring my hand to the back of my neck and massage the tension building there. As much as it kills me to say this, I think it might be the only way. "What if we..." I groan, dreading the rest of my sentence. "What if we don't make any big decisions about us—good or bad—until you're done with the Flames gig? That will give you some peace about the job situation, and it'll give me time to sort all this shit out with... everyone."

I planned to say Jane, but the truth of the matter is, I'll have a lot more people than my all-business P.R. manager to answer to if *Drew Anderson* plans on changing his tune. I'm not so worried about my coach and teammates. Monte would probably be happy to see me out of the gossip, and the boys would understand eventually, I know that. But my dad will damn sure have something to say when his limelight player simply fades into the game.

"And what?" she asks. "Bang in secret?"

"Sure, sounds good to me," I quickly answer jokingly. Brooke slaps my arm, and we both smile. "I'm kidding. Well, I mean, we can definitely do that. But I also want to just be with you. Hangout. Eat food."

"Wow," she says bluntly. "You really were telling the truth, weren't you?" She scrunches her face and sticks out her chest. "I don't know, Brooke. We could like hangout and eat food," she says, mocking me in a voice two octaves lower than her own. I snatch her up, her body collapsing in on me as I pull her close. "You really *don't* find your own dates." She laughs, throwing her arms around my neck.

"Hey, I'd do just fine on my own." I dip my hand up and past her cheek, pulling her lips mere inches from mine. "But yes, I was telling the truth. And now, it doesn't matter." Pressing my mouth to hers, I inhale deeply, the obstacles bound to come somehow lighter already knowing she's in my arms.

"Okay, so a few weeks, huh? We'll just give it a shot and see how it goes?"

"A few weeks," I echo, wanting the time to speed by and drag on simultaneously. "But I'll warn ya, baby... I score on most of the shots I take."

There's no hiding the smile that spreads on her face, or mine that forms in reaction.

I kiss her again, hard at first but then softly, shoving down all the uncertainties that creep to the surface. My dad's latest idea, Jane's calendar, my teammates' questions—all of it just hurdles.

And I'd climb mountains if it meant getting to hold her like this.

"Okay, Twelve. I'll give it to ya. I didn't know you could be so persuasive."

Bringing her mouth to mine once more, I run my tongue past the seam of her lips. When she opens, I dip back in one last time, sucking her bottom lip as I pull away.

"I told you, Brooke," I say, running the tip of my nose up from the line of her jaw to the base of her ear. "There's a lot that you don't know about me."

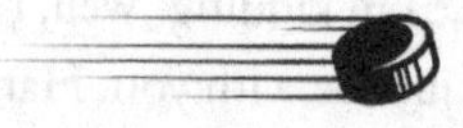

"Offsides!" Monte yells, and almost immediately, the ref blows his whistle.

The Hurricanes' forward throws one hand in the air and shakes his head before skating over to his bench with the rest of his team. There are three and a half minutes left in the third period, and this will be the last TV timeout.

The boys and I head to our bench to wait out the break, when the jumbotron starts with the Look-Alike-Cam.

"Oh, bullshit!" Burnsey calls over the noise. "That dude looks nothing like Michael B. Jordan. He's a three at most. MBJ is an easy eight."

"If Jordan's an eight, name a ten," Ward says, tapping his stick to the beat of the song.

Brett peers over at him, one brow raised.

"You?" Carter laughs. "Yeah, fat chance."

"Dude, look at me! I..."

Burns's voice drifts off as I lock eyes with a ten of my own. Brooke is sitting with Coach's girl and Cooper in their usual box in the stands. The three of them seem to be in some sort of heated debate, possibly similar to the boys' considering their pointing at the Look-Alike-Cam. Even from here, Brooke's smile lights up the room—and my goddamn senses, even when it's not directed at me.

After we left the bay earlier, my head was fucking spinning even more than it normally is. I get to be with Brooke. Maybe not openly or with titles involved, but I get to spend real time with her after all these months of craving her. She may not have shoved me down on one knee, but my mystery girl, who is stubborn and sarcastic and full of excuses, finally let me in just a little.

The conditions are honestly what's best for us—we both need time to figure things out. She needs to see that I'm serious about changing my ways while keeping things professional. And I... well, I don't exactly have a plan to do this without having Jane and my dad and the rest of the world on my fucking back.

The ref's second whistle interrupts my thoughts, signaling the end of the TV timeout. I glance up at the jumbotron as the Dance Cam fades out and look back at Brooke. Alex and Cooper are now sitting back down, but she's still standing... her eyes on me.

My instinct is to burn a hole into her—not moving back to my spot on the ice until she knows exactly what I'm trying to say with just one look. But my line's already moving into position, and the last thing I need is to draw attention to myself and my lingering gaze up to the box in the sky. Instead, I wink quickly, hoping that alone will tell her everything she needs to know.

Brooke smiles softly as I push off the bench, my mind habitually resetting back to the game. Peering up at the scoreboard, I'm given the unnecessary reminder that there's still a little more than three minutes left and we're only up by one. Like clockwork, a wave of adrenaline-laced anxiety washes over me. My body's amped just the right amount, but my mind kicks into overdrive.

Luckily, I now have someone worth performing for.

It never used to be like this. Hockey used to be the easy part. I never made it a point to stick handle more than I had to. Never went out of my way to make a goal into an epic celebration. But once upon a time, I still had fun.

I'd make the occasional trick-shot or do some sort of inside joke of a celly with my teammates. But that was my natural enjoyment shining through. The general happiness I felt in my escape during a time that would be hard on anyone, let alone a young teenager. And I think people recognized that.

I was a personality on the ice, but that wasn't *who* I was, just *how*. Now, it's all different. Those things are what's expected, but all over the top. Now the "fun" is more-muscle memory than innate behavior. All of my natural joy for making the game my own, lost among the rest of it.

To be this close in score doesn't typically help with the heaviness. But then again, I don't usually have *her* watching me. Not like this, at least. I take note of the way that even the thought of Brooke calms that uneasiness. It doesn't matter if I have to lie to Jane or hide from my dad or sneak her into the back of my car like I'm seventeen again. In four minutes, I get to have her. And that's all the motivation I need to end strong.

Bending over my stick, I get into position, the ref hovering between our center and the Hurricanes'. The whistle starts the clock again as the puck is dropped between them, hitting the ice with a smack. Their sticks tangle together as they both push for possession, and I glide forward toward our opponent's net.

The puck sails backward toward our zone and Burns steps up, cracking it up the boards. Petrov is there to receive it, two of the Hurricanes' defenders heading toward him. He skates behind the net as the rest of my line and I get into position to shift the puck around. Alexei deeks right but sails left, and instead of dumping it into the net himself, he kicks it out to Burns as one of the defenders rams into him. Burns pulls his stick back and fakes a shot, following through past the puck and tapping it to me behind him.

I inch toward the blue line, unnecessarily close. My skates cross over into the neutral zone, the puck nearly touching it. It hovers so close that if the incoming Hurricane skated any quicker, the breeze he'd cause would push it out, forcing my team to recover. I play with the puck for an extra beat before passing it to Petrov by the boards and sprinting past my defenseman. In one fluid motion, Alexei sends it to me—a tape to tape pass under two players' sticks—and I rip my shot.

As smooth as butter, the puck sinks into the corner of the net, and the horn blasts through the arena. Like Pavlov's law, I fall into a rhythm after the sound, cruising toward the boards and skating past the bench. All the while, I sweep my stick past me on either side of my body, "rowing" myself past my coaches and teammates. When I clear the blue line, I throw my hand to my helmet, my pointer finger running along the top of my shield as if I'm searching the stands for a safe landing from the ice's rough waters.

And maybe I am.

I spot her once more, but just as I do, I also find a rip current from the corner of my eye. My dad tips his chin up at me from his usual seat at center ice—pride and annoyance both present on his face—and it's no surprise that a weight settles in my chest again.

It hasn't always been like this. I used to look up to my dad—aim to please him. But that came from wanting him to be proud of me for succeeding in something that I know he loves. But after Mom died, I realized it was never about me. And if anything, losing her just made it worse.

I could be drafted into the NHL, win Rookie of the Year, make captain for our hometown team, and I'd still never be enough to fill the holes left in his heart from his first two loves. I tolerated it for years—busted my ass to get here so *Dad* could finally see Anderson on the back of an NHL jersey—but lately I've realized he brings with him some of the loudest noise that I'm trying to avoid.

"Nice," Petrov says as I step through the boards. He tips his chin down at me, his hands wrapped around his stick that sits between his legs.

"It'll do," I pant, squeezing water into my mouth. I hand my stick to Max, knowing at this point I won't be going back in, and slip my helmet off before running a hand through my sweat-locked hair.

"Good shit, Drew," Monte says, tapping the pad at my shoulder.

I wipe the dew off my brow with the sleeve of my jersey, then nod back at him. "Thanks, Coach."

With my body turned away from the ice, I glance up and immediately lock eyes with Brooke. She arches one brow at me seductively, and my jaw tenses, my racing heart settling into a slow pounding rhythm.

I don't normally celebrate a win like I used to. Game nights off are one of the exceptions with my deal with Jane. But something tells me that I won't be soaking in my ice bath at home, listening to music, and decompressing from the last two hours like I'm used to.

Well... at least not alone, I hope.

21

Brooke

Standing at the end of the hallway that leads to both an exit and the locker room door, I have to make it a point to do something for "work." The truth is, I've been posting stories on Instagram and Facebook all night, have a reel and TikTok both scheduled to go out of footage I took from the first period, and a list of ideas to dive into next. But I can't just wait here for Drew without looking busy. What if his teammates notice? Or worse—what if whatever we're doing doesn't include seeing me after a game?

So, instead of setting myself up for possible failure, I pulled out my phone when I rounded the corner from the equipment office and walked past the locker room to the end of the hall. I have my camera app up and have been asking the players that don't look completely wrecked to show me their "big win face" before they walk out the door.

Only two guys have left so far, one of which was Hughes—who I have learned to differentiate from Ellis off the ice by his eccentric style—and the other was Carter Ward. I didn't expect that the goalie would be the first out the door, humming *The Macarena* may I add, but I've come to the conclusion in my first week here that my research is right. They're totally strange.

I'm looking at Carter's picture, one eye winking and two finger guns aimed at the camera, when a man I don't recognize rounds the corner at the other end of the hall. At the same time, the door between Drew and me blows open, and my whole body stands on edge as it has each time it could be him walking out. Once again, it's not. Instead, Petrov's massive body charges into the space and nearly swallows the man behind him, who I barely had time to look over before he blocked him from my view.

I smile at Petrov, whose usual stone-cold expression erases the mystery man from my mind. *One day I will get this guy to smile.* I wait for him to approach me, and as he does, I can finally see past him. Drew must have snuck out right behind him because he's standing with the man looking six kinds of gorgeous in his full game suit, the slate blue color taking me right back to the gala. He starts talking to the guy, his voice so low I can't hear a thing, but I do notice that he and the man bear a striking resemblance.

"Brooke." The Storm's voice rumbles through me like thunder during a... *huh... fitting.* It catches me off guard and draws my attention back to him.

"You remembered my name," I say, surprised and impressed.

He continues to stare at me blankly. "You have only one."

My eyes run down the length of him in his jet black... everything, as I attempt to figure out how this poetic version of him fits into his overall picture. I purse my lips when I fail to see it, but am still just as taken aback by him. "That I do, Alexei. That I do."

He moves to exit through the door, and when he does, I spot Drew out of the corner of my eye. He throws an arm in the air pointed in the opposite direction, a faint whisper of anger trailing through his low voice now bouncing off the walls. When he starts heading my way, he adjusts his jacket, huffing through his nose. I try to pretend I don't notice.

"Oh, wait," I say, grabbing at Petrov's arm. It's obviously massive under my very average grasp, but *damn*—his bicep could eat my hand for a snack. He steps backward into my space. "Show me your big win smile," I say cheerfully. As expected, his expression doesn't change, but he looks into the camera as if he's giving it all he's got.

"Uh, thanks." I smile, and he busts through the door just as Drew finally reaches me.

"Mystery Girl," he says, his voice more depleted than I expected after such a win.

"Twelve," I answer with a grin. I'm not exactly sure how to approach this, and it hits me harder now that waiting for him after his game might have been a little presumptuous.

"So, Anderson," I say, pivoting my thoughts. "Show me your big win—"

"Let's get out of here, Brooke," he whispers.

A warmth grows on my face, but it's nothing compared to the one that starts between my legs. *God, he really does have an effect on me.*

I tip my chin down nonchalantly, waiting for him to direct me on how I should do this.

"You drove here?" he asks, his voice still low. I nod just once, as if somehow the walls suddenly have ears. "Alright, there's probably going to be cameras outside. Can you meet me at my place?"

Suddenly it all feels real—the last six hours and everything that came with them, rushing past my mind. Surprisingly though, it's not anything but excitement that hits me. Almost as if past-Brooke is taking the driver's seat once again.

"Sure," I say confidently.

He smiles that genuine smile that I'm telling myself is reserved just for me, his adorable dimples finally joining the conversation. Drew slings his backpack around to the front of him, unzips it, and reaches inside.

"Here, take this." He pulls out a ball of black fabric from his bag, wafting his usual, welcomed scent toward me. "Put this on before you walk up to the building. Hood up. I'll wait for you in the lobby and tell the doorman to let you in."

That realness hits me again, bringing with it a few nerves this time. Swallowing it down, I mask it in my usual way. Gesturing to my tight black long-sleeve v-neck, I say, "What? You don't like *my* shirt on me?"

He steps closer so we're just inches apart, and my whole body senses the shift in mood. Drew makes no attempt to hide the way he can undoubtedly see down my top and into my cleavage from this proximity.

"Oh, I fucking love that shirt on you. And I bet I'll like it even more *off* of you. But for at least the next few weeks, I need you to blend in." He blows a heavy breath through his lips. "And, baby, you do not blend in with *that* on."

Pulling my bottom lip into my mouth, I let my teeth run over it. "Well, okay then," I say, taking it from him.

"I'll meet you there."

"Should I give you some sort of head start?" I ask, suddenly desperate to avoid waiting outside of his billion dollar building in a black hoodie with my head covered and no one inside to vouch for me.

"Nah," he says, taking one step forward. As he does it, he grazes my hand with his pinky discreetly and winks. "I rode the bike."

Once again, my anticipation suffocates the possible anxiety of reality as I picture Drew on his bike, the jacket he's wearing, stretched across his back as he hovers over the handlebars. I instantly find myself wishing these next few weeks had already passed so I could be behind him, my hands slipped underneath the fabric, the bike's motor vibrating between my legs.

"You good?" Drew asks right before I completely slip into my fantasy.

I answer, my voice floating out accidentally suggestive. "Oh, I'm good."

The corner of his lip curls upward as he wraps his hand around my wrist. "I'll see you soon," he all but growls.

I inhale deeply. "See you soon."

"So, who were you talking to outside of the locker room?"

Drew presses the up arrow on the wall to signal the elevator, and I mentally curse myself for picking nosiness as my form of small talk.

"Oh, uh, no one," he says as the elevator doors ding open to let us in. *Saved by the bell?*

We step inside as I brush off his dismissive answer.

"That's not true actually," he adds before I have enough time to feel awkward about it. "I probably shouldn't start this whole living my truth thing out with a lie." I inhale quickly as the doors close in front of us, and Drew swipes a card in front of a sensor. "That was my dad."

Curiosity causes my thoughts to race, but Drew stares straight ahead, clearly uncomfortable. If anyone knows a complicated relationship with a parent or the deep desire to avoid all feelings, it's me. So, instead of asking for more information, I coat the topic in humor instead. "Wow, okay. Came extremely close to meeting your parent on night one."

He looks at me side-eyed, offering a grateful smile.

"Great game," I say, continuing the topic change.

"Yeah, thanks." He slips his hands into his pockets.

"You had the whole stadium out of their seats straddling the blue line like that at the end there."

He turns toward me and winks casually. "That's the point."

The floor number in front of me continues to rise as I face him. "So, you really do all of that showboating intentionally? How? I can barely keep up with the game as it is."

He laughs, shrugging his shoulders. "Honestly? It's habit at this point. I used to do that goofy shit all the time for fun in Juniors and stuff. Now, it's more about appearances. Forced. It's like singing a song that you hate just because it's stuck in your head. It's annoying as hell, but you remember the words."

"Is that where you learned that little celebration you did too?" I ask, chuckling softly, wondering how the chill guy in front of me is the same one that used his stick as an oar an hour ago.

The elevator settles at what I know from the last time is Drew's penthouse floor, and the doors chime open. "That little celebration will cost me a couple grand," he says, using his arm to hold the door open.

"What? As in thousands of dollars?" I ask, still standing in my spot.

"As in three probably, yeah."

I stare at him, my mouth open and his closed nonchalantly. After a few seconds of his arm still slung over the opening, he looks into his apartment, then back at me. "Are you gonna..."

"Oh, shit, yeah, sorry," I stammer, stepping into his place, still wrapping my head around his comment. "So, let me get this straight. You did a dance you didn't even want to do, and it's gonna cost you three thousand dollars?"

Drew steps off and the doors close behind him. "Yeah, it's not considered the most sportsmanlike."

"Why do you do this again?"

He raises his eyebrows as he steps toward the kitchen. "Give the people what they want," he says over his shoulder.

"Would they really care if you stopped?"

"Oh, they'd care," he throws back.

I cross my arms over my chest, suddenly defensive of him. "Well, what about what *you* want?"

Drew freezes right as he reaches the island that was covered in smoothie the last time I saw it. He stands with his back to me for just a second before rounding the counter and leaning his forearms on the granite. He hangs his head between his arms briefly before looking back at me. When he does, his eyes hold a mixture of amusement and sadness.

"What?" I ask, walking over to him, leaning on the opposite side of the island, playing with the strings of his sweatshirt that I'm still happily drowning in.

He shakes his head shortly, inhaling deeply. "No one's ever asked me that before."

My eyebrows shoot up. "Ever?"

His lips turn down as he looks off in the distance as if he's trying to recall if he's missed an instance. "Not since my mom died."

His words, and my assumptions about him, hit me unexpectedly. I know what it's like for people to shove you down a path that you aren't interested in traveling. I've just been lucky enough to dig my heels in hard enough to avoid the forward momentum. But I've also had people like Blake and Aunt Ivy always on my side. It may be infrequent, or behind closed doors, but their voices live rent free inside my mind, reminding me that what I want matters. And that they'll love me either way.

I think of Drew and how thousands of people judge him daily. Thousands of people, me included, assume that what we see is who he is. But we're wrong.

"So, what *do* you want, Twelve?"

He smiles with his eyes before standing back up. "I used to love it, ya know? Fuck, I think I still do. Hockey, I mean. But the rest of it? The rest of it just feels like something completely different. It's not sport at all. It's a game. And I tried the whole lying low thing after my suspension last year," he says, continuing to circle around the question. "It was sort of necessary, so I used it to my advantage and cut out all that shit. No ego or extras on the ice. No parties, extravagant trips..."

He turns his lips in and narrows his eyes.

"It's okay, you can say it. Believe it or not, I have slept with men before you," I tease.

His jaw grows tight as he cracks his neck to one side. He clears his throat, then nods. "Yeah, no wild one-night-stands." He places his palms on the island and leans into them. "Turns out, I loved it. That was never who I was until I got here. The fans hated it though. They want me as the guy they painted or not at all I guess, which is my own fault in the first place so... here I am."

"Why would they care?"

Drew scoffs, pushing off the counter. "They care about everything." My face must read my hesitation because he sighs heavily, then continues. "Brooke, I once got hate for cutting my hair."

"Well, why'd you cut it?"

"I didn't!" He rubs his forehead with his first two fingers, then looks at me with sorrow in his eyes. "But that's my point."

My brain slowly catches up to the Drew that I've seen over the last week or so. The one that's hidden underneath the showman antics and bad boy lifestyle. I think part of me knew he was there the moment we locked eyes at the gala. It's why I really felt drawn to hide who I was. Part of me knew that I would fall for him—despite his reputation, despite his age. And yet... here *I* am.

Before I realize it, I'm rounding the island, my eyes—and my heart—set on my prize. Drew turns to me when I reach him. He peers down at me sternly, as if he's waiting for my judgement, but it won't come. I'm all too familiar with feeling like you have to please everyone else but yourself. I just never thought I'd be considered the lucky one.

My whole life has been built on top of their disappointment. It's a quiet friend that tags along, but it doesn't steer my way. In Drew's life, *he's* that friend. Someone else is driving, and he's just along for the ride.

"So, what do you want, Twelve?" I repeat my question, but this time, I expect another answer.

He raises one eyebrow slightly and searches my face. "I thought I just kind of told y—"

His words drop off when I dip the tips of my fingers into the waistband of his pants, shaking my head. His eyes shoot to my hands, then back up to mine as I echo the same words. "What do you want?"

Drew's gaze grows heavy, his lips just barely parting, and I tilt my head as if to say, *well?*

After a quick pause, and a deep breath, he finally answers. "A banana," he says seriously.

I pull my head back, trying to gauge if that's some sort of weird kink or double entendre that I'm missing. He must read my confusion because he chuckles softly as his hand sinks past my cheek and into my hair. "To eat," he clarifies.

I can't help but smirk as my brows knit together tightly. "Okay, not what I—"

"So I don't cramp like a motherfucker when I finally get to you."

22
Drew

All innuendo aside, I've never downed a banana so fast in my life. I almost didn't even mention it—Brooke standing there asking me what I wanted is just about the only thing that could derail my recovery routine. But considering I knew the foam roller and ice bath were out of the question with her here, I had to at least keep myself from cramping while inside of her. Nothing says *ruin the mood* like a charlie horse mid-fucking-thrust.

Luckily, Brooke excused herself to go to the bathroom and take a look around, which gave me the three minutes I needed to at least push off any spasms. Maybe I am losing my touch a little bit with all these dates Jane's been making for me.

Nah.

Heading out of the kitchen, I search for Brooke. My penthouse is definitely more than I need, but it's not so big that she should have gotten lost on her way back out. Not to mention, the last time she was here, she spent most of the time washing smoothie out of her clothes in the very spot she should be now. It's been a few minutes though—I even had time to chug another water—and she hasn't come back from her little self-guided tour.

Taking the few steps it takes to get to the bathroom, I peek my head in—no signs of Brooke. I push off the doorframe, moving further down the hallway, and almost walk right past her sitting on my bed, the comforter tossed over her lap.

"I've always wanted to fuck on sheets with a thread count this high," she says coolly, her palm stroking the fabric beneath it.

"Oh, yeah?" I ask, slinking over to her. "That can be arranged." I throw the blanket to the side, revealing Brooke's naked lower half, and my hand immediately flies to my mouth before it drags down my chin.

"You ready to tell me what you *really* want, Twelve?"

My whole body reacts to her, my chest and pants both equally tight, and I blow out a breath as I hover over her, straddling my arms on either side of her body. "You, Brooke. I want you."

She bites her lower lip, and I can't stop myself. I take it between my teeth and do the same. "Good answer," she says when I pull away.

My eyes trail down the length of her again, my hoodie still on and pulled down just low enough to cover what I want that she's hiding underneath. "God, I could get used to seeing you in my clothes."

She takes the strings around her neck into her hand and trails her fingers down them. "And I could get used to wearing them."

I shake my head, ripping the cords from her grasp and tugging her toward me, so close that I can feel her quick breath on my lips. "Fuck that. Take it off."

Brooke pulls her knees up and wiggles her hips below me, hiking the hoodie up over her waist, proving me right. *Fucking flawless.*

She crosses her arms, yanking the fabric up and over her head. The shirt she has on underneath goes with it, and she tosses both to the other side of the bed where I could guess her jeans and underwear are hiding too.

Standing back up, I place both hands between her thighs and rip them open. "You already wet for me, baby?"

Brooke shrugs, not even remotely shy being on full display. *My girl.* I reach for the top button of my shirt, wishing I had already taken it off with my jacket, and nod toward her hand sitting next to her ass. "Check."

Brooke once again drags her teeth along her bottom lip, but this time, I stop myself from doing the same. Instead, I let my shirt slide off my arms and down to the floor as she walks her fingers up the inside of her thigh.

I unbutton my pants, freeing myself, rock hard for her, and at the same time, she dips her fingertip inside her pussy. Brooke gasps, either from her touch or the view of my throbbing cock, and holds her pointer up to me. "Soaked."

I snatch a hold of it with one hand, grabbing myself with the other. Taking it in my mouth, I taste just how wet she really is. My dick twitches against my palm in response, and a growl creeps out around her finger.

She smiles and reaches for me. "I think I know what you want."

"Jesus," I groan as she strokes the length of me.

It's funny how my dad can try to dictate my life, Jane can tell me who to date, but here, I call the shots. With Brooke though, I don't have to take the reins. It's like she already knows what I need. Like she already knows *me*.

And fuck if that doesn't turn me on more.

"Why don't you take a break and let me perform for you for a change," she suggests. I roll my tongue past my lips and inhale with anticipation. "That okay?"

I answer with a kiss, bending down and smashing my mouth to hers. I try to tell her with my tongue how *okay* that is—how refreshing it feels just to be with her. She whimpers her acceptance as she stands, still holding me tightly. My dick aches against her touch as she uses her free hand to push against my shoulder.

I turn with her movement until my calves are backed against the mattress. Suddenly, she pulls away from our kiss and shoves her hand into my chest. "Sit," she commands.

My lips curl at the change of pace, but I oblige without hesitation. Following my movement, Brooke drops to her knees between my legs and locks eyes with me. She holds my stare, my begging body growing more and more impatient for her, then parts her lips. I wait for her words, but she doesn't speak. Instead, she spits on my cock like a goddamn angel, then takes all of me into her mouth at once.

"Fuck, baby," I shudder, bracing my weight on my hands behind me, my head lolling backward.

Brooke hums with her lips wrapped tightly around my base, and I feel the vibration everywhere. She works her mouth up and down, her tongue swirling against my tip, her cheeks hollowing as she slides back and forth. Her hand lands at the sensitive spot below my belly button as she glides it up my abs already tight in reaction to her fucking mouth.

My hips flex beneath her as she drags her fingernails back down the length of my torso, and I come dangerously close to finishing before I even get to be inside her. Reluctantly, I slip my hand past her ear and tug at the hair at the nape of her neck.

"Come here," I say, pulling her to me, both of us now standing. Brooke digs her grip into my sides as she presses her hips against me. "Tell me what *you* want, Mystery Girl." I kiss her once, then drop next to her collarbone and nip up her neck.

"I want to get on top," she answers, clearly breathless.

I scoop her up as she instinctively wraps herself around my waist. "Say fucking less."

Sitting back on the bed, I throw one arm around her lower back and shuffle both of us toward the headboard. "Your show, baby," I say, settling us both into the mattress.

Brooke untangles her legs from underneath me and pushes up on her knees. I grab her hips, expecting to help guide her onto me, but instead, she shifts forward. "Think I'm still wet for you, Twelve?"

My cock flexes at that name falling from her lips. "You better be," I say, following her movement.

"Check," she says cockily, her pussy now hovering just above my chin.

When I realize what she's doing, I shake my head in disbelief, then lick my lips. "God," I draw out. "I knew you were bad."

I force her to sit, my mouth diving into her slick middle. She tastes exactly like I remember—sweet and like a fucking escape. I slide my tongue up the length of her slit, massaging her ass with my hands as I do it. Brooke leans forward, grabbing a hold of the headboard, moaning and riding my face like my goddamn Ducati. My cock protests behind her, my own body jealous of itself, my breathing quickening as Brooke's rhythm increases.

"Holy shit," she cries.

Just when I think I can't take it anymore—that I can't wait one more minute for her to slide so easily on top of me—my name falls from her lips, her legs quivering beside my head. I decide right there that I'd stay here forever, but as if they heard my thought, her muscles tense around me as she slows her movement. I keep my lips in place, sucking up every bit of her as she soaks in every second of her high. As her body relaxes, I turn my head, kissing the inside of her thigh, then gently biting the other.

"Soaked," she says suddenly, sitting back on my chest.

"Best recovery ever."

She tries to hide a smile and arches a brow. "Better than a banana?"

With that, I sit up, wrapping my arm around her waist and lifting her upward. With my free hand, I line my cock up with her drenched entrance and settle her weight back down. "So much better," I groan, falling back to the mattress.

Brooke whimpers as her legs clutch around me, her knees digging deliciously into my ribs. She leans forward, placing her palms on my chest, sliding them over my shoulders and down my arms.

"I didn't even know you had sleeves that night at the gala," she says softly, beginning to rock gently up and down.

I grab her hips and quicken her pace as she claws at my inked biceps, flexing underneath my hold on her. "You should have let me take my shirt off," I quip.

She pants. "No time, remember?"

I buck my hips into her, our bodies meeting at the perfect tempo like they always do—like they were made for each other. "How about now? You got time for me now?"

Her head rolls backward as she grinds even faster.

"Don't play with me, Brooke," I growl, stopping our movement, holding her body in place against me. "Answer me." I finish my thought while fighting my need. "Do you. Have time. For me. Now?"

She snaps her eyes back to mine, reading them like I intend for her to—bold and honest. I want to know if she's in this for real. If this is still happening. If she's still giving us a chance.

"Yeah, Twelve," she answers, shifting forward and placing her forearms on either side of my neck. She leans down and kisses me hard, our damp chests pressing against each other. When she breaks our kiss, she keeps her face just inches from mine. "Yeah, I have time for you."

My lungs fill with air I didn't realize I was missing. Air I probably haven't had since the gala, when she breathed life into me with just her words. I know we just met again a few weeks ago, and I know today is just the first of us, but it feels like my body's been missing her for more than ten months now. It doesn't seem like the beginning. It seems like the end—the end of my life without her and the start of, hopefully, so much more.

Brooke drops her lips to the side of my neck, her lower half swirling in slow circles as she nips at the sensitive skin by my collarbone. Once again, I can't stop myself from telling her exactly what I'm thinking—exactly how I feel. "Something tells me you're going to change everything, Mystery Girl."

Her teeth graze my throat as she smiles against it, but when she pulls back, she tempers her reaction. "Is that what you want?"

I consider her question, my body naturally meeting her steady movement, and search for an alternative answer. One that doesn't sound selfish or ungrateful. One that isn't full of grief or angst and doesn't wish away this life that so many people would kill for. But I come up short of anything other than the truth once more.

"More than fucking anything."

Brooke kisses the corner of my lips gently before sitting back up and taking her throne as the queen of every inch of me. "Good," she says confidently, riding me again. My cock responds to her words, and her movement, growing even harder inside her.

"Yeah?" I ask, bouncing her higher.

Brooke turns her lips in as she hums through her building pleasure, her voice almost a whisper. "Yeah."

With that, I fill beneath her, the sight of her at the edge, her promise—the whole thing—making it too hard to hold on. "Fuck, baby," I groan, a guttural sound following behind it.

She brings one hand to the base of my throat and squeezes gently, using me as her anchor as she falls apart.

And the image is everything.

The majority of my life, it's felt like I'm floating. Like I'm surrounded by a universe full of shit I don't belong to. My dad always told me I was meant for this, but I've learned that I'm the type of person who needs something to ground me. A form of gravity to anchor me to... anything meaningful. And maybe now I've found it in her.

And maybe she'll find that too.

In me.

23

Brooke

The last few days have been a whirlwind. The Flames had two back-to-back away games that I didn't travel for, which left Drew and I separated for the first couple of days since our second time in the shooting bay. It's also the longest we've been apart since the start of the season. It's crazy to think that less than three weeks ago, almost ten months separated any time we spent together. And now, I already really miss him.

We finally exchanged numbers that night at his house, but our few flirty texts—and the one topless photo that a certain one of us sent—have only made me realize how much I've liked having him around. Past-Brooke, or future-Brooke for that matter, would have never guessed I'd feel this way. They'd never believe that Drew Anderson—the same guy who just a few hours ago held a finger to his grinning lips, shushing an away-team crowd when he scored—would not only want to be with someone looking to settle down, but buried underneath his image, he'd seemingly fit the mold.

I know I still have a lot to learn about who Drew really is, but so far, I'm pleasantly surprised. We actually have a lot in common—our love of music, the way we are in the bedroom, our parental and good-old childhood trauma. But is it enough to actually make this work?

I'm doing pretty well right now. I'm steady and focused—I stopped going out and hooking up which really says something. So, that's what I still need to figure out. If he and I stand an actual chance or if falling for him would be a setback. Another one of my what-I-want-in-the-moment opportunities disguised as a risk I'd be taking on a guy who claims he's not who I thought he was.

"Brooke, what are you doing here?" Tessa's voice rings out from behind the wooden counter of The Gilded Pub as I cross through the front of the dining area toward the bar.

This is my usual shift, so I not only knew that Tess would be here, but I also knew that the managers wouldn't be. I've been so swamped with going to and from the rink, posting pictures and videos, and creating content ideas—not to mention actively learning the game of hockey and the Flames team in general—that I haven't had a chance to check in with Tessa. I don't miss the job at all, which is not surprising in the least, but this is the first time in ten years that I've missed this many shifts in a row. I knew The Pub would function fine without me, the same way I'm thriving without its greasy food and tipsy patrons. But I am a little curious about what's been going on.

"I knew you'd be here," I say, sliding onto a stool. "I thought I'd check in."

"Did Trish see you?" she asks anxiously.

I scoot closer to her and lower my voice. "No, thank God. But I may or may not have waited outside until a party of seven had to be seated."

"Genius," she draws out before pushing off the bar.

"So, how's it been today?"

Tess finishes wiping up a crumb-littered spot, tossing the bar rag over her shoulder. "Oh, it's fine. You missed the rush earlier when the Flames game was on. Those college kids came in again. The ones with the polos and the pastel pants."

"And sweaters tied around their necks?"

"Yep, as usual. Feels like they may have been watching the wrong sport."

I shake my head. "I don't get it. They know scarves exist, right?"

Tess shrugs her shoulders. "Maybe all that hair product is going to their brains."

A laugh breaks out between us, and I prepare to once again thank her for taking that misery away from me for these few weeks, when her giggle fades out and her eyes go wide.

"Oh, shit."

"What?"

"Damn," she says, impressed.

"Tess?"

"Isn't that..."

Her voice fades as I try to decipher her mumbling. I swing around on the stool to catch a glimpse of what's caused her sudden glitch. "Maybe the product went to your... brain... too."

My words trail off as I land on what—or rather *who*—has snagged her attention. All six foot two inches of my newest life decision struts through the door of the sports bar. He's wearing an open soft-shell motorcycle jacket with a black t-shirt underneath and jeans that hug the solid thighs I've been dreaming of sitting on top of again. His hair is pushed back, a piece falling onto his forehead as he scans the room with his helmet in hand and his backpack hanging off his shoulders. When he spots me, his face lights up, but only through his eyes—only in the way I would know.

He strides toward me easily, tucking the lock behind his ear, his boots seeming to thump against the floor to the same rhythm as my heart. "Hey, Brooke," he says when he's close enough.

Anxiety flushes my belly, a slow heat creeping up my chest as I realize this is supposed to be a secret. I curse him internally for exposing us already, even if Tess is pretty low on my list of people to hide this from.

It's only when Tessa chirps a friendly, and not the least bit suspicious, *hi*, from behind me, that I realize us recognizing each other would be expected. She knows why I gave up my shifts at The Pub. Of course we would know each other. So, apparently I'm the only one making this a big deal.

But why is he here?

I clear my throat, removing the foot I so quickly shoved down it, and try to smile casually, thanking the universe that my back is to Tess to hide whatever residual face I'm still making. "Hey, Drew. What are you doing here?"

He looks over my shoulder and grins at Tess. I follow his gaze and watch as she lifts a hand to wave, yet remains oddly calm compared to most people around him—and considering her temporary malfunction when he first walked through the door.

She spins around to restock glasses, her blonde hair swinging behind her, and I mimic her movement, turning back to him. I watch as he brings his thumb to the chain around his neck and drags his fingertip across it, his eyes now piercing through me as usual.

"I missed you," he whispers, his voice low enough that even I can barely hear him. My chest swells as I kick my toe against the bottom rung of the stool, punishing it for inserting itself in the first place.

I go to reply with whatever words I'm able to muster considering the shock I still have of seeing him here, when a group of twenty-somethings walk in and immediately scan the idol in front of me. "Don't you think this is a little suspicious?" I ask, my eyes flitting back and forth between them and him.

"Let's get out of here then."

There's a pulse between my thighs from his words alone, plus the fact that it's been a few days since I've gotten to have him. It's wild that I went ten months before because now I think I might be addicted.

I shift on the stool, and Drew's gaze drops to my legs. He runs his tongue along his bottom lip as if he knows exactly the effect he has on me. Trailing his movement does nothing to help my situation.

"Hey, Tess," I call over my shoulder, my eyes locking with his, telling him my answer.

I hear her bracelets lean over the counter behind me, and I spin back around. "I'm gonna head out. We have a uh, a thing to do for the Flames."

She looks up at Drew, then back down at me with a knowing expression written all over her face. "Oh, okay," she says just a bit too cheerfully. "You *do* your *thing*, girl."

I don't have to look to know Drew is not helping with whatever reaction he's having, but the fact that Tess acts unfazed otherwise only adds to the list of things I love about her.

"Thanks again," I say, squeezing her wrist. She winks at me, and I take the easy out before she suddenly finds questions.

With one last deep breath, I pop off the stool and step up to Drew. A silence sits heavily between us, but I know better than to have any conversations here. Instead, I hold his stare as I step toward the exit, only for my eyes to land on one grouchy looking Trisha when I get to the door. I offer her a half-smile, watching as her face only scrunches harder when she spots Drew behind me. She may be the only one unaffected by his presence, and honestly, that tracks.

Pushing through the familiar wooden door of The Pub, the cold air washes over me like a much-needed cold shower. I freeze on the sidewalk when I see Drew's Ducati, that sudden breeze instantly gone. *Shit, why is that thing so hot?*

As if on cue, Drew steps up behind me, our bodies not quite touching, but my every nerve is on end just waiting for contact. His head dips forward, his hair brushing past mine, his warm breath on my ear traveling south instantly. I brace myself for his next few words, the unexpectedness from his visit still throwing me off my game.

He makes me wait just another second as I hold my breath before he finally speaks.

"That hostess scares me," he whispers honestly. I snort out a laugh, my hand flying up to cover my sound as he walks out from behind me. "I'm serious, man. I face some of the toughest guys in the world—toothless maniacs, massive defensemen, guys put on the ice to just throw people around. But that girl?" He blows a breath through his lips and switches his helmet to his other hand. "Somethin' else."

I nod in agreement, my entire body relaxed again. "Right? And she always pops up out of nowhere."

"I could see that." Drew flashes me a smile, and we both look at each other grinning until he steps a few inches closer. "I missed you," he repeats.

"You said that."

"And yet I still haven't heard you reciprocate." He peers down at me, his expression a cross between amused and punishing, and my body reacts all over again.

"I missed you, too," I say, my voice thick.

His jaw grows tight, almost as if he's controlling the reaction he really wants to make, and he tilts his head toward his bike. "Get on."

"But I have my c—"

"Get on, Brooke."

My face falls into one of anticipation as I nibble my lip, considering his words for maybe two seconds before obliging.

When I get to the bike, I turn around, only to bump right into the helmet Drew is holding out for me. I take it, slipping it over my head, watching through the shield as he slings his leg over the seat. I climb on after him, hugging him tightly right before he wraps his arms under my thighs and yanks me closer. I gasp when he starts the bike, my legs so widely set around him that it's no longer even my ass that's touching the pad of the seat.

Drew keeps one hand on the throttle, trailing the other up my inner thigh as he revs the engine beneath us. The vibration hits me in all the right places, the mixture of that and his touch sending goosebumps to every inch of my skin. He backs out of the spot slowly, navigating the bike between a car and an SUV. As soon as he's cleared all possible obstacles, he rolls toward the exit, then peels out of the lot at triple the speed.

I tighten my grip around his waist, his abs flexing from the position—or maybe he's as on edge as I am. Drew stops at a red light and drops his arm, massaging the outside of my thigh. I attempt to shift even closer to him, squeezing my legs around his. I'm desperate for more. Needy for him.

I can't help myself. This man knows exactly how to light me on fire, and I might combust if I don't have all of him. Slipping my hands between the flaps of his jacket and underneath the hem of his shirt, I run my fingers over his muscles. Drew sucks in, which because of the rumble of the engine, I only know based on the way his whole torso lifts. I drag my fingertips over the rises and falls of each peak and valley, and he presses harder into the flesh of my leg, turning his head, cracking his neck to one side.

For a second, I contemplate telling him to pull over. Suggesting that he just turn the ignition off altogether and set up traffic cones so other drivers know to go around us while we get to what I really want. But before I'm too tempted to offer an idea, the light turns green, and Drew floors it down the road. The vibration continues, a dull trembling encouraging my need. I can't resist continuing my exploration, walking my fingertips lower and lower until I reach the waistband of his jeans.

There's no way that from this angle I could so much as even dip a hand inside, although that's exactly what I'd like to do. So, instead, I drop them altogether, only for one to land on his bulging cock strained between the seat and his right thigh. Just the feel of it makes me wetter, my nipples overly sensitive as they brush against his firm back. I press my palm against it, and Drew groans loud enough to hear over the bike's roar causing my hand to squeeze tighter as if I could somehow move it closer to where I need it most.

My other five fingers cling to the hem of his jacket, white knuckling it as I rest the front of my helmet on his shoulder, biting my lip so hard it hurts. Suddenly, the bike veers to the right, gravel from the side of the road crunching below the tires as Drew cruises onto the shoulder. Adrenaline rushes past me thanks to the quick change of pace, my heart-rate beating through my chest once we come to a stop.

Drew shuts the bike off completely, smacking the shield up on his helmet and twisting his torso to face me.

"I will fuck you over this bike if you so much as breathe the word, but I give it about two minutes before someone recognizes my ride and starts snapping pictures."

I stare at him in shock, which he probably can't even see through the tinted guard on my helmet. I stay quiet, torn between pretending I have no idea what he's talking about and actually accepting his offer.

"Your move, Mystery Girl," he continues impatiently, as if he didn't walk me right into this. "This is the kind of shit people expect from me. Honestly, you'd be doing me a favor."

Past-Brooke goes to speak first—to point out that technically if I left my helmet on, no one would know it was me he was pounding against the back of the bike. But future-Brooke pops onto my other shoulder, arguing that this is not the kind of behavior someone in their thirties trying to settle down would partake in. Sex? Sex is fine—I hope senile-Brooke is still getting laid. But I'm supposed to be taking all of this more seriously. And as serious as indecent exposure can be, that's not exactly what I had in mind.

"Take me home," I say, reaching forward and sliding his shield back into place. Drew hesitates for only an instant, then spins back around. He reaches to restart the engine but before he can, I palm him once again—with purpose this time—touching the side of my helmet to his. "But then, this is mine... however I want it."

24

Drew

"You knew this was going to happen when you pulled up to The Pub tonight, didn't you?"

"Oh, I sure hoped it would." I wrap my arms around Brooke, who against my wishes, searches her tan dresser drawer for a pair of pants.

"Well, Twelve, you sure fuck like you're twenty-five. I'll give you that," she says, turning around in my hold with a pair of those sleep shorts girls wear that are just a step above underwear.

My eyebrows shoot up as I suck my teeth, pulling her close. "And what's all this say about you, huh? You started it."

Her mouth drops open in disbelief, as if she took no part in the highway foreplay we admittedly both initiated at about the same time. I roll my eyes playfully, continuing to tease her.

"Brooke, you practically groped me from the back of my bike." Her face scrunches up as she pushes me away. "Just admit it. I'm irresistible, baby."

My hands open wide as I gesture to myself, only in my boxers. She shakes her head, bending to step into her shorts, and avoids eye contact. "Yeah, yeah, whatever," she mumbles sarcastically, peering up at me with a smirk on her face. "No one said putting down roots had to mean giving up getting laid."

"Just getting laid by anyone but me." My words shoot out quicker and more stern than I mean for them to, but I'm definitely not sorry about it. I was serious when I said I wanted Brooke. And I didn't mean for only that night.

"You keep doing that thing that you did with your tongue just then, and I don't think we'll have any problems with that."

I huff out a laugh as she smiles coyly, then I throw her a wink. "All part of my charm."

Brooke's eyes look toward the ceiling as she walks through her bedroom door. I follow her, studying the photos that line the navy blue wall, documenting everything from candids of a damn cute baby, to pictures of her with Coach's girl. There are also photos of her with a guy that looks like he's probably her brother and even one of her with the blonde from the bar—the one that didn't scare me shitless.

When we reach the living room, I really see it for the first time. We had to cross through to get to her bedroom, but when we busted through her apartment door like the hallway outside was on fire, my mind—and my eyes—weren't on anything but Brooke. My jeans may be strewn over the back of her fluffy, cream-colored couch, but I wasn't watching where they landed an hour ago. With her in front of me, my vision tunneled as it usually does.

I knew Brooke and I were compatible in more ways than one when we first locked eyes at the gala. Something in my bones told me she was different. But since then, I've realized just how alike we really are. Just how much we have in common. Starting with the bedroom.

She and I are both insatiable. I can never seem to be near her enough, on her enough, in her enough. And I know realistically, I *can't* be sure being that she keeps things close to her chest, but I am—the same way I was sure before—she feels it too.

It's the reason both of us felt the energy shift the second we stepped outside on our own at The Pub. The reason our hands started wandering the second my tire cleared the lot. One glance at each other and it's all either of us need. And it's not even physical. It's just a pull between us, drawing us together. One I never experienced before she walked into that ballroom.

"So, talk to me about this charm," Brooke says, settling into the corner of the couch.

I reach over her, purposefully leaning down a little more than necessary to grab my pants from just above her head. She kisses my chest gently before I pull away, and I swear it hits my soul.

"What about it?" I ask, ignoring the urge I have to take her here all over again.

"What parts of the *Drew Anderson* the world knows, would I actually be getting?"

I step into my jeans, Brooke watching my every move, as I contemplate my answer. "Why don't you tell me what *you* think?"

She rolls her tongue over her top teeth and sinks a little further into the cushion. "Well, I know the goal celebrations aren't you unless you like just throwing cash down the drain."

I laugh, my eyes on my jeans as I zipper them up. "Yeah, no. They used to be, back when I was a kid. But that shit is typically a dick move in the league. Hockey's a *we* sport, so showboating like that only really flies because I know how to toe the line."

"And because that's what the people want."

"Exactly." Plopping down on the middle of the couch, I pull her calves onto my lap and throw my arm over her legs.

"And the parties, the world traveling, the ladies-man thing. You're saying all of that's for appearances?" Her tone's not accusatory, though she wiggles her eyebrows like she's giving me shit.

"I mean, don't get me wrong—I like a good party or trip as much as the next guy. But I'd much rather kill a case with my friends or lay low in the mountains somewhere than close down the club or rent out an island."

She nods slowly, taking it all in. "And the women?"

I heave a deep sigh and trace a wave she has tattooed on her ankle. "I like to fuck, I think that's obvious." I glance up at her, her expression not giving me any reaction. "But those women you see me out with, a different celebrity every few days, that's not me. They're fine, I guess, but I don't like them like that. Hell, sometimes they don't like me either."

"But it looks good?"

"It paints a sexy picture. Keeps me relevant off the ice. It's the whole "women want me and men want to be me" thing. It's good for branding and marketing and shit, and all of that brings the Flames more attention. But they're not my type."

"Uh huh," she says, playing with the string of her shorts. "And what is your type then?"

"You."

My answer is quick and definitive and causes that faint blush that every so often creeps up her neck. But this is the first time anyone's ever talked this through with me. The first time anyone's ever really cared. And I'm not wasting it by tip-toeing around my thoughts.

"So... brunettes. Tattoos, nose rings, hilarious..."

"No," I say sternly. "Just you."

She smirks deliberately. "You think you're smooth."

"Well, yeah," I quip. "But I'm also serious, Brooke." I drag my hand up her leg, stopping just above her knee and brushing circles on the bottom of her thigh with my thumb.

She shuffles in her spot, wedging her hands between her legs. "Okay, so the angsty music is definitely yours. And so is the bike. I would have assumed you owned like a dozen different Lambos instead." I go along with her topic change, allowing my eyes to grow wide, impressed and agreeing that she's right about the ride.

"And the style..." She continues, sitting forward and looking me up and down. "The clothes and tattoos are you—badass but not flashy about it. But I'm gonna say the signature hair and gold chain are for the *look.*"

Out of habit, I run my hand through my overgrown locks. "You got the hair right. That's one of the first things I changed. I was told to *grow the flow.*"

She giggles, and I clear my throat before continuing. "But the chain, no, that's uh, that's me actually." She pulls her head back in surprise as I pick up the necklace and brush my thumb along the metal before dropping it again. "My mom gave it to me when I started high school. It was the last thing I got from her before she died."

She doesn't respond, not verbally at least. Instead, she reaches out and places her hand over mine that's resting on her knee. My eyes land on her touch, and I realize Brooke might know more about me after this short time than any other living person. It's surprising in a way, but also not at all. What does shock me, though, is how good it feels to be known. Seen. Listened to.

"She had pancreatic cancer," I continue unexpectedly, spinning the thin gold band on her middle finger. "Late-stage. We didn't find out until she only had about six months left. It all happened really fast, which is good and bad, I guess. She was my... my rock, really. My dad was always a lot, constantly pushing me. But my mom, she was—she was just different." I finally meet her eyes. "She kept me grounded."

Once again, Brooke stays quiet until she sits up and runs her hand past my cheek. I lean into her touch, my eyes closing softly when she pulls me to her and kisses me firmly. I sink into her lips. The wave of guilt that typically crashes in my chest when I think about how different I was when Mom was alive, only ripples by.

When we separate, I leave my forehead pressed to hers. "You're a good listener," I whisper.

She smirks and pulls back. "In case you were wondering, I like the chain."

Her avoidance once again hits me like whiplash. And this time, I'm not breezing past it. "You know, for what it's worth, I don't usually do this either."

"Do what?"

"Open up. Talk about feelings and shit."

She blushes before offering a shy smile. "Am I that obvious?"

I pick up her hand and lace my fingers through hers. "Only to someone who does the same thing."

"Oh, so you also avoid most emotions by shoving them down or blowing past them with humor?"

I shrug once and nod. "I usually lean more broody than funny but yeah, same idea."

She gives me a knowing look, and I cock a brow. "Angsty shit," we say simultaneously.

She snorts, and I huff out a quick laugh before I grow more solemn, pulling her hand back into my lap.

"You've been pretty open with me," she says, brushing her thumb across mine.

"Exactly," I say simply. "Because I'm trying here. But I'm not usually like this."

She nods without looking at me. "I'm just not big on... feelings."

"But you can be with me. I'm not even sure why I seem to be able to talk to you about shit literally no one else knows, but I clearly do. And fuck, it feels good. It feels like... like how I'm supposed to be. Which I guess is the whole point."

She responds by glancing at me and smiling with only her eyes. I narrow mine and reach forward, grabbing her by the waist and sliding her into my lap.

"Hey," I say, peering up at her. "I told you, I want this. I want *us*." I brush a loose hair behind her ear and search her gaze for understanding. "It won't be that simple out there. It's gonna take a little time and a whole lot of bullshit. But here with you, it's pretty damn easy. And that's what will help with the other stuff. You just have to let me in. Let me be *this* for *you*. Even if you are my mystery girl."

She arches her brow, dropping her hands around my neck. "You keep doin' that thing with your tongue—"

"Brooke, I'm serious."

She lets her lids fall shut with acceptance, before lifting them again. "Okay, okay, I know. You're right." I look at her smugly, and she rolls her eyes. "You're wise beyond your years, Twelve."

I consider pushing her. Asking her questions or forcing the issue so that she'll at least tell me how she feels about us. But I know better than anyone that just because you don't talk about a feeling, doesn't mean it's missing. So instead, I keep it simple, reminding myself that she's hiding it because it's there. And because it's big. Intense. Deeper than she probably ever expected.

"And you're scared I'm too young," I joke with a shake of my head.

Brooke visibly settles, pulling herself closer to me. "I mean, I don't know if I'm *scared*."

"You're scared."

She tilts her head sideways and looks at the ceiling. "Eh, hesitant maybe."

"Terrified."

"Skeptical."

"Straight up panicked." I plant a kiss on the side of her throat, and she opens up for me. "But I told you, you're worried for nothing."

"Let me guess," she starts, her words vibrating against my lips. "Your favorite cliché... actions speak louder than words."

"Exactly."

"Well..." She digs her fingertips into my shoulder muscles as I continue pecking up her neck. "There's still plenty of time to prove me right."

I pause my lips, hovering right next to her cheek. "Don't bank on that, Mystery Girl," I whisper, nipping her ear as my warm breath floats past her skin. "I've built a whole career on being pretty damn convincing."

Brooke hums, resisting every urge I know she has to simply submit. "We'll see."

I slide my hand under the flimsy material of her shorts to where I know she's naked underneath. "Yeah, baby," I say, brushing the pad of my finger past her middle. "You definitely will."

I'm dragging a little this morning, the lack of proper recovery from my game not quite mixing well with mine and Brooke's long night.

We didn't go to bed late—she had a meeting with Sadie, our community relations director, this morning—but by the time we were finally finished with each other and got back to her car, I could have slept for much longer than I was able to.

But my alarm rang at my regular hour, and as much as I'd love to take a day off, that's just not a luxury I have. Plus, I haven't been able to visit Mom all week thanks to my away games, so there's no way I'm missing this morning's run.

I've got a lot to catch her up on.

Approaching my mom's site, I swear I see the silhouette of someone kneeling by her tombstone. I wipe sweat from my eyes, assuming it's my mind playing tricks on me, but as I get closer, I know I'm wrong. It's not a trick. But still a joke.

"Dad?" I rip my headphones from my ears and shove them into my pocket. "What are you doing here?"

"You left so quickly yesterday, and you aren't taking my calls. I figured this might be the only way to talk to you."

I take a deep breath, my head lolling backward as I set my palms on my hips. "How did you even know I'd be here?"

Dad rests his hands behind his back. "It's sort of my job to know this stuff, Drew."

"You do know you're not my manager, right? I pay someone else to do that."

He scoffs, crossing his arms over his chest. "You do know I'm still your dad, right? And since you went dark on me, I've had to stoop to chasing you down—showing up outside of the locker room and at your mother's grave for Christ's sake."

"Yeah, God forbid you come on your own," I mumble under my breath, making a mental note to remind my people who they work for. "I told you I just need some space."

Dad hangs his head as if *I'm* the one causing *him* grief. "Well, did you at least give some thought to what I said?"

"Dad, no!" I yell at a volume that's definitely not cemetery etiquette. My frustration over his relentlessness these past few weeks, finally rips through me. "I'm not leaving the Flames."

He tilts his chin down calmly and raises a finger. "I didn't say leave necessarily. I told you to keep your options open."

I shake my head at his technicality. "Well, I'm not doing that either."

Dad takes one step closer to me, his hands up in surrender. "I just think you're missing out on an opportunity to make more money. To lead another franchise to a Cup. To be a bigger fish in a smaller pond. Golden City's organization is grow—"

"A bigger fish? Dad, are you serious?" I ask, interrupting him. "My God, you don't fucking get it. I don't *want* to be a bigger fish. I barely want to be *a* fish anymore. All this shit—the on-ice antics, the media, the headlines, the paparazzi—it's too much."

"Drew, this is what we built."

"We? You're kidding me, right? *We* didn't build—no. No, you know what?" Now it's me who holds my hands up, only not in surrender—in finality. "I'm not doing this. Not here."

Dad attempts to close the gap between us again, but I counter his movement, stepping back once more. "Listen, son, I don't want to fight with you," he says, his voice defeated. "I just want you to have what's best. Everything you're capable of. Everything you deserve."

I contemplate jumping in—telling him that I don't want any of what he thinks I deserve. But it's not worth my breath. It'll never get through. "Just consider not signing your contract until the end of the season and see what offers come in."

I glance at my mom's tombstone, wishing more than anything that she was here to jump in and defend me. But she's not. She's gone. And this is all that I have left of her. "Yeah, Dad, sure," I agree, knowing damn well that despite how good starting over may feel, I'm not going anywhere.

He strides over to me with a closed-lip smile and places his hand on my shoulder, giving it a tight squeeze. "Thank you, son."

He continues moving past me, his footsteps growing fainter as he walks away.

"Hey Dad," I call to him without looking back. When the crunching of the grass under his shoes stops completely, I finally turn to face him. "You know you can come here other than to trap me, right?"

He looks at me blankly, his expression unchanging, until he offers me that same hesitant smile from before. He goes on his way at the same time that my phone rings, Jane's name flashing across my screen.

"Holy shit," I say to myself, rubbing my forehead with the palm of my hand. I silence my phone and sit down in my usual spot, ignoring the world and turning my attention to one of the only two people lately that I find myself running *to* instead of *from*.

25

Brooke

Twelve
Can I see you?
Ugh, on my way to have dinner with my parents and brother.
Twelve
Should I be offended you didn't invite me? You did almost meet my dad the other night.
Trust me, I'm doing you a favor. Blake's cool, but my parents would just bore you with how big of a disappointment I am.
Twelve
I can't even imagine your name and disappointment in the same sentence.

> That's what I'm saying. I'm great. They're just crazy. Mostly my mom.

Twelve

> That sucks, I'm sorry.

> How about after?

Twelve

> As tempting as you are, I should probably sleep tonight. Early game tomorrow.

> Good call. Rain check.

Closing my phone, I hop into my car to head over to my parents'. I flick on the radio, and the first song that blasts through the speakers seems like something Drew would like. The beat is quick, the vocals loud, but the lyrics are deeper than you'd expect them to be for something so lively. Honestly, it's a lot like him.

I never expected that he'd open up to me the way he already has. Or that he'd see that I struggle with doing the same—and call my ass right out on it. I'm not used to airing out all my feelings—or any of them, really. But my playmaker seems to be keeping score.

My entire life I've been told that what I want—what I *feel*—is wrong, immature, atypical. That if it wasn't what my mom expected, then it wasn't worth acknowledging. I guess somewhere along the line, I decided it was easier to keep the heavy stuff to myself. And now, it's almost uncomfortable talking about those things at all. I guess, like anything, if you don't practice it, you can't get better. All I know is that when people press me to open up, I get physically uncomfortable. Maybe it's made me a little guarded—it's definitely made me funnier—but it's also shielded me from any more judgement or criticism.

Despite my *one* flaw, I really do like Drew... a lot, actually. I think a year ago I was enamored with him. What girl wouldn't be with a working lady part between their legs? But that night at the gala really changed things for me. I saw him differently than I had before, and that pulled me in even more than the flashy surface stuff ever could. I just never expected that I'd see that version of him again.

But I have. Over and over.

And I'm learning that's who he's been all along underneath the uniform he wears. Not the one with twelve stitched across the back, but the armor he sports for the world. And the truth is... I could actually see myself falling for him.

He's everything past-Brooke wanted—sexy, badass, amazing in bed. But he's also everything future-Brooke needs—thoughtful, reflective, self-aware. And I don't think I've ever had a man see me like he has before. I don't only mean that he's attracted to me, although our chemistry is undeniable. But I mean really understand who I am. Without me having to bare my soul. And sometimes before I even admit to myself what's going on inside my head. It's refreshing and liberating but also, scary as hell.

I'm not used to getting this deep with someone so quickly—or at all for that matter. Most guys would rejoice in the fact that I'm "unemotional" or "easy going," and we'd live in the shallow end until the whole thing fizzled out—if we even made it past the bedroom. But Drew? He sees through it. And he's pushing me for more.

He's only twenty-five, and I worried that meant he wouldn't want to settle down—that he wouldn't know how to. But now, I think Drew's showing me that sometimes wisdom doesn't come with age. Maybe you get wiser the more life throws at you. And if anyone's been dodging life's shrapnel these last few years, it's him.

With sharp projectiles in mind, I pull into my parents' driveway. I really need to start getting out of these again. The Flames did me dirty these past couple weeks not having a game on Family Dinner Night, but hopefully, the work I've been doing will be enough to get me through this meal without my mother passive-aggressively cursing my name across the table.

One last song plays before I kill the engine, dragging my mind right back to Drew. It's funny how such a big personality to the rest of the world is so impacted by the smallest things. The silence in the shooting bay, the seemingly meaningless chain he wears around his neck—how his whole demeanor changes when music's involved. I picture the way his face lit up in the showers that day during our tour or how settled he was in the gym once his songs came on. Not relaxed exactly but focused. Present. As if music was the one thing that could soothe the chaos in his mind.

The realization hits me. We're actually so alike. Two totally different people—different worlds, different reputations, different ages. And yet, all we want is to be seen, loved for who we *really* are. I guess that's true for anyone. People just want to be themselves and not feel wrong or unaccepted. But some of us just say, *screw it.* And we live life on our own terms, throwing out the ideas people have in their heads for who we're *supposed* to be—or shoving them deep down until we're ready.

Others, like Drew, don't get that luxury. For me, the stakes are personal. It's just my family, and I've spent the past thirty-one years letting them down. What's one more disappointing dinner? Plus, my change will actually work in my favor.

But for Drew, the stakes are higher. His image isn't just his own. He has the weight of his team, his coaches, his fans—all of Golden City on his shoulders. And he's not just looking to live his truth. He's looking to tear it down, brick by boisterous, bad boy brick. I thought uprooting *my* life and changing everything I've come to know has been hard. I can't imagine how difficult it will be for him to do the same.

With that in mind, I push open my car door and slide out, shutting it loudly enough for my mom to know I'm here... two minutes early. Of course, this is the one time she chooses not to accost me at the door. Instead, I walk into the house like a peasant, with no greeting at all.

Until I hear *her.*

"Ivy?" I whisper to myself.

I bound towards the opening at the end of the hallway, and when I step through it, my eyes land on Mom assembling plates as she always does. But yep. There it is. Her tight-lip, high-brow, hostess smile.

Peering through the dining room, past where the usually empty spot next to mine is set with a napkin and silverware, I glance into the living space. There she is, sitting on the loveseat across from Dad and Blake.

"Aunt Ivy!" I call, darting toward her, dodging Amy and Selah on the floor playing blocks.

Ivy pushes her red glasses up her nose before opening her arms to receive me. "You're glowing," she whispers in my ear.

"You say that every time I see you," I softly say back.

She holds me in our embrace a little longer than usual. "But this time it was the moose, wasn't it?"

My cheeks immediately warm as I clear my throat and pull away from her. I offer her an awkward smile, full of warning that, no doubt, tells her everything she needs to know. "I didn't know you'd be here," I say, my voice slightly higher than normal. I catch a glimpse of Mom's side-eye as she fills bowls with salad, and I can't tell if it's because she assumes I'm being rude or if she's suspicious of my behavior.

"Oh, well, the last time I breezed through, your mama convinced me to hit a doctor for once. Handsome fella, but a little old for me." She winks in my direction before leaning back into the cushions. "They said they wanted to run a few more tests—I think he just wanted to see me again. But either way..." She raises her voice a notch or two higher, calling over the dining room to Mom. "I knew your mother wouldn't let it go if I didn't come back for them." Lowering her voice to a whisper once more, she leans into the space between the couches. "I think she just wanted to see me again, too."

Blake and Dad both huff out a laugh as Selah whacks the tower of colorful blocks that Amy just meticulously stacked one on top of the other. "Boom!" she yells, throwing her hands in the air. The group of us start laughing, and when she finally scans the room, she locks eyes with me.

"Book!" she calls, her little face lighting up. "I build."

"It looks like you break," I reply cheerfully, my eyes just as wide as hers. She giggles and returns to watching Amy intently as she reconstructs the pile again, a hint of mischief in her expression.

"So, is everything okay?" I ask, turning back to Ivy. "With the tests?"

She waves me off, sliding one leg under herself. "Oh, enough about that. Tell me how the job's going."

"I second that," Blake chimes in. "My autograph collection's still a little light."

I roll my eyes, noticing Dad's impassive expression as he sits indifferent to my next response. "It's going really well, actually," I answer confidently, making sure to hold eye contact with both Mom and Dad as I do. "Monte actually told me the owner himself commented about how good the content has been lately. He says I'm doing a great job at getting the fans involved."

"Aww," Amy says, her face full of concentration as she finally places the last block. Selah instantly throws her tiny fist into the finished product, and Amy sighs, an easy grin on her lips.

"Dude, that video you posted of Anderson was cool. That guy's curling at least double what I do." Amy peers over, quickly attempting to cover up her curiosity about Drew's obvious muscle. "Didn't know he was a Tom Ford guy, though. Maybe I'll have to switch it up."

"From what? The same cologne Mom got you for Christmas senior year?"

Blake looks at me blankly, his chest puffed out, but after half a second, his shoulders fall. "Yes," he admits.

Ivy snickers next to me, and I shake my head. "Yeah, that was, uh, an interesting day."

"So, what's next? I know you said this is only temporary, but you seem to enjoy it?"

"I do, yeah. I told them last week that I'm thinking about finding something in this field permanently. Really start to build a career doing something I actually enjoy."

Ivy places her hand on my knee and gives it a light squeeze. "That's great, Brookie."

"Maybe the Flames would let you stay on after this sort of trial period," Blake says, leaning forward and placing his forearms on his thighs.

"Oh, no, I don't think so. Levi already has someone permanent starting soon, and I don't think they're looking to fill anymore positions—especially with someone just starting out."

My mind snaps back to Drew. We all know that, technically, I *could* work for the Flames and still be with him. Hell, Alex helps Sadie run Spark the Flame, and she's banging—and, okay, is spending her life with—the head coach. But I don't want to finally start a new job that I hope will turn into my life's career and always wonder if I got it as a favor. More importantly, I don't want my parents to be able to hold that above my head every time they get nostalgic and are tempted to throw my job in my face for old time's sake. I want the roots I finally grow to be *mine*. And that's the real reason I don't want this thing with Drew coming out until after these next few weeks.

"Have you applied anywhere else?"

I nibble on my lower lip, pretending not to notice Mom's piqued interest from across the room. "Not exactly. It's all still new, and I haven't seen anything come up just yet."

I glance up at Mom, who makes a poor attempt at hiding an eye roll as she heads toward the table with two plates in hand. "But I'll be look—"

"Dinner's ready," she calls. "Let's eat before the food gets cold."

Dad springs off the couch as Blake offers me an empathetic smile before standing and scooping Selah off the floor. Amy follows them, leaving Ivy and me as the last ones in the room. When I turn toward her, she's still looking at me. I tuck my lips in and raise my brow, attempting to stand, but before I lift off the couch, she stops me, a firm hand back on my knee.

"It's all going to work out, Brookie. I can feel it."

I exhale heavily, squeezing her hand and hoping she's right.

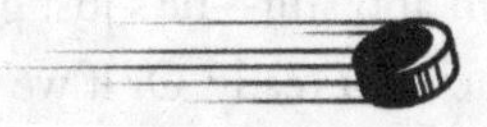

"Aunt Ivy!" I run through my parents' front door, careful not to fall down their steps as I chase after my aunt. As soon as dessert was done, she threw her patchwork satchel over her shoulder and announced her exit, and I was elbow deep in Cool Whip thanks to Selah, my worst influence.

Ivy turns back around just as she's about to step off of the sidewalk to round the front of her current ride—a burnt orange pickup with a rusted bumper and a pink elephant air freshener.

"These tests..." I say once I finally reach her, my breathing heavier than I'd like to admit. *Damn.* It'd be nice if all this time near professional athletes would rub off on me in some kind of way. "Everything's okay, right? You didn't give us much detail."

"No results yet! Can you believe it? All these body scanners and beeping machines and you still have to wait to get your answers." She opens the passenger door and sets her purse on the seat. "But I'm fine, Brookie, really," she continues, slamming it shut.

"You're sure? You feel okay?"

"Oh, I'm fine. You know doctors, always poking and prodding." Ivy scoops my hands into hers. "Now quick, tell me about the boy." Her subject change catches me off guard, but the thought of talking about being with Drew to, well, anyone, is all it takes to rattle my brain enough to move past it with her.

I drop her hands and bring my fingertips to my forehead, massaging away the nervous energy. "It's him—the hockey player." She claps her hands together quietly, then brings them just below her chin, a full smile spread above them. "God, I think I really like him. But Ivy, it's so... complicated."

"Why, darling?"

I blow out a breath. "Just because of who he is." *At least to the world.* "He's younger than I am and still—he's just got a lot going on. I don't want to get invested if he's not ready. Or if we're too different."

Ivy tilts her head in the way that she always does when she's about to say something that she wants to stick. "I believe in timing more than anything, you know this. There's a reason the universe put you two together now, even when things feel messy or unexpected."

I glance down the quiet street, the sun just starting to set, that Golden City glow forming in the distance. Drew's smile pops into my mind—cocky, but real—and I think of the way he looked at me that first night at the gala like I was the only person in the room. Back when the last thing I thought I wanted was to settle down.

"What if I let him in and it doesn't work out? Then I've just wasted more time."

My eyes make their way back to Ivy's as a lump forms in my throat. I realize I'm once again second-guessing myself, flipping back from my decision earlier in my car and hoping her answer will convince me one way or another.

My aunt leans forward and takes my hand again. "But what if it does and you waste no time at all."

Her words settle in my chest, warm and weightless—a little terrifying—but exactly what I needed to hear.

26
Drew

I woke up this morning to possibly the sexiest notification I could have received. The kind that makes me want to start my day off with an actual bang and turns morning wood into something that *needs* to be handled. Rolling over, already battling the usual mixture of nerves and adrenaline about today's game, I read the one message that stopped everything cold:

Brooke Larkin has sent you a playlist.

I paused where I was, my face—and my heart—lighting up at the gesture. *I knew this girl was special.* Clicking on it, a million other thoughts ran through my mind as it loaded. Which songs did she pick? Why did she pick them? What made her think to make this in the first place? When it finally downloaded, I scanned the list, snickering at the ones that I knew.

The first few were some of the songs that played at the gym the morning that she shadowed me. Then, there was the Blink 182 song that I almost forgot existed until she cracked that joke at the gala. A couple were about being yourself and not giving a shit—ones I already know and love. And then there was one that made me laugh out loud just because of the name—the last one on the list that I had never heard before. At least not until it became my new favorite song.

The whole list has been playing on repeat my entire ride to the arena, but stopping at a red light, I pull out my phone and tap the last track again. I roll into the arena's lot as MGK's *Cliché* plays through my headphones, and let the words rush over me for what feels like the millionth time already this morning.

It's more upbeat than some of the songs I listen to regularly, especially before a game, but it has all the same familiar bottom lines. The sound is uplifting, but the lyrics are raw and deep—a heartfelt confession that he knows he's flawed.

And a quiet plea for her to take a chance on him anyway.

It makes me wonder why she added it. Was it just the title? The one that must remind her of our new inside joke. Or did she hear something in the lyrics that made her think of me? Because it's as if I wrote the words myself—took a play out of Petrov's book and put my thoughts on paper. For her.

I sit on my bike after parking for a little longer than I should, letting the song play until the end. The chorus lingers in the back of my mind as it rings out for the last time—words about how he and his girl could run away or build a home, even if technically, she's better off without him. If only she would wait for him—until he has it all together.

I know I should get in there—warm ups start in an hour, and I like to be early enough to not feel rushed. But for a second, that doesn't matter. Because it finally hits me. And as the playlist ends, I repeat the song again.

Technically, Brooke could have chosen it because she thought it was funny. Or because something about the word cliché just reminds her of me now. But the lyrics hit too close to home for it to be so simple. It can't be. Because it's everything I haven't said out loud.

I'm trying to be open and show her I care—in the small gestures and the quiet details that I'm sharing about my life. But despite giving more of myself to her than anyone else, I haven't told her all of it.

The fact that I'm fighting to maintain my confidence with Brooke and that I'm scared the real me isn't good enough—for the world or for her. I'm scared that she's right—I'm too young to have it all together like she needs. And I'm terrified that if I don't figure out how to show her I do, that she'll move on without me, and I'll be left more trapped than I am now.

But she sees that. She sees me. And this song is proof. It has to be. This girl, with her curated confidence and strategic silences, made *me* a goddamn playlist. And she knew exactly what she was doing—this is her way of opening up.

The thought sends a heat both to my chest and further south. I thought Brooke was sexy as my mystery girl, but that was before I got this side of her. The vulnerable side—even if it takes some reading between the lines.

Eventually, I take my headphones out, kill the engine, and swing my leg over my seat, setting my helmet on the cushion like I always do. It's time to lock in—to gather myself for the game and put on the face I need to wear in an hour. But right now, the only thing on my mind is showing Brooke how much I loved her gesture. And how much it fucking turns me on that she's finally comfortable giving me a little more.

Walking toward the locker room, I pull up our text chain. I consider telling her exactly how I'd like to repay her for the playlist, but I decide I'd rather *show* her after the game instead. I begin typing out my message, a cheesy smile on my face, when a familiar voice catches me off guard.

"Son."

My head flies up, my eyes landing on a set of blue eyes that perfectly mirror my own. My dad's standing there, his silver hair perfectly gelled away from his face, his beard trimmed and sculpted as always. He pushes off the wall he's leaning on, his hands tucked into the front pocket of his Flames hoodie, his fresh Nikes brushing against the pebbles on the pavement as he walks toward me.

"Dad, not now," I say, trying to save any residual buzz from my ride over while attempting to finish my text to Brooke.

"Did you hear about Cam Rourke?"

"Nope," I answer bluntly, my fingers hovering over the letters I can't seem to focus on.

"He just called a press conference."

I fumble through a word or two before losing my train of thought. "Okay."

"Drew..."

I sigh, stopping next to him in front of the door and surrendering, shoving my phone back into my pocket—text unsent. I know Dad's dancing around the real reason he brought up Washington's star forward. And rather than waste anymore time with this conversation, I decide to get it over with.

"So, he's retiring."

Dad tucks his lips in and nods. "Looks like it."

"And what does that have to do with me?"

He tilts his head, questioning me. "You know the shoes the Titans will have to fill. They'll need a new goal scorer. A new personality. Someone to lead their team and bring the recognition to their organization that Cam did."

I hike my backpack up on my shoulders and tuck my hands into my suit pants, my jacket suddenly warmer than it was before. "And you think that should be me?"

"Don't you? Scott sure does. He said—"

"What the fuck?" I yell. "Why are you talking to my agent?"

He waves me off as his eyes flutter toward the sky. "It was just casual, relax." I scoff as if that's the point, but he continues. "Think of what they'll be willing to give you, son. How much of an impact you could make there. They've got a good team, but they need fresh eyes—new skates. You could make huge moves over there."

"In Washington? Dad, why would I want to leave Golden City?"

He exhales, dropping his head briefly before meeting my gaze again. "You've made your mark here. Got your Cup. You don't want to stay stagnant."

"Stagnant? What? It's called foundation. Roots. Loyalty."

"Loyalty? What about that test they never let you forget?"

My eyes grow wide in disbelief. He can't possibly mean the same test I failed trying to avoid his judgement. "Are you serious? These guys are the *only* ones who have let that go."

He opens his mouth to speak, but then closes it again, keeping his initial response to himself. "Just keep it in mind like we talked about, okay? This could be your shot to move on from here. To start somewhere fresh and still be that big fish." He steps forward, placing his hand on my shoulder. "Think about it, son. Change might be good."

I suck my teeth, my blood pumping and his words echoing in my mind, but not the way he intended them to. I realize Dad's thoughts aren't relevant anymore—they're just noise. Because if there's anything I need to outrun, it's him.

"Yeah, I agree," I say, Brooke's playlist humming in my chest like a second heartbeat, her face at the forefront of my mind. "I definitely think a change would be good."

Dad looks at me satisfied, assuming that we're on the same page, and I don't bother correcting him before I clap him on the shoulder. "I'll see ya in there, Dad," is all I say before heading through the door.

I barely make it halfway down the hall toward the locker room in search of some sort of distance from him—some sort of relief in general—when my phone pings in my pocket. I groan, holding my breath as I pull it out, waiting for a follow-up text from Dad. Instead, Brooke's name flashes across my screen. I suck in a full breath for what feels like the first time since stepping off of my bike, and swipe it open immediately.

Mystery Girl

Good luck today!

I bite my lip, stifling a smirk as that ache to thank her creeps back in below my belt at full force. Without checking the time or overthinking it, I respond with my natural reaction.

I need her.

Where are you?

I bust through the locker room door, waiting for a response. A handful of guys throw me a, *yo* or *what's up?*, but I respectfully brush them off as I stride to my stall. I shrug off my backpack and suit jacket, hanging them up as my phone vibrates again.

Mystery Girl

Just leaving the social media office. Gonna head back toward the tunnel to prep.

I freeze, immediately searching my mental map of the facilities, calculating which rooms fall between where she is and where I am. I quickly unbutton my white shirt and pants as I figure out my answer. Everything's connected somehow, but there's one room I can get to in less than a minute, that would open up to exactly where she is. I slide out of my shirt and pants, tossing them carelessly into the stall, then grab my phone again.

Don't move.

I don't even bother putting my gitch on first. Instead, I dart toward the hall at the other end of the locker room, and right before I hit the showers, I step toward the room that *should* separate me from Brooke. Scanning my finger, I wait for the lock to click open like waiting for the final seconds of a penalty kill to wind down to zero. When it finally does, I dip inside, speed walking over the tile floor.

My heart rate quickens. I'm grateful my briefs are black and tight enough to do a half-decent job at concealing my body's reaction to the anticipation of seeing her. My breath grows heavy despite the short distance to the opposite door, but when I push it open, all of it stops.

She's here.

"Hey you," I say, my voice low. There shouldn't be a lot of traffic on this side of the facilities so close to a game, but the last thing I need today is anymore unwanted attention.

Her face brightens, a mixture of surprise and amusement, as she quickly glides toward me. "What are you—wait, why are you in your under—?"

"Would you just get in here?" I practically beg as I slide my hand behind her back and pull her past my body propping the door open. We both slink into the room, and I close the door behind me, turning back to see her, my mood instantly lifted.

"I thought you weren't much of a spa guy," she says as if it's a question.

I grab her hand and lead her to the sauna tucked in the corner of the room. Popping the glass door open, I pull her inside before shutting it again, my need for her growing more intense by the second now that she's in such close proximity.

"I'm whatever kind of guy gets to have you," I say, my voice huskier than before as we move toward the wall-to-wall, two-tiered benches at the back of the cedar box. When my shins hit the wood, I spin around, yanking her into my arms.

"I take it you liked the playlist then?" she asks, her voice laced with humor as she gives me an obvious once-over.

"Loved it," I say, mine dry with desire as I dip down to kiss her neck.

Brooke hums, and the vibration hits my lips, then shoots right to my cock sitting between us. "Mmm, good. Which song was your favorite?" I continue sucking at the skin just below her jaw, and she giggles as she continues. "Let me guess, the NF song."

"No," I growl, nipping her ear. "The last one."

Brooke gasps, maybe because of my answer, maybe because my hand is now gliding under her bra. "I'm obsessed with that song."

"You got a thing for broken blonde guys?" I ask, standing back up and looking her in the eyes, one brow arched high.

Her face falls slightly, her irises growing darker. She pauses, scanning my expression.

"You aren't broken, Drew," she eventually says. My heart and my cock both swell from her words, the fire that was once building inside me threatening to burn this fucking place down if I don't put it to use.

I dive into her, doing my best to tell her with my lips exactly how she makes me feel. How that one statement alone could piece me—the *real* me—back together. Brooke dips her tongue in to meet mine, and they dance in perfect rhythm. Her palms land on my chest, her fingertips dragging down my torso until they reach the waistband of my boxers. She grazes her hand over the tight material, moaning into my mouth as she touches me through it.

As if on instinct, I grab her hips and spin both of us until we've switched spots, throwing them around until she's facing the benches, her back flush against me. I reach around, wrapping my hand around her neck and pulling back until her ear is next to my mouth.

"Thank you," I whisper, pressing harder into her.

"It's just a playlist," she pants back.

I slide my hand back into her bra, rolling her nipple between my fingers. "Sure it is," I say, knowing damn well that this was her first way of giving me more—of unraveling just a little in a language she knows I understand. It was more than a song list. Shit, it might as well have been a goddamn love letter.

Brooke looks over her shoulder at me knowingly, and the thought urges me on, the ticking clock in the back of my mind reminding me I have a game to play. As if she hears it too, Brooke pushes back into me, grinding her ass against my cock. I exhale loudly as I drop my hands, groaning when I reach for the button of her jeans and find them already open.

"You're always ready for me, baby."

I yank them down, leaving them in a pile at her ankles, then press between her shoulder blades until her palms find the highest bench. My dick begs for release at the sight of her as she waits for me, bent-over—no questions asked.

Pulling it out, I place one foot on the lowest bench, bringing us as close as possible as I slam right into her pussy. A guttural sound rips from my throat as I finally slide into her, her walls slicked perfectly for me without any warm up. "Always fucking ready."

Brooke whimpers as I pull out and drive back in again, her knuckles white as she grips the wood in front of her. I continue that rhythm at a relentless pace, the two of us meeting in a perfect collision. When Brooke arches below me, her head lolling back, I lean down, placing my hands on either side of hers and framing her in my arms. With my chest to her back, I continue moving until I can feel she's close from the way her walls are closing in on me even tighter than before.

"Look at me," I demand in her ear. She snaps her head to the side, her hooded eyes meeting mine. "See what happens when you let me in."

Even in this vulnerable position, she tries to brush me off, her gaze floating away from me. "It was no big deal," she argues, her voice desperate.

I freeze, my cock still buried inside her, and her eyes grow wide, her muscles tensing as she holds tighter onto the bench. "It was to me."

"Drew," she whines, her pussy clenching around me.

I groan as she squeezes and releases again, forcing myself to hold still. "It wasn't all the way, but it's a start," I say, pulling one hand back and sucking on my first two fingers. I wrap my arm around her waist and dip them between her legs, rubbing slow, steady circles on her clit. "And I fucking loved it, baby."

Brooke cries out, the sexiest sound, as I spread her and drag my thumb down her center. "Okay," she pants. "Good. Now keep moving."

"You gonna keep that up, Mystery Girl?" I ask, brushing one finger over her most sensitive spot. I somehow grow harder from her begging, but I need this answer. I need more of her. "Or are you gonna pull away again?"

Brooke hangs her head between her arms and breathes heavily. When she turns back to me, the corner of her lips are curled upward, her eyes hungrier than ever. "I'll tell you what, I'll give you more if you give me more."

"I've told you so much—"

"Actions," she interrupts, dropping one hand over mine between her thighs. "I want to see you be *you* out there today." My jaw clenches as her words settle in, and she guides my fingers to move in quicker strokes. "I'll make it worth your while."

This fucking girl.

I pull out of her just a little before slamming back in, our fingers still moving. "Is that a challenge, Brooke?"

She lets her eyes flutter closed as our hands circle faster, my cock throbbing for release inside her. "It's a promise," she gasps, her legs starting to quiver.

Throwing her hand from mine, I slap her pussy right where our fingers left off, sliding out of her simultaneously before driving back in, harder than ever. Brooke cries out, her whole body tensing. Her walls grip my cock like the two were fucking made for each other, and it's all that I need to empty inside her.

I slow my pace as we both recover, my mind replaying her last words. But before I pull out completely, I lean back down to her. "Don't leave," I whisper.

She tilts toward me, resting her head on my shoulder, her breathing still labored. "You're literally still inside me, Twelve."

I huff out a laugh as I wrap my arms around her waist, tethering myself to her without her even realizing it. She smiles and rolls her eyes as she lays her arms on top of mine, but all I can think about is the aftermath I know will come if I follow through with what she said.

I can tell myself I don't care—fuck it, you can't hurt me when I'm numb to it all. But I'm not numb to Brooke. Not even a little. And I don't want her backing out because of what they say. Or because of how she sees me.

"Just do me a favor. Promise that, too."

27

Brooke

Watching Drew Anderson on the ice is always mesmerizing. Watching him not even an hour from the last time he was inside of you is a totally different experience. Not to mention the fact that I now know how hard he's working to make this all look effortless. It's amazing to think he's performing twice every time he laces up—amazing, and yet, still so sad. But hopefully not something that will go on much longer.

I knew he'd like the playlist. I didn't realize it'd mean as much to him as it seemed to, but I know music is his love language. What I didn't predict was how aware he'd be of why *I* made it. How lyrics seem to explain the things I think or feel in ways I would never be able to say aloud.

I am trying though. And I do want to let Drew in. I just didn't realize when I set out to settle down with someone seriously, how hard it would be to open up. It should be obvious—being in a relationship means giving someone your heart and trusting them not to completely destroy it. But I'm realizing that's the reason committing never seemed to appeal to me. Going all in is scary as hell. I get shit on every day by people who are supposed to love me—talk about a love language. Why would I willingly allow someone else to do the same?

"Alright, spill."

I practically throw the camera in my hands into the boards thanks to the jump scare Alex causes from sneaking up behind me. "Holy ninja! Warn a girl."

She shrugs standing in front of our seats, glancing over my shoulder at the boys as they skate to the bench for the final ice cut before puck drop. "Tell me whatever it is you're not telling me."

I stare straight ahead, hoping she'll suddenly get amnesia or lose this sixth sense she seems to have. *Damn her and her parental instincts.*

"You slept with him, didn't you?"

"I have no idea what you're talking about."

She inhales slowly, her eyes trailing Levi behind the bench. "Mhmm. Where was it this time? A kitchen, a laundry room... maybe a nice foyer."

"The shooting bay."

"The shooting bay?" she hisses back at me, turning her body so it faces mine.

I stay where I am, but take a deep, steadying breath, knowing the rest of this conversation's inevitable. Alex is my best friend. We don't keep secrets. Or at least not well.

"And his place," I add quickly.

"What?"

"And mine."

"B!"

"And the Flames' sauna like forty-five minutes ago."

At this point my words are just spewing out as quickly as possible to get the whole thing over with. I watch her mouth fall open from the corner of my eye before twisting to face her, waiting for any kind of verbal response. She holds that position, pausing briefly with her eyes narrowed and her lips still parted, until she finally leans in slightly.

"Was it on?" she whispers, her brows fully creased.

I roll my eyes as I face the ice again, escaping momentarily into the satisfaction that is the sleek lines that trail behind the Zamboni. "No, it wasn't on," I answer after it curves around the corner. Suddenly my head snaps back to her, a more important detail on her end yet to be mentioned. "But what gave it away?"

Now it's Al who rolls *her* eyes as she brings her attention back to our team's bench. "Please, B. I've known you for how long? And all but the last six months have involved seeing you quite frequently in your post-coital glow."

"Dammit," I mumble. "I do glow, don't I?"

Alex chuckles under her breath, crossing her arms over her chest. "Yeah," she says confidently. My whole face scrunches up as I curse myself for not preparing better for this conversation when she speaks again. "But you also smell like man."

I instantly raise my shoulder, inhaling deeply as I stuff my nose into the cotton of my gray Flames t-shirt. The all too familiar scent of my favorite player hits me, and I instantly ache between my thighs... and surprisingly, my chest. Drew's cologne takes me back to where we were just before this, his body pressed flush to mine, his warm breath lingering past my ear as he tried to punish me with his strong hands and flawless cock—his movements anything but cruel. I shiver at the memory of him pleading for me not to leave him, and my gaze coincidentally—or *not*—lands on him.

"Just be careful, B," Alex says, as I watch Drew talk to her husband, his helmet in his hands revealing his slick hair and boyish grin. For a second I wonder if he's smiling because of me until Alex brings me back to earth. "You're a tough one to crack, but once you do, you're total mush on the inside."

I look at her sideways, defensive but also reluctant to fully look away. "Am not."

She scoffs. "Mhmm. Tell that to my teenage son who has you eating out of his hand."

I suck my teeth and shake my head, my eyes following Drew as he walks down the bench, the entire front row of spectators banging on the glass beside him trying to get his attention. *Man, this really is a boy aquarium.*

I clear my throat of the annoyance—and slight jealousy—that's building in my chest from their relentless pursuit of him while he sits trying to prepare for his game. "That doesn't count," I eventually rebuke. "Cooper's young and adorable."

Alex laughs. "Yeah." She looks at me and smiles slyly as I stare at Drew. "That's exactly what I'm afraid of *here*."

Before I can argue that she makes me sound like a total creep, the lights dim slightly, and the announcer's voice booms through the arena as the players skate to their respective blue lines for the anthem. The crowd around us rises as I press my lips into a firm line and hold the camera up in front of my face, finally getting to the reason why I'm here in the first place.

Behind the lens, my focus drifts back to Drew standing at the end of the line. His stick is in one hand while his other arm hangs loosely by his side, his head bowed. The music starts playing, leading in the singer standing by the announcers' box, and for the first time since the sauna—where he froze while buried deep inside me—he's completely still.

Throughout all of warm ups he seemed to pace, occasionally diving into a stretch or spinning his stick as he caught a puck on the blade. He still gave the crowd his usual show of pouring water down his hair or spraying ice at the glass as he came to a stop. But his energy was shifted slightly. Even if I'm the only one who would have noticed.

Attempting to focus the lens with my mind on his well-being, I slowly lower my pointer on the shutter button. Just as it clicks, Drew raises his head and brings his eyes right to me as I snap the first shot of the day.

I lower my camera to meet his gaze, but that quickly, it's back on the ice. Instead, I scan the image that's momentarily up on the preview. It's Drew—a little blurry and slightly off-center—but it's him.

And maybe that's the perfect start to the game.

As the clock winds down to the end of the first period, I look at Alex who has been straining to keep quiet this whole time. Admittedly, Drew has been playing... not his best. He's fumbled a few passes, missed the net on the only shot he's taken, and turned the puck over more than a couple times. Nothing outlandish—the Flames are still up by one—but definitely not his norm. *And maybe that's the problem.*

I follow him as he lines up for the last minute of play, his body language slouched in defeat, and Alex peers over at me, her eyebrows high but her lips sealed shut.

"Don't," I say bluntly, my heart-rate kicking up.

"B..." she presses.

"Al..."

She stares through me until I look at her. "Did you break him?"

"No!" I shout, quickly glancing around to make sure I didn't draw any attention. "No," I repeat quieter, but more definitively. Alex holds my gaze as everything about Drew's situation and his feelings toward it—as well as our last conversation—runs through my mind.

His dad, his attitude, his PR manager.

"I'll tell you what, I'll give you more if you give me more."

"I want to see you be you out there today."

"I promise I'll make it worth your while."

"I don't think so," I whisper under my breath.

Alex smacks me with the back of her hand. "Brooke!"

"No, that's not what I—here." I toss my camera in her lap and jump from my seat. "I'll be right back."

I hit the stairs, rushing toward the main concourse. Thankfully, during my meeting with Sadie from Spark the Flame, she gave me the inside scoop on how to get back to the facilities quickly from the stands in case I needed any last minute pieces of equipment. *Thank God for that woman's attention to detail.* Luckily for me, the directions still apply even if what I need is worth a little more than a tripod.

As I bound down the first turn toward the offices, the buzzer sounds throughout the arena signaling the end of the first period of play. Frazzled, I spin around, gathering my bearings, knowing that somehow this hallway leads me to three places—the exit, the rest of the facilities, and the tunnel I need to be at in just a few seconds. Holding my breath and making my best guess, I stride down the longest hall, knowing if I'm wrong, I won't make it in time.

My heart pumps as I move as quickly as possible, the full weight of skipping a half dozen classes at *Beats & Barbells* hitting me quite literally in the center of my chest. The thumping of skates on rubber bounce off the walls of the corridor as I finally make it to the far side of the tunnel, my ear pressed against the only barrier between me and the team like I'm some sort of spy. Voices begin floating under the threshold, mostly grumbling, until I finally gain some insight on where Drew could be in the mix of the boys. Thanking God for Brett Burns's ridiculously loud voice, and his insistence on calling him Cap, I crack the door open. I watch as he pats Drew on the shoulder and hustles by him, leaving him last in the lineup like I knew he would be.

With my heart hammering inside my rib cage, and my hands border-line trembling, I push the door open further just in time to grab Drew by the sleeve of his jersey and yank him inside.

"What the fuck?" he snaps, stumbling through the doorway.

I quietly click it shut before turning around, and—

Holy hell. This was a terrible idea.

Standing—no, *dominating*—over me is a sweat-glistened, two-inch taller, twice as broad Drew, with heat behind his eyes and his chest still heaving. He looks about four shades of confused, but all I can think about is if it's possible to get a quickie in before anyone notices.

Swallowing hard and sweeping the crazy—*maybe possible?* No, definitely crazy—idea from my mind, I snap back to reality. "What are you doing?"

Drew's eyes grow wide as a bead of sweat drops from his forehead. "What am *I* doing?"

I huff out a breath, starting over. "What's going on out there?"

He shakes his head, his focus shifting away from me. "I'm playing like shit is what I'm doing."

"You're in your head, Twelve."

"What?" he barks.

"You heard me. You can do this. Just play as *you*."

He tucks a glove under his opposite arm and slips his hand out. Sliding it under his shield, he drags it down his face. "I can't. I'm freaking out. When I get the puck, I'm so busy overthinking not to play with it that I lose it altogether. When I take a shot, I'm so hyper-focused on not over-celebrating, that I miss the whole net in the first place." He shifts his weight on his skates and drops his head forward. "I don't even fucking know *how* to play as myself anymore."

A lump rises in my throat as I watch this massive man with confidence and swagger stitched into his jersey, slowly crumble—the weight of everyone else's opinions, criticisms, and expectations on his shoulders. Drew is cracking in front of me, the ego that typically defines him in this uniform, slowly collapsing.

My heart breaks for him. He's not trying to outrun a rumor or recover from a mistake. There's no failed drug test looming over his head. Drew's just trying to play the sport he loves the way he was made to. Not the way the world thinks he should.

"My aunt's sick," I blurt, the words flying out as my stomach sinks. Drew pulls back, the dread in his eyes morphing into something closer to concern. "Well, I think she is. She's had all these tests done which is saying something in the first place because, well, she's kind of a... free spirit."

Drew steps closer to me as I pick at the skin around my nails, continuing to ramble. "Anyway, she says it's fine but... I don't know. Something just doesn't feel right." His fingers graze my forearm, his touch settling my slight panic just a little. "It could be nothing," I continue, tracking the brush of his thumb across my skin. "But if it's not, I..."

I peer up at him, still silent as he gives me the space to keep going. I lose myself in the blue of his irises and the truth that I haven't allowed myself to think about until this very moment. Tears threaten to form behind my eyes, but I blink them away. "I'm just really scared."

Drew shifts the glove under his arm, preventing it from falling, then reaches forward with his free hand. He tucks a hair away from my face, then drags his thumb down my cheek before sweeping it across my lips. "Wow," he says so delicately it sounds foreign coming from someone who looks like he does right now.

Heat slinks up my neck as I realize the emotional spew I just poured onto him. "Yeah, sorry, I—"

Drew interrupts me by pressing his lips to mine, and it takes my body all of half a heartbeat to sink into his kiss. He pulls away too quickly for my liking, a smug, yet adorable, smirk on his face.

"There she is."

My whole body relaxes as I let out an unexpected breath. The thing about swallowing your emotions is that when you share them, it's like spilling your darkest secrets, but also like hearing them for the first time. You never really know what you're hiding because before you allow yourself to feel much of anything, you tuck it away, hoping you can keep it concealed forever. Or, at least until you're ready.

Drew just experienced me processing Aunt Ivy's words for the first time, and the relief his reaction provided is what allowed me to finally let them surface. I have no idea how he feels out there—the burden he carries every day—but if I can be even half of what he's being for me by just showing up—by listening—then I'll do whatever it takes to provide him that support. Even if it means facing fears myself.

"I knew you had it in you, my not so mysterious girl." He smiles softly, pulling me into his padded embrace. He places a gentle kiss on the top of my head as he holds me tightly. "And I'm so sorry about your aunt."

The tears from before now threaten to burst, but I've dumped enough on him already, and he has two more periods to play. Pushing off of him lightly, I clear my throat. "Alright, well, now you owe me, Twelve. A deal's a deal."

He chuckles through a sigh, bringing his hand to the back of his neck. I close what little gap sits between us, and slide my palm past his cheek. He instantly leans into my touch as he takes a deep breath.

"You got this," I say. He raises his arm and grabs my wrist, letting his eyes blink closed slowly. "Like playing in the driveway in middle school." That boyish grin returns, and it hits me everywhere. "Except with like nine other giant men—half of whom are trying to hurt you."

He laughs a sweet, genuine laugh and shakes his head. "Eleven," he says. "There's twelve guys on the ice."

"See," I quip. "You can picture it already." He blows a serious breath through his lips and nods once, such a human fear behind his eyes. "Now go!" I reach around and smack his ass, my hand bouncing off his pads.

He jolts into gear, his whole demeanor sparking back to what I see on the ice. "Thank you," he says, wrapping his palm around mine and squeezing it tightly. He leans down and kisses me on the cheek before letting go and shoving his hand back into his glove.

I smile as he reaches for the door. "Hey, Twelve," I say quickly before it's opened too far. Drew peeks out into the hallway, then back at me. "I'm not going anywhere."

"I'll find you after the game."

"Sure," I nod. "But that's not what I meant."

He drags his bottom lip between his teeth, then dips into the hall, taking the real promise of my words with him as he goes.

28
Drew

"Granger had it comin', huh Stormy?" Brett slaps his arm over Petrov's shoulders as we step into the locker room.

Alexei shrugs Burnsey's hand off instantly, but tips his chin down at him. "Our opponents will respect our goalie."

The team erupts in claps and whistles, celebrating the two minute cross-checking call that Petrov took after the Lightning's forward snowed Ward at the whistle in the beginning of the third period.

"Yeah, thanks, brother!" Carter calls from the opposite side of the room. Petrov grunts and tosses his gloves into his stall as Brett sits on the bench next to me to untie his laces.

"Way to go, bud," Burns says, sliding his first skate off. He gets to work on the other as he scoots closer to me, his voice low. "What was with you out there, Cap? Awfully quiet today."

Anxiety bubbles in my chest despite knowing it was coming. He's the first to mention it, but he damn sure won't be the last. After my run-in with Brooke, I spent the next two periods doing everything I could to play *my* game. I scored once, a backdoor goal, and rather than the throwback dance that Jane suggested earlier this week, I kept my head low, high-fived my team, and skated back to my position on the line.

I avoided eye contact with my dad as the fans shouted their usual low, drawn-out "Drewww." But they all went quiet almost immediately when I gave them nothing in return.

The rest of the time was spent making simple plays, sending safe passes, and taking clean shots. It was hard at first to lose the act, but when I started to struggle—falling back into step or worrying about the repercussions—I held onto Brooke's words. I pictured her face.

Having her close is like hearing my favorite song for the first time all over again. She envelops my senses, each look like the bass hitting me right in the chest, each touch like lyrics I didn't know I needed to hear—intimate, electric. Her smile is the chorus I could never get sick of, her laugh the melody I never want to forget. Being near her doesn't just feel good, it fucking resonates. Like I've been waiting for her rhythm my whole damn life. I know there will be fallout from making the changes I started tonight, but having her by my side might be the perfect sound to drown out the noise.

"Just trying something different," I say flatly, grabbing my jersey between my shoulder blades and dragging it off over my head.

"Do I have to worry about you?" he asks, his focus still on his laces.

"Nah, man. I'm good."

Burns slips his other skate off and springs to his feet. "Alright, then." He turns, ripping his own jersey off. "You let me know if that changes, eh?"

As if on cue, Emma Dean walks into the locker room, all legs and tits, her usual cameraman on her six-inch heels. She locks in on me and saunters over, her high ponytail swaying with her hips.

"Drew Anderson?" she questions, her voice dripping with sarcasm. I spin around, nothing but my gitch still on at this point, but she doesn't care. She prefers it that way. "Oh, it is you. I wasn't sure after what I just watched out there."

"We lost 4–2, Emma," I say through a sigh. "We were down by one, pulled Ward with a minute left, and the Lightning scored an empty net goal. Games like those are a dime a dozen. Come on..." I narrow my eyes and tilt my head knowingly.

"Oh, I didn't mean the game," she persists. "I meant you."

My gaze lingers on her as I slide my thumb under my chain and brush it back and forth, my learned arrogance coming to light. "Oh, I knew what you meant."

She smiles sweetly, looking back at the balding cameraman at her service and finally pulling the mic up from her side. "So, Drew, we didn't see much of your usual performance out there today. Any insight?"

I lick my lips, looking right into the camera. I lean down so my mouth nearly touches the microphone and paint a cocky smirk. "None, actually."

Emma squints at me coyly, her free hand landing gently on my bicep. "Oh, come on. There's absolutely no reason for the complete one-eighty? Not even... one line? One little bump?"

Heat burns behind my eyes and rage swirls in my gut as she points the mic back at me. Emma and I hold our stare, my jaw tight, her expression perfectly relaxed—neither of us wavering. For a second I contemplate laying it all on the table—spilling the truth or at least giving her and the world a piece of my mind. But when I part my lips to speak, my hands both balled into fists outside the view of the camera, there's a forearm on my shoulder.

"It was nice of Cap to share the spotlight tonight. He's so generous, aren't ya bud?" Burnsey's eyes burn a hole in the side of my head, but mine are still piercing through Emma. "Humble too, huh, Em?" Brett tosses the reporter when my motives are clear.

Her eyes dance back and forth between the two of us until Burns steps closer to her, boxing me out. "I—"

"I know you saw that top-shelf goal," he adds, cutting her off. "Dirty dangle then popped it up glove-side. Goalie's still lookin' for it, am I right?"

I miss Emma's undoubtedly lackluster response as I turn back to my stall and pretend to be busy searching in my bag. My teeth are clenched so hard I'm afraid they might crack, my nostrils flaring with each sharp breath. I grab a hold of a roll of tape in my duffle and squeeze it with everything I have, crushing the tube in the middle so the two separated parts collapse in on each other. I search my mind for a song, one off of

Brooke's playlist or the fucking ABC's at this point, but nothing tunes out the ringing in my ears.

Time moves in slow motion as a list runs through my head of every person, reporter, or profile I'll hear from if this were to continue. Emma's just the start. This was one game.

And already, I can't take the heat.

"Yo!" Burns calls just feet from me as if it wasn't the first time he tried to get my attention. I exhale all of the air in my lungs to the point where my chest burns and my abs are so tight I think they may cave in before twisting back around.

"You have two choices here, bud. Start talking or start drinking. And honestly, I'm good with either."

"Yo, Drew! Where the hell ya been?" Jace Holloway, the Gators' rising rookie, slaps his palm into mine and claps me on the back. The motion sloshes the beer in my hand, causing droplets to splash from the can and run down my wrist.

"Just busy, man," I explain, bringing the metal to my mouth. I run my tongue up the side to catch the last drip and slurp up the beads that sit along the rim. With the signing bonus I know Jace got, he can afford to have someone clean up my mess. But it's not the mess I'm worried about—it's the waste of the alcohol I so desperately need.

Jace laughs as he spins his Golden City baseball hat, then nods. "Yeah, I feel you. Good to see you out though, brother. Caught the last two periods earlier... you seemed a little off, I can't lie."

I slug down another two gulps of the cold, bitter liquid and hold the can out to him as my only response before a group of his teammates pull him back toward the kitchen.

Scanning the room, I spot the back of Brett's head behind the black leather couch, probably losing at Chel against Ward and another one of the Gators. There's a group of guys playing pool in the massive game room through the door on the right, a woman hanging off of each one, and some dude I've never seen before messing with the laptop hooked up to the speakers.

Brett and I have been drinking since after the game, starting with just a six-pack between the two of us at his house to take the edge off. I wasn't sure what else could fix this day besides seeing Brooke. She found me after, and told me how proud of me she was, then kissed me like she meant every word. But apparently Coach's girl asked her to take Cooper for the afternoon, and she had to agree—something about her owing her one after the secret she's kept. The way her eyes sparkled when she said it told me that *I* just may have been that secret, and there was nothing discreet about how that affected me.

The alcohol has been a close second as far as relief goes, though it definitely doesn't hit like it used to. A guy my size would need a lot more than three beers to numb any pain, but as I stand here attempting to chip away at it, I'm realizing nothing will work like she does.

My anxiety kicks up as I once again feel completely alone in a fucking room filled with people. This isn't my scene. It never was. But it feels even more foreign now that I've gotten a taste of the old me—of the real me that I haven't seen in so long.

Sipping again at my half-empty can, I continue to let my eyes wander the room. They land on a girl now posted up by the couch that I recognize from these types of parties. A puck bunny or cleat chaser—doesn't matter, really. They all seem to run in the same social circle, just like us athletes. She's objectively good-looking with strawberry blonde hair that flows down in waves past her shoulders. She has a tank top on despite the weather that looks at least three sizes too small, and she's staring through me, lust in her eyes, tempting me to approach her.

I run a hand through my hair as I blow out a breath before taking one last sip of my beer. Slowly striding forward, I set my can down on the narrow table that runs along the back of the sofa. I drag my thumb under my chain, letting her look rush past me. It hits me in the chest as I lean down, lowering my voice.

"Hey, I'm gonna get out of here."

"Are you sure?"

"Yeah... definitely."

I pull my phone out and turn it on. I powered it off after my dad's third call and Jane's fifth all-caps text. There was no way I was screening those notifications—and so many others—the whole time I was here.

"Alright, bud. You okay to get home?" Brett pauses his game and looks over his shoulder as I glance up at my newest admirer.

"Yeah, man. I'm good. I'll call the car service."

"You that buzzed?" he asks, his brows creased together.

I huff out a laugh, nudging his shoulder. "No, dipshit, you drove me here."

Brett snorts, rubbing his forehead. "That's right."

"*You* good?" I chuckle.

"Oh, yeah." He jerks a thumb over his shoulder at the TV screen where his player is still frozen mid-stride. "Brutal O.T. Brain's cooked."

I shake my head and grin, dropping my hand onto his shoulder. "I'll see ya later, buddy. Thanks for the hang." He slaps me on the arm and winks before turning back toward the screen.

When I fully stand up, I lock eyes with the girl. She's staring straight through me—even deeper this time, and once again, it hits me between the ribs. It's not lust or desire or even curiosity that drills me. What knocks the wind out of me is ache, longing, maybe even need. Her attention doesn't make me want *her*, it reminds me of the girl I *actually* crave.

Tapping on the screen, I light up my phone. It's riddled with missed calls and texts from everyone—Jane and my dad, one from my agent and even a couple of the guys. My heart sinks as I scroll through them. They may not all be related to the game, though I'm sure my P.R. manager and father will have notes. But I don't even get a chance to read them. Wedged between a voicemail notification from dad and a missed FaceTime from Jane is a text that stands out amongst the rest. One that starts my heart beating again.

Mystery Girl

> Coop left early to go to a friend's. Am I losing my touch as the cool aunt? Text me later if you want to hang out now that I'm free apparently.

That ache in my chest snowballs into something deeper. More primal. Once again she's able to drag me out of the trenches of my mind—of my whole fucking life. And exactly when I need her most.

In the time it takes me to pull up the number for our team's 24/7 confidential car service Monte put in place his first year here, I completely change my plan. I know where I am, and I know where Brooke lives. And thanks to not giving a single shit about what I looked like at this party, I'm in joggers, a hoodie, and the sneakers I created with my last brand deal. I can get to her place in less time and miles than it takes for me to complete my morning run. And if I'm lucky, I'll be just sweaty enough that she won't see the tears of relief that may happen to fall as I sprint toward my one place of solace.

29

Brooke

"Just tell me that Levi doesn't have anything to worry about. Because we all know how that ended after Drew's... after last season."

"Al, I told you at the game," I say, moving toward the window, faint screeching coming from outside. "He doesn't. Drew's good. He's just... figuring some stuff out."

"Okay," she sighs. "And you? Are you good?"

"Is it supposed to rain?"

"B..."

"What? I just heard Frank yelling like he usually does like three minutes before the first roll of thunder. Man, that guy has some sort of sixth—"

"Brooke!"

"Okay, okay. I'm sorry. Yes, I'm good."

Alex hesitates before asking again. "Are you sure? Have you heard from Ivy?"

I exhale heavily. "No, I texted the last number she messaged me from, but you know how she is. That was probably a phone she won in a poker game that she used once, then dropped into the guitar case of some subway busker."

She laughs, and I roll my eyes at the thought. "And your mom doesn't know anything?" she asks next.

"Not that she's told me at least."

Alex is quiet in agreement on the other end of the phone. "Okay, and back to the Drew thing. How are you doing with that? Have you seen some of the headlines?"

I scoff, but swallow hard, glancing out the window just in time to see Frank's unkempt locks flopping behind him. *Have I seen them?* How could I not? At this point, though only temporarily, it's my job to keep up with the Flames' presence on social media. Not to mention that my phone ads and click-bait articles are now completely geared toward Golden City Hockey. Every time I open the internet, there's a new gossip headline or short clip of the game or a link to the Emma Dean interview. And the hardest part is I haven't even gotten a chance to talk to Drew about any of it.

It broke my heart to see his raw reaction online, though no one else would quite understand it. The last time I saw him was after the game, and that was before this all unfolded. But for this much to be happening because of one game is mind-blowing to me. I've read some unavoidable comments and people aren't holding back, that's for sure.

All of it only lends itself to his massive hesitation.

"People seriously need to get a life. It was three damn periods for God's sake."

Alex chuckles on the other end of the phone. "You clearly don't understand your boyfriend's influence in our city, my friend."

"He is *not* my boyfriend." *I texted him earlier, and he still hasn't answered.*

"That is *not* the point. B, hockey fans are intense—borderline crazy. And Drew is like some sort of god around here. It may seem like one game to you, but after last season, any off-day for Drew Anderson triggers panic."

The image of Drew from earlier flashes through my mind. The panic on *his* face because of what he knew was coming—because of exactly what Alex is talking about now. These people put him on a pedestal.

They see him as a hero and an icon, but what they don't realize is that he's just... human.

He's a friend, a teammate, and somebody's son. He's a guy making his living off of a sport that he loves, but that has been slowly molded into someone he hates. He's not my boyfriend despite what Alex says, but he's also whatever he is to me. And as I sit here wishing he'd text me already, I'm reminded of just how quickly the idea of that is growing on me.

"Well, I think it's bullshit," I say simply, rather than repeating all of that aloud.

Alex clicks her tongue. "And so do I, but we don't make the rules."

"Which is also bullshit."

A roll of thunder cracks through my apartment, interrupting my latest complaint. The pitter patter of rain on my windows quickly follows, and I hum through a heavy exhale as the noise fills the room. "Frank's never wrong," I say softly.

"Well, let's hope you aren't either. I'm all for you figuring this thing out with Drew, but if you know anything... please give Montgomery a heads up before it flies out of left field."

Moving toward the kitchen, I swipe the bottle of red from the counter and yank the cork out. "That's the wrong sport," I say, filling a glass. "Or the wrong brother, depending on how you look at it."

Alex chuckles, but something about this conversation has put me even more on edge about not hearing from Drew—each drip on the pane like a ticking clock since the last time I saw him. Maybe the wine will help weather both storms.

"Just keep me posted," she reiterates. "And thanks for taking Coop. Sorry again that he sort of bailed."

The word *bailed* hits me right in the gut as I attempt to swallow the gulp I just took. I know Drew isn't ditching me. Hell, I'm the one who made plans in the first place. But I thought maybe with everything going on, he'd seek comfort here. That he'd escape the chaos and run to me.

"Yeah, of course," I answer.

"Love ya, B."

I smile despite the faint gnawing in my stomach. "Same here."

With a light click, the line goes dead, and my teeth find the inside of my cheek. I almost can't tell what's eating at me more—the fact that I miss him or that I could guess how he's handling all of today's aftermath alone. It's funny, I used to be so afraid of my own emotions—still am in so many ways—but it's almost as if feeling them doesn't hit half as hard as empathizing with someone you care about.

I down another large sip of the wine as the realization that I *care* about Drew rolls past me. Maybe subconsciously, this is why I never got too deep. Maybe my body—my heart, my soul—knew that when I did, I wouldn't just slip into feelings I've tucked away for so long. I'd fall. Hard and fast. The way I think I'm falling for *him*.

Suddenly, a chime rings out from the intercom, causing me to nearly throw my glass against the backsplash. It takes me a second to gather myself before hesitantly setting down my wine and making my way toward the door. Part of me wants to be excited. Could it be Drew waiting down on my steps? But another part has been here before and is half expecting Alex to come barreling through my door with more alcohol and a greasy bag of tacos.

For the millionth time, I curse myself for choosing an apartment that doesn't have a video system, and slowly bring my finger to the microphone button. "Hello?" I ask suspiciously.

"Hey you," a voice pants through the intercom.

"Twelve?"

"Yeah, Mystery Girl. It's me."

My shoulders sink as the emotional energy I was clearly holding onto from the events of the entire day, drains to the floor. The ache in my chest quickly turns to more of a glow. Is this what the Grinch felt like when his heart grew three sizes that day? Is the man waiting out in the rain my own little... Cindy Lou Drew?

I cringe to myself for even thinking it when another thought hits me—*the rain.*

"Oh my God, wait, sorry. Get in here!"

With that, I press the button on the system that clicks open the door at the main entrance. My mind swirls with everything I *should* be doing in the time it takes Drew to trek up the steps to my apartment—check my hair, grab my wine, put a bra on... or not. But it's like my body's frozen. Drew has this effect on me that no one else has ever had. He paralyzes me but in the best possible way.

If you ask people to describe me they'd probably say something like: bold or independent. Also, desperately funny... obviously. If you ask my mother, she might give a slightly less positive version of the same—like unattached. But Drew's changing me. It's as if I can literally feel the pull he has on me. Like my heart is tethering itself to his. And knowing he's just on the other side of the steps, knowing he probably needs my support, I don't care about anything else right now besides waiting for him to get to me.

With one deep breath, I pull the door open, just in time to see Drew standing with his fist raised, ready to knock. His free hand is tucked into the pocket of his grey joggers that are now darkened and clinging to him in all the right places, the front piece of his damp hair hanging onto his forehead.

The smile he gives me is all the answer I need as to whether or not I'm falling for him. It used to hit me between my legs, but, *shit*. Now, I feel it all over.

His gaze drops to my chest, and his expression darkens, his throat moving up and down. "I thought you might leave me out there," he says, slowly dropping his arm to his side.

"I didn't know you were coming," I quickly explain, unapologetically looking him over.

Drew's jaw grows tight, his eyes burrowing through mine with an intensity that tells the story of how things have played out since I saw him last. "Neither did I."

I attempt to hide the heat that flushes my body as I pull the door open further, but I doubt it works. "Well, come in. You're soaked."

Drew steps inside, and the scent of his cologne fills the room, the moisture on his clothes amplifying the smell. He reaches for the hem of his hoodie and pulls it over his head, taking his undershirt with him the first couple of inches. His V makes a brief appearance, and it takes everything in me not to drop to my knees in front of him. But is that what he needs right now?

"How are you feeling?" I ask, my mouth suddenly dry.

Drew hangs his sweatshirt on the hook by the door, then runs his hands through his over-grown hair. He pauses with his hand resting on the back of his neck and runs his tongue past his lips.

"Honestly?" he asks, stepping closer to me. I nod, desperate for his answer, meeting him halfway. "Like I've wanted to be inside you since you slid into the tunnel after the first."

A sigh leaves my body like I've been holding it all afternoon—because maybe I have—and Drew swallows the end of it, pressing his mouth to mine. I melt into him, dragging my hands down his back, only now realizing that despite the cold rainy evening, his once-covered shirt is still damp, his skin warm.

"Are you sweating?" I ask between kisses.

Drew nods with his lips still on mine as he turns me around and presses me against the door. "I ran here," he says without pulling away.

I freeze, slowly leaning back. I look between his eyes as he creases his brow, his chest heaving. "You ran to me," I whisper.

He sweeps his lips past mine gently. "It was the only thing I thought would help."

Without thinking, I drop to my knees like I've wanted to since the moment he got here. Drew inhales sharply as his palms naturally fly to the door behind me. His joggers do nothing to hide the way he feels about me being trapped between his steel thighs and the wall, which only encourages me more.

Bringing my mouth to the outline of his cock through the cotton, I blow out a warm breath from the back of my throat feeling him twitch underneath me. "Oh, shit," Drew hisses as I dip my hands into his waistband. "God, I fucking missed you today."

"I'm sorry I couldn't stay after the game."

"Don't be," he pants as I slide the back of my fingertips across the sensitive skin below his drawstring. "You just make everything better."

I peer up at him, and he slides one hand past my cheek into my hair. "You do," he reassures, his voice and his eyes both full of sincerity.

He brushes his thumb past my cheek, and I white-knuckle the fabric. Dropping my gaze to his chest briefly, I lick my lips before rubbing them together. "I think I just might like you, Twelve," I say matter-of-factly despite the burn in my chest as I admit that out loud.

I peer back up at him, and when I do, the corners of his lips are turned up, his blue eyes steady on me. "Oh, I definitely *like* you, Mystery Girl."

With that as momentum, I drag his sweatpants to his knees and take his cock in my hand. Drew groans as I push spit through my lips, letting it drip onto his tip before taking all of him to the back of my throat. Bringing his palm back to the door, he hangs his head between his arms, watching as I slide my mouth back up, rolling my tongue up the length of him. I drag my teeth gently past the last inch before reaching around and pulling his firm ass toward me to thrust him back in.

"Fuck, baby."

Drew lets his eyes fall closed as his lips part, short breaths passing them in quick bursts. His voice is borderline breathless, his brow creased, momentum causing his hair to sway in front of his face.

I bob my mouth up and down as I scan his expression, realizing each time I do, I'm taking away a piece of his pain. Each stroke's an opinion. Every lick and suck is a comment or headline or somebody's assumption. Drew needs this. He needs *me*. And I'm realizing just how much *I* need *that.*

I get lost in the thought, continuing my motion at a relentless pace, and Drew's legs tighten on either side of me. "Holy shit, Brooke. Don't stop," he begs, bringing his hand to the back of my head.

Emotions swirl inside of me, this whole experience—this whole damn day—somewhat transcendent. I take him as far as I can once more, his cock hitting the back of my throat, and tears brim my eyes for maybe both of those reasons. Drew holds me to him gently as he empties inside me, and when he's finished, I swallow all of it—his release in more ways than one.

Drew pulls out slowly, his hand cradling the back of my head, then he rakes his fingers into my hair and tugs me upward. I stand to meet him, and he kisses me hard, swirling his tongue inside my mouth to meet mine.

"God, I really fucking like you, baby." He kisses me once more. "And I fucking *love* tasting my cum on your lips."

I hum into him, reaching for the hem of his shirt, then pull it over his head. "Better?" I ask. Drew drags his joggers back around his waist, and when our gaze meets, I know he understands what I'm asking.

"Not really," he sighs, pulling me to him. "But fuck it. And fuck them. If you keep showing up, that's all I need."

With that, he wraps his arms around my ass and lifts me up. I fold my legs around his waist, and he carries me through the living room. As we move down the hallway, my eyes trail each frame hung sporadically, and my thoughts from earlier jump to the forefront of my mind.

My mind told me to panic. That I never get this deep with others like where I'm headed with Drew. But this wall is full of people I've completely let in. There's Blake and Selah of course, who has my whole heart. But there's also Alex, Cooper, and even Tessa in these frames. It might not come naturally—maybe I'm harder to crack—but I'm capable. And when I do, you're in for life.

The people on this wall are stuck with me. I've opened up my heart to them, and they've burrowed inside to make a permanent spot. But what does scare me now, is that I find myself looking for a spot to put Drew.

"Stay over," I blurt as we make it to the bedroom and I fall from his arms.

Drew lets out a chuckle that's almost a growl as he walks to the bed and sits down. "You couldn't kick me out if you tried," he says, extending his arm.

My eyes drop to his hand, and without hesitation, I leap for it. He smiles as he pulls me between his legs where he's already hard again for me. "You *do* like me, don't you?" he says, leaning forward and placing a kiss on my hip.

I rock into him, needy for more and drop my arms around his shoulders. "Yeah, Twelve. I definitely do."

30
Drew

"Dad, enough. I'm not talking about this," I say, my heart pumping way too hard because of him this early in the morning.

"Drew, you just completely flipped. The last time this happened—"

"It's not like that, okay?" I move toward the window, raking my hand down my face. "I'm just over the bullshit."

Dad clicks his tongue. "That bullshit is what made you, son."

"No, Dad," I snap through gritted teeth. "*I'm* what made me."

There's a pause on his end that gives me the slightest bit of hope. Until it doesn't.

"Drew, all I'm saying is—"

"Don't." I pace back through the living room, peeking into the bedroom to find Brooke still sound asleep. "The only reason I even answered is because you won't stop fucking calling me at the ass-crack of dawn," I whisper loudly.

"I'm sorry, I thought you'd be getting ready to run," Dad says, almost hesitantly.

"Yeah, well, I'm not."

He inhales deeply and blows out hard. "Well, just stay focused, okay? If you want any shot at going to Washington, they're going to want to see consistency from you."

My whole body freezes, my grip growing tighter on my phone. "Washington?" I scoff. "*That's* why you're concerned I played differently last game? Why you're worried something's wrong? Because it'll ruin my chances to replace Rourke on the Titans?"

"I mean, yeah. I thought—"

"Fuck, Dad" I groan louder than I mean to, glancing behind me to make sure Brooke's not standing in the doorway. I run my free hand through my hair instead of continuing my response.

What I want to add is that he doesn't know me. That he clearly stopped giving a shit about me or what I wanted when Mom died—if he ever really cared at all. I want to tell him that *he's* high on the list for why things were different yesterday, but that nothing is *wrong* with how I played. If anything, besides Brooke, it was the only thing that felt right in a long fucking time.

But I don't admit to any of that.

Not because I can't *say* it.

But because he won't *hear* it.

Instead, I sigh. "Just drop it, Dad. Please."

He takes a steady breath on the other end of the phone, and I think for once he might listen. He might actually think before he speaks. "I can't promise that, son. It's my job as your father to help you decide what's best for you."

No, Dad. It's your job as my father to love me either way.

"I have to go," is all I say before tapping on my screen to end the call.

I squeeze my phone so tightly in my hand that I'm afraid it might crack. But then for a second, I think, maybe that'd be the best thing to happen yet. Peering out the window of Brooke's apartment, all I can think about is how I wish I could call my mom so she could undo everything that he just did. So she could remind me of who I am—and who I'm not. A lump crawls up my throat as the sound of footsteps creak behind me. Swallowing it down, I turn to find Brooke in my t-shirt from yesterday, the soft fabric hitting her mid-thigh.

"Hey you," I say, my shoulders falling as soon as she offers me a smile.

"Hi," she answers, her voice still full of sleep. She slinks over to me with her arms across her chest and burrows her face into the crook between my neck and collarbone. She fits there perfectly, her lips against the pulse at my throat, and it takes everything in me not to tell her that she's the one thing keeping it alive.

"Did I wake you?"

Her cheek brushes against my skin, still warm. "No, I just rolled over, and you were gone."

My heart throbs in my chest. *She missed me.* "Do you have plans for the day?" I ask, avoiding sharing any information on the reason I was up in the first place.

"Most of my posts for this week are already planned out. I had a lot of free time to fill yesterday before you got here thanks to Cooper being *too cool* for me now." She peers up at me and rolls her eyes. "But I was gonna head to the rink to film some sort of content. Brett said he'd meet me."

"Brett?" I ask, jealously clearly lacing my tone.

Brooke gives me a suggestive grin. "I can't just post you, Twelve. People will get suspicious." I narrow my eyes, but she ignores my instant possessiveness. "I'm just trying to batch-make some posts this week, or at least collect pictures and videos for whoever's starting permanently." She inhales slowly, releasing it gently. "So they aren't starting with nothing when they get here."

Brooke stills, taking a deep breath. I press my lips to the top of her head and close my eyes, letting the quiet between us settle, my previous envy now meaningless. "It's coming up fast," I murmur, turning my head to rest my cheek against her hair.

I don't need to explain. I can tell from her body language that she knows what I mean.

"I know." She drops her arms around my waist like an anchor, and it's all the confirmation and reassurance I need.

We haven't talked about what's next—what it will mean when we're finally able to be seen together. To *be* together. I don't want to spook her, and I've had so much other shit on my mind the last few days. But even with it all looming, I'm not worried. Because with her here, next to me, all of it—the image, the opinions, my dad's relentlessness—feels a hell of a lot lighter. Like maybe I could actually survive the fallout because for the first time in years, I'm not alone in the spotlight.

With that in mind, I don't stop the next words from pouring from my mouth. "What if I gave you some content?"

Brooke's head pops up. "This is not that kind of show, Twelve."

I chuckle, nudging her cheek with the tip of my nose. "No, I think I want to cut my hair."

Her eyebrows hit the roof as she scans my face. "Seriously?"

I nod, rubbing the back of my neck, the locks sweeping against my knuckles. "Yeah, I've been over it for a while now. It's never really been me." My eyes meet hers. "Unless you like it."

She shakes her head, her wide eyes narrowing with sincerity. "I just like *you*, remember?" She winks as a brush off, then reaches up and combs her fingers through my hair. "Are you sure about this? That's a statement for Drew Anderson." She cocks a brow and tilts her head.

I blow a breath through my lips considering her words, regardless of how ridiculous it is that she's right. "I think that's the point."

Brooke tips her chin down definitively. "Then, it's settled." She rakes her hand through my hair, gripping it at my nape and yanking me toward her in the sexiest way. "Looks like it's makeover day."

Just hours later, Brooke and I are standing outside of a barbershop on her side of town that's wedged between a sandwich hut and a laundromat. "You, uh, do know I usually have someone come to my house to cut my hair, right?" I smile politely at a man with a face tattoo as he walks past us on the sidewalk. "It's one of the things about this job I actually like."

Brooke jabs her elbow not as gently as I'd like into my side and shushes me. "Trav's been cutting Blake's hair since he was small enough to sit in the racecar chair. He's the best. And I called in a favor." She reaches for the handle of the door. "He owes me."

Before the words even fully leave her mouth, I place my palm on the door to stop it from opening. "I'm gonna need you to explain that one to me."

Images that have no business flashing through my mind make their presence known in my head. Did they sleep together? Date? Did Trav fuck over my girl, and now, I have to kill him *and* keep my long hair?

"I save him the corner booth at The Gilded Pub every year on Fantasy Football Draft Night. Trust me when I tell you, it's a hot commodity."

Relief flies from my chest and is quickly replaced with embarrassment. I clear my throat and lower my hand, shoving it into my pocket and hoping Brooke doesn't realize I thought she was banging the barber. "Cool," I respond with attempted ease.

She hesitates before pulling on the long metal handle, then smiles coyly. "Oh, and we banged that one time," she says quickly, ripping the door open and leaving me frozen.

I catch the bright red wood just before it swings fully shut and walk in after her, my heated gaze landing on a guy at least sixty-years-old, with a gray handlebar mustache and two silver braids framing his face. Brooke turns back to me with a smirk and says, "Drew, this is Trav."

I suck my teeth at her idea of a joke before stepping forward and extending my hand toward the very stylish, but very not-Brooke's-type barber. "Nice to meet you, man. Thanks for doing this."

"Yeah, of course," Trav says, draping an apron over his neck. "Brooke here is a saint for saving my guys and me that table each year. People are vicious out there, ya know?"

"Yeah," I say. I glance into the mirror in front of his black swivel chair and run my hand through my hair one more time. "I get that."

"Well, listen, I'm just gonna wash you up real quick since you got some length to ya, and then you can talk me through what you're lookin' to do today."

My eyes dart to Brooke nervously who, with one look, reassures me that this is all going to be okay. "Sure. Sounds good, man," I choke out.

Trav nods as a phone rings in the distance from what must be his office in the back. "Shit, give me a few minutes. I've been waiting for my supplier to call me since yesterday."

"Take your time," I say.

"I can get him started," Brooke chimes in quickly. We both give her our attention. "With the wash, I mean. I can wash his hair while you handle that, and then he'll be ready to go when you're done."

Trav pushes his bottom lip out and nods before spinning his heel on the black-and-white checkered floor and leaving me with an anticipatory hard-on.

"Don't look at me like that," Brooke says, walking over to the station in the corner of the room. There's a cushioned chair that's attached to a shampoo bowl and a small shelf above it that's lined with just a few simple products.

"What look?" I ask as I follow her.

She taps the chair and stands behind the sink. "You know what look."

I slide into the seat, letting my head fall back into the cut-out groove and peer up at her. "I have no idea what you're talking about. *You're* the mystery, remember?"

She gives me a knowing grin and turns the water knob until it slowly trickles out. I watch as she reaches below the sink and pulls out a thin rectangular towel.

"You know, I've never had my hair washed before a cut," I say, still confused about this part.

Brooke giggles. "Well, if you haven't noticed, Trav's a little... different."

I leave my neck cocked at the uncomfortable angle just to see her smile. "What gave it away? The braids or the mustache?"

She huffs out another laugh as she pushes on the back of my head. "Up," she says simply, but I have to remind my dick she's not talking to him.

Brooke slides the fabric beneath my shoulders before I lay back down, then drapes the ends over my shirt on either side of my neck. Testing the water once more, she pulls the hose from the holder on the sink, the zip of the chord echoing off the basin. When the warm rush touches the back of my head, the hairs on my neck fight it to rise. Once it's soaked, Brooke massages her fingers into my scalp, digging them into the nape of my neck and dragging them upward before swirling them behind both ears. She sinks her nails into the hair just above my forehead, combing it backward in quick, short strokes, taking a tantalizing amount of time to do so. When she pulls on the ends just a little more roughly, I reach my arm behind me and slap my hand around her wrist.

"Don't play with me, Brooke. You know exactly what you're doing."

She giggles, then leans down and exhales a warm breath on my ear before responding in a low, painfully-fucking sexy tone. "Don't worry. It's working for me too."

My eyes snap shut as I let out a groan. The sound of her reaching for a product on the shelf teases my senses, knowing she has to repeat that whole process in order to actually get the job done. The next five minutes are spent painfully thinking about anything besides the way Brooke's hands feel in my hair, and how I'd like to tease her back.

Thankfully, after another few seconds, Trav reappears. He steps in front of my chair, twirling the corner of his mustache, his braids dangling over his shoulders—apparently the exact remedy I needed.

"Alright, Brooke. You gonna look at me?"

With her back still to me like it has been for the last twenty minutes, she responds. "Oh my God, I don't know why I'm so nervous."

I can't help but laugh as I flick my fingers through the front of my hair, the only part that's still remotely long at all. "Gotta be honest, you're not making me feel any less anxious about this."

"No!" she says quickly. "I'm sure it looks..." She whips herself around, her breath hitching when she sees me. "So fucking hot."

I run my tongue across my teeth as I glance shyly at Trav. Brooke strides toward me slowly, reaching out and petting my hair with her mouth dropped open. "So. Fucking. Hot," she repeats, her voice breathy. I chuckle as I lean into her touch, then wrap my arms around her waist.

"You're not being very mysterious," I say, tilting my head to the only person who has ever seen us interact like this.

Brooke tears her eyes away from my new look, her hand still in my hair, just long enough to find Trav observing us, his chin resting in the curve of his hand. "I'll throw in an order of sliders this year if you forget this ever happened."

He tilts his head back and forth in contemplation. "Make it potato skins and you got yourself a deal."

Brooke nods once, and Trav turns toward his office as she slams her lips to mine. It takes my body a second to catch up, but when it does, I dissolve into her, any worry I once had about making the change totally gone—or at least completely worth it. My tongue meets hers, and Brooke sweeps her palm over my new fade. "So hot," she repeats once more.

Pulling away reluctantly, I press my forehead against hers. "You should probably cut this part out of your time-lapse."

Her eyes fly to the tripod set up just feet from us on the other side of the chair. "But don't delete it," I add swiftly. "Just, you know... maybe send it to me instead."

The corners of her lips turn up as she playfully rolls her eyes. "I promise I'll run it past you before I post it later."

I plant a kiss on her forehead. "Perfect."

"So, what now then, Twelve?"

I inhale slowly, going through my usual routine. I skipped my run which threw off the rest of my morning, but there's still time before practice later to get some of it in. "Actually, there's something I usually do that I'd like to not skip." I bring my hand to the back of my neck, the bare skin foreign to my touch. "Especially after all this."

"Oh, okay," she says casually. "Well, I have to meet Brett at the rink later, but maybe I can see you after."

"Or you could come with me," I shoot back before I can even fully process it. "Now, I mean. It won't take long."

Brooke grows a slow smile and shrugs. "Yeah, sure. Where to?"

31

Brooke

"I hope this is okay," Drew says, taking my hand and walking me down the quiet path. A cool breeze blows past us, and I try not to overthink the chill it sends up my spine. "You don't have to talk or anything."

"It's a little unexpected, but..." I drop my free hand onto the one holding mine. "Definitely okay."

His eyes fill with relief as he smiles softly, leading me further into the cemetery. This isn't a place that I frequent—I'm lucky enough to not have any tombstones to decorate or deceased friends or family to visit. I assumed I'd be majorly uncomfortable—maybe minorly nauseous—but surprisingly, I'm only borderline uneasy. I think the idea of Drew taking me to see his mom is numbing all possible negative emotions. I know how much this means to him. And that in turn, means more to me than I realized.

"Right over here," he says, pointing through the lush scenery toward a site that's well-kept and looks freshly polished. I read the name written across it, Joy Anderson, and my heart-rate picks up. I know I'm not meeting his mother in a traditional sense, but it still feels big—colossal considering our current situation.

As we approach the tombstone, Drew drops my hand, stepping in front of me as he gets closer. "Hey, Mom," he says, touching the marble. All of my nervous energy dissipates as my entire being swells for him. "I brought someone I want you to meet."

He glances over his shoulder at me, and I take in his new look for the hundredth time. He really does look different, but it's not so much the hair that's changed. It's as if the light I see in flickers is slowly coming back to stay. "Hey, uh, hi, Mrs. Anderson," I stutter awkwardly. "I'm Brooke."

Drew sinks into the grass, pulling his knees to his chest and leaning back on his palms. He taps the spot next to him, more relaxed than I've ever seen him. For a fleeting moment, my heart aches. I'll never actually get to meet the woman that he talks about with such reverence—the one who shaped him into who he really is. But then I remind myself... if this is as close as I'll ever get, I can't waste it being inside my head.

I sit beside him, choosing to lean in like he asked me to before—feelings and all this time. If this is hard for me, I can't imagine what it's like for him. The least I can do is give them both my best.

"So, what do you think, Mrs. A?" I ask, my voice stronger now. "Do we like the hair?"

Drew laughs quietly and nonchalantly slides his hand closer to me, curling his pinky over mine. "She'd like it. She liked everything. I don't think I ever heard her criticize anything about anyone."

"My kind of lady," I say, thinking about my own mother's habits. Guilt washes over me as I consider the lingering dread I always have for going to my parents for Family Dinner Night, when Drew has to visit his mom here.

"Brooke's the girl I've been telling you about."

My head whips his way, and he flashes me his boyish grin. "It better all have been good," I grind quietly through my teeth.

He leans into me as if his mom can hear us. "It was... mostly." He slides his vibrating phone from his pocket as I slap his arm before turning back to the stone.

"I've heard a lot about you, too."

Drew taps my shoulder and nods his head toward the open field behind us before standing. I watch him walk away as he brings his phone to his ear, but besides a *What's up?* I can't hear much of anything else.

When I twist back around, I realize I'm alone at the gravesite. It's interesting how even though she's not really here, the same anxiety pools in my belly as it probably would if Drew left the two of us together. It feels like I should keep talking—I probably would if it really was just her and I.

"Drew really misses you," I start, picking at the thick grass by my ankle. "He's a lot like me in the sense that he doesn't come right out and say it, but I can tell. It's in the songs he listens to and the way he talks about you. There's a hole I think he's gotten used to, but the emptiness is still there."

An all too familiar lump begins forming in my throat as I continue. "I'm sure you can tell that he's not necessarily happy. That there's a lot going on right now that's eating at him." The mass grows as I pluck a long blade and begin rolling it between my fingers. "I mean, you're his mom, I'm sure you can tell. But he's really working on it, ya know?" My voice breaks as tears build behind my eyes. "The hair's pretty obvious," I laugh, sniffling back what I can. "But there's other stuff too—the things you can't see." I tear the piece of grass in three pieces before reaching for another one.

"I'm proud of him," I add. "*You* should be proud of him. He's doing everything he can to step out of his comfort zone so he can exist in this world without judgement or retribution for being himself—whatever that looks like." A tear rolls down my cheek that I can no longer hold back. "But I don't have to tell you to celebrate that, do I? You just know. And you'd love him regardless." I wipe away new tears that fall and tuck my hair behind my ear. "Most moms would."

I sit there awhile, so lost in my thoughts and comparisons to my own life that I miss the crunching of footsteps as they approach.

"Sorry, that was Scott, my agent. My—hey." Drew searches my face as I look up at him, my cheeks wet, my makeup most likely starting to run. He kneels down beside me. "Hey, what's wrong?" He pulls me into him, and I seek comfort in his familiar smell and the way I fit perfectly against his chest.

"I'm good," I answer, nuzzling into him.

"Brooke..." Drew places his hands on my shoulders and pulls me away from him. "Talk to me."

I shake my head, wiping at my cheeks. "No, your mom's just..." I bring my eyes back to the light gray marble, her first name sticking out even more to me now. "I bet she was a really good listener."

He glances at the stone as well and smiles. "She was," he says. "With a heart of gold." I nod thoughtfully. "Kind of like someone else I know." I tilt my chin up to him, smiling, and he brushes the corner of my eye with his thumb. "I definitely like you, Brooke Larkin."

I huff out a laugh, glancing down toward my lap. "Hey, you didn't call me Mystery Girl," I throw back, my tone dripping with sarcasm.

Drew drops his head, and when his eyes meet mine, the blue is so clear I can almost see my reflection. "Well, yeah. That's because I've finally got you all figured out."

"Oh, do you?"

"I do."

"Huh..." I roll my tongue over my teeth. "Well, that makes one of us."

Drew grins and stands, extending his hand to me. I take it, and he yanks me up, but rather than stopping when I land on my feet, he continues the momentum and throws me over his shoulder.

"Don't worry," he calls over my squeals. "I can carry the team."

"Okay, Brett, tell me about yourself."

Burns glances around the players' lounge, his knee bouncing as he sits at the edge of the black leather couch. He tosses an M&M into his mouth before bringing his attention back to me. "What do you want to know, InstaBrooke?"

I huff out a laugh as he scans the room again, shaking the bag of trail mix in his hand. Trying to get his attention, I snap in his direction. "Well, first, I'd like to know what is happening right now?"

Brett looks over his shoulder, clearly still distracted. "I, uh..." He clicks his tongue. "I'm just—where's Cap?"

I throw my hands in the air, then press stop on my recording app. "What?" I ask slightly exasperated. We've been sitting here for ten minutes already, and all he has done is munch snacks and kill time.

"Where's Drew?" He wrinkles his forehead but smiles as if he's completely unbothered.

"No, I understood the qu—nevermind. I don't know where he is. On the phone or something, maybe. Why?"

Brett clears his throat, searching for another piece of chocolate among the mixed nuts. When he finds one, he throws it into the air, catches it in his mouth, then chews before responding. "Maybe we should wait."

"For Drew? So *you* can tell me fun facts about *your* life?"

He shrugs and twists to study the other guys around the room. A few players I don't know well, because they rarely touch the ice, are posted up on the high-back stools by the bar counter, eating sandwiches and watching game film on the flatscreen TV. Hughes and Petrov sit together at opposite ends of the conference table, both of their heads buried in their phones, and Ward is on his back on the floor, his eyes closed and his legs up on the wall.

Brett finishes his scan then shifts closer to me on the loveseat next to him, tucked in the corner of the lounge. "Cap's my best friend, InstaBrooke. If he sees you flirting with me—"

"What? Brett, this is for social media. I am not flirting with you."

"Well, not yet. But that's why we need him here. So you don't get swept up in the Burns' Effect, eh?"

I stare at him blankly, wondering what twilight zone I've somehow entered—and why he'd say that anyway. "Okay, first, I think we're probably good on *that*." I reach forward and pat his shoulder. "But I appreciate the concern."

He smiles, and it's admittedly adorable, but, especially after today, I'm too far gone for his captain for it to have any greater effect on me. "Second..." This time it's me who leans in, curious. "What would even make you say that?"

He takes a long swig of his purple Gatorade, grinning at me beneath the bottle. He lowers it and swallows, then spins the lid back on and settles into the cushion. "Like I said, Cap's my best friend."

For the first time since we started talking, Brett makes direct eye contact with me without any sort of playful expression. My face relaxes as he stares at me knowingly. "You're good for him." I stare back, unsure of what to say, a slight case of whiplash hitting me from his two opposite sides. "Different than what people would expect," he continues. He lowers his voice. "But so is he. I'm just not supposed to know that."

My chest tightens at the thought of the Drew I know. The one who deserves for his true self to be seen. The one who, according to Brett, might be more understood than he thinks—at least by his best friend. "And how would you know that?"

He pretends to search the bag again, his hand digging aimlessly around as he stares at the light gray carpeting on the floor. "I just do."

I offer him a slight smile, and silence grows between us. I'm not sure how to respond, especially considering Drew's and my situation, but I want to hug Brett. To tell him he's right. Drew *is* different than he pretends to be—and in the most beautiful way. But I don't. It's not my secret to tell.

"What's your favorite color?" I ask, hitting record again and moving on from the current topic.

"Cyan," Brett says without hesitation.

"Favorite food?"

"Peanut butter and jelly."

I glance down at my list. "Fav—"

"Strawberry jelly," he adds decisively.

I nod slowly, brows high. "Favorite season?"

"Winter."

"Least favorite season."

"Winter."

I pause my series of rapid-fire questions. "But you just said—"

He holds up his palm to face me. "It's a love-hate relationship."

I tilt my head and turn my lips down. "Actually... I totally get that." Brett smiles, either at me or at the fact that he fished another M&M from the bag of mostly nuts. "Okay, favorite childhood memory?"

"Pass."

My eyes perk up from the list in my lap and meet Brett's as he chews the chocolate. "What? No, you can't just pass. Where's the fun in that?" His shoulders lift as he takes another sip of his drink, then swallows down his gulp. "Come on, what's your favorite memory from when you were a ki—?"

"I said pass, Brooke."

He wipes his mouth and replaces his lid. His tone and expression are both stern, a complete contrast to his usual merriment, and before I can react, the door behind us clicks open. Brett's head swings toward the noise, but my eyes are still stuck on trying to read him.

When he tips his chin up toward the entrance to the lounge, I finally pull my eyes away. They land on Drew, who looks unbothered, his body relaxed, coffee in hand. Brett and I both smile at him, and the corners of his lips curl up as he passes. Burns waves and sinks back into the couch. I, however, am stuck with the image of him with his new hair and same swagger, and now, thanks to Brett's words, have a growing urge to show him just how much I care.

Our time after the cemetery was brief. I had to meet Brett back here, and Drew was getting calls left and right the entire ride over, which he actively denied. But I felt closer to him today than I ever have. I never realized *that* would make me want him even more physically—I guess I never let myself get to this point. But since we got to the arena, melting into him is all that I can think about. I was doing a good job at ignoring my need until now—until he entered my space and brought with him our usual, unbearable tension.

"So, what else you got for me?"

Brett's question pulls me back, but now I'm the one distracted, no longer able to disregard my pull to Drew. I follow him as he walks toward a seat in the opposite corner of the room, falling into the chair and propping his feet up on the coffee table in front of it, his eyes lingering on Brett and me. "Uh, tell me about something your fans might not know about you. Something fun."

I drag my gaze back to Brett in time to see his face light up, but I can still spot Drew from the corner of my eye. Tapping my knee, Burns stands and plops down next to me, pulling up the Photos app on his phone.

For a second, I worry that I might regret this whole thing. Once because I suddenly can't focus with Drew seducing me by merely existing and once for the fear of what Brett may be preparing to show me. Both of my worries are calmed—at least momentarily—when the picture he clicks on is of a cream and orange tabby cat, with piercing yellow eyes and a tiny pink nose, sitting on a windowsill.

"Oh my God, Brett," I squeal. "You have a cat?"

"That's Sid," he says, his smile growing from ear to ear. "Sidney Clawsby."

I scoot closer and take the phone from his hand, and when I do, the thump of Drew's feet sliding off the table grabs my attention for just a second. I glance up to find him now leaning forward in his seat, his forearms resting on his knees—slightly less unbothered. I ignore his sudden shift and zoom in on Sid's little face.

"How did I not know about him?"

Brett shrugs. "Honestly, I don't know. I talk about him all the time."

"Wait, I thought I told you to tell me something the fans *wouldn't* know about you."

He holds his pointer finger in the air. "Uh uh, you said *might*. And I don't pass up any opportunity to talk about my boy here."

I shake my head, swiping on the photo to another one of Sid, and momentarily getting lost in Brett's feline friend—or family maybe with how he's talking. This one is of him in Brett's arms, the two of them wearing matching bow ties. "Shut up," I say loudly, bringing my knee up on the couch and turning toward him. I look at Brett, my mouth hanging open, and he winks before nodding toward the photo.

I nudge my shoulder into his, and he reaches over me casually. "Oh, just you wait." He scrolls to another photo of Sid wrapped up in a lush white blanket in the middle of a king-size bed. "I treat my pussy right," he says.

Laughter rips out of me that has nothing to do with his innuendo and everything to do with picturing Brett Burns, NHL defenseman, wrapping a cat up in a throw. I bring my thumb to the screen and slide to the next image, expecting to see a picture of Sidney Clawsby in shoes or a stroller. Instead, I not so gracefully stumble upon Brett in possibly the tiniest boxer briefs known to man, pulled so low that he might as well not be wearing them at all.

"Woah."

"Whoops!" Brett says, snatching the phone and shoving it between his thighs. "Sorry about that."

My hand flies to my mouth as my head snaps up, and when it does, I lock eyes with Drew, who's now standing, nearly crushing the cardboard cup in his hand. My whole upper-half grows warm as his burning gaze mixes with my memory of an all but naked Brett.

"I didn't mean to turn you on like that," Burns whispers in my ear, my face clearly pink.

I swing in his direction, my eyes wide. "Oh, no. Brett, you didn't—"

"I told you, InstaBrooke... the Burns' Effect is strong."

I snort out another laugh despite my growing awkwardness, but don't get a chance to argue his point. Instead, Drew's shadow hovers over me, and when I follow it to meet his face, it's heated and hungry—completely bothered.

"Burnsey, I need to steal her for a second." He speaks to Brett, but he's looking at me. I scan the room, anxious that someone may notice his presence, but if they do, they don't dare say a word to their captain.

"Oh, yeah, no worries, bud. Sorry, you know how strong the Burns' Eff—"

"Now," he says in my direction. "Please."

I look at Brett, who gives me a coy smile. Deciding there is so much more to him than meets the eye, I squeeze his arm before standing. I look to Drew for direction, and he nods toward the door. When he places his hand on my lower back, every memory of the day we had, and my conversation with Brett, comes rushing back to me.

All wrapped up as one needy reminder.

32

Drew

"**W**here am I going?" Brooke whispers from over her shoulder.

With my hand still on her lower back, I guide her further down the hallway. "Just keep walking," I grind out, casually grinning at the janitor emptying the trash can in the trainer's room.

She continues speed-walking, yelping when I pull on her shirt and drag her down the next hallway. "God, this place is like a freaking maze." Brooke searches the walls for any clues as to where we might be headed. I move in front of her when it hits a dead end and scan my thumb over the sensor. "See, I thought this hallway led to the..." Her voice trails off as the door swings open to exactly where she expected it to. "Drew, why are we in the tunnel?"

Pulling her through the opening, I slam the door shut and press her back against the wall. "Because the ice is the only place my team won't be on an off day." I search her eyes for understanding, but before my point can register, I crash my lips to hers.

Brooke inhales sharply, then reaches for my waist, scrunching up the hem of my shirt at either hip.

"This is killing me," I say, reluctantly pulling back.

She pauses. "I'm sorry, I didn't realize my lips were so deadly."

I huff out a laugh. "Oh, they are." I bend forward, taking her bottom one between my teeth and biting gently. "But I mean *this*." I throw my arms out and look around. "Keeping you a secret."

"Not much longer," she pants, dragging her nails down my back.

I arch into her touch, pinning her hips to the wall behind her with my own. "Thank God. I can't even fucking look at you with someone else knowing they don't understand you're mine."

She brings her palms to my chest, blocking my movement to kiss her again. "Wait, are you talking about Brett?" She giggles, and I clench my teeth—all the response she needs. "Did you know he has a cat?"

"Yes," I say bluntly, fighting her resistance for another kiss.

"He's funny."

Kiss.

"I know."

Kiss.

"And a good friend."

I freeze. "That better be all he is."

She smiles, and my irrational hostility fades. "I mean to you."

I sigh, brushing my thumb across her cheek. "I know he is."

"See, you have more people in your corner than you think, Twelve."

"Yeah, well..." I take her hand in mine and pull her toward the boards, first double-checking that we're in the rink alone. "As long as I have you, that's all I really need." I snap my wrist, yanking her toward me and put my mouth on the exposed skin below her neck.

"Well, you have me," she says softly, her chest rising and falling quickly. "But there's only a few more days until we get this for real, and I don't know if we should be risking that."

"What do you mean?"

She scans the arena. "I mean I know we're no strangers to public places, but this is so... open. And I swear there's like a million doors to get here from the facilities."

I smirk. "There's only two, Mystery Girl."

She looks at me like she's unconvinced. "Feels like more."

Tugging her to me, I slide my hand into her hair and drop my forehead to hers. Brooke lets her eyes fall closed, only popping them back open when I dip my hand into the waistband of her jeans. "You tell me what you need for this to happen, and I'll do it," I say. I groan as I slip a finger inside her, and her walls clench around it. "But fuck, I have to have you, Brooke."

It's true. I've needed her since she ran her fingers through my hair at the barbershop. Then, again, at the cemetery when she nearly fucking broke me talking to my mom and being so vulnerable. Seeing her with Brett was the final straw. I know he's not a threat—Brooke and I know where we stand and somehow so does Burns. But having to just sit back and watch her be so casual with someone else—how I want to be with her, not just behind closed doors—was all I could take before instinct took over.

"Can we just go somewhere—anywhere—less obvious in case someone comes walking through the tunnel?"

I search the rink, almost as desperate to find somewhere fitting as I am for her. I glance across the ice, and it clicks. Getting there may be riskier than the bench, but once we make it, the chances of being caught will be so much lower.

"Do you trust me?"

I don't mean for the words to come out so weighted, but Brooke's expression tells me she's searching for an answer to the general question, even outside of this moment. "I'm leaning in, remember?"

That's all she answers with, but in *Brooke*, that's good enough for me.

My smile says it all as I take her hand again and open the boards to the bench. She follows me blindly until I step one foot onto the freshly cut ice.

"What the hell are you doing?" she hisses, digging her heels in. "Drew, I'm up for a lot, but banging on freaking ice might be where I draw the line."

"The only way to get to the box is by crossing it," I state matter-of-factly. "Perfect for seclusion, but... we gotta get there first."

Her lips part, her eyes wide, the perfect expression of excitement—in more ways than one—washing over her. She nods, and I set my second foot onto the slippery surface. "Just go slow."

Brooke braces herself on the boards and places her feet one at a time onto the ice. We shuffle together, her hand entangled in mine like the two were made to fit inside of each other. I smile over at her, and she does the same, both of us letting a quiet laugh slip between us.

It's a silly moment—charged and arousing—but completely ridiculous. The funniest part though, is that this moment is the first I've had on the ice that's brought me joy in too damn long. Sure, winning is fun, and I love my team and hockey as a whole. But for me, individually, here with her is the happiest I've been coasting across ice for years.

When Brooke's toes hit the box, I reach past her, lifting up on the lever. The door unlatches, and she shuffles backward into me, allowing it to open. I still, wrapping my arm around her waist and pulling her flush against me. She whimpers when her ass hits my cock that's been ready for her since this morning and drops her head back onto my shoulder. I slip my hand underneath the hem of her shirt, her covered skin warm against my chilled palm.

Brooke's nipples are already peaked from the temperature, tempting me to play with them, when I slide underneath her bra. I do, rolling one between my fingers, and Brooke grinds into me, her back arching away from my chest. I repeat the motion on the other side, bending down to nip up her throat, but when she moans the sweetest of sounds, I can't wait any longer.

"Get in," I demand.

Brooke immediately steps into the penalty box, turning around to face me as I grab the door behind us. "Still very exposed," she says weakly.

I laugh and pull it shut, the sound from the latch echoing around us. "Did you hear that?"

"Hard to miss."

"Exactly." I step to her until the back of her legs hit the bench. "There's no noise in here. Well... besides yours." I kiss her neck again, and she hums like I knew she would. I lick my lips and smile. "If someone comes in, we'll hear it and can hide behind the boards."

"You've thought of everything, haven't you?"

"I told you, you can trust me."

Brooke holds my gaze and reaches for my joggers. "I know I can."

A fire lights inside of me hearing those words—and knowing I can finally have her. "Come here." I snatch her wrist from my waist and kiss her hard once before moving my hands to the elastic around her hips and pulling her leggings and underwear both down at once. "Sit," I bark, and Brooke obeys, a smile on her face I wish I could frame.

I kneel between her thighs, lifting one over my shoulder as she places her palms on the bench and settles her weight backward. "I guess this is why they call it the sin bin," she snickers, letting her neck loll back.

"No one calls it that," I correct her, peering up.

She drags her head back up to face me. "Uh... yes they do."

"No." I dip down and kiss the inside of her thigh. "They don't."

"Mmm... I've done my research, Drew. People absolutely call it that."

Leaning forward, I drag my tongue up her middle, and she hums as she bites her bottom lip. "The media maybe," I concede, nipping at her clit. Brooke shifts her hips up toward my mouth, and I laugh at the contrast of her actions with her argument. "But you call it whatever you want, Mystery Girl. Just let me eat this fucking pussy like I've wanted to all day."

Brooke gasps as I dive into her. "Holy shit," she cries, her words bouncing around us and egging me on.

I flick my tongue, guiding a finger inside and hooking it at just the right angle. Brooke exhales heavily and slides her hand into my hair. "Oh my God, I forgot," she says, attempting to grab a hold like she's used to. "It's gone."

"Do you miss it?" I ask, adding another finger.

Brooke moans, her lids closed, and digs her nails into my fade. "No, it's just different." She opens her eyes, and I get lost in them. "Still perfect." She shifts her weight, switching hands and letting her head fall back again. "I can totally work with this."

I shake my head and grin as I vanish back into her, devouring her like she deserves. Brooke knows exactly what to say to put me at ease, but not because she's telling me what I want to hear. She just understands me. It's part of why I like her so much.

And I really fucking like her.

One thing I've learned throughout this whole experience with hockey is that when you truly care about something—or some*one*—you shouldn't feel nervous or worried. People talk about how heightened anticipation and positive anxiety's a good thing, but I call bullshit. When your heart is involved, you shouldn't be hoping for approval with warning signs in your gut disguised as butterflies. You should be at ease—yourself. And not afraid of the reaction.

That's what Brooke does for me. She makes me feel accepted. Seen. And it's all that I want. Hell, it's all anyone could ask for. And that's why being that for her is so important. She's changing my life every day that she embraces the *real* me—and helping me embrace him too. Her opening up to me means everything. And I plan to get that from her in every way I can.

"Drew," Brooke whines softly, my fingers working inside her as I suck on her most sensitive spot. My dick twitches from the sound as it always does. And from seeing her so raw with me.

"Don't hold back, baby." I continue at my relentless pace, flattening my tongue against her center. "I want all of this." *All of you.*

Brooke pulls my head closer to her with one hand, her fingers on the other, curling around the bench. I continue my movement, my cock growing harder—selfishly, her undoing is as much for me as it is for her. I reach up under her shirt, brushing my thumb across her nipple, and when I squeeze it gently, her thighs begin to quiver.

"God, yes. Keep going."

"I need you to come for me, baby. Before I fucking do."

She whimpers at my warning—or confession. "You like this, Twelve? Watching what you do to me?"

I blow out a long steady breath just inches from her middle, centering myself but also adding to her pleasure. "You know I do," I answer, pumping both fingers in and out of her, then dipping back in, swirling circles with my tongue.

Brooke moans, tightening around me, the lower half of her leg wrapping around the back of my head. I continue licking and sucking until her pussy pulses against my lips, and my cock strains so hard against my joggers it's borderline painful.

When she finishes riding out her high on my mouth, I slide up from my knees, standing tall above her. I take her chin in between my thumb and forefinger and lift so that her eyes meet mine. "I could watch you come for me all goddamn day."

Her lips part as her breathing continues to spurt out in short, quick breaths. "I need more of you," she whispers, sliding off her shoes and leggings.

I growl, tightening my grasp. "You have no fucking idea, baby."

With that, I pull my own pants down, and Brooke and I switch places, her standing above me now seated. We both rip off our shirts as she straddles my legs with hers, slipping each foot past the bench on either side of my hips. At a torturously slow pace, she lines me up with her entrance, and sits on my cock, aching for exactly this.

I groan as she takes all of me easily, my head drooping forward onto her chest. Brooke throws her arms around my neck, and I wrap mine around her lower back, pulling her as close to me as I can manage. She begins shifting her hips, her range of motion limited from my grip, but it somehow feels even better than if she were bouncing on top of me.

With her feet planted on the floor behind me, Brooke rocks back and forth, lifting herself off of me just enough before dropping back down. I hold her tighter, and she meets my intensity, our bodies moving passionately as one unit. Both of our breathing increases, the only noises in an otherwise silent rink, intertwining with each other just as *we* are.

"Look at me," Brooke says suddenly, separating our chests now slick from our closeness.

I peer up at her, and she kisses me, her tongue eager to meet mine. When she pulls back, she searches my eyes. "What's wrong?" I ask.

She shakes her head. "Nothing." She gulps down a breath. "I'm just so proud of you."

My body freezes, my mind racing a mile a minute. I press my lips to hers in an attempt to stop myself from saying something I shouldn't—something she's not ready to hear. Something it's way too early for.

But *fuck*. How else do I explain this feeling?

"You're changing everything for me," I say back.

"No, Twelve," she says. "You're changing for yourself."

She starts moving again, but I'm still stuck on her words. She's right. I'm finally doing things *my* way. For *me*. But I wouldn't be able to do it alone. Not without someone in my corner who knows the truth. And it's been way too long since that was the case.

I used to think I wanted to be left alone. To be just another face in the crowd—lost. But what I'm learning is, all I ever really needed was to be found by someone who saw me for who I truly am—by her. And the rest of it started to melt away.

"You gonna be with me for real after all this?"

Brooke laughs. "Are we really talking about this *now*?"

I slide my arms behind her, reaching up to pull down on her shoulders, holding her in place. "Yeah, actually. We are."

She tries to continue riding me, but I have her unable to move. She clenches around me on purpose, and a guttural sound rips from my throat as my cock begs for its release. Brooke raises one brow, but besides a moan, I still don't waver.

She sighs. "Are you asking me to be your girlfriend after all this is over, Twelve?"

I chuckle, but it's short-lived as the slight movement it causes brings me that much closer to the edge. "Fuck, I guess I am."

Brooke sucks her teeth trying to smother her smile. "Well, I guess I do know you after all." I grin, then she continues. "But, I'm gonna need a little more than *'Fuck, I guess I am'* as we bang in the penalty box. Maybe you can use some of those performance skills for good."

She winks, and I drag her lip between my teeth. "You want a show? I'll give you a fucking show." I finally release her shoulders, and this time, I *do* bounce her in my lap.

Brooke cries out as she slides off of me, then sinks back down. "But only for me," she pants, grabbing her chest and massaging her own nipples.

Her head drops back as she falls apart, and I fill beneath her. "Yeah, baby" I groan, then I empty inside her, thinking of everything from these last few weeks. "Only for you."

33

Brooke

"**G**ood game, Twelve."

Drew walks through the door to my apartment and smothers me in his arms. "You think?" he asks, resting his head on the top of mine.

I nod, my hair rubbing against his chin. "I do."

Sighing, he releases me and slides his thumb under his chain. "Well, you're probably the only one."

I scoff, walking to the couch. "Drew, you scored twice."

"Yeah and both times I was quiet after. And so was the crowd." He sinks into the spot next to me, throwing his arm across the back of the cushion. I scoot closer to him, sliding my fingertip along the seam running down the side of his jeans.

He's not wrong. This game was as rough as the last, but Drew has kept to his word and stayed true to himself—no parties, dates, celebrations—much to Golden City's dismay.

"They'll get over it. And they'll get *used to* it."

"By tomorrow at 11a.m.?"

My lips turn in as I hide my doubt. "You keep doing what you're doing, and they'll move on to someone else's drama before you know it."

Drew grins in that way that makes my heart melt and my panties wet. "I think you underestimate your future boyfriend's fan base."

My cheeks grow much warmer than they should as a thirty-one-year-old woman. Drew's used that term so frequently this past week that the crazy is finally starting to wear off, but it's still so wild to think about for the two of us.

"You're ridiculous," I answer.

"It's true."

Remembering Alex's words from just last week, I smile. "So I've been told."

At almost the same time, both our phones buzz, his from his pocket and mine from the coffee table in front of us. We reach for them and groan simultaneously.

"Jane," he says, his voice full of annoyance.

"Is she still begging you to go out with that troll?"

Drew tilts his head down and looks up at me from under raised brows. "You mean, supermodel, Samantha Gray?"

"Isn't that what I said?" I deadpan. We both laugh softly. "I'm kidding. She's literally gorgeous."

"She is," he says. "But she's not you. And yes, that's what Jane's text was about." I nod understandingly as he tucks his phone into his pocket, ignoring her message. "What'd you get?"

I sigh loudly. "My mother."

"Another dinner reminder?"

"As if I could forget," I say, rolling my eyes.

Drew drops his palm onto my thigh, and my body responds as if it's always belonged there. "Is it really that bad?"

I tuck myself under his arm, pulling my legs up onto the couch. "I mean, probably not. It's just my mother's constant reminders and passive-aggressive comments about how I've repeatedly gone against her wishes my entire life."

Drew chuckles, and I pretend to be insulted. "Sorry, it's not funny. I just always thought I was the only one royally fucking with my parent's plan for me."

"Oh, no," I say quickly. "The only difference is, I'm finally coming around to the path my mom wants me to take, and you're just veering off of your dad's."

He goes quiet for a second before he finally replies. "That's because I let him call the shots for the last ten years. At least you were strong enough to do your own thing from the beginning."

I turn my body to face him. He looks at me, and his eyes are full of sadness that I recognize. I've seen the same upset reflected back at me in the mirror countless times. "Drew, I..." Playing with the strings on my sweatshirt, I fight my natural urge to blow off what I'm feeling and replace my true thoughts with something lighter.

But I'm not just doing this for me.

"I don't really think strength had anything to do with it. Sure, it was hard to take the hits, and being an outsider in your own family is, well—it's shitty. But going against the grain doesn't take any less strength than hiding who you really are."

"Yeah, well... I guess we all start somewhere."

A silence slips between us until he pulls away. I shift in my seat to find him looking down at me, his expression serious. "What?" I ask.

"I'm proud of you, too. You know that?" My eyes fall to my lap, twirling one string around my finger. "Hey, look at me."

Drew tilts my chin up and cradles my face in his hands. "I'm serious," he says, his eyes burrowing through me like they did that first night. "You never gave in—never settled. You held steadfast until *you* were ready. You took hold of your life and never fucking let go." He brushes my cheek with the pad of his thumb. "And your mom will be proud too when she comes around."

"So will your dad," I say quickly. Only, this time, I'm not deflecting. I mean it.

He gives me a small and unconvincing smile, breezing past my comment. "But until then—even after that—I'll be here."

Turning my neck, I press a kiss to his palm. "Don't leave," I say, grinning up at him. It's a play off of what he said before, but as soon as the words are spoken, I realize how much I truly mean them.

He kisses me deeply without a hint of levity. "Not a chance," he says. Slowly, my favorite smile grows on his lips. "I'm about to be your boyfriend, Mystery Girl, remember?"

I roll my eyes. "You're still ridiculous."

"You like me," he argues.

As if on instinct, I kiss him again, and our teeth graze each other as we both smile through it. My heart swells as it always does when Drew and I give another little piece of ourselves to each other.

"Yeah, Twelve. I definitely like you."

"So, how many more days left on the job?" Blake asks, as he gets down on all fours.

"Just this weekend," I answer as my head yanks backward. "My last game will be tomorrow..." My voice trails off as the timeline hits me.

It's coming up fast.

"Then, I'm pretty much finished." With that, Selah rips the doll brush she has in my hair so hard, I see stars. "Ouch!"

"Selah," Blake warns. "Be gentle."

"Sha sha, Book," she says sweetly, patting my head to apologize but hitting it almost as hard as she pulled.

"It's okay, Say Say."

As if my mother finds joy in throwing salt in my wounds, she joins the living room at the perfect time. "So, what is your plan for after the weekend then?" she asks, refolding a blanket that I'm pretty sure hasn't left the couch in three years. Blake sprawls out on his stomach, pulls out his phone, and checks out of the conversation. *Traitor.*

"Um, I'll go back to The Pub while I continue looking for other jobs like this one. I haven't heard back from the few places I've applied—a couple of hotels, a gym across town, some smaller businesses. The problem is, not everyone has a social media team in their budget."

I peer over just in time to see my mom press her lips into a straight line. "I really loved it, though," I continue. "It barely felt like work, honestly." I picture Drew's face, and although he was part of it, I'm telling the truth. My whole time with the Flames has been so fulfilling.

"Well, that's definitely something to consider," she says as she sits on the couch.

Selah, who must have the opposite sixth-sense as my mother, eases off of my scalp and starts playing with the actual babydoll instead. I quickly take advantage of my release and pull myself up on the sofa across from Mom.

"How's Aunt Ivy," I ask, watching as Selah attempts to gather the doll's hair into some sort of ponytail. A song bursts through the speakers of Blake's phone I don't recognize.

"Sorry," he says, quickly silencing whatever social media video he's escaping to.

Mom shakes off the noise and sighs. "You can ask her yourself if she ever shows up. She told me she'd be here fifteen minutes ago."

"Again?" I ask, surprised. "I think this is the most I've seen Ivy in the last few years."

"Yeah..." Mom says, her voice distant.

I wait for her to go on, and when she doesn't, I sit forward on the cushion. My mother may not often emit positivity, but there's something about the crease in her brow that causes tension in my shoulders. "Mom... is there something you aren't telling—"

"Holy shit!" Blake calls out, pushing himself up into a sitting position. "Did you know about this?"

My eyes—and my mind—dart back and forth between desperation for answers from Mom and curiosity about what Blake's going on about.

I try to ignore my brother's antics, but when I look back at him, his phone is turned toward me, and the image on the screen grabs my attention.

"What is it?" I say, leaning forward to read the headline written above a familiar face.

"Is this really Anderson's last season in G.C.?" Blake asks his question looking at me, but my vision tunnels as I reread the words on his device.

Drew Anderson's Talking Titans Trade.

"The Titans?" I whisper. "But they play in—"

"Washington? Yeah." Blake pulls his phone back and shakes his head. "What the hell, man? I didn't even get my damn autograph."

All the blood in my body rushes to my feet, and my chest constricts, my ears ringing despite the silence between us. Without thinking, I reach forward and snag the phone from his hand.

"What the—"

"Brooke, what are you doing?" Mom questions. "Do you even know this boy?"

"Everyone knows him, Mom," Blake explains. "He's the Flames' star forward—their captain."

Amy pops into the picture from the other room. "Ooh, are you talking about—"

"Hey, hey, hey. Don't even start with his muscles. He—"

"Can everyone just please shut up!" My words spew from my mouth much louder than intended, but between their comments and the thoughts in my head, I can't focus enough to even read the damn article.

It is rumored on good authority that Drew Anderson is looking to make a big change at the end of this season. Cam Rouke, right wing on the Washington Titans, who holds the same position as Anderson, announced his retirement earlier this week. This, in turn, sparked assumptions about who Washington would pick up to replace him.

A source, who would like to remain anonymous, but is admittedly very close to Anderson, shared earlier that "Drew has had a great run in Golden City, but is looking to venture out west to join the Titans in their pursuit of a Cup."

Speculations could be made that the move makes sense, especially after the Flames' forward has unexpectedly changed his tune recently, which hasn't happened since his failed drug test last season. His typical on-ice personality was clearly toned down during his last few games, and his own team's Instagram advertised a major change in his iconic image.

Although a haircut and lack of showboating aren't guaranteed evidence that number twelve plans to leave Golden City, one could argue that these may be small steps toward a greater change. It's possible that this franchise player is looking to build a new empire—or maybe he's simply a fallen hero looking to out-run an old mistake.

When I finally stop reading, my eyes stay frozen on the screen as it fades to black. I attempt to shove down the emotion in my throat, but my mouth is so dry I can barely swallow. My mother's voice seems to grow from a distance until her once faint words push through the fog and pull me back to reality.

"Brooke! Hello? What is going on?"

"I, um—"

"You okay, sis?" Blake asks cautiously. He grabs a hold of the phone as it slips from my grasp, and before I know it, I'm moving toward the door.

"Where are you going?" my mother shouts from the couch, but her voice barely registers. All I can think about are these last few weeks.

The kiss in the street.

Him blowing past my excuses.

The shooting bay. The sauna. The penalty box.

The cemetery.

Everything we've admitted out loud.

Don't leave.

Was he planning this the entire time?

Am I just another adjustment to his image?

My instincts say no. Drew's never been who *they* say he is. But maybe it wasn't calculated. Maybe this opportunity came up, and he didn't know how to tell me.

Ivy always says that timing is everything. Maybe this is just the universe's way of ending things for us. A quiet way of telling us we're wrong—it won't work. Of saving us from even more pain.

But then my biggest fear floats to the forefront of my mind. That none of that's true, and this has just been his most convincing performance of them all. My heart drops through my feet as they carry me toward the door, and I attempt to reassure myself.

He told me he'd be here. He wouldn't say that if he knew this was coming.

Or would he?

It hasn't been that long. Sure, we have history, and we didn't meet a month ago as strangers. But Drew's young. Maybe he got swept up in the *idea* of us—of someone sticking by him while everything else shifted.

I couldn't even blame him. As much as he's shaken my world, he's also been the one steady pillar as I navigated this new path in life. I thought this all happened so fast because we were drawn to each other. Understood each other. Were meant to be.

But maybe I was wrong. Maybe that pull wasn't an anchor.

Maybe it was an anvil.

I try to decide where I stand as I throw open the front door, but I'm saved from making any decisions. Or just thrown into a new one.

"Ivy!" I yell as I race toward my aunt lying face down on the sidewalk. "Oh my God." I reach her after what feels like an eternity and brush her matted hair from her face. Her eyes are closed—unresponsive—and blood trickles by her temple. "Ivy," I say again—a whisper this time.

All the emotions from the last ten minutes mix with the ones surfacing now, and the floodgates open, tears blurring my vision and rushing from my eyes. I open my mouth to scream, but nothing comes out. Instead, I hear my own name ring out around me.

"Brooke!" my brother calls as he flies down the porch steps. He's followed by my mother, who screams at the sight in front of her house. "Amy, get out here!"

The two of them rush the two of us, and I'm stuck between running from all of this and freezing in place. When my sister-in-law emerges from the house with my dad behind her holding Selah, I finally back away. Amy wobbles down the stairs as I hold on to my aunt's limp arm like if I don't let go, it won't be real.

None of it will be.

34

Drew

Striding into the locker room, I once again look at my phone sitting shattered in my hand. The spider-webbed screen taunts me as it has every other time before I shove it in my pocket.

I can't believe this is happening despite all the arguing with my dad and all the money I pay Jane to keep my personal business private. All of the changes I'm trying to make and somehow *this* is still the story.

Waking up this morning to a text from my agent, my P.R. manager, *and* my coach, all asking if there was something they should know, was like the fucking hat trick from hell. I'm not sure how the rumor started exactly—well, besides knowing my dad must be behind it—but it's out now, and I can't even imagine what the headlines are saying.

I haven't looked. In fact, after I left Brooke's last night, I turned my phone on airplane mode and spent the night listening to her playlist on repeat and wishing she didn't have dinner with her parents. I thought the last few games were bad—that maybe it was only up from here. But apparently, I was wrong because I passed out to that dream and woke up to a real-life nightmare.

I should have thought twice about smashing my phone to the floor first thing this morning after turning all of my messages back on. It's made getting a hold of Brooke difficult. I rode over to her place before the rink this morning, but she was already gone by the time I got there. My only hope now is that I can find her here before warm ups start.

I can't imagine what she's thinking. She finally lets me in—I tell her I'm not leaving—and now she hears that I have plans to do exactly that? I'm trying not to panic as much as I probably should—Brooke and I just get each other. She has to know that this wasn't me. That it isn't true. Or at least that's what I'm telling myself.

"Yo, you doin' alright, Cap?" Burns claps me on the back the second I get to my stall.

"Yeah, man," I say quickly, nerves still budding up my chest. "Hey, have you seen Brooke?"

"InstaBrooke?"

I pause, annoyed more than I should be by the random pet name. "Yeah, sure. Have you seen her?" I throw my backpack into my stall and continue walking through the locker room.

"Uh, no, not since the other day."

I stop outside the showers and exhale heavily, contemplating my next move. Brett steps up next to me before I can decide and places his hand on my shoulder. "What's wrong?"

I shake my head through a sigh. "Nothing, I just—I need to talk to her." Saying the words out loud tightens the knot in my stomach and increases the pulse in my head. My hand flies to my forehead in an attempt to rub out the tension as Brett bites at the inside of his cheek.

"Does this have anything to do with the rumors?" I peer over at him, dragging my palm to the back of my neck. The breath Brett blows through his lips fills the silence between us until he speaks again. "You, uh—there's no truth to that, is there?"

My body whips in his direction. "Fuck no," I say boldly. "That's all my dad. He just won't fucking quit."

He nods, bringing his eyes to his hands, then positions his body in front of mine. Ward walks past us, and I tip my chin up at him, but Brett doesn't move his gaze off of me. "Listen, Cap," he continues once Carter's gone. "For what it's worth... your old man probably just wants the best for you."

"Ha, right. He's an asshole, Burnsey," I rebuke, taking a step toward the hall to our right. Burns steps in front of me again, stopping me in my place as I attempt to squash the irritation building inside me for my best friend.

I need to see Brooke.

"Or maybe..." he continues hesitantly, his hands up in surrender. "Maybe he's just failing at trying to love you the only way he knows how."

I burst out in laughter. *He can't be serious.* "Not sure this calls for your usual Canadian positivity, buddy," I quip, but Burns doesn't crack a smile.

My brow creases as I search his face for any sign that he's joking, but the expression shining back at me is stone-cold. "Wait, you're serious?" I throw my hands to my hips and shift my weight. "You think him pushing me to be... pushing me so hard all this time is because he *cares*? That he started this rumor not to strong-arm me but because he doesn't know how else to *love* me?" Brett shrugs, and I cross my arms over my chest. "No shot."

"All I'm saying is that sometimes how someone treats you..." His voice drifts off as Ward walks past us again. I roll my eyes, waiting for the rest of his sentence. "It isn't personal."

I scoff, dropping my arms back to my sides. "No offense, bro, but it feels pretty fucking personal."

Burnsey gives me an empty grin, then shakes his head. "Yeah, no, for sure. I totally get that," he relents. "Just, uh—just give it some thought, eh?"

I nod and smack my palm against his shoulder. "Sure, man."

His face falls, and I realize that, for some reason, this means something to him. As I study his expression, I become more sure. Me understanding this is big—important.

"Hey," I say seriously, my annoyance morphing into reassurance. "I will. Okay?"

He smiles, genuinely this time. "Love ya, bud," he says, shoving his hands into his pockets.

"Yeah," I say, still taken aback by our entire conversation. Brett is always good for throwing me off with the shit he says, but this hits harder than it usually does.

I give his arm a squeeze, looking at him with my full attention. "Love you too, Burnsey."

He finally steps out of my way, but I can't shake his words as they stick with me like he meant them to. For the millionth time this morning,

Brooke's face drifts into my mind, but this time, it's for a different reason. When she and I reconnected, she shot me down so fast my head spun. She was short and closed-off and acted like she wanted nothing to do with me.

But I didn't quit.

I knew that deep down those actions weren't directed at me. I gave her the time she needed—the space she *deserved*—to let me in. And the grace to do it the only way she knew how.

So, how come with my dad it's different? Instincts tell me that it's because he's *supposed* to love me unconditionally—I had to earn Brooke's feelings. But maybe Brett's right.

That's just really fucking hard to believe right now.

I spent every second I had before warm ups, searching for Brooke. I checked the offices and the tunnel, the shooting bay and the gym. I even checked the goddamn sauna, which only made me fucking hard on top of everything else. She's not here. So, either she bailed on the game or she's doing one hell of a job avoiding me.

Both options worry me. She should be here. This is her last game with the Flames. Did something happen? Or is the other possibility the only reason for her absence? Maybe she's not avoiding me in the arena. Maybe she's gone, and she's avoiding me altogether.

I tried convincing myself earlier that if anyone would understand that this is all bullshit, it'd be her. Our... whatever it is now... was built on her learning about how different I am from how the world sees me. But doubt creeps into my mind like the tune of an obnoxious song you can't outrun. I can't lose her right now. *Fuck*, I can't lose her ever. And if anything good has come from this, it's the solidification that there's not an ounce of doubt in my mind about that.

Glancing up at the countdown clock, the rapid-fire numbers tick past at the rate of my heartbeat. I've spent most of warm ups avoiding all people in the stands, looking for the only one I care to talk to right now. As the horn sounds to call us back to the bench, my eyes still don't find Brooke, but they land on what might be the next best thing. Sprinting to the boards while the team piles off of the ice, I pound my glove on the glass off to the side of the boys.

"Coach's girl!" I yell, my voice muffled by the wall between us. When she doesn't look, I tap my stick against the glass. "Alex!"

With that, her head spins toward me, then to Monte who's busy talking to Max. When she looks back at me, I pull my helmet off and throw my head back, telling her to move closer. She stands almost hesitantly, but I don't have time to overthink if that's because she's confused or knows something I don't. Or because she's trying to avoid coming between me and her best friend.

"Where is she?" I call when she reaches the boards.

She once again looks to Coach, whose back is turned to the both of us. "At the hospital, I think."

I stand paralyzed, pulling a Petrov and racing through every word I know that rhymes with hospital, thinking I must have misheard her. When I come up empty handed, I try to blink away the worry.

"Sorry, no," Alex adds before I can respond. "She's fine." My whole body deflates, and she definitely notices. She grins and raises her brows in... admiration? Acceptance? "Her aunt was taken there yesterday. I think she's been with her."

Once again, I'm up in arms as Brooke's words from before seem to echo off the walls.

I'm just really scared she's not okay.

My mystery girl is not fine. She's worrying and panicking just like I am, but she's shoving it down, swallowing it, and carrying it all by herself. She's pretending she's alright so she doesn't burden anyone else. So she doesn't have to feel what she's trying to tuck away.

But she does.

Even if she won't say it out loud. Even if she seems *fine* to the world.

"Fuck," I whisper as my last teammate steps off of the ice.

"What?" Alex yells.

I shake my head, my mind racing a mile a minute as I push off toward the bench. "Thank you," I call back to her, holding my helmet up and over my head.

Stepping past the boards, I calculate how much time sits between now and the time I can get to her. Every fiber of my being says to leave. To skip the game, find my girl, and make sure she's okay. Make sure *we're* okay. But I can't do that. Especially now. Not with the narrative already working against me.

"Drew! Drew!" The sound of my name floats above me as I step into the tunnel. I avoid searching for the source, but instead, I find Emma Dean waiting for me as I take just a few paces toward the locker room.

"Not now, Emma," I say, brushing her off. I take one step forward, but her trusty cameraman blocks my way. "Seriously, dude?"

He shrugs, hiding behind his equipment, as Emma tries again. "Oh, come on, Drew. Before the game—give us the Anderson Exclusive. Are you leaving Golden City at the end of this season?"

I part my lips to speak—or fucking tell her off—but the same voice from earlier answers first. "No, he's not."

I turn to see my dad standing behind me, and his eyes meet mine differently than they usually do. More genuine.

"I, um..." My head's fucking spinning. I can't keep up.

"Drew is happy where he is. The Flames are his family," he says into the camera. Emma's eyes dart back and forth between the two of us before Dad turns to face me. "One he desperately needed these last few years."

"And how do you know our star forward?" Emma asks, but I can't seem to tear my eyes away from *him*.

"I'm his father," he says, looking at me.

"Anything to add, Drew?" Emma shoves the microphone in my face, and I shake my head, still looking at a man I haven't seen in years. "Well, you heard it here first, G.C.—looks like we'll get number twelve a little longer."

I shoot her a look when she finally signs off, but Emma barely notices as she turns to walk away. With her out of the picture, I bring my attention back to Dad, questioning him with just my expression.

"I went to visit your mother's grave the other day, which was long overdue," he says, not quite making eye contact.

I tilt my head, curious about what he's getting at and how this relates to the rumors. "You were there. I saw you with that girl outside of the locker room the last time we actually talked in person." The creases in my forehead flatten. "Are you seeing her?"

"Uh, yeah," I stutter, still so thrown. "I am. Sort of. I guess." *Hopefully.*

Dad grins without showing his teeth, his eyes fluttering. "I barely recognized you between the hair and the smile. You looked happy there. With her." He clears his throat before continuing. "Happier than I've seen you in a long time."

"I am, Dad," I shoot back.

"Does she have anything to do with the changes you've been making?"

"Yeah," I jeer. "She actually does. And those *changes* are—"

"They're good," he interrupts.

The end of my sentence gets stuck in my throat. "They are?" is all I manage to say.

"Yeah, son. I—I didn't think so at first. But I see it now. That's why I've been trying to call you."

"My phone's broken."

He nods. "Well, I figured you'd assume I was the one who started that rumor, but—"

"Wait... it wasn't you?"

He sighs heavily, looking down at his feet. "I don't blame you for thinking that. It's shameful really, but I get it. It wasn't though, Drew. I swear. When I saw you at the cemetery, it all clicked for me. Something else overdue, I guess. The fact that you talk to a tombstone more than your father probably should have been a hint all along... not that it's a bad thing. You know what I mean." Dad cracks his neck to one side and nervously rubs his arm. "But I haven't seen you laugh like that since freshman year. Then, after the last few games, it all started to add up. The play changes, the hair, the girl... it's like I saw a glimpse of who you were before... when your mother was still around."

I want to say so many things. Ask so many questions. But I can't seem to sort them out. So, instead, Dad continues. "This person you've become—the one I've forced on you—that's not *you*. "

My shoulders fall, the weight I once carried instantly gone. "It's not, Dad. It hasn't been for a really long time. I'm not sure it ever was."

"No, I know," he says, brushing the tip of his toe across the rubber flooring. "And I'm sorry for not seeing that. When your mother died, I... I didn't know what to do—how to carry that grief and still be there for you. I think it was easier for me to just get lost in it all. To avoid my new reality. To convince myself that I was doing what was best for you so that you didn't have to acknowledge it either. Like if you were just bigger, better, more successful, that you'd somehow manage to forget that your entire world was uprooted when you were supposed to be at your most carefree."

The locker room door slams shut, and only then do I realize that we're alone in the tunnel—the two of us left to soak up the silence. I picture Brooke again for the same reason as I did with Burns—who apparently was right—and I tell him exactly what I'd say to her.

"I didn't need to get lost in it, Dad. I needed to feel it. To live through it in a way that would make her proud."

"Oh, she's proud of you, son. That I'm sure of. And this..." He flicks his fingertips through the top of my hair. "This would make her happier than anything."

"The hair?" I ask, brushing my glove past my fringe.

"All of it."

I swallow hard—pain, happiness, frustration, peace—all of it passing through me at once. "I don't want to leave Golden City, Dad. I'm not going to."

"I know, son. And I'm done pushing for that. Hell, I'm done pushing for any of it."

His words settle over me, and for a second, I'm a teenager again. My mom is gone, but my dad's still here. And despite all of my disheveled pieces, it's as if he's helping me to press them back together. All of them but one.

"I don't know what's going to happen."

He looks at me, his eyes full of emotion, and the corners of his lips curled slightly. "With the girl, you mean." It's not a question. It looks like my dad still knows me after all.

"Brooke."

"Brooke," he repeats, and I'm taken back to the day I first heard her name spoken out loud.

"Yeah," I sigh, remembering how much has changed since then—since she came back to me. "There's just a lot of shit going on."

"Has she seen the rumor?"

I inhale, narrowing my eyes. "She might have."

"Well, is she mad?"

"It's possible."

He pauses, squinting at me. "Okay... what'd she say when you talked to her about it?"

My face scrunches up as I respond. "I haven't." Dad's lips fall open. "No phone, remember?"

He scratches the back of his head, then heaves out a deep breath. "Drew... do you love her?"

I smile genuinely for the first time all day. "I definitely like her," I answer coyly.

He purses his lips and smothers a laugh. "Then I think you should get the hell out of here."

"Dad, I can't just—"

"Yes," he says bluntly. "You can."

"I can't. I'll get—"

"Anderson!" My head snaps up to find Monte at the locker room entrance. "What the hell are you doing?"

I look at my dad, and he tips his head toward the door.

"Coach," I move toward him, my heart-racing in my chest. "Brooke, she's..."

"I know," he says. Then he exhales deeply. "Go."

"Wait, are you sure?"

"No," he answers, blowing another breath through his lips. "But Brooke's like family, and you... well, just don't fuck this up, okay?"

I don't need him to explain that he means more than just her. "I won't, Coach."

With that, he holds the door open for me, but before I step through it, I turn back to my father. Tears threaten to well at the sight of him. For the first time in a long time, my chest doesn't constrict when he looks back at me. Anger doesn't burn in my chest. Bitterness doesn't swell in my gut. For the first time in a long time, when our eyes meet, all I see is Dad.

"I love you too, son," he says, staring back at me.

I turn to leave, but at the last minute, I twist back around. "Wait... if you didn't tell the reporter then..."

He takes a deep breath. "There's only one person who would benefit from stirring up drama with you. And who would be pissed that you aren't listening to her."

I scoff. "I guess I have a few calls to make then."

Dad pulls his phone from his pocket and tosses it to me. I rip my glove from my hand, and it lands in my palm with a smack. "I don't have Brooke's number, but I have the rest of the ones you're probably looking for."

"Thanks, Dad," I say. He smiles at me, and I finally leave.

To fix this mess.

And get my girl.

35

Brooke

"*F*" *alling down toward her, I roll her thighs so her knees point out-ward. She glistens between them, and I force myself not to dive right...* alright, I think that's enough for today."

I glance up at Aunt Ivy over the pages of her latest read to find her eyes closed and her breathing steady. She's out cold. I'm glad she's resting, she needs it, but I am questioning how *that* scene is the one that put her to sleep. Then again, I'm always a little curious about the things that Ivy does.

The doctors say she has a weak heart. I guess cardiac strength isn't measured in kindness or adventures. She's lucky she was on her way over yesterday—or maybe not, if the mere *idea* of my mother was enough to make her heart skip a beat. But my free-spirited soul of an aunt could have been anywhere when she collapsed to the ground.

Setting the book in the bag that it came from, I quietly scoot my chair back and stand. Draping the white hospital-grade blanket over her toes, I study the way her chest repeatedly rises and falls, her breaths low and slow with heavy sleep.

I wish we were somewhere else—anywhere else. I wish we were sipping coffees together while I listened to Ivy tell the story about her trip to the nudist colony or that time she supposedly shared a cigarette with Dolly Parton at a bus stop. I'd laugh, and she'd hum the song they sang together under the overhang until she realized it wasn't Dolly after all because *her* vibrato would never sound that pitchy.

I wish we weren't stuck in a hospital room surrounded by stark white walls and beeping machines. But in a strange way, I'm also grateful for the distraction. Those headlines last night hit me like a train off its tracks, and I'm still not sure what I'm supposed to believe. The worst part is, I haven't talked to Drew. Not once. I was too distracted to reach out about something that suddenly felt so insignificant in comparison, and he either didn't know about the stories or didn't care enough to call me.

I stopped checking my phone after things settled down here. Alex and Levi both know where I am. The team's content is scheduled for the rest of my time with the Flames. And the only things waiting on that screen are headlines I'm avoiding and messages that don't seem to be coming. I'm trying not to jump to conclusions, but between his acting skills and the radio silence, things aren't adding up in my favor.

I was upset at first—frustrated, angry, hurt. Still am. But now, most of it is directed at myself. This is why I don't open up. Why I keep things surface level—easy. Why I avoid commitments—in jobs, relationships, all of it. Because the second you let yourself believe it could actually work out—you might get the guy, land that job, maybe even make your mom proud—it doesn't.

Leaning down, I place a gentle kiss on Aunt Ivy's head before tip-toeing out of her room. I reach back to pull the door shut, and when I turn around, I find my mother standing mere inches from me.

"Shit," I whisper-yell, bringing a hand to my chest. "Good thing I'm not the one with the weak heart, Mom. You scared me half to death."

With a roll of her eyes, she peeks through the window of the hospital room door. "How's she doing?"

"She's asleep. I was, uh, reading to her."

"A sex scene?" she asks emotionlessly, walking back toward the waiting room. I follow her, cringing at those last two words coming from my mother's mouth. I nod anyway, and so does she. "When we were teenagers and would sneak erotic novels from the library, she used to tab those scenes to reread at night. It's a mystery how that woman lands so many men without falling asleep underneath them."

A laugh bursts from my throat and catches both of us completely off guard. "Sorry," I say, covering my mouth with my palm. "It's just—this is somehow the most normal, yet most ridiculous, conversation we've ever had."

Mom's face falls, humor slipping from her eyes as she slinks into an empty chair. I follow her lead, taking the seat next to it, but she doesn't look over. Instead, she picks at the frayed corner of the blue cushion overtop of the armrest.

"I didn't mean anything by that, Mom. I just... you know. We aren't exactly the Gilmore girls."

She lets out a deep breath like she's been holding it for years and finally turns to me. "You know, I've never admitted it out loud," she says. "But I was always jealous of Ivy."

I blink at her, caught completely off guard. She sees my confusion and gives me a smile that doesn't quite reach her eyes.

"I was," she says again. "She's carefree and open-minded. The fun one. Always dancing through life like there's nothing holding her back—like gravity doesn't apply to her like it does the rest of us. She doesn't care about jumping in lakes fully clothed or catching rides with strangers because their car smells like wildflowers. There are no risks with her. No hesitations. Ivy's the one who will hop on a boat and chase the horizon, and I'm the one standing on the shore charting riptides and undertows."

A laugh seeps through my lips as I picture the scene. "She sure is something, isn't she?"

Mom chuckles too, but there's no weight to it. "You're a lot like her," she says.

I frown. "Me? No way."

"You are," she insists. "Deep down. You have more Ivy in you than you do me, that's for sure. And, Brooke, that's always scared the hell out of me."

"Really?" I ask, surprised.

"Yes. Why do you think I've been so hard on you? So desperate for you to choose something—*someone*—anything that meant you were anchored. Ivy's life, it looks beautiful, but there's a darkness to that kind of freedom. It's lonely. Dangerous. I never know where she is or when I'll hear from her. I mean, look at yesterday. If she hadn't collapsed on our doorstep, would I have even heard about it? Would anyone?"

For a moment, I stiffen, ready to jump to my aunt's defense. Of course she would have heard. But then I think of how I can't even be sure her number's still the same each time she reaches out. "I guess I never thought of it like that before."

"I know I've pushed you to settle down..."

I throw her a side-eye that I temper with a grin.

"Relentlessly," she adds. "I'm sure it's felt like I'm trying to steer you in *my* direction, and I know it's come between us. But I think, selfishly, I couldn't take worrying about someone else that I love in the same way that I worry about her. I don't know if I could have done it again."

"But Ivy's always been fine, Mom. I don't think I've ever seen her sweat—unless she was talking about the guy from Morocco with the two Pomeranians."

That earns a smile, but it's fleeting. "She performs well, but I see her. The looks she gives you and your brother when she comes around—like she's trying to memorize each moment before she disappears again. She wears armor, but Ivy's not wandering, Brooke. She's running. She clings to her sovereignty like it's her shield, but is she independent? Or is she alone?"

My jaw grows tight as I fight the burning rising in my chest. It's a sadness I didn't expect. For Aunt Ivy. For Mom. For me—for the fact that I could ask myself those same questions. She gives me the space to connect the dots and smiles softly when I do. "I always just thought you were disappointed in me."

Mom's eyes fall shut as she exhales. When she opens them, they're heavy and wet. "I was never disappointed in you, Brooke. I was scared. And fear builds walls nearly impossible to tear down—made of control and opinions." She blows out a shaky breath as her lower lip begins to quiver. "I'm so sorry that you've felt that way. That I let my worries show through as anything but love. I just... I don't want you to be alone, Brooke. I don't want you to run from life and relationships and genuine connections. I don't want commitment to be scary. I want you to put down roots and enjoy it—flourish."

Tears prick at the corners of my eyes as Mom drops her hand into mine and squeezes gently, wiping away the dampness on her cheek. For the first time, I see her not as my hypercritical mother, but as a person. A woman. A sister. Someone who has been holding on to too much for too long—masking her own fears as something more tolerable.

And, for the first time, I see myself through her eyes, too.

"I've been seeing Drew Anderson," I blurt out.

Mom sniffles, then sits up straighter as if she's contemplating how to respond. "He's the hockey player Blake was talking about, right?"

"Yeah," I admit. I wait for her judgment—a look, an eye roll—but nothing comes.

"So, that explains the escape," she finally says.

I smile awkwardly. "We met last year, before the Flames job started. He's younger than me, and we're so different. But actually... so alike."

"What did he say when you talked to him?"

I clear my throat, avoiding her eyes. "I, uh—I didn't."

Mom's go wide. "What? Brooke, why?"

I glance obviously around the waiting room, then bring my gaze back to hers. "We've been a little busy, Mom. This was so much more important. Besides... he hasn't tried to reach me either."

My voice softens as the weight of that settles. Mom nods, her brow furrowed, but to her credit, she doesn't jump in.

"Anyway, I think it's over now. He's leaving—or he's not. Either way, I think it might just be a sign that it wasn't meant to be."

"Is it?" she presses quietly. Her tone is gentle, but the question cuts deep. I narrow my eyes, preparing to answer, but before I can, she strikes again. "Or is it just safer to let him go and pretend that it won't break you than to let him leave you first?"

Her words land with a force I wasn't expecting, and Alex's echo in my mind.

"You can cut people out easier than anyone I know."

I part my lips to respond, but nothing comes. No excuses. No defenses. She's right. It's my reflex to shut people out—at least emotionally. To guard my heart from those who threaten to hurt it. It doesn't make it right. But it's helped me survive.

"You don't have to be scared, Brooke," Mom reassures. "If you learn anything from me, please don't let it be timelines or correct paths. Let it be this—don't allow fear to make you walk away from the very thing you're the most afraid of losing."

My chest is somehow suddenly both too full and airless at the same time. "I'm not *that* scared of losing him," I whisper mostly to myself. But even I don't believe it.

Mom tilts her chin down and gives me that mothering look. "Right or wrong, many things have been said in my house that should have gotten a reaction out of you, Brooke. But only one landed so hard you had to run. And that is Andrew—"

"Just Drew."

"Right. That is Drew Alder—"

"Anderson."

Mom looks at me blankly. "Mhmm, Drew Ander—you know what? You get what I'm saying. You brush everything off, Brooke. And this—*he*—was the only thing that challenged that."

I swallow hard, scared to admit the truth. "Yeah... I guess you're right."

"Well, there's something I've never heard you say."

I peer up to see her smiling at me, and I smile back. "Here's something else you've probably never heard—I really am looking to settle down, Mom. With the job thing."

"I can see that. And I am so proud of you."

Her words hit with more edge than they should. *He was right.*

"It's hard, but I'm trying," I say, defeated.

"It'll come."

"And with relationships."

She nods. "I see that too."

I take a deep breath, choosing my words carefully. "I *am* scared," I finally admit.

Mom presses her lips together and brushes the pad of her thumb across my hand. "Yeah... I know a little something about that."

"Relationships are hard enough, but this is all just... *a lot*. His image, the age difference, these rumors. I've spent all this time holding on to who I am—guarding myself from everything. I thought when I found someone, it'd be simple. This isn't. And I'm afraid I'll get lost in the... in the *muchness* of it all."

"Oh, hunny," she coos. "That's where you're like me. But that's the best part of finding someone—finally being able to be Ivy. At least with *him*. Letting go just enough to not have to carry it all on your own. Despite outward appearances, you've spent your whole life trapped in here." She drops my hand and reaches forward to tap my temple, then gently presses her finger against my chest. "Because you're afraid of what living in *here* might be like."

The corners of my lips curl up slightly, and she nods as if she's been waiting for it. "I know I've had a lot to do with that."

I shrug my shoulders, then wave her away half-heartedly. "I think a lot of it is just who I am."

"It's not though," she says quickly. "Look at Selah and Alex and that friend from your work. You met them after decades of 'guarding yourself,' and you still let them in. That heart of yours that you think is so easily distracted by humor and sarcasm... it's not. At least not as easily as your mind might be. It knows what it wants to hold on to. And trust me..." her voice fades as she looks towards her sister's room. "That's one thing you won't ever outrun."

Sliding my zipper mindlessly up and down the front of my jacket, I soak up her thoughts. The idea of letting Drew fully into my heart is scary as hell. But I think if I'm honest with myself, he's already there. Just like Say Say and Alex and Tessa. He somehow fought his way in, and now? Now, I wouldn't just be *keeping* him out, I'd be *throwing* him out. And something tells me that Mom's right again. That would be a lot harder to do.

Especially when it feels so right with him there.

"Do you know what I'm saying, Brooke?" Mom asks, searching my face for her answer.

I huff out a laugh, looking down at my zipper, then bring my eyes back to her. "All I got from that is that you think I'm funny..."

She slaps my arm before grabbing my hands again, and we both sink forward in our chairs. "No, I hear you," I say, then I bite my lip trying to decide how much to give.

She notices. "Tell me," she says.

I contemplate it for another few seconds before finally giving in. "I do really like him, Mom." She smiles softly and nods. "And this is what I wanted—to settle down. To build something. But what if he *is* leaving? What if I finally lay a foundation and he's gone before anything can grow?"

She doesn't answer right away. Instead, she traces soft circles on the back of my hand with her thumb. "Then you still built it," she argues gently. "You still proved that you're ready. That you're capable."

"Yeah," I say, still not quite convinced.

Mom sits up straighter. "You're not fragile, Brooke. You never have been. And I might have taken advantage of that, but it's true."

Her voice cracks so slightly that at any other moment I might have missed it. But I don't. "And you're intuitive," she adds, catching me by surprise. "You know yourself, and you read others better than most people I know. Something tells me you wouldn't have gotten this far just chasing hope."

My brows crease together as a wave of something I can only explain as reassurance washes over me. "What do you mean?"

Mom shakes her head. "I think it's more of what I'm asking. Do you think Drew would do this, Brooke? Just decide he's leaving without any warning?"

She pauses, giving me time to think, but I don't need it. The answer is already waiting. "No," I say easily. "No, I really don't think he would."

Mom gives me her infamous *I Told You So* look, but for the first time, I'm grateful for it. "Well, there ya go." She drops my hands and holds hers open. "You are whole all by yourself, hunny—always have been. And that's one of your greatest qualities." She peers down at me as she has so often. "But talk to him. Let him explain for himself."

I nod, already knowing I will.

"And for the love of God," she adds, her tone lifting. "Go get your damn man."

My mouth falls to the floor, and Mom simply raises one eyebrow in my direction. "I love this version of you," I finally quip.

She reaches for my shoulders and pulls me into a tight hug. "And I love every version of you."

I squeeze her back, reveling in quite possibly the most genuine embrace we've ever had. This is one of those moments, I think, where there will be befores and afters. I smile, holding her just a little longer, then let go.

I can't wait for the afters.

"Now, leave!" she says, her volume at an absolutely inappropriate waiting room level. An older man behind us, who I just now am realizing is asleep in a chair, snores loudly and clicks his lips, his eyes still heavy.

Adrenaline courses through me as I prepare to obey, but then my whole body melts. "There's really no rush. He has a game. And I have no car—we drove here together."

"So, take mine. And go wait for him."

I shake my head. "It's just starting. Those things take hours. What if you or Dad or Ivy needs something?"

"Then call one of those car services—Lift or Huber."

I snort. "I'm sorry, do you mean an Uber?"

She rolls her eyes playfully. "Will you just call already?"

"Okay," I say, taking a deep breath. "Okay, fine. Yeah, I'll call."

"Good." She stands, presumably to go check on Aunt Ivy. I join her on my feet, suddenly full of energy. "Hear him out. I'll be rooting for you."

My vision blurs as I hug her again. "Thanks, Mom," I whisper.

"No, hunny," she says, holding tight. "Thank *you*."

"Yeah, I saw it. The one with Liam Montgomery's perfect. I'd say go with that for now, and we can tweak the others to post throughout the rest of the week. Yeah... uh huh, right. Okay, perfect, talk then."

My eyes shoot back down to my phone as I pretend my ears didn't perk right up at the sound of Liam's name. The man standing in front of me outside the hospital doors turns around, and we nearly collide.

"I'm so sorry," he says as I fumble my phone in my hands.

"No, don't be. I wasn't paying attention." *To anything but your phone call.*

"I get so lost in work calls, sometimes I forget I don't actually live in a baseball bubble."

I offer him a forced laugh, glancing back down at my screen. I tried Drew twice since I got out here despite knowing he's already on the ice. Both calls went straight to voicemail, which is not unexpected, but doesn't help to fill the pit in my stomach.

So now, I wait.

Seven more minutes until Robert arrives in his black sedan.

"I get that," I say, though my mind is still looping through every possible scenario with Drew.

"Do you follow the Gators?" he asks, sucking from the vape in his hand.

"I'm, uh, more of a hockey girl," I answer, distracted.

My words tumble out before I can filter them. And my stomach flips at how easily they do.

Drew.

"But I know Liam," I add quickly. "He's great."

"Highest baseball IQ on the field."

"Yeah." I smile, pretending that's exactly what I meant. That I'm impressed by his stats and not that he's an incredible father, loyal brother, and one of the kindest souls I know.

"I've actually been working with his brother for the Flames recently."

The second I say it, my chest tightens. I've been so caught with what's next with Drew that I forgot to worry about what's next for *me.*

"Oh, what is it you do?"

"I've been filling in as their social media manager until their new hire could start permanently."

"No way! Wait, so you're the one who made the post of the guys reenacting pictures from their childhood?"

I smile thinking of Ward sucking his thumb at the ripe age of twenty-seven and Petrov wearing an ushanka as Burns played his babushka, spoon-feeding him mashed potatoes. "Yeah, I did a question box asking the fans what they wanted from the boys, and couldn't unsee that idea."

He hits his vape again and blows the sweet smoke behind him. "It was hilarious," he says, turning back to me. "Seriously, gold. If you're ever looking for something else outside of their organization, give me a call." He reaches into his back pocket and pulls out his wallet, sliding a business card from the clip.

"Oh, uh..." I read the name and title written across the middle: Miles Whitaker - Director of Digital Content. "Honestly, that's all the experience I have. It was just temporary—a favor, really."

"Well, it's sort of my job to keep tabs on all the media for the Golden City teams. You know, make sure we match up. And your stuff has been good. Funny. People probably eat that shit up. We're currently looking for a fan engagement specialist. It may not pay as much as a social media manager position, but there's room to grow. And honestly, just going off of what I remember seeing, that's your specialty."

I'm left speechless, his offer taking me aback and a low rumble in the distance distracting my thoughts.

Miles takes another puff, raising his brows and hollowing his cheeks. "Think about it and give me a call. This might sound bad, but we haven't had much interest. Between that and references from Jack and Levi, I could all but guarantee you the job."

Flicking the card rhythmically in my hand, I nod. "I will, thank you."

And I mean it. Maybe this is what I need.

Maybe this is all I'll have.

"You got it," he says before heading back toward the entrance.

I shove the card into my jacket pocket and click my phone screen on, bouncing on my toes with more nervous energy than ever. "Four minutes," I whisper aloud, but I can barely hear my own voice as the same thunderous sound from before grows louder.

Suddenly, there's an all too recognizable popping sound that sends shivers down my spine. My head jerks up just in time to see a familiar bike rolling to a stop in front of me, and my heart stops as the rider pulls his helmet off, revealing himself.

"Hey you," he says, killing the motor.

I step forward, not quite convinced it's really him parked in front of me. "Twelve?" I question under my breath.

Drew's shoulders fall as he heaves a huge sigh, the corner of his lips turning up. "Mystery girl."

36

Drew

"Wait, what are you doing here?" Brooke slowly slinks toward me as I round the front of my bike to meet her.

Grabbing her shoulders, I give her a once over. "Are you okay?" I ask, my voice full of concern.

"Drew, don't you have a game like..." She wedges her wrist between our chests to check her nonexistent watch. "Now?"

Sliding my hands behind her ears, I cradle her cheeks in my palms. "Brooke," I say sternly. Her eyes snap to mine. "Are *you* okay?"

She shakes her head and swallows hard. "Yeah, my aunt, she... fell. She has some stuff going on, but she's going to be okay, I think. And I'm... um..." Tugging her toward me, I wrap my arms around her and hug her tight. "Fine," she finishes through a breath.

Her body is rigid against mine, all of my fear about how she'd take the rumors resurfacing and pushing through the concern. "You saw them didn't you?"

"Saw what?"

My jaw grows tight as I pull back and look at her deeply. "The headlines."

Her lips part as she shakes her head. "Yeah, Drew. It's fine. We knew this might not go anywhere and—"

"What? No," I cut her off, my pulse pounding. "Don't do that."

"I'm just saying," she tries again, her voice weak. "I know this is a lot—you're making changes, I'm making changes. Maybe the two just don't... mesh."

My stomach drops, an intensity building in its place. "Are you serious?" I shoot out, the pain and frustration twisting my words before I can stop them.

Brooke's eyes go wide, then her brow furrows. "Well, I just mean... I thought that..." She drops her head into her hands and continues speaking, her voice muffled by her palms. "Fuck, I'm messing this up."

I stand frozen, forehead creased, trying to make sense of what's happening. I thought *I* was the one screwing with this—the one ruining everything we've built.

I pull her hands away from her face, lowering myself to meet her eyes. "Talk to me," I say, my voice calmer now.

Brooke raises her head slowly, her shoulders sunken. "I promised my mom that I wouldn't just write this off because it was easier."

"Easier than fighting for it?"

"No," she whispers, huffing out a laugh under her breath. "Than losing it."

I exhale, my chest caving under the weight—or maybe the relief. "Brooke," I say, inching closer. "I'm not leaving."

She stands taller, her eyes darting between mine. "You're not?"

"No." I shake my head slowly. "I never was."

"I read the article, and—"

"It's all bullshit, Brooke," I explain, taking both of her hands in mine. "You have to know that. Hell, you would know better than anyone that what those people say about me isn't true. It was fucking Jane," I scoff. "Can you believe it? Her little tantrum, I guess because of me going rogue."

"For not dating the troll," she adds with a nod. A smile slips past her lips, and it radiates through me like goddamn lightning.

"Maybe," I chuckle. Her face tightens again, and I rush back in. "I handled it, baby," I continue. "I told you I'm not going anywhere, and I'm not. I called my agent before I even left the arena. The papers are already drawn up and with my lawyer. They're all but signed, Brooke. I'm staying in G.C."

She goes to speak, but I cut her off.

Because I know her.

"I'm not just doing this for you either," I add. "This is my home. My team. My city. My friends are here. My *mom* is here. And yea..." I tug on her wrist, pulling her just a bit closer. "You're here too, and that means everything to me. But, honestly, this is about *my* life, Brooke, and for once, I'm taking charge of it."

Her shoulders relax for the first time since I've gotten here, and looking into her chocolate eyes, I see *her* again. *My not so mysterious girl.*

"God, I was so sure yesterday," she says, glancing down at her feet. "About us. About everything. But then I saw the article, and the accident happened with my aunt, and... I want this, Drew, I *do*. That's the point. But apparently I have no clue what the hell I'm doing."

"And you think *I* do?" I ask through a sigh, tucking a hair behind her ear. "There's a reason you're the only person I've let see this version of me—the real me."

She sucks in a breath, and her hand slips around my waist almost instinctively. "I don't want the giant scissors anymore," she mumbles, leaning her head against my chest.

I laugh, and the rumble moves through both of us. "Am I supposed to know what that means?"

Brooke stands up and loops her arms around my neck. She runs her fingers underneath the cool metal of my chain and brushes gently. "You don't really need to." Her amusement is swallowed by a breath that catches in her throat. "Just know I definitely like you, Twelve. And it feels good." Her eyes glaze over, but her lips turn up. "Really good."

The final weight that sits on my shoulders disappears as she strokes the back of my neck with her thumb. I drop my forehead to hers, eyes closing, lungs filling, words pouring out before I can overthink them.

"You have no idea what it feels like to be falling in love with you, Mystery Girl."

Brooke gasps softly, but I pull her in tight before she can respond.

I don't need her reaction. I don't want it right now.

I just want her—us.

Like this.

I've gained a lot of things in these last seven years—money, fame, notoriety. Cars, bikes, brand deals worth more than both of those combined. But I lost myself along the way. When I think about my time as a rookie—an eighteen year old just getting his start, the one willing to do whatever it takes, whatever he's told—I want to scream at him not to worry about the noise.

I want to tell him that winning the hearts of a million fans isn't worth anything if you don't love yourself. I want to stand behind him and whisper in his ear every time he forces himself to attend the party, do the dance, or take the date. Remind him that at the very least, he should find someone to hold on to throughout the chaos. Someone who will be there for him despite it all. Who will trust *him* no matter what the world says.

Because that—*this*—is all that really matters.

Picking up my head, I look into her eyes. She stares back expectantly, like she's asking for guidance on what to say next. But she doesn't need to say anything.

The fact that she's still here says it all.

"So, are you officially done with the Flames then?" I ask, suddenly needing the answer.

Brooke lets her eyes wander, then shrugs. "I guess, yeah. I already scheduled posts through the weekend, and the new girl starts Monday."

I nod, and both of us look at each other knowingly. "Alright then," I say vaguely, a smirk on my face.

After a few quiet seconds, she asks, "Are you going back to finish the game?"

A dull throb of guilt pangs in my stomach that I know I have to deal with. "Nah, it'll be all but over by the time I get back. And they would have already scratched me anyway."

She cocks a brow, then glances behind me at my bike. "You wanna get out of here then? Maybe pull over on the side of the road somewhere?"

I nibble my bottom lip. "Fuck yeah, I do." Brooke giggles, and the sound makes it so I almost don't finish my thought.

But I have to.

"But can I take a rain check? I should probably get back so I can talk to the boys after the horn. Explain myself at least for bailing. And for the rest of it."

Sliding her hand past my cheek, she nods. "Sure. How about I meet you at the rink in a few hours, and you can give me a ride? Maybe get a little handsy on the way home."

A growl slips from my throat as I shake my head. "How many times have I told you not to play with me, Mystery Girl?"

She moves so that her mouth is only inches from mine. "Apparently not enough."

I crash my lips to hers before pulling back. "Then it's a good thing we've got nothing but time."

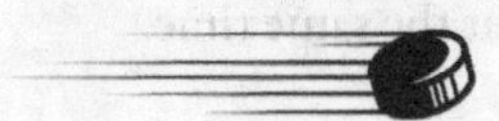

"Thanks for hanging back, guys."

"Yeah, no worries, Cap. Everything okay?" Burnsey asks.

He's sitting with Ward and Petrov on the couch in the lounge, his hair still wet from the shower. I asked the three of them to meet me after they were done getting changed. I have a lot to explain that I don't really want to, but they deserve to hear it all.

"Yeah," I answer. "For the most part. I just wanted to apologize for today. For not being there. And for all the shit that's come with these last couple games." I clear my throat as I search the boys' faces, all of them sterner than I expected. "I figured it was best to start with my A's and my goalie."

"What's been going on, man?" Ward asks.

"Yeah," Brett says. "Talk to us, bud."

I inhale deeply, waiting for Alexei to join in. Instead, he leans back on the couch and crosses his arms.

"Well, it's been a long time coming, but I'm just so done with all of the showman shit. The elaborate celebrations, the risky puck handling, the cocky attitude that no one asked for."

Burns chuckles. "But that's just you, Cap. We know it's not meant to be anything serious."

"Yeah," Ward adds. "As long as you keep the puck down ice, I don't really give a shit how you perform." He smiles nonchalantly and looks at Petrov. Again, my assistant captain doesn't speak.

"I get that," I say. "But *I'm* done with it. It's not me—it never was. I got wrapped up in it all when I was a rookie—the parties, the trips, the girls, the attitude. But I don't want any of it anymore." I sigh as I lean my forearms on my knees. "I just want to play the game I used to fucking love."

Ward nods. Brett shrugs. And Petrov creases his brow just slightly. The three of them speak all at the same time.

"That makes sense."

"You do you then, Cap. No worries."

"So, what changed?"

Petrov's deep voice cuts through the others, his question coming out as a command to answer.

"Before or now?"

He sits up again, placing his hands in his lap. "Both."

Now *I* sit back, rubbing my chin between my first two fingers. "Before?" I repeat tentatively. "My mom died and..."

My mind goes back to my conversation earlier with my dad. Normally, I would put this all on him—blame him for steering me wrong. But I get it now. Brett was right. We were all just doing the best we could with a grief that no one is ever prepared for.

"And my dad and I both did what we had to do to survive it."

Brett's eyebrows lift, and so do the corners of his lips.

"But that ended with both of us fully diving into the game—with doing whatever it'd take for me to rewrite my future, on and off the ice. And now? Now I'm just realizing that I don't need that to feel alive anymore—I don't want it. I have the team and you guys and..." My voice fades away.

"And who, Cap?" Brett pushes.

I move my gaze to see him smiling from ear to ear. "And my girl," I say confidently.

He drapes his arm across the cushion and throws me a wink. Carter looks at Petrov, but he doesn't react.

"But that's no excuse for how I've gone about it. I should have kept you guys in the loop. Hell, I should have done that a long time ago. But I guess I was afraid that I'd lose you too. Or just afraid of admitting that I lost myself."

Burnsey and Ward both nod in understanding as a silence falls between us. I think that might be the end of it when Alexei chimes back in.

"You are man before player. You must take care of your heart and your mind before you can carry the team."

The three of us all go wide-eyed, glancing back and forth between him and each other.

"Wow, Stormy," Brett says in shock.

Ward shrugs simply. "What he said."

His statement replays in my head a few times before I finally add my thoughts. "I think that might be the most words I've ever heard you string together, Storm." He sucks his teeth, and I laugh before my face grows as serious as my next few words. "But thank you."

"And there's no truth to the rumors?" Brett asks quickly, his voice hopeful.

"None. In fact, I signed my contract for next year before you guys got here. Scott just left."

Ward and Brett both grin, Burnsey reaching his fist out to me. I meet it with mine, and I swear I see the faintest of smiles from Petrov as I do.

"So, uh, what happened today, then?" Carter asks, sitting forward.

I blow a breath through my lips. "Yeah, so... that's where the girl comes in."

"Wait," Ward says, his hands in front of him. "Who's this girl?"

Brett looks at me, and I feel my cheeks flush. They all wait in suspense as I work up the courage to finally say it aloud. So far, Brooke and I have lived in a bubble away from the rest of the world. A bubble where, if I'm honest, part of me would like to stay. But I also know that a girl like her—a relationship like ours—deserves to be seen from the suites, shouted through the speakers, and witnessed by everyone in Golden City.

"It's Brooke."

"InstaBrooke?" Carter asks, unconvinced.

My forehead creases like it always does when I hear the nickname. "Where the hell did that name even—nevermind. Yes, InstaBrooke," I mock.

Ward scoffs, his lips parted. For a moment I think he doesn't approve—not that I'd give one fuck if he didn't. But I finally feel like I'm getting *my* life back, and I never even considered that she might not fit into it.

"How the hell did you score InstaBrooke?" he finally asks. I huff out a laugh as I lean back on the couch. Carter stares at the carpet before he continues. "InstaBrooke," he repeats. "Damn, I bet that girl is a freak in the..."

Petrov and I both shoot forward, not a hint of amusement on either of our faces. Carter holds his hands up in defense, and I turn to Storm and tip my chin down in gratitude.

"Anyway..." Brett chimes in. "So, are you guys like... I don't know. Official?"

I roll my eyes, but my stomach swirls, nerves and excitement both mixing together. "Actually..." I draw out, almost embarrassed to continue. "I was hoping you guys could help me out with that."

The boys all look at each other, and I hold my breath for the teasing to come.

But it doesn't.

"Hell yeah!" Brett yells without question.

"I'm in," Ward says.

Petrov cocks a brow and points a finger at his chest. "Me?"

I nod, laughing and shaking my head. I can't believe I'm about to do this, but for Brooke, I'd do anything. "Yeah, Storm," I say, scratching the back of my head. "For what I have in mind, I'll definitely need *you*."

37

Brooke

"Hey, Brooke!"

Walking toward the locker room, a voice calls from behind me.

"Max?" I ask after spinning around to find the Flames' equipment manager jogging down the hall.

"Yeah." He continues toward me as he talks. "Drew asked me to find you and let you know that he and a few of the guys are getting some reps in on the ice."

"After the game?"

Max stops in front of me, exhales heavily, and places his hands on his hips. "Yeah, something about making up for lost time today. You know how the boys are."

"Oh, uh, okay." I look around unnecessarily as if the walls might tell me what to do now. "Did he say if I should wait?"

Max nods, his eyes bright. "He actually said you should join them when you get here. Behind the bench or whatever."

"Um, alright."

I clear my head of all the expectations I had for when I finally saw Drew again, my mind racing as it attempts to pivot. Max shoots me an easy grin like he always does despite the situation and turns on his heel.

"It's propped open!" he calls from over his shoulder.

It takes so long to realize what he's talking about that he's almost out of sight before it clicks. "Thank... you..." My voice fades off as I yell to him, waving awkwardly to the back of his head as he rounds the corner of the hall.

Shifting in a half circle, still thrown off, I turn back around. I walk past the locker room, continuing down the hallway toward the door Drew and I so recently escaped to.

The door that leads to the ice.

And to the penalty box.

After Drew left this afternoon, I felt on top of the world. He came. And he's staying. And he's... falling in love with me? *That* I didn't expect. All of it was a toss up really, but to hear those words come from his mouth, took me by surprise. Since then, I haven't stopped thinking about what he said.

"You have no idea what it feels like to be falling in love with you, Mystery Girl."

Just like Drew, it was bold and unexpected. But also like him, it was familiar and comfortable. I would've thought hearing that would scare me—especially after the last twenty-four hours and everything we've been through. But instead of wanting to run, I wished I could wrap myself in his words like a blanket.

The truth is, I'm not sure I knew how I felt until he said it out loud. I want to fall in love, that's been my plan all along. But I guess I didn't realize it would feel the same as it did when I met Alex or saw Selah as a newborn. Every relationship I mistook for love in the past, I had free fallen into—heart racing, head spinning—a complete loss of gravity. But maybe those weren't real. Or this is just what growing up really feels like. Because when Drew told me how he felt, it wasn't a cliff dive. It was a warm, steady hum.

And just like that, I knew.

I feel the same.

But now, nerves hit that I wasn't expecting. This will be the first time the guys are around us since that moment. And since we can be together.

How do I act?

What do I say?

Why do I suddenly not know what to do with my hands?

The palm hooked around the handle of my bag grows clammy, a slight panic taking over as I get closer to the tunnel door. I start to overthink if I should even join them—considering the conversation I know he planned to have, maybe this calls for a bit of a boys day. But just as I begin to hesitate, the faint sound of music seeps through the crack in the door.

"What the... ?"

I take a few more strides, and the noise grows a bit louder, the vocals calling me closer.

Sticking my fingers through the inch of space that separates the door from the wall, I pull it open. A folded piece of paper that must have been wedged in the frame to prop it open, falls to the floor. I pick it up, humming the familiar tune to a song I've listened to a million times in the last month—one off of *the* playlist. I shove the paper in my pocket and step into the tunnel, the sound of the door slamming shut, ricocheting off the walls around me. *Damn, Drew was right.*

Moving toward the ice, I expect to see Drew and the boys taking shots on net or passing the puck back and forth across the blue line. Instead, Drew, Brett, and Alexei stand at center ice in street clothes and skates. And they're all staring directly at me.

"Hi, guys," I say hesitantly, stepping onto the bench.

Drew skates forward as the other two stay put. Brett and Alexei both wear straight faces, Burnsey clearly struggling more than Storm with the task. When he gets to the boards, Drew stops on a dime.

"Hey you." He smiles that boyish smile, and just like that—despite the weird freaking circumstances—all of my nerves disappear again.

"Twelve," I say back, my voice still wary. "What are you doing?"

He raises an eyebrow, attempting to maintain his confidence. His cheeks grow rosy, though, and something tells me that it's not from the temperature of the ice. "It seems you're officially off the Flames' clock."

He tips his chin up toward the stands behind me as the song fades out. I turn around to see a very giddy Alex sitting in the third row, her phone in her hand.

"Al?"

"Hi, he's right. I just met the new girl, so you're no longer needed," she explains quickly.

I scoff, faking offense. "Well, damn. Thanks a lot."

She rolls her eyes playfully. "You know what I mean. You're no longer employed by the Flames, and therefore, free to see whoever you'd like." She wiggles her brows at me, and I narrow my eyes in her direction. "Not that it really matters," she mumbles under her breath.

"Where *is* McHottie?" I ask, passive aggressively.

"Who now?" Drew hurries to lean forward, but I ignore his question, my attention still on my best friend.

"I don't know, reviewing film from the game or something. But you're good, I promise! And I'm here to document." She shakes her phone at me, and I spin back to Drew.

"Document what?"

He pulls his bottom lip in and drags it between his teeth. Between that and the way he's looking at me—mixed with my full reign to kiss him in public—I'd be turned on if I wasn't so confused.

"Well," he starts, resting his forearm on the boards. "I remember something about you asking for a performance."

My eyes go wide as I consider all the ways he could possibly mean *performance*. "No."

Drew nods, glancing at the boys over his shoulder.

"No," I say again, this time dragging out the last letter as several dots connect in my mind.

"Let 'er rip, Ward!" Drew yells.

His voice echoes around the rink until it's replaced by music—the opening to my, and now *Drew's*, favorite song.

"No," I deny for a third time as he bends over the boards between us and grabs a pile of hockey sticks. Drew throws one to Brett and one to Alexei before kissing me on the cheek and skating back to center ice.

Machine Gun Kelly's voice rings out, and when it does, it mixes with Drew's as he sings the lyrics into the butt of his stick. "Oh my God," I whisper.

I stare in awe as he belts out the whole intro, Burnsey and Petrov bopping behind him. They mix in a few spins here and there—Alexei still stone-faced despite his pirouettes. But no matter how ridiculous they look, I can't seem to fully rip my eyes away from Drew.

When the first verse starts, he pushes off his back foot and glides toward me, his hockey stick microphone still in hand. He stops at the boards, and slides his hand past my cheek, serenading me with a pop song and two backup dancers who are doing surprisingly well prancing around on skates.

I can't hold in my laughter as he dramatically sings the words I know so well just inches from my face. Drew smiles, breaking character completely, and I almost cut him off with my mouth, endorphins rushing through me like I'm actually on stage.

But I don't want to stop whatever's happening here.

As the hook begins, he moves back to center ice where the other two boys join him again. I look over my shoulder at Alex, who is staring wide-eyed and open-mouthed, her phone in front of her face as she watches through the screen.

I turn back around just in time for the chorus—and air guitar—to start. All three boys belt out the words, Petrov's low grumble the perfect anchor to whatever stage voice Brett seems to be using. The group of professional hockey players in front of me, swing their arms over their sticks—complete garage band style—and Drew melts me with his piercing eye contact and flirty grin.

He sings the lyrics like a question—asking whether or not I'd stand by him despite his imperfections. If I'd take the risk on us even though it might be safer just to walk away. His performance is pure comedy—full of off-key harmonies and grown men dancing on ice—but tears still sting my eyes. I don't know if he chose this song because it's fast-paced or we both like it. Or if the lyrics mean as much to him as they do to me. But I picked it for his playlist because *he's* all I think about when I hear it.

And now I'm reminded of why.

Drew has a lot going on. And no, he hasn't always made the right choices. But he's filled with so much good—so much kindness and quiet empathy—that he's hidden all these years behind an image that he has had to maintain. But if you know him, you see it right away.

You feel it when he's with you.

Or at least I do.

He's taught me that we're all navigating how we want life to unfold. That it doesn't matter if you're twenty-five or thirty-one, sometimes it's not about knowing what you want. It's about going after something real. I thought because he was younger than me, that there was no possible way that he'd be ready to settle down. But what I didn't consider was that readiness doesn't come with age—it comes with intention. And Drew, with all his chaos and charm, is intentional with me. With the way he looks at me, the way he listens.

The way he lets me in.

I used to believe that settling down meant having all the answers—a steady job, a stable relationship, a five-year plan. And all of that felt so big—so possible to fail at. But Drew Anderson, Mr. Showman himself, has proven to me that it's not about perfection or appearances. It's about what's on the inside—whether or not you let your heart grow roots.

It turns out there's no age requirement for the real thing. No perfect timeline or magic moment for finding someone who makes you feel seen for the first time. Love isn't about a number or a date or a checklist. It's about being there—showing up. And in the middle of this rink side concert with hockey player rockstars, I'm even more sure—that's exactly what Drew does for me.

As the second verse starts, he comes back to me, smiling as he pants and tossing his stick behind the boards.

"You're insane," I yell over the music.

Drew laughs, glancing back at the boys who are skating toward the side wall. "Insane... ly talented?" he asks, his dimple making its usual appearance.

"Something like that," I chuckle. He presses his lips together, puffing air through his nose as he grins, and all of him—all of *this*—overwhelms me. "Insanely easy to fall in love with."

Drew's eyes double in size, his grin blooming into a full-blown smile. He looks like he might speak, but instead, he dives into me and kisses me hard—saying nothing and everything all at once.

"I like the song choice," I say when he pulls back.

He winks at me, tucking a hair behind my ear. "Angsty shit."

I nod, the lingering weight of this moment settling into the space between us. "So, was this just a fantasy you've always had with the boys or... ?"

Drew tilts his head, narrowing his eyes. "Not quite."

"So, what then? A joke? A dare?"

Suddenly, he pauses. "How did you get in here?"

Confusion washes over me as I reach into my pocket and pull out the folded paper. "Max told me the door was propped. This was shoved in the frame."

Drew looks at the square in my hand and tilts his chin up toward it. "Open it," he says.

I hesitate, but his face is serious, so I do as he says and unfold it crease by crease. The small cube expands to a full sheet of paper, words scribbled across the center. I peer up at Drew, who raises his eyebrows, encouraging me to read it.

So I do.

Brooke,
You've always been my mystery girl,
but you've become my whole damn world.
I see clearly who you are,
and you see me despite my scars.
Together we're the perfect team.
A power play—a real-life dream.
The shots against us? There's a few—
But sinking shots is what I do.
Together we will build and grow,
but there's one thing I need to know.
Brooke, you've changed my life somehow.
So, can I be your boyfriend now?

"Wait, did you write this?" I ask, my eyes darting from the poem to him. My voice carries now that the music has faded, but I don't care who hears.

He cocks an eyebrow coyly. "Ehh, I may have had a little help."

My forehead creases until it clicks.

"Petrov," we both say together.

"God, there's so much more to all your friends," I mumble, shaking my head. I place my hand on his gripping the boards. "And to you."

Drew smiles, then opens the door and joins me on the bench. "So, what's it gonna be?" he asks, taking my hands in his. I reread his note quickly then peer up at him. "Your move, Larkin."

I stare at him, attempting to memorize his face more than I already have—his crystal blue eyes, the new fade of his hair, the indent in his cheek. He's beautiful. And for the second time today, I'm experiencing a moment that feels like the start of something new—better.

"You sure about this, Twelve?" I joke. "Rumor has it I'm a little older than you."

Drew laughs in an attempt to hide the growl that crawls from the back of his throat as he closes what's left of the small gap between us. "Haven't you heard that I no longer give one single fuck about rumors?"

I drape my arms around his neck and push to my tip-toes, our mouths nearly touching already. "Well, in that case," I whisper. I press my lips to his, and it's just as natural—and as life-altering—as it was that night last year at the gala. "Yeah, Twelve. I'm good with that if you are."

Drew lights up, and as if it was planned that way, the song starts over. The volume increases as a low rumble mixes with the introductory notes.

"Oh, please tell me there's an encore," I quip.

Drew laughs and rubs his forehead with his first two fingers. "If Brett had his way, there would be several."

With that, the nose of the Zamboni peeks out from the storage room. I look at Drew trying to decide if this was part of the plan or if we're being not so subtly kicked out of the rink, and he breathes in deeply.

The full machine comes chugging onto the ice, and I freeze, stunned, watching Carter Ward drive it, with Brett Burns straddling the top, a massive speaker lifted above his head.

"What the hell is happening?" I yell over the music.

"Jamboni!" Brett calls back as Carter continues driving past us, a sleek strip of glossy ice left behind them.

"Jamboni?" I question, turning back to Drew.

"You're lucky. He wanted to add strobe lights and a disco ball."

I laugh for what feels like forever before growing more serious, my heart so full from these last few hours. "You did all of this for me?"

Drew leans down and kisses me gently. "I'd do anything for you."

I glance at the poem again before returning my eyes to him, taking the time to soak up his words. "So, uh, I guess you're my boyfriend now, Twelve," I finally say.

He slips his arms around my waist and picks me up. I squeal as my legs curl around his hips like they always do, his eyes branding me like they always have.

"It's about damn time, Mystery Girl."

Epilogue - Drew

"Hey you." I lace my fingers through the net in front of me and smother a laugh when Brooke spins around, scared shitless.

"My God, Drew." She drops the camera she was holding, and it bounces off of the strap around her neck as she throws her hand to her chest. "How the hell did you get back there?"

I wink at her and smirk. "I have my ways."

"Jace let you in?" she asks blankly.

I stare at her for half a beat before clearing my throat. "Maybe."

Brooke rolls her eyes then turns back to the field, picking up her camera again. "So, what are you doing here, Twelve?" She aims the lens at one of the Gators on first base in front of her and snaps a shot before looking over her shoulder. "Did you miss me already?"

I drag my tongue over my bottom lip and mentally curse the netting between us for stopping me from showing her exactly how much. "Actually, yeah," I admit through gritted teeth. "It felt like we were gone on opposite days this week."

She shifts and takes one more photo of Jace at second, then removes the strap around her neck and sets the camera in her bag by her feet. With her hands free, she walks back toward me. "That's because we were—stupid schedules. But the first game's next week, so it feels like *my* first official chance to prove myself, ya know?"

I nod, my chest swelling with pride for her like it always does. "I know, I know. And you're gonna kill it."

She smiles sheepishly.

We're still working on her accepting how perfect she is.

"I do miss you, though," I have to add.

Brooke slips her fingers through the net and intertwines them with mine. "I miss you too. Hopefully, after you win me a Cup we can look into... maybe... moving in together?"

I fake surprise, pulling back, my eyes growing wide. "Brooke Larkin, did you just ask me to move in with you?"

She winds up to smack me in the chest, but drops her hand when she remembers the barrier between us. "Oh, shut up. We've only been talking about it for weeks."

I laugh, incapable of hiding my shit-eating grin as usual. "Oh, I know." My demeanor grows serious as I shove my hands into my pockets. "I can't wait."

She rolls her eyes and looks back toward the field.

So much has changed since that little rink side performance I gave my now *girlfriend.* I haven't played a game as anyone other than myself, and my new P.R. manager helped me to phase out all the other shit. Turns out, Brooke was right. Once I spoke my piece, the fans moved on to someone else's drama. Some of them are still coping with the fact that I'm an openly taken man, but if backlash over Brooke is all they have to throw at me, I'll cover myself in glue and make sure that shit sticks.

Brooke called Miles once everything settled down with her aunt. After a ten minute interview, she had gotten the job and was already in deep conversation about movies with the Gators' owner. Ivy, who is a total fucking trip, is fine as long as she remembers to take her medication while she's metal detecting across ancient ruins or sword fighting with medieval reenactment groups. Brooke gets to see her more regularly now, thanks to her routine doctor's appointments, and the two of them usually grab coffee together with Mrs. Larkin.

Blake's cool as shit—I finally got him the autograph he's apparently been wanting. I wrote it out to Selah though because, man, that little girl is just about the cutest thing I've ever seen. Her little brother Sawyer is too—Amy told me I have to get him on the ice as soon as he can walk. But there's something about Say that draws me in.

Maybe it's that she reminds me so much of her aunt.

Brooke waves to someone in the dugout, and it pulls me back to the present. "Who's that? Do I have to worry about you around all these players?"

"Why?" she asks, spinning back toward me. "You afraid I might fall for one of them?"

She winks at me, and my teeth clench through my closed-lip smile. "Just kidding," she sings. "It's Ruthie."

I lean in, attempting to look inside, but am blocked by the angle. "Liam's kid?"

Brooke nods. "Yeah, apparently he fired another nanny."

I cross my arms over my chest. "Do I need to call Burnsey?"

She rolls her eyes and shakes her head, smiling and walking back toward her bag. When she reaches for it, I all too quickly step up to the net. "Are you done?" I ask eagerly.

She slows her motion slightly, peering up at me. "I can be," she says. Then, her eyes slink lower, and she licks her lips. "Did you bring the bike? Cause you know, it's been months, and you still haven't cashed in that rain check."

I suck my teeth and nod slowly. "Oh, I brought the bike." Her face lights up as she grins flirtatiously. "And trust me, Mystery Girl. I have all sorts of plans."

Rolling back into town, Brooke's arms squeeze tightly around my waist in excitement. Her legs are snug around mine, and her chest is pushed flat against my back. Each turn I take or street I dip down, I can feel her holding her breath, wondering if *this* might be where I pull over. I've almost caved a few times already—it's taken all of my self-control not to give in to the moves she's been putting on me the entire ride in. But despite how much I always want her, I have to stay level-headed right now.

My dad and I have been working on this for months. We've had many long conversations and shopped around more than I care to admit. It's something that I can't believe I'm finally doing, but the moment I saw Brooke at that bar in Grand Oaks, I hoped this is where it would lead.

There's a reason that we were brought back together—I like to think maybe Mom had something to do with it. I wasn't lying when I told her that she was changing everything for me—my life, my game, my heart. Turns out I might have found even more of a home in her than I thought.

"Wait... " Brooke calls over the roar of the bike. I roll to a stop at the next red light and look over my shoulder. "Why are you heading downtown? This is *not* the highway shoulder I expected."

I chuckle under the shield of my helmet. "Oh, come on, you're way too classy for the shoulder," I toss back. "We're going residential, baby."

She doesn't respond, and I smile, picturing the confusion that's undoubtedly etched into her brow. The light turns green, and I zip around the next turn, decreasing my speed as we reach an all too familiar street. Brooke's arms loosen around me as I pull over toward the curb, and I grin, trying to decipher her lessened grip as curiosity or disappointment.

"Drew, I love you," she whispers as I cut the engine. "And that rain check has been burning a hole in my pocket, but I'm not sure the families in these houses would care to witness us having sex across your bike."

Swinging my leg over, I take my helmet off and straddle the seat in the opposite direction to face her. Brooke takes hers off and tosses her hair, her cheeks pink from either the spring sun or her anticipation.

"I thought you were bad, Mystery Girl." She tips her chin down and tilts her head, glaring at me in an adorable way. I lean forward, kissing her gently, and her lips curl beneath mine before I pull away. "I'm kidding, Brooke. That's not why we're here."

She creases her brow, and I wait for nerves to shoot through me now that we've reached our destination.

But they don't come.

They never do with her.

If anything, she calms my chaos.

Things with Brooke are easy, and not in the sense that we never argue or that everything is perfect. Life didn't just become simple because she suddenly fell into it. But my love for her outweighs any fear I've ever known. It's stronger than any doubt or pressure I've taken on. Truer than any expectation the world has thrown my way.

Being with Brooke feels as natural as hockey once did when I was first handed a stick. And that doesn't mean it's without its bumps and bruises and jagged edges, but it's steady. And it's real. And even when it's hard, it still feels pretty fucking right.

And *that's* what makes it easy.

That's what makes it everything.

"Brooke, I..."

She stops her eyes from wandering when she hears her name—and my shift in tone—and the way she looks at me expectantly physically draws me closer.

"Brooke," I continue again, shifting forward. "Since I met you, my life has completely changed."

"Drew..."

I hold a finger up and blow out a slow breath. "And some of that had to do with my own choices—finally taking back control of my life. But so much of that is thanks to you."

Brooke's jaw grows tight as her throat moves up and down, her eyes darting back and forth between mine. I smile slowly, then reach for her hand before continuing. "I used to feel alone—so alone—even surrounded by people, but when I laid eyes on you last year at the gala, I finally felt connected again. Like I was part of something."

Her gaze drops to our interlocked hands, and she brushes her thumb back and forth over mine. Dipping down, I curl my first finger under her chin and bring her back to me. "Brooke, I used to think that true love was something that had to take your breath away. But it's not like that with you."

"Gee thanks," she says through a laugh, her voice nearly breathless, her eyes now glossy.

I exhale through a soft chuckle, swallowing the emotion rising in my throat. "It's not like that with you," I repeat. "Because with you, it's like I can finally breathe for the first time in too damn long."

Brooke's eyes fall shut, and when she opens them, a single tear rolls down her face. I lift my hand to brush it away, but at the last second, I change my mind. I don't want to wipe away her emotions—the ones she gives me so willingly now. I want to see her feel everything. And still know she's safe with me.

Instead of reaching for her cheek, I drop my arm and look over my shoulder at the brownstone we're parked in front of. The one I've dreamed of living in for as long as I can remember. That I want to turn into a home—*our* home. That I want to fill with art and decorations and pictures... so many pictures.

The one I bought for Brooke and me.

"Brooke Larkin, will you—" I lift the leg of my jeans and slip my hand into the ankle of my sock.

"Wait, what are you doing?" she asks anxiously.

I hold up the shiny gold key I pulled out. "Will you move in with me?"

Brooke sucks in a breath and rips it from my grasp, holding it in both hands, examining it. "Oh my God. Drew, I—" She smiles and shakes her head, looking back down at the metal. "I thought you were gonna ask me to marry you."

I huff out an almost awkward laugh. "And what would you have said to that?"

Brooke's eyebrows shoot up briefly before settling back down. Her shoulders sink slightly, but not from disappointment or devastation—from ease and comfortability.

"I mean, honestly?"

I nod, nerves just now threatening to creep in.

"I would have said yes."

Now it's my body that relaxes as I dip back down into my sock. "Well, good." I hold up the gold-banded, admittedly over-size single oval-cut diamond ring, and it shines almost as brightly in the sun as Brooke does behind it. "Because that was next."

She gasps, taking it in, her palm flying to her mouth. "What is happening?" she whispers.

I pull her wrist back and hold her hand in mine. "I was hoping to change your life too, Mystery Girl."

"*Our* life, Twelve," she shoots back.

I nod, my chest tight with everything bubbling to the surface—happiness, adrenaline, eagerness... love. "Is that a yes?" I ask, looking into her chocolate eyes.

She smiles, and everything settles again. *My perfect anchor.* "Yes."

"To both?"

Brooke inhales deeply, looking down at the ring. "To both," she says, then she looks up at me and arches a brow. "God, I'm such a cougar."

We both laugh as I slide the ring on her finger.

"No big performance this time," she says definitively.

I peer up at her and fill my lungs with air, shaking my head. "Nope. Just me."

"Good." She leans in and kisses me like she always does, our lips connecting like they were meant for each other—like they always did. "That's all I ever wanted."

The End

The Playlist
ft. Drew's Angsty Shit

1. Lonely – Justin Bieber & Benny Blanco

2. Electric – Alina Baraz ft. Khalid

3. Falling Up – Dean Lewis

4. Headlights – Alex Warren

5. Pretty Eyes – Bryce Savage

6. Let You Down – NF

7. Fine – Kyle Hume

8. The Kill (Bury Me) – Thirty Seconds to Mars

9. The Search – NF

10. Winter – HART

11. Keep to Myself – Caleb Hearn

12. Hero – Family Of The Year

13. Brown Eyes, Brown Hair – Caleb Hearn

14. Young Blood – Noah Kahan

15. Blink Twice – Schaboozey & Myles Smith

16. Helium – Sia

17. Lose My Mind – Dean Lewis

18. Cliché – MGK

19. All That Really Matters – ILLINIUM & Teddy Swims

20. Home – Good Neighbours

Acknowledgements

Dear Reader,

If you've made it here, it means you stuck with Drew and Brooke—and me—until the very last page, and that means more than you will ever know. I've learned that writing can be lonely and messy. It's a process that is often full of worry and self-doubt. But knowing that people like you exist makes the sleepless nights, endless editing, and imposter syndrome worth it.

To my friends and family, who have stuck with me since day one—listening to my groaning, brainstorming with me, and reminding me of my worth and talent—*you* have carried me through.

To my Chaos Crew, beta team, and loyal readers—you just keep showing up. It is nearly impossible to feel like I have no one in my corner with you in my life and my DMs, and I'm not sure you realize how much you keep me going.

And to you—the one holding my dream in your hands—thank you for being here. For choosing this book. For choosing *me*. And for giving my words a home. None of this happens otherwise.

In short, thank you to everyone helping to change my little corner of the world. No message, voice note, coffee run, or page read has ever gone unnoticed.

With lots of love (& tons of angst—the good kind, obviously),
Cassandra

About The Author

Cassandra Moll is a hockey wife and girl mom to three little ladies who are the inspiration behind her imprint name - *Three Bows Books*. When she's not chasing them around, Cassandra loves to be outside, lift weights, and read. After falling back in love with books, and hearing other authors' stories, she was inspired to finally write her own. Cassandra's books are filled with love and angst and sprinkled with banter that keeps you coming back for more.

For more information about Cassandra and her books, please visit cassandramoll.com.